A BLAZING NEW SAGA OF GALACTIC
COURAGE BY THE AUTHOR OF
THE HELMSMAN SERIES
CANBY'S LEGION

✷

COMMANDER GORDON CANBY: Hero and
helmsman, he'll protect his troops by winning
back the pride—and power—they've lost . . .

KAPITAN NIKOLAI KOBIR: An outcast warrior
with a lust for life can be a very lusty warrior
indeed . . .

CYNTHIA TENNIEL: She does what she
must—and what she does, she does too
well . . .

SADIR, FIRST EARL OF RENALDO: The mon-
strous glutton who craves everything—except
his just desserts . . .

CREW CHIEF LELA PETERSON: A ground-
bound optimist with sky-high connections, she
knows how to get things done—and how to
get her man . . .

**MINISTER OF THE ADMIRALTY DAVID
LOTEMBER:** A whiz-kid politico who can lie,
scheme, blackmail, threaten, wheedle—the
only thing he can't do is his job . . .

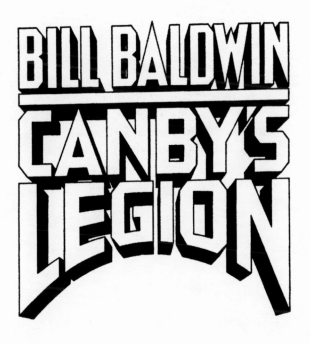

BILL BALDWIN

CANBY'S LEGION

iUniverse.com, Inc.

San Jose New York Lincoln Shanghai

Canby's Legion

Published by iUniverse.com, Inc.

For information address:
iUniverse.com, Inc.
620 North 48th Street, Suite 201
Lincoln, NE 68504-3467
www.iuniverse.com

Originally published by Warner Books

ISBN: 0-595-14138-2

Printed in the United States of America

PROLOGUE

Aboard KV 388 #SW799, in space • off Khalife

"All hands to stations for landfall! All hands man your landfall stations. Secure from HyperLight Operations. . . . "

Nikolai Kobir, Kapitan in the Novokîrsk Fleet, peered into SW799's forward Hyperscreens as he slowed the ship through LightSpeed, waiting for the Transition to end. There . . . the planet's actual disk was rapidly coming into view. The Screens were still projecting their HyperLight simulation of what was ahead, but even while he watched, they became more and more transparent as the ships' two big CNX-801E SpinGravs fought the terrific momentum they'd built up on the three-Standard-Day journey across the galaxy.

Through the starboard Hyperscreens he watched wingman Émil Lippi flying his Kvlokov KV 388L close in, as he had through nearly six years of savage warfare. Below and slightly aft, Jano Quadros and Georges Roualt completed the foresome, with Roualt flying Quadros's wing. A half kilometer to starboard, four more of the angular 388s flew in formation. All eight ships had come through LightSpeed at exactly the same instant—after flying halfway across a storm-racked galaxy. Kobir smiled. He expected nothing less. These were among the finest crews and helmsmen in the whole Volpato Confederation, no matter which of the Confederation's eleven affiliated dominions one considered. They were also the last survivors of Task Force Eight's Flotilla Twenty-one, a detachment that only two Standard Years previously had numbered 263 ships, not including spares.

Presently, light photons from forward began to arrive at speeds the human eye could translate, and the Screens became transparent, revealing the remote planet itself, orbiting a third-rate star along with three rock-barren siblings, little bigger than asteroids. "Khalife," the Kîrskian whispered dolefully, and shook his head. "A bleak place for such a gallant dream to end."

"All hands to stations for landfall!" the blower repeated—smashing aside his somber thoughts. "All hands man your landfall stations. Secure from HyperLight Operations. . . . "

From the aft companionway, the 388's cramped navigation bridge filled with sounds of thudding feet, the dull bang of airtight doors and hatches, crewmen hurrying to their stations, and the general cacophony associated with securing a starship from deep space.

Kobir scanned the information flowing from his readouts, eyes roving professionally from group to group in a practiced manner. All normal, as they should be in a magnificent machine such as this. Only a small number of the advanced killer ships had been built—or ever would be, now that the armistice was no more than a few Standard Hours away. He shook his head.

A Standard Week ago—at what remained of Koris-29, their final base, orbiting a lonely cinder only thirty light-years from Novokîrsk's capital planet of Megiddo—he'd ordered two of their trusty old KV 72 transports loaded with the few surviving civilians, provisions, and spares, then sent them on ahead along a safe route. Three days later, once defeat was an absolute certainty, he'd scuttled the base, then led his remaining eight 388s through the tightening globe of enemy ships—probably the last to escape before the presiding officers of all Confederation member states accepted an armistice with Imperial Earth—on *its* terms. The end was now only Standard Hours away, but he—with the brave men and women who'd fought at his side and survived—had escaped.

Escaped to *what*, though? Kobir had no deceptions about the future of the Confederation—it was finished, once and for all; the Imperials would see to that under the terms of their armistice. However, with this little squadron of powerful ships, he and his people might well carve themselves something worthwhile from the postwar chaos that would soon descend upon them. It was certainly better than sitting around waiting for something to happen. If nothing else, he could provide them a few options—sure to be scarce commodities in Novokîrsk following the armistice. After securing their ships, the two-hundred-odd Kîrskians would scatter throughout the galaxy for two or three years—long enough for things to settle down. Then, at his signal, those who still wanted to—or who could—would regather to begin a new career, whatever *that* might turn out to be at the time. . . .

The deck trembled momentarily beneath his boots, focusing his tired mind on the ship once again. It was a last send-off from the series of powerful gravity storms they'd encountered along the way. The violent tempests had dogged them every parsec from Megiddo, but they'd also provided cover from fleets of Imperial warships that filled space these days. Most Imperials skirted the big graviton cyclones that periodically rumbled out of the galactic center. They were dangerous, to say the least, but Kobir had long ago discerned their value and learned to fly in them. Passing the experience on to his crews was paying off today.

Beside him, Dorian Skoda, his cohelmsman, glanced his way. "You will fly the landfall, Kapitan?" he asked.

Kobir nodded. Below, the planet was already taking on added dimension. Their proximity warning systems showed nothing in the area. Khalife and its star, Sa'anto, were deservedly considered a galactic backwater. But with space almost totally ruled by Earth, there was always the possibility of meeting a chance Imperial ship, so he dove at much higher speed than normal. In moments, all eight ships were blazing through ever-thickening atmosphere like meteors—heating rapidly to temperatures just short of explosively diffusing the metal that formed their hulls. Simultaneously, they were decelerating near the very cushioning limits of their internal gravity systems. At these insane velocities, even the best helmsmen found themselves greatly challenged, for the ships twitched nervously as they passed through changing atmospheric pressures—and the slightest swerve could crumple their hulls. To starboard, Lippi, Quadros, and Roualt were keeping steady company. At the far edge of his vision, he checked the other four ships: Haidar, Gutzkow, Rosenberg, and Jabir were also keeping perfect station.

Suddenly, Kobir's heart jumped in horror as Rosenberg's 388 suddenly came apart, then exploded like a puffball. Everything forward, including the flight bridge, flew off to one side; the aft section with its heavy power chambers and SpinGravs went on falling like a great comet, while debris followed in every direction. The bridge filled with groans of dismay.

Kobir bit his lip. Rosenberg and his crew had come so terribly far to end up like that . . . only minutes short of safety. He forced them from his mind, reminding himself that he and his crew were *also* minutes from safety yet—*dangerous* minutes, at that. At least ancient Calabria, the planet's single—and stubbornly *neutral*—city was still considerably 'round the horizon, so their arrival was still probably unobserved. He wasn't terribly worried about his reception there. The Calabrians, heirs to a civilization founded more than a thousand years in the past, were an odd-lot people more interested in profit than alliances. But the fewer who knew about the hidden ships, the better.

Down he led them toward shapeless, smoothed-over cloud banks that quickly became moving, grayish masses fringed with color, hurtling toward them at truly frightening speeds. The flight bridge had gone tomb-silent—all he could hear on the intercom was breathing, and an occasional gasp. He silently wondered how many of the crew were as apprehensive as he was. At only a few hundred feet above the first cloud layers, he carefully nursed the steering engines and pulled out of the perilous dive with the spaceframe groaning and creaking. A glance through the Hyperscreens verified that the remainder of his flock had not only come through safely but in some semblance of formation. Now, all that remained was to find the caves—and the transports, if indeed their crews had brought them safely through the dangerous journey unescorted.

They descended through a solid bank of clouds nearly as large as the continent it covered. Only a few hundred feet below, Kobir picked out at least four more layers of dirty, gray-looking clouds—detritus of a frontal system moving slowly down from the icy polar regions of the planet.

Momentarily, it seemed strange not contacting some sort of Planetary Center for landing instructions. But the Imperials now owned the lot of those, such as they might be on a planet this size—without even a satellite warning network. He listened to the steady beat of the SpinGravs thundering away in their housings on either side of the hull. No trouble there. He glanced beside him at Skoda, who was straining his eyesight at the surface. "Anxious to be down, my friend?" he asked.

Skoda smiled. "Anxious to begin our beginning," he replied, looking across the center console. "I have become sated by trouble over the last two years."

Kobir felt himself smile. "But Skoda," he bantered, "once we make landfall and conceal our ships, then our troubles will *truly* begin, for we must survive until things settle out."

"Ah," Skoda replied, "but the troubles will then be ours, not those passed down by an incompetent high command."

Kobir sighed. "You may have a point there, my friend," he said, increasing the lift augmentors and feeding in ten degrees more power to take up the load. A series of slight bumps shook the deck as they descended through the first cloud layer, then things smoothed out again and he returned his attention to the controls. The atmospheric radiators were already in operation according to four graviton temperature gauges and . . . moments later, his AutoHelm disconnected, as the ship began to buck and twist through increasing turbulence. Flying with the light touch that identified him as a master helmsman, he casually turned to the COMM officer behind him. "Kruger," he said calmly, "are you ready with our signal to the transports?"

"I am, Kapitan," Kruger replied. "I have downloaded three of the agreed-upon codes into the burst transmitter."

"Good," Kobir said over his shoulder. "Send one immediately." Another layer of clouds was beginning to close in when he noted some lightning out to port and veered slightly to starboard, still losing altitude at about sixty meters per second.

Moments later, Kruger spoke excitedly. "Kapitan," he said. "We have an immediate reply."

"Well?" Kobir asked with a little smile. He too was excited, but didn't want to show it. "What do they say?"

"'Welcome to the Kingdom of Boredom,'" Kruger quoted. "'Beacon on 14273.'"

Laughing for the first time in days, Kobir nodded. "Do you have that beacon setting, Skoda?" he asked.

"I have just entered the value in our course direction," Skoda replied evenly.

A ruby light began to glow in Kobir's forward screens, then separated into horizontal lines. As he corrected to starboard, the light shimmered into vertical lines. One final correction to port and it coalesced to a steady point—on centerline. A glance to starboard confirmed that the other ships were also lining up on the beacon.

Increasing the lift augmentors to nine, he checked the nav switches and set the airspeed APR bugs to just under one fifty—then followed the light to a new course while powerful downdrafts caught the ship from starboard and threw her on her side. "Perhaps we might have picked a hideout with better weather, eh, Skoda?" he joked while he leveled out again.

"Perfect weather—" Skoda commented in his normal deadpan, "for hiding starships from prying eyes."

"Another good point," Kobir declared.

Clouds broke for a moment to starboard, and he spied the ground—dense forest as far as he could see. He'd visited only once before, years in the past. At the time, the planet's remote antiquity had seemed irksome, along with the bizarre architecture of its only city and the whimsical denizens who lived there. Now . . . if the place hadn't changed all that much, it would be a positive *haven*.

Overspeed warning horns sounded momentarily as the ship was once more swallowed up in the dirty gray, turbulent cloud. They squawked again moments later in another violent downdraft. Kobir stoically kept to his course, losing altitude gradually. After six years of wartime flying, it took more than a little dirty weather to ruffle him. Abruptly they broke out from the last cloud layer. One moment, they were wholly consumed by it; the next, they were clear. Ahead through the stormy atmosphere he could see a long, narrow lake at the foot of a low mountain range. The ruby beacon was at the far left of its long axis. The caves—and the transports—would be nearby.

Dropping to 150 feet altitude above what appeared to be more forest, they flew through a few gray wisps of haze. Then, the mist quickly thickened, and rain began to pelt their Hyperscreens, boiling to vapor on contact with the white-hot crystal surfaces. Instinctively, the ships' pilots closed up the formation to maintain visual contact. Any radiating source such as a transmitting/receiving position indicator might alert the city to their presence.

"We shall start the approach check, if you please, Skoda," Kobir said.

"Aye, Kapitan," Skoda acknowledged. "Continuous boost?"

Kobir scanned the 'Grav panels. "On," he said as the ship bounced in the cloudy turbulence.

"Radio nav switches?"

"Set on RADIOS."

"Auto flight panels?"

"Checked," Kobir said. His seven remaining ships had now moved into line-ahead formation that curved around aft to starboard. "Let's get everybody down now," he added.

"Aye, Kapitan," Skoda said. Moments later, his voice was on the blower: "All hands secure personal stations. All hands secure personal stations. . . . " Then, "Nav radios?"

Kobir focused on the COMM panel. "Manual—" he replied, "—as if we need them anymore."

"Too true, Kapitan," Skoda commented. "Altimeter, flight, and nav instruments?"

"Ah . . . set and cross-checked," Kobir replied. They were rapidly approaching the lake now. Ranks of whitecaps marched toward them like some great, gray-haired army.

"Airspeed EPR bugs?"

"Reduced to one thirty-nine—and cross-checked."

"Speed brake levers?"

"Locked."

Lining up on the beacon for final, they thundered over one of the planet's mysterious ruins—an eyeless, bristling octagon whose entire surface appeared to be constructed from a smoked mirror. The ship jinked from a sudden updraft, then suddenly they were ready to land. At the far end of the lake, Kobir could see openings in the cliffs that formed the shore there. Inside one, a beacon was flashing. Journey's end.

"Er . . . verticle 'Gravs?" Skoda asked.

"Verticles on. Three green."

"Lift enhancers and extras?"

"Thirty-three, thirty-three—green light."

"That does it," Skoda declared.

Kobir nodded. "Everybody down, back there?" he asked.

Skoda paused a moment, studying one of his panels. "Everybody's down," he said.

Off to starboard, a stand of great trees slid by the rain-streaked Hyperscreens. Only a hundred feet altitude, now. Kobir walked the steering engines carefully. All 388s were slippery on landing, but she lined up and mostly stayed where he put her despite the stiff crosswind gusts. In the Hyperscreens, the ruby vector was flopping back and forth between vertical and horizontal. Kobir was now concentrating on the ranks of waves marching at a slight angle to the ship's track. They'd make things a little harder . . . but not *that* much. He checked the instruments once more: glide path . . . descent rate . . . speed . . . angle of attack. None perfect, but close enough in this kind of turbulence. Throttles matched. He called up a little more thrust—should be about two to four knots fast—then eased off the steering engines. The bow swung to windward, then he slanted the deck a little for drift. Nose up ever so slightly. Judging the wave troughs, he held her off . . . deftly leveling the deck only an instant before cascades of gray lake water shot skyward in the side Hyperscreens, diminished as they slid through a trough, then shot skyward once more and stayed that way as Kobir gently plastered the ship's hull to the surface. They sliced through two more of the big rollers before he gently pulsed the gravity brakes, sending two long streams of gravitons out ahead that flattened the waves while they slowed the ship. Moments later, the ship was stopped, rolling on the surface of the storm-roiled lake.

Half a galaxy away, on a planet known as Earth, it was 9:14 A.M., G.M.T., November 21, 2681. For a number of unsuspecting people, the future—such as it might be—had begun.

Book One

DREAMS AND HOPES

Brooklyn Sector, New Washington • Earth

Another Armistice Day, marking acceptance of Allied terms by the Volpato Confederation. That momentous ceremony, aboard a common IL-271 starship, ended nearly six years of vicious warfare between the two intragalactic coalitions. Now, eight years afterward, Gordon Bernard Canby recalled the occasion well as he toted a worn shopping bag along the Brooklyn Sector's noisy Seventh Avenue. He'd commanded the formation of DH.98 killer ships escorting that very IL-271 to landfall on the Confederation's inner sanctum Megiddo, capital planet of Novokîrosk.

It all seemed so heroic at the time. Subsequent ratification by both parties of the Treaty of Houdak had kicked off a year of general Allied celebrations—crowned on Earth, herself, by perhaps the greatest victory procession in human history.

10

Canby remembered *that*, too. His famed 19th Star Legion had been prominent in the gigantic flyover of New Washington—bureaucratic capital of Imperial Earth, a sovereignty extending across thirty distinct star systems, nineteen habitable planets, and uncounted asteroid reefs rich in the mineral building blocks of intragalactic commerce.

A brief eight years later, however, the once-celebrated, (now thirty-one-year-old) Star Legion Commander Gordon Canby was merely citizen Canby—and had been for nearly seven of those eight years. Under Imperial Earth's GNO, or Grand New Order, his once-great Imperial Earth had become a kingship in the guise of democracy. Presiding atop the now "perfected" regime was an Emperor, elevated to this lofty post by dint of accumulating more wealth than anyone else who wanted the job—and would be replaced speedily when that affluence was surpassed. He (or she) chaired the House of Nobles, a largely ceremonial body of Peers comprising the Empire's most wealthy citizens. They controlled nearly all capital in the Empire, and could sell their titles or pass them to heirs, who were not required to be blood relatives.

Lawmakers—principals of the Political Class—existed considerably beneath the Nobles, upon whose largesse they relied for money to finance their gaudy, extravagant election campaigns. In consequence, Nobles had largely become exempt from the laws passed by their elected patrons. Naturally, the latter—when they managed to appropriate sufficient wealth and capital—often joined their more fortunate mentors by purchasing a title of their own from the Emperor.

Managers of commercial enterprises existed at virtually the same social plane as did Lawmakers. Invariably, their success was measured—and rewarded—by profit generated for their Noble owners, with no regard for niceties whatsoever. Managers could also purchase titles from the Emperor.

These few—Nobles, Politicans, and Managers—formed a de facto monarchy that was primarily dedicated to maintaining maximum productivity among the employed, minimum unrest among the unemployed, and strict observance of various laws that—at any given time—were most beneficial to themselves. They ruled nearly seven billion "Enfranchised" or "Freemen" citizens scattered throughout the galaxy.

At the war's conclusion, veterans had been seen as a real threat to the entrenched monarchy as millions of victorious soldiers and spacemen returned to civilian life trained for independent action. A far-seeing coalition of conservative Politicians, wealthy Nobles, and religious zealots of the most doctrinaire persuasions recognized the threat even before the armistice was signed. They set to work immediately, enacting laws that would safely control these men and women—and were successful beyond their wildest dreams.

Predictably, their triumph produced a cheerless environment for people like Gordon Canby, native Imperial and honor graduate of Imperial Earth's Military Fleet Academy at Annapolis. Seven years after demobilization, he still kept himself physically in shape, although he certainly had no "official" reason to do so. He was of medium height, chunky, and carried himself as if he were still a member of the armed forces. On this late autumn afternoon, he wore his old flight jacket—long bereft of military ornamentation—over a heavy woolen sweater, nondescript gray trousers, and war-surplus boots, shined as if he were going on parade. Hatless in spite of cold, damp wind off the nearby Upper Bay, he was bald except for a swath of curly, graying hair that extended from each ear to meet at the nape of his neck. He had a prominent forehead, deep-set blue eyes that often sparkled with humor, a button nose, and a mouth whose routine configuration was a grin. That same mouth, however, could assume a tight-lipped aspect of grim determination when Gordon Canby was afoot on dangerous business—as he was today. And predictably, it had to do with frustration of the self-serving, self-righteous charlatans of the Political Class.

Canby's one bright hope for the future was Nemil Quinn,

a fellow veteran of the Fleet, whose enormous family estate allowed him to independently finance his own successful election campaign with no obligations to the Nobility. The man was presently Chancellor of the Exchequer, but he had recently let it be known "unofficially" that he would be a candidate in the next election for Prime Minister, espousing a movement of centrist reform. Because he was the only member of the Political Class who could speak out (however carefully) against the excesses of both Nobles and their lackeys, he had become more than a little unpopular among his Political Class peers. To most veterans, that made his possible candidacy even more attractive.

Canby's eyes swept across Seventh Avenue to an unkempt row of faceless, six-story public housing apartments whose filthy, unadorned windows seemed to reflect the hopelessness of the semi-educated "Freemen" who lived there. Ex-enlisted people for the most part, they had been unceremoniously dumped by a government with little further need of armed forces—especially when maintaining them in fighting trim took credits from the coffers of Politicians who were no longer threatened by Kîrskians. Many of the residents were once members of his own 19th Star Legion—and continued to serve in a new and completely illegal organization he'd gathered to thwart the new government's obvious campaign of subjugation. Over the years, they'd quietly named themselves "Canby's Legion" despite his most vehement protests.

Twenty miles beyond the apartments, a stately liner soared up from the distant spaceport at Idlewild. Canby watched enviously as it banked onto a tight, climbing turn and thundered into the overcast, bound for deep space and the stars. He was an excellent starship helmsman who not only flew with a natural grace but also understood the arcane physics of true HyperFlight as if he had been born on a flight bridge. However, the last time he had set foot in a starship was the day he and a skeleton crew docked his battle-worn DH.98 at a breaking yard outside Karachi.

He'd then returned to New Washington on the HyperTube for his reluctant demobilization and discharge—only the most independently wealthy and influential officers managed to retain their uniforms after the "Big Demob," as it had come to be known. Since then, he'd discovered that thousands of similarly qualified starship officers were also out of work. And berths on civilian starships were invariably filled by their former civilian occupants or people with sufficient influence or wealth to bribe their way—with "Tributes"—into the tightly controlled system of guilds and corporations. A dedicated military man before the armistice, Canby was neither influential nor wealthy. Born on Artemos-8 of two hardworking asteroid miners who quickly went their own ways, he spent most of his youth in the prisonlike confines of cheap boarding schools, then went directly into the Fleet—which quickly became the only real family he had ever known.

He was a natural leader who rarely needed to raise his voice, graduating near the top of his class in the Fleet Academy, then rising swiftly through the wartime ranks by dint of a natural aptitude for spaceflight. But, like the majority of his fellow veterans, he was now only a castoff with little hope of future employment of his best talents. By winning the war, he—and most of the people whom he commanded—had literally worked their way out of their jobs. Inevitably, and ironically, the reward for their success was unemployment.

" . . . as you draw to the close of your distinguished career in our Imperial Fleet," declaimed one of the senior officers with sufficient wealth and political influence to remain, "you take with you the appreciation of countless people, including all of us with whom you served. . . . "

So he had turned his energies elsewhere, as had lanky ex-Lieutenant Norton Peter—once a Gunnery Officer aboard a 19th Star Legion attack ship—who signaled from across the street that the way ahead was clear of the ubiquitous Vice Police, or V-Pols.

Halfway along 65th Street, Canby passed one of the National Soup Kitchens maintained to keep Freemen dependent for their very sustenance on government and its dole. In an age of almost complete industrial automation, there were no vocational jobs, as such, for semiskilled workers, although millions were available as a cheap pool of brute-force labor when such might be necessary for large government-sponsored projects. The men and women in line shuffled zombie-like, with heads down for the most part, avoiding eye contact with one another. Canby was reluctant to believe the government actually *drugged* food it fed the Freemen. But he had yet to eat in one of the Soup Kitchens—even though he had gone hungry a number of times when he'd failed to stretch his officer's Stipend from one of the euphemistically named "paydays" to the next.

An arrogant black limousine skimmer whispered past on the street. Its mirrored passenger windows would conceal sleek, young Managers at the top of the Enfranchised Class returning from an afternoon of sport in one of Brooklyn's nefarious unlicensed "Frolic Houses," enjoying aberrations unavailable even in the most specialized fleshpots of "The Square" in midtown Manhattan. Many of Canby's closest associates worked the Houses, including one Madam, ex-Lieutenant Commander Olga Confrass, a black helmsman who once commanded one of his 19th Star Legion warships. He watched the big skimmer disappear into a side street and scowled. Limousines seldom came to Brooklyn for other purposes; their occupants resided elsewhere with wearisome, pious spouses in the very odor of officially endorsed—hypocritical—sanctity.

As a member of the "Enfranchised" Class, himself, Canby was a lucky man indeed. He and his fellow ex-officers were permitted to hang on at the very bottom end of this economic bracket by virtue of the government "Stipend," periodically distributed at "pay stations" in amounts determined by one's previous military rank. Recipients could also collect their lifetime stipend in one payment. calculated according to actuarial tables. And many did, living a short life to the very hilt, then reporting to one of the government-sponsored Euthanasia Centers before their funds ran out. Soup Kitchens were off-limits to "paid-out" pensioners. However, because steady employment was nearly impossible to people with neither assets nor political connections, they inexorably tumbled into the unofficial subclass of thieves and fugitives from the law. A case in point was ex-Chief Pearly Madder, who attempted to avoid the inevitable, and failed. . . .

At an inconspicuous signal from bearded, ex-Petty Officer Carlo Nunn. who leaned casually—but watchfully—against a rusting lamppost, Canby turned east where Sixty-fifth Street terminated at First Avenue. In the distance beyond, ancient towers rose from the Manhattan Sector, a polluted and overcrowded hell like most of the New Washington metropolitan area. On his right, he was separated from the tossing gray waters of the bay by a row of deserted starship wharves that followed the shoreline in either direction as far as the eye could see. Isolated by a rusting electric fence. the sprawling, ghostly complex once supplied a war effort so vast it embroiled twenty-two separate civilizations and nearly all of the 483 planets known to contain starflight-capable sentients. Now, everything on the bay side of the fence was deserted— largely abandoned—and rapidly deteriorating. Great warehouses stood silent and empty, with whole floors of broken windows and unkempt facades; trash blown from littered streets tumbled in the wind over rows of darkened tram guides to collect in ugly drifts against the sheds and buildings; huge, brooding dockyard cranes rusted like the rotting corpses of colossal birds. The tattered wharves themselves had suffered the worst deterioration from both weather and water; some were already collapsing through their rotted pilings.

After his demobilization, Canby had settled on Staten Island for lack of anywhere else to go—military people seldom put down deep roots. As a "retiring" officer, he'd had his choice of transportation to any planet on which he might legally reside. But he'd chosen to stay where he was and added the unused transportation costs to his Stipend. It had seemed a good idea at the time, and still did—but for enormously different reasons.

Unfortunately, the life to which Canby had retired was no life at all, at least for people whose prior lives were defined by at least some significance in the scheme of things. Before the war, he'd delighted in hopes and dreams like any other determined young man. In those days, he'd even aspired to voyage beyond the galaxy—and before the Armistice, he had once flown a DH.98 prototype swift enough to make the trip. Now dreams of that magnitude were things of the past—unless perhaps Nemil Quinn's campaign for Prime Minister prospered. But that was in the future, and the odds of an election victory were a million to one, even for someone with Quinn's resources.

For the first years after demobilization, Canby had done everything in his power to find some sort of meaningful employment. In the end, however, he had few qualifications outside the starflight disciplines, and no one was interested in an ex-military officer past twenty-five. Finally, he'd given in, as had millions of other veterans throughout the Empire. To survive, he'd learned to trade self-respect for the Stipend—but with his "Legion" he fought the oppressors using every ounce of courage and cunning he could muster.

The abandoned wharves ended just before First Avenue became the Shore Parkway and took a more southerly direction—into the ancient Bay Ridge section. It was here that ex-commander Namron Amps—one-time 19th Star Legion Chaplain—promised that Madder would be waiting. The bustling streets would provide necessary cover from V-Pols, ever vigilant for felons like the Chief, who had been apprehended after stealing food from one of the National Soup Kitchens: one of many crimes punishable by death.

Canby glanced around him, searching for a familiar face in the bustle of life swirling noisily around him: a crew of cable repairmen in fancy monogrammed coveralls, two muscular women driving a great construction lorry belching acrid smoke, a skinny prostitute on a park bench with his trousers open displaying himself to three prospective customers in miniskirts, plumbers lugging ten-foot lengths of heavy pipe between them, a muscular brewery man rolling barrels into a taproom cellar, little boys dodging through the crowd as they boisterously played out games known only to themselves, a trio of old men puffing thoughtfully on sweet-smelling pipes, a ragged gang of tough-looking Freemen up to no good, empty-faced ladies driving expensive street skimmers, a pink-haired executive with a row of five self-propelled brief-cases bobbing in his wake, umbrella vendors who disappeared like wraiths when V-Pols approached. Brooklyn's ancient Bay Ridge neighborhood was a world teeming with action and diversity—one to which Canby found himself more attracted each time he visited. These people were more real than all the sleek, stylish Politicians in New Washington.

From the littered entrance of an alleyway beside a dingy storefront, a heavyset, bearded figure nodded to him: Amps. The man had a colossal nose, bull neck, and totally unsupressed hair. Beside him, a familiar round face with large ears materialized from the shadows, eyes darting nervously here and there like a housecat about to emerge from a doorway. It was Madder. The eyes fastened suddenly on Canby, and an anxious smile appeared where only the grim line of a mouth had shown.

At the same time, Amps smiled, patted the man reassuringly on his shoulder, then disappeared into the crowd, his mission accomplished.

Returning Madder's cautious smile, Canby checked once more for V-Pols, then sauntered casually through the crowd into the shadows of the alley. Madder was hiding behind a tumbledown shed. Lord, how he'd changed! Filthy and disheveled, he clearly weighed only a fraction of his service heft; his stubbled face was drawn; and his eyes bore the haggard look of a man in constant fear for his life. His clothing was in rags, and he smelled as if he had slept in a sewer—which probably he had.

"Skipper," the wretched man whispered hoarsely, "thank God you've come!"

Canby put a hand on Madder's trembling shoulder. "Looks like it's been bad, Chief," he said gently.

"Aye, Skipper," Madder replied in a weak voice. "Worse than I ever imagined—an' now they won't let me near the Euthanasia places. They want me for their public executions. If I'd known, I never would have—"

"Don't look back, Chief," Canby interrupted, giving the man's shoulder a reassuring squeeze. "You've got your future again—all you need do is take it." He drew an envelope from his flight jacket. "I have a HyperTube ticket here in my name to Bombay. They've never subscribed to INTERPOL's tracking network there."

"Bombay." Madder pronounced it as if he could hardly believe his voice. "Then they can't trace me there, can they?"

"That's right," Canby assured him. "Everything's arranged. All you need to do now is catch the HyperTube."

"But how will I do that?" Madder asked, as if he were about to discover that everything was too good to be true. "I can't get on a train dressed like this. I . . . stink."

"That's what I brought *these* for," Canby said, holding out the shopping bag he carried. "The SterileWipes and clean clothes in here will take care of your, er, *unusual* accoutrements," he said with a chuckle. "Although, I'm afraid they'll be a little large. You've lost a bit of weight since I last saw you. Chaplain Amps forgot to tell me about that."

Madder shook his head. "My God, Skipper," he said, fingering the clothes. "Don't matter how well they fit. Lots of clothes don't fit well these days. An' they'll make it harder for the V-Pols to recognize me."

"I brought *these* for the V-Pols," Canby chuckled, producing a wig, false beard, and eyeglasses. "With these, you're on your way for certain."

"Jesus," Madder gulped, his eyes filling with tears. "I can hardly believe it."

"You asked for help, didn't you?"

"Yeah," Madder replied in a low voice. "I asked a lot of other people first, an' all of a sudden they didn't know me anymore. Only you an' Commander Amps." He shook his head. "I didn't get into trouble because I planned things that way—"

"Forget the others, Chief." Canby said. "Everything's going to be all right now. Just get yourself to Bombay. change your name, and start a new life. It won't be easy, but it shouldn't take much more than a couple of years' hard work until you can register there as a Freeman."

Madder nodded. "Yeah," he said, "I can survive if they're not lookin' for me—and I've never been afraid of hard work. You remember that, don't you, Commander?"

Canby smiled. "It's why I'm here, Chief—" he said, "and glad to help you."

"God bless you, Commander Canby," Madder said, clutching the envelope in his hands. "Someday. somehow, I'll pay this back to you—with interest."

"Get that new life for yourself, Chief," Canby said. "Anything that beats these rotten Politicians is reward enough for me." He looked at his watch. "The HyperTube to Bombay leaves in less than half an hour. Duck into the alley and put this stuff on. Then we'll walk to the station together. It'll make things easier. . . . "

By noon, Canby was on his way home. His remaining funds would carry him through—frugally—to the next "payday" *if* he went easy on food and put off the rent (with heavy interest) until the following month. Braving a fierce wind, he rode in one of the small ferries plying the "Narrows" beside the ancient wreck of a colossal bridge. He smiled. So he'd be a little hungry; everybody in the Legion sacrificed once in a while when a fellow veteran veered into trouble. It was worth both the effort and the risk—if for no other reason than to subvert a government gone totally out of control.

Belgravia Sector, London • Earth

Late that afternoon in London's Belgravia sector, just off Belgrave Square where Grosvenor Crescent meets Halkin Street, Sadir, First Earl of Renaldo, stormed across the second-floor bedroom of his elegant mansion, hurling curses in the direction of two butlers and a footman as they beat a hasty retreat from the room. During a moment of inattention, Gertrude, the assistant butler, had dropped one of Renaldo's favorite cuff links. It had promptly rolled into one of the ancient town home's "authentic" hot air registers, where it rattled down a pipe whose very origins were lost in time. "Out, you bloody, *bloody* idiots," the Earl screamed. "And stay out, until you can use your goddamn stillborn brains!" Panting as much from anger as his exertions, he plopped heavily into an overstuffed chair, glaring at the empty doorway. Cheap, lowlife bastards, he thought dyspeptically. It was the same in so *many* phases of modern life. Hired help simply couldn't be trusted. Of course, one couldn't trust *anyone*, these days. Petulantly, he glowered at his reflection in an ornate standing mirror—today of all days! The whole week he'd looked forward to attending the charity reception at the Barbican Gallery in his new Elizabethan ensemble, and now this.

He was partially dressed in knee-length breeches of russet satin (with an extra full cut for his considerable girth), yellow silk knee stockings, garters trimmed with white lace, a white undershirt, and a lace ruff around his neck. A gold brocaded emerald doublet—authentically padded, puffed, and slashed—was draped on a dressmaker's dummy next to the mirror. Atop an ornate nightstand was a high-crowned, be-plumed beaver hat; nearby, a pair of wide, soft black leather boots with buckle and riding spurs. A large, circular cloak, in the manner of the three Musketeers' d'Artagnan, lay in a heap where one of the footmen had dropped it in his haste.

Groaning, Renaldo struggled out of his chair—the corset he wore to reduce his huge stomach and puff his normally sunken chest could be painful at times. And now that the worthless servants were spooked, he would have to finish dressing himself, often a difficult task with the complex historical garb customarily frequented by Imperial Earth's nobility.

As were his highbred father and grandfather before him, he was short—less than two meters tall—with stubby fingers, a protruding belly, and thin, spindly legs. Attending London University (at prestigious Beesley College), he'd once been somewhat of a sportsman, but high living and acute addiction to good food quickly transformed a once-promising athlete into the corpulent, crimson-faced ruin he became before he turned thirty. Today, at some fifty-eight years of age, half a lifetime of tobacco in one form or another stained his neglected teeth; his face—round and white as uncooked meat pie—was pockmarked from the many venereal diseases he'd sampled as a young man; and his cheeks showed the network of tiny, blue capillaries associated with overindulgence in a number of substances. Only his small, close-set eyes—mistrusting and unyieldingly avaricious—revealed any life at all.

He glanced about the room, displeased even by the seventeenth-century grandeur around him. The ceiling was a magnificent trompe l'oeil painting by Verrio depicting ancient England's Queen Anne as the allegorical figure of Justice, attended by Neptune, Britannia, Peace, and Plenty. On the walls hung five of six Battle-of-Solebay tapestries that were woven by the Poyntz family at Mortlake and Hatten Garden during the 1680s. A spectacular marble fireplace by James Nost (originally intended for George I's bedchamber) blazed odorlessly with holographic images of a coal fire across from a huge, canopied bed designed for Charlotte, George III's queen. The bed was, as yet, unmade—the Earl spent most of his morning and early afternoon hours delighting in certain "distractions" provided by individuals of the mansion's staff.

Waddling to the nightstand, he groaned as he bent to retrieve his boots—*Goddamn* corset!—then set course once more for the chair. Another unhappy groan accompanied his return to the cushions, after which he dropped one boot on either side of himself, then sat puffing unhappily and wondering—only momentarily—if he should jettison the corset. Of course he couldn't. He'd never fasten his breeches without it, much less close the vest for which the bloody tailor Bartholomew had made him pay so much.

Letting out his breath, he canted dizzily sideways, retrieving the right boot with his fingertips and placing it beside his leg. Now came the hard part. With extreme effort, he grasped the top of the boot in both hands and painfully began to raise his right leg, with the corset cutting cruelly into his chest. But the foot wouldn't go high enough. Giddy with lack of oxygen, he tried to gain a toehold by tilting the boot backward. But just as he felt his foot slip over the top, he simply *had* to breathe, and dropped the whole thing, sprawling backward in the chair while air burst into his grateful lungs.

Panting weakly while tiny points of light danced before his eyes, he cursed the butler for her clumsiness—and for the horrible circumstances in which he now found himself. Damn! He paid the simple bastards a living wage to serve him, and by God, serve they would. "Mrs. Timpton . . . Gertrude," he roared. Come here. *Immediately*."

An older woman's face peered cautiously around the corner.

"Yes, you, Mrs. Timpton," Renaldo said. "You and young Gertrude. In here. Immediately."

"You won't punish us, my lord?" Timpton asked.

"I didn't say that," Renaldo answered peevishly. "My cuff link *is* gone, after all."

Timpton disappeared.

"Goddamnit, you two. In here, I say. Now—or you lose your jobs. You both know what it's like on the Dole." He laughed to himself. *That* would get to them—nobody wanted to be a Freeman.

The women cautiously made their way into the bedroom, heads hanging, eyes on the floor. They were dressed identically in long red jackets trimmed with gold braid, white satin breeches, white stockings, and black slippers decorated by huge brass buckles. Gertrude Kress, a skinny teenager with the eyes of a frightened doe, held little interest for Renaldo; he could hire her clones for his pleasure whenever he wanted. On the other hand, Dorothy Timpton was a handsome, statuesque woman in her mid-forties with long straw-colored hair, an ample bust, and a pleasant face. Over the years, he'd rather overlooked her among the household staff as he would a familiar, agreeable piece of furniture. A servant, but never a woman—staff whores were hired through an altogether different process. On closer inspection, however, she was . . . pleasing. . . ."Stop right there," he commanded when they were halfway across the room.

Both came to a halt without looking up.

"Now," he demanded, staring reprovingly, "where is that footman you had with you?"

Neither responded.

Renaldo felt a sudden rush of annoyance. Servants were paid to *answer*, by God. "Did you hear me?" he demanded in a high voice.

"Y-yes, my lord," replied Timpton, glancing momentarily at the Earl's face but never meeting his eye.

"Then where *is* he?" Renaldo demanded, continuing to stare at Timpton—she *did* have a decent figure for a servant woman her age. A bit hefty, but definitely interesting, especially her large bosom. Despite the quite recent ministrations of an expensive whore, he felt a definite stirring in his loins.

"He is in the hall, my lord," Timpton replied uneasily.

"You'll call him here, old wench—immediately."

"Yes, my lord," Timpton mumbled, her face betraying a moment's anxiety. She turned toward the door. "Gunter!" she called. "Come here!"

Gunter Beck, a rough-hewn man of some thirty hard years, limped into the bedroom, his eyes also on the carpet. At some time in his life, he had obviously injured his left leg and seemed proud of the wound, as if it made him more of a man.

Renaldo remained frowning for a moment, then an idea began to form. He smiled. "Take off your clothes," he ordered, "all three of you."

"M'lord, please . . . " Timpton pleaded.

"Silence, old woman," Renaldo said, "unless, of course, you want to go back to the Dole, where I found you."

"No, m'lord," the woman said, and began to unbutton her jacket. Soon all three were standing nude in the middle of the floor.

"Well, Beck," Renaldo said with a chuckle, "looks as if *you're* ready to play, aren't you?"

"Yes, m'lord," Beck said, his eyes eagerly exploring the two women.

"Which one pleases you, lad?" Renaldo inquired with an evil leer.

"Either of 'em, m'lord," Beck replied with a coarse laugh that revealed a number of missing teeth. "I'm not proud when it comes to women."

"My lord," Mrs. Timpton interposed, "Gertrude has never . . . "

"Never what?" Renaldo demanded.

"Never . . . been with a man, m'lord," the woman replied wretchedly, keeping her eyes on the floor.

"Gertrude," Renaldo inquired, turning to the younger

woman with obvious surprise, "you claim you're still a bloody virgin?"

"I am a virgin, m'lord," the young woman replied in a whisper. By now, she was blushing so intensely her cheeks looked as if she were running a fever.

"With looks like that, can't say I'm surprised," Renaldo commented. He turned to the older woman. "Very well, Mrs. Timpton," he said, "I shall save her for later. But only *you* are left to service poor Gunter, here—and you can see as well as I that he requires relief in the worst kind of way."

Gunter gave a deep laugh. "Oh, I do, m'lord," he said. "I do."

"Gertrude," Renaldo ordered with a smirk, "would you be so good as to fetch that padded chair for Gunter and Mrs. Timpton?" He pointed to an ornate antique beside the fireplace. "Bring it here in front of me so I can watch."

With a look of utter dismay, the young woman dragged the chair across the room and placed it in front of the Earl.

"Excellent," Renaldo said, motioning to Timpton and Beck as his face broke into a great smile. "Well, you lovebirds—to the chair. You certainly know what to do next." He sniggled. "Yes, and Gertrude," he added as an afterthought, "stand close to me here so you can see firsthand what you've been missing. . . . "

In the first hours of the following day, after a genial evening with peers at the old twentieth-century Barbican Center—where he donated a quarter million credits to the World Opera Society—Renaldo eagerly hurried home and retired to his study. Other, more interesting business had been on his mind all evening—business whose fruition, by now, should have been reported on his private message system. In his haste, he hardly noticed the magnificent dark walnut paneling that surrounded him. The shelves contained more than a thousand handsomely bound volumes, some dating to the mid-fifteenth century. Carelessly tossing his plumed hat atop a rare twelfth-century globe—added to his collection only weeks ago—he settled heavily into an ornate chair before a colossal nineteenth-century desk carved for the young Edward VII when he was still Prince of Wales.

A touch of a button revealed that the great desk had been gutted for a more modern role. Noiselessly, its top slid open to reveal a powerful workstation that brought a smile of real appreciation to the Earl's rouged countenance. He was exceedingly proud of his grasp—however superficial—of "modern" technology. And, truth to tell, Renaldo had indeed managed to acquire a certain skill in topics related to information sciences. He found the knowledge, or at least its exhibition, to be useful in his semi-official status of First Patron of the Admiralty.

Everyone knew, but no one admitted, that each member of the Political Class was ultimately controlled in one way or another by the vast wealth of the Nobles. And the most powerful Nobles—those controlling the really gigantic fortunes—usually specialized in a particular governmental area. Renaldo's area of interest was the Fleet. Since purchasing the title of First Patron of the Admiralty from the late Earl of Gloucester some years ago, he'd directed considerable wealth to campaigns of favored politicians for positions controlling or affecting the huge bureaucracy that ran Earth's Imperial Deep Space Fleet. In fact, his latest protégé, one David Lotember, had only recently taken office as Minister.

Tonight, however, other ships—very *private* ships—occupied Renaldo's mind. With no particular occupation to occupy his mind, save collecting wealth and pursuing pleasure, the Earl had been dabbling in the extremely profitable occupation of slaving.

Shortly after achieving HyperLight travel, Earth's occupants were surprised to discover that they were not at all alone in what soon became known as the "Home Galaxy." Stranger yet, most of their sentient neighbors looked a great deal like themselves. A general consensus attributed this to mysterious beings known only as "Gods" who had, unknown ages past, seeded numerous planets with organisms that would ultimately develop star-shaped, "humanoid," body configurations. Because these peculiar "GodSeeds" continued to evolve at random rates, many of the developing cultures were still in primitive states, incapable even of perceiving the intergalactic commerce that flowed around their planets. And—as might be predicted—various occupants of Earth had been raiding lesser planets for slaves, much as their enterprising, surface-bound ancestors had plundered the coast of Africa centuries before.

The fact that the odious practice was highly illegal—carrying a penalty of death that had been upheld many times over the years—frightened even Renaldo. Though his position in the House of Nobles would probably save his life should he be apprehended, such was never a certainty. Over the years, a number of lesser Nobles had been publicly executed for the crime. And even if he did manage to avoid the primary consequence, his defense would cost a ruinous fortune and destroy his reputation besides. To this end, he kept a huge sum in escrow for use by the captain of his ship in case he found himself apprehended. It could buy freedom from nearly anywhere—with enough left over to make the captain's silence well worth his trouble.

With this sort of protection in place, Renaldo dabbled, and dabbled profitably. One of his slaver ships had recently made a fine catch on the planet MT80'9A987-3, bagging nearly eight hundred prime slaves from a presteam society that included a number of nubile children who would bring tremendous prices on the pedophile circuit. The cargo was to be auctioned off that morning and—if everything had gone according to plan—the Captain's report should be waiting to be decoded.

Launching into what promised to be a pleasurable task, the Earl located an incoming message signed by Georges A. Cortot, an obscure composer. It described progress on a new opera he, Renaldo, had commissioned. The text—if slightly long—was certainly innocent enough in its content and subject; Renaldo commissioned many legitimate works of art, especially operas. However, when the message's complex encoding was deciphered—a task requiring the space of some few seconds, even on Renaldo's powerful Elton-IV workstation—it described not an opera but an economic triumph. According to Cortot, nearly the whole cargo brought top prices at market, with wastage limited to a few cripples put down in space or sold to the gaming worlds for hunting targets. Renaldo felt himself grin. The special pedophile auction alone nearly doubled his contribution to the World Opera Society.

Working rapidly, he set up a number of special accounts in banking institutions scattered throughout the Empire, then composed a message of "congratulations." The latter contained coded account numbers into which his owner's share was to be allotted—along with a most generous deposit on the composer's next "opera," which, he instructed, should begin immediately. Then, chuckling, he shut down the terminal, locked the desk with a thumbprint, and made his way to his bedroom. A deliciously terrified Gertrude Kress would be waiting for his ministrations upstairs—with two wiry matrons to assist him should she prove *too* uncooperative.

NOVEMBER 29, 2689, EARTH DATE

Rayno Talphor • Nephalii

At the far edge of known civilization, in a ramshackle city where nearly anything—including anonymity—could be procured with enough money, Nikolai Kobir and Dorian Skoda, his cohelmsman, strode purposely over the cracked tarmac toward their use-burnished personnel shuttle.

Tall and powerfully built, Kobir had the broad forehead and high cheekbones of his Slavic ancestors, with straight black hair and the impassive look of one whom life has tested so often and so vigorously that he was beyond confidence. Son of a Kîrskian Admiral, he had the enormous hands of a peasant, an eagle's nose, thick black hair. and wide-set sniper's eyes. Since his early days as a ranking cadet in the Kirov Academy, he had progressed from an Ensign specially assigned to the Emperor's own *Tzigane* Squadron to a command position in the Kîrskian Fleet.

Beside him, Skoda was a wiry man of medium height and remarkable physical endurance. He had dark thoughtful eyes, an immense mustache, and black curly hair. He was also one of the steadiest helmsmen Kobir had ever encountered. Lighthearted and at times loud-voiced, he was often prone to bursting into the ancient Komaroff songs of his ancestors, inspiring sympathy and friendship everywhere.

Perhaps half a kilometer distant, the odd, bullet-shaped control tower of Rayno Talpohr's Municipal Starport cast three separate shadows across the featureless plain. As far as the eye could see, a perfectly level gulf of bright purple grassland extended in every direction to a jagged horizon of saffron mountains. The latter appeared to be formed from billions of flat plates that sparkled and flashed as three of the planet's nineteen moons rushed overhead through the black dome of space. A breeze swept up from the center of the great depression, bringing with it a spice-laden odor slightly redolent of pepper, to which neither Kobir nor Dorian Skoda paid much attention. They were much more taken with a transaction they had completed only moments before—one that Kobir had accomplished with the aplomb of a lifelong finagler. "A fine bargain, my friend," he said judiciously, squinting up at Nephalii, the triple star that provided light to the planet at this time of day.

"A *fine* bargain indeed, my Kapitan," Skoda agreed with a grin, "especially since according to the Empire's most recent interdominion legislation, the entire transaction cannot have occurred in the first place."

"True. my friend." Kobir said. "But is it not surely wonderful how cash money can instantly make possibilities from the impossible?"

"And modify laws as well," Skoda added, keying open the shuttle's carefully polished hatch. "Especially amazing when one considers that we—citizens of defeated Novokîrsk—have just purchased fourteen KT 88-E, beta-torqued disruptor cannons, the most advanced weapons in the known universe. Technology that—by the strictest treaty—is not permitted to persons of our nationality."

"Ah, blessed corruption—" Kobir sighed facetiously, deftly reactivating the seal as he followed his cohelmsman through the hatch, "where should we be without it?" Inside, the little ship belied her age-dulled exterior. The tiny control bridge was equipped with the most up-to-date readouts and navigation equipment money could buy. Kobir insisted on maintaining equipment in the best manner he could afford—and budgeted much of his organization's "earnings" toward this goal. Back on Khalife all seven of his surviving KV 388s looked and flew as well as—often better than—they had when they were new. Only the two plodding KV 72 transports looked their age, and then solely in places such as their exterior hull cladding that might be observed by "outsiders." Otherwise, they were also maintained in better-than-new condition.

While Skoda radioed the orbiting transport crew for a cargo shuttle, Kobir eagerly scanned confidential starship-movement schedules he had also purchased in Rayno Talphor.

His interest in the movement of starships was no passing whim. Indeed, such tables were of extreme interest to him—as well as to his entire organization—for Kobir operated one of the more successful squadrons of space pirates, or "freebooters," as he chose to term their operations. He had not selected the vocation happily, but during the past five years had inexorably been starved into it by the draconian terms of armistice imposed by Imperial Earth's Treaty of Houdak. However, the fact that Kobir's most frequent targets were starships of Imperial Earth had nothing to do with his politics. Ever pragmatic, he attacked only the most richly loaded targets—and inasmuch as Imperial Earth presently controlled most of the galaxy's rich commerce, their ships became his targets by default. It made sense to Kobir; it provided a good living both for himself and the people who depended on him.

"Hmm," he mused, still studying the tables as Skoda taxied out onto the grassy surface for liftoff, "fat targets appear to be awaiting our ministrations in the next few weeks." He nodded to himself. "We have been most conservative so far this year, Skoda; only five raids."

"We have been patient indeed, Kapitan," Skoda agreed, easing the little ship into the air and setting her controls for best-climb-to-orbit. "Our financial people are anxious for another raid; investment opportunities are at a peak next month in many parts of the galaxy."

Kobir nodded appreciation for the man's words. "I understand," he said. "But keep in mind that one reason for our success has been a dearth of greed. And as a consequence of our latest patience, these, er, unwilling *patrons*, shall we say, will be most ill-prepared for our visits, both in amount of potential spoils in their holds *and* their preparations to counterattack."

They surged past their cargo shuttle—looking just as age-polished as their own ship—at a little beyond thirty miles altitude. Approximately six Standard Hours later, fourteen disruptor cannons were secure in the holds, and the old KV 72 moved out of orbit into deep space. setting course for Khalife, eight days' journey distant.

NOVEMBER 30, 2689, EARTH DATE

Columbia Sector, New Washington • Earth

Back on Earth in the ancient Columbia Sector of New Washington. David Lotember, Minister of the Admiralty, relaxed amid musty splendor at the grand Hall of Parliament. Surrounded by baroque decorations and trappings of the approaching XmasTide holidays, he carefully regarded the important men and women around him as they debated fine points of the Empire's new Universal Entitlements Act. He was tall, slim, and—no other word would fit—aristocratic looking: the very embodiment of a career legislator. His alert brown eyes were set deep beside a long, patrician nose that perched within the confines of a narrow, clean-shaven face, complementing flawlessly his thin, patrician lips. His practiced demeanor bespoke calm dignity, intelligence, and concern, from his fastidiously coifed sorrel hair to his luxurious Edwardian ensemble—a hallmark of success in the Political Class. He wore a gray frock coat, fitted close to his body with a slight flare at the bottom and velvet lapels forming a deep vee to his waist. Attached to his left lapel was a tiny wreath of jeweled pine boughs, signifying his recognition of those *tiring* individuals from the Revised Imperial Church & Spiritual Authority who constantly clamored for observance of the holidays as sort of a religious occasion. Beneath his coat, a figured, double-breasted vest matched his suit and mostly covered his pleated white shirt whose stiff, winged collar complemented a large, puffed ascot tie with a gold stickpin in its center. Narrow gray trousers with distinct creases above side-buttoned gaiters and patent-leather shoes completed the apparel. He cut an imposing figure for his age, and he knew it.

The Entitlements bill—an important issue nearly everywhere—would be up for a vote in the very near future. Entitlements was an issue that Lotember was glad to leave for others. It was a subject dear to the hearts of the voters, especially the swarms of Freemen—and therefore one that had to be handled carefully. Not that voters had any real power. Elections at any level merely decided which members of the Political Class were in office and which were not. Office-holders wielded more power and could accumulate more wealth than their less fortunate colleagues. The latter spent their between-election days in reasonably gainful pursuits such as lobbying, a term that translated into earning money by passing "campaign donations" (and other less subtle inducements) to officeholders in the name of business interests. But no matter how comfortable out-of-office politicos made themselves between elections, it was not the sort of life that appealed to persons who were accustomed to (or would-*like* to become accustomed to) power. Therefore, the business of politics was a very serious one indeed—especially on those rare issues that caught the public eye.

Luckily, today's issue was quite beyond the realm of Fleet politics (a deadly serious game itself, involving tremendous personal "complementary fees"), and Lotember's interest lay only in guarding against possible threats to his own power.

He'd come to this exalted position recently, after investing his entire life to achieve it—only the office of Prime Minister was higher. He'd begun during the war as a lowly Lieutenant—a supervisor of clerks—in the Ministry of Supply, but rose swiftly due to a penchant for unerringly diverting supplies to destinations where they would do the most good—for himself.

By war's end, Admiral David Lotember found himself rubbing elbows with some of the Empire's most powerful Nobles, who promptly returned to civilian life and resumed their normal activities—managing the tremendous resources accruing to their titles He stayed on just long enough to help them on their way, then moved swiftly to the Political Class, ran for State Treasurer of Greater Europe, and pulled in enough unwritten IOUs to outspend his competitors and win the election.

It was in this office that a number of discreet fund transfers won the appreciation of Renaldo. With the Earl's financial backing, the onetime supervisor of clerks began his final ascension to Minister of the Admiralty—into which lofty post he had settled only the previous month. A wholly visceral feeling of exultation was still with him, as if his election victory had taken place only the previous evening. And the experience was surpassed only by the luxurious existence that attended his newfound power. The fact that he had absolutely no aptitude, education, or experience for the job counted little with Renaldo—or with Lotember himself. His ability to deliver under the table had won him the office—and barring the outbreak of war or like requirement for a Fleet of any great fighting competence, that ability would keep him in office for years to come.

Lotember smiled comfortably and settled into the cushions of his chair. Below, on the floor of the great semicircular room in which he sat, men and women dressed in Edwardian grandeur took the speaker's podium, presented short discourses for distribution to the voting masses, then blusteringly upheld their points against the equally blustering attacks by the other attendees who had their own points to make. The fact that these so-called "debates" had absolutely nothing to do with the actual running of government was nevertheless the basis for all Imperial rule. And though the actual voters instinctively knew that their ballots decided no more than which politicians were in office and which made their livings peddling influence, they patiently followed each campaign and voted their choice with a false hope characteristic only of human beings—at the same time the most intelligent and most witless sentients in the Home Galaxy.

Dorthea Pollard, the present speaker—an attractive woman in her thirties wearing an outfit with an uncomfortable-looking high-boned collar and great, puffed shoulders—was in the midst of declaring her "belief" that ordinary Freemen should have more of a voice in the intellectual workings of government. She'd find few who would argue against *that* before the media, Lotember thought with a laugh, even though he—and everyone else in the room —knew she didn't believe a word of what she said. She tended to voice her *true* opinions when she was under the influence, which was quite often, these days.

" . . . Here, then, the advocates of intellectual liberty have a clear dilemma proposed to their choice," she droned on and on and on. "They must ascribe this freedom, this imperfect conjunction of antecedents and consequents either to our voluntary or our involuntary actions. They have already made their determination. . . . "

In spite of his best efforts of concentration, Lotember's attention drifted to thoughts of the Grand Knight's XmasEve Divertissement he would attend with a select group of Nobles and high-ranking members of the Political and Managerial classes. He had always before attended these elite entertainments as a Mendicant; this time he would be initiated as a full-fledged Knight Reveler. If that were not excitement enough, however, this particular Divertissement came in the middle of the Holiday season *and* would be hosted by Nemil Quinn, a man also deservedly famed for the nubile youths of both sexes who participated in his previous entertainments and tournaments. . . .

These pleasurable musings were suddenly interrupted by a gentle touch to his forearm. Irritated by the intrusion, he turned in his seat to confront a senior Captain of the Imperial Fleet. The man's ramrod-straight posture, dauntless bearing, and piercing eyes were a familiar sight around his offices, but Lotember had never bothered to learn his name. "Who are you?" he asked imperiously, raising an eyebrow.

"Lyle Jennings, Minister. Captain, Imperial Fleet," the man replied. "I was assigned as your personal aide when you took office."

"Yes . . . of course, Jennings," Lotember grumbled, pointedly tenting his fingers to parry any possibility of a handshake. Bad business to encourage familiarity with a military type—especially one who had the temerity to open a conversation. After the war, the top tier of officers had been quickly dismissed to their Stipend, but some, of course, had escaped expurgation. All in all, the House Review Board had done a good job, but then perfection had been impossible during the victory celebrations. Clearly, this stiff-spined idiot was among those who had slipped into an unfortunate crack. "Well?" he demanded. "Do you have anything to say?"

"Minister," the Captain whispered in a respectful undertone, "I have been instructed to inform you that space pirates attacked the starliner E.S.S. *Queen Anne* this morning just off Nolon-31 in the Vega Sector."

"Space pirates?" Lotember demanded irritably. "Attacking our *Queen Anne*?" He frowned. *Anne* was one of the Empire's newest and most palatial express liners—a huge starship, capable of crossing the entire galaxy in less than two weeks.

"The *Queen Anne* herself, Minister," Jennings assured him. "Attacked by pirates."

"Yes, I got that," Lotember said with a scowl. "But what does it have to do with me? Certainly someone in the Admiralty has been designated to care for such emergencies without direct orders from a Minister."

"To be certain, Minister," Jennings replied. "Admiral Kendall has already dispatched a destroyer flotilla to lift for the Vega Sector within the hour."

"Then why bother me?" Lotember asked sarcastically. "Am I required to lead the chase or something?"

"Oh, no, Minister," Jennings said patiently. "But under the orders you personally laid down following your second briefing on our new weapon systems, you were to be immediately notified should an unauthorized 'foreign' agency make use of advanced technology."

"I see," Lotember said as a feeling of unease began to creep into his afternoon contentment. He remembered the briefing, all right. A number of powerful, top-secret weapons had been developed as a result of wartime research and had only recently reached production. He understood little of warfare, and even less about weapons, but one of them, a new disruptor system—something "beta-torqued," if he recalled correctly—had caught even his half-bored attention. So powerful and so compact were these disruptors, they could furnish the firepower of battleships to vessels the size of a light cruiser. It didn't take much of an expert to understand what mischief they could cause were they to wind up in the wrong hands. "I take it some technology turned up with these pirates," he said at some length.

"Yes, Minister," Jennings replied.

"And?"

"You mean the weapons, Minister?"

"For God's sake, man, what else would I mean?" Lotember growled contemptuously.

"They are rather secret to discuss in this room, Minister," Jennings suggested.

Lotember felt his face flush with rage. "And who gives a mere Captain authority to question the wishes of his Minister?" he demanded.

"An error, Minister," the officer said, taking a deep breath.

"You may continue. . . . "

Jennings squared his jaw, then brought his face close to Lotember's—rather too close for a common serviceman. "Our new KT 88-E disruptors," he whispered. "Admiral Sir Thomas Crandall was traveling aboard the liner at the time and identified the weapons aboard the pirate ship. All beta-torqued. Er, you *do* remember the term from the briefing, Minister?"

"Of course I do," Lotember growled through clenched teeth. He was angry, now. The new disruptors had found their way into the criminal network already. God, talk about corruption; it was everywhere. And, of course, since it was Fleet equipment, the whole bloody affair might reflect badly on himself. Indifferently dismissing the Captain with a wave of his hand, he waited fifteen minutes to ensure he would appear calm and unruffled, then sauntered back to his suite of offices to spread the word that anyone assigned to tracking down these pirates—from the highest to the lowest—would find themselves court-martialed and on the streets as lowly Freemen should they fail. It was early in his regime, and this offered an excellent opportunity to demonstrate that David Lotember was a strict disciplinarian who brooked no excuses for failure.

Book Two

THE SHIPS

Manhattan Sector, New Washington • Earth

Grand or mean, subways all over the galaxy smelled pretty much alike to Canby, whether they served as commuter transportation beneath the streets of a city or connected two megacenters through the center of a planet. In a word, they reeked of filth, blending the faintly sweet redolence of decaying organic matter with ordinary detritus from the abrasive process known as civilization. "Things went pretty well, considering," he remarked thoughtfully, following Nik Kellerwand and Pete Menderes onto a squalid, debris-strewn platform from the Naples–New Washington Express. The coach's sides were still hot from the speed of their passage through the Earth's mantle and outer core. Around them, age-grimed tile walls echoed the babble of at least ten languages as departing passengers crowded a single working escalator to the surface.

39

"Went well *considering*," Kellerwand allowed in a grumble. "But takin' chances like that worries me, Skipper. Naples was full of those blue-suited V-Pol bastards." A powerful, broad-shouldered black man, Kellerwand originally hailed from New Britain, one of the first star systems colonized after the discovery of the HyperLight Drive. He had enormous feet, a broad nose, bristly black hair, and the narrow eyes of a gunner—which was precisely what he had been, before demobilization. Extremely precise in his ways, he had once served as Gunnery Officer aboard Canby's number-six ship, with some eight confirmed kills to his credit.

"And you *know* the place was lousy with the V-Pols' plainclothes buddies who we *couldn't* see," Menderes added. He had a pink, open face, red, curly hair, and green eyes. A popular starship commander in the old 19th, his countenance was open and humorous, inspiring sympathy and friendship everywhere.

"In spite of all that, we made it *and* accomplished the mission we set for ourselves," Canby reminded them with a little grin as they stepped from the musty warmth of the station into Manhattan's damp December cold. "Five guys and nine women safely off to Marmaria, halfway across the galaxy. And without us, all of them would be dead." He shook his head and glanced at at least a half dozen blue-suited V-Pols who lined the sidewalk, openly scanning people on their way out of the station. "Unless Quinn wins the next election, a lot of people are in a heap of hurt," he said from the side of his mouth. "It's pretty clear the V-Pols are under orders to trim out the old Fleet types who actually saw combat. All you gotta do is look cross-eyed at them and you're in jail."

"Headin' to the gallows for a public execution," Kellerwand added as they started down the street. He turned to look Canby in the eye. "It's only a matter of time till the bastards wise up to what we're doing, Skipper," he said. "Then it'll be *us* they're cookin up charges against—and who'll be around to save *our* bacon?"

"Maybe no one," Canby said, looking the ex-gunner in the eye. "But *our* skins aren't the point. Fact is, we're saving people who don't deserve to die. If the risks are getting to you, then it's time to bail out of the Legion. A lot of people need help out there, and we can't afford anyone who's busy looking over his shoulder. They're the ones who get tripped up and blow missions. Right, my friend?"

"Yeah," Kellerwand admitted grudgingly. "guess you're right, Skipper."

"Still with us, then, Nik?" Canby asked, stopping at the entrance to a subway station.

Kellerwand thought for a moment. "Yeah, of course I am, Skipper," he said. "I've just gotta blow off steam every once in a while."

"We all do," Canby reassured him with an encouraging squeeze to his arm. He looked at Menderes. "You all right, Pete?" he asked.

Menderes nodded. "I'm all right, Skipper," he said. "But, by God, I know how Nik feels. I'd just as soon tackle a whole squadron of Kîrskian 388s than try to outwit those V-Pols. Nothing worse than enforcement fanatics—especially when they think they've got some sort of holy writ behind 'em."

Canby nodded. "Hang in there, guys," he said. "Maybe we can help get Nemil Quinn elected. Things ought to get better then."

"If he even runs," Menderes said. Then he clapped Canby on the shoulder. "I've got to catch a train, Skipper," he said. "Don't worry about us or the Legion. We're in it for the duration—whatever *that* turns out to be."

"I've got to go, too," Kellerwand added. "I'm with you— hell, we're all with you. If you hadn't gotten us together, somebody else would have had to. We can't just let the bastards run roughshod over us without puttin' up a fight."

"Thanks, guys," Canby called as the two strode off down the street toward midtown. Just as he was stepping to the sidewalk, an alarm sounded from the subway entrance. Simultaneously, the filthy lamps over the stairway dimmed, then slowly regained their dismal glow.

Moments later, a trio of women stormed out of the entrance. "Goddamn subway," one of them growled as the trio pushed past Canby. "Can you believe *another* bloody power failure?"

"What's to believe?" another said. "That's what the bastards do for fun!" Laughing, all three dashed for the curb, where they hiked their already short skirts and began shouting for a HoverHack. They got one in record time.

Grinning, Canby took mental stock of his own hairy legs and pronounced them hopeless, at least for the task of attracting a HoverHack—ninety-nine percent were operated by men. Instead, he started off at a brisk walk for the river walls, where he could catch a surface ferry to Brooklyn and then home.

Around him, Manhattan thundered through eternity in its own peculiar manner—much unchanged through the centuries. It was still mostly a vertical city, though many of the original steel-trussed palaces were no longer habitable—and many more had been replaced by even taller structures glistening like the purest crystal that, in clear summer air, seemed to stretch all the way to the stars. Today, they disappeared into a shroud of soft, gray vapor only a thousand feet or so above littered, HoverHack-filled streets. People hurried around corners, burst across streets in suicidal dashes, shouted their wares, stormed through doorways grand and small, flounced on spike high heels, laughed in a million tongues, and babbled every dialect of the galaxy. Everyone, even obvious bums, seemed to be hurrying somewhere, as if the world was scheduled to end when clocks struck the next hour. As always, Canby was fascinated—invigorated—by the colorful pandemonium, a protean, gleaming surge of colors splashed almost at random on forms and geometry that influenced—and were influenced by—every human-habitable city in the known universe. It was at the same time frightening and comforting, humbling and euphoric, depressing and stimulating—old and incredibly new. Dirty beyond belief, the old city still managed to sparkle in Canby's eyes. Denied the grand, limitless vistas of outer space he'd loved so well, he settled as close to Manhattan as he could afford. It was as near to the ends of time and space as he could manage without a starship.

At the East River, he turned south along the stone sea wall. Beyond the huge Fleet Salvage Yard was a ferry dock where he could see plumes of steam and smoke rising from a few old-fashioned ferries that still plied the river among the wreckage of once-mighty bridges, fallen into disuse, then disrepair, by virtue of myriad tunnels honeycombing the riverbottom. He checked his watch: more than an hour before the next boat departed—if, indeed, it left at its appointed time. Smiling, he followed the slowly crumbling concrete bulkhead, enjoying the riverside and its relative solitude. Out on the odorous gray-green water, a giant barge, prickly with rusting derricks and giant mechanical claw-arms, picked its way through the tangle of fallen bridges. Nearby, a large decomposing mass of tangled skeins and matted hair moved slowly downstream in the eddies. Canby filtered out the ugliness, striding easily along the shore and allowing his mind to connect with the peace of the river itself—or at least its unconquerable essence. Though the great stream had been a virtual sewer for nearly a thousand years, not even man could kill its spirit. Canby loved the water as he loved space.

On he trod, humming tunelessly, until the rusting, angular buildings of the Fleet Salvage Yard intruded on the seawall like a giant barricade. He smiled at himself as he detoured inland; no matter what his mood, the place never failed to conjure a feeling of excitement. It was where they put surplus starships up for sale before sending them to the breakers. Behind two courses of rusting wire fence and evilly flickering laser slashers, long, decrepit quays reached out into the filthy river like the gray, rusting fingers of some giant, malformed hand. During the first years of peace, these quays had been crowded with surplus military starships of every conceivable description. Most had been sold to lesser dominions, or eventually scrapped, but a small number had also been purchased for conversion to various peacetime roles—or sometimes, it was rumored, to become the vehicles for private mercenary fleets, or even space privateers. Like many other veterans, Canby had been a frequent visitor in those days, roaming the wharves and quays, gazing longingly at the graceful forms moored there and imagining—just imagining—what it might be like to purchase one of the powerful ships for his own use. Most were bargains, priced at a fraction of their real worth. A number were even within Canby's reach—provided he cashed in his Stipend. Unfortunately, then he'd have a serious grocery problem, not to mention an embarrassing inability to maintain his purchase. So he only dreamed while all eventually disappeared to their various fates.

These days, like as not, the great wharves were nearly empty as the Space Fleet completed its task of downsizing for a peacekeeper's role. Today, only a few dozen forlorn vessels bobbed gently beside the huge empty piers, testing their berths in the cold breeze.

As he approached the Yard entrance, Canby glanced toward the ferry dock, then checked his watch. Probably not enough time to go in and look around, he considered, even though there were so few ships to look at. Replacing his hands in his pockets, he was about to stride on, when a half-familiar shape—until now obscured by a warehouse—caught his eye. Frowning, he turned to peer through the gate. Couldn't be. He took a few steps forward, staring intently.

"Hey, mate, it's still eight credits to go in, even on a cold day!"

Canby jumped, startled to reality by a guard's voice. "Those DH.98s down there?" he asked, still staring intently.

"What's a DH.98?" the man asked with little interest. Tall

and angular, he had a thin face, long jaw, and mean, narrow-set eyes.

"Those little starships over there—behind the warehouse."

The guard shrugged. "Oh, them," he said. "I donno what they are. They've been here a coupl'a weeks now—nobody seems interested in 'em, 'cept you. Off to the breakers soon, I'll wager."

"Yeah," Canby mused, "I guess so." He took one more peek at the starships parked nose-in to the quay. Their bows and flight bridges were still mostly obscured by the wharf itself, but no ships he knew of had two Drive nacelles the size of those. He reached into his pocket for a worn money clip. Peeling two Quads from his thin reserve, he handed them to the guard, absently took his receipt, then strode through the gate and made straight for the quay. They *had* to be DH.98s . . . and there were two more moored beside them, floating side-by-side behind the warehouse. Brawny-looking ships, they had huge nacelles to house huge powerplants and Drive units. One, the prototype, he remembered, had even been rigged for intergalactic travel. He'd flown that one at a factory rally during the war, but no further development had taken place. Nevertheless, with all their aspect of tremendous power, they were also among the most graceful starships ever designed. And it was this external shape, with a truly magnificent internal structure, that was the key to their weapons-carrying ability and speed. The chief reason they had never been placed into large-scale production was that they completed their testing schedule relatively late in the war. By then, the production pipeline had been filled with the lesser—but still quite effective—ships that actually won the victory. Too, by the time the powerful little ships were ready for manufacture, the Kîrskians' Deep Space Fleet had been much reduced in strength, so they had little chance to show their full potential. And certainly the builder of the little ships, Geoffrey Ltd. of Salisbury Hall, near London, had never been much favored by the Nobles in the first place. So unless it had become evident that the Empire was about to lose the war, there was little need for a better ship, especially one whose profitability in manufacture had yet to be proven.

Geometrically, the DH.98 was the outcome of a development chain that started with an outstanding intragalactic racer. Geoffrey's DH.96 aimed at extracting the maximum cruising speed from minimum power and maximum range. Minimum size, neat packaging, and above all clean design for atmosphere maneuvering enabled the Geoffrey designers to achieve this aim while wrapping the DH.98 around a huge weapons complex that, with a little extension, could accommodate more firepower than many a light cruiser.

Few starships had been designed with such fidelity to their original concept, but the end result was not achieved without some cost. The small mass, mighty Drive units, and delicately harmonized steering engines unquestionably laid the foundations of the ship's astonishing performance, but at the same time they also bequeathed pitfalls for unwary or poorly trained helmsmen. The DH.98 was a slightly nervous thoroughbred that would—and did—perform impressive feats in the hands of the courageous and competent, like Canby and his minions of the 19th Star Legion. However the ships could also deal out an occasional kick or bite as well; a number of "average" helmsmen had lost their lives in them, frequently taking the other nineteen members of the crew with them.

Nevertheless, as real connoisseurs of space flight knew, DH.98s without a few quirks would have been starships far less optimized for maximum performance above all things, and would have been just another class of combat starships among others rather than the outstanding machines that they turned out to be.

Surprised at the fervency of his reaction to the remarkable little ships, Canby frowned. He hadn't been this close to one for years. The few that survived the war had been snapped up quickly by smaller governments, and until today, not a one had appeared at the yard. Descending the ladder to the pier, he set off at a brisk walk, stopping only when he was at the short brow leading to the nearest ship's boarding hatch. He peered up nearly twenty feet to the small flight bridge near the nose, where two gray-white seagulls were soiling the raked Hyperscreen windshields while they covetously watched a third devour one of the misshapen creatures that managed to live in the polluted river. Canby pictured the helm and flight controls, just out of sight below the coaming. It was a tight little bridge, room for only a small flight and weapons crew. But proximity made for close teamwork, and the close quarters had been credited with at least some of the ship's phenomenal battle success.

All the Hyperscreens were filthy, but then, so was the whole starship. It mattered little to Canby; no amount of dirt could hide those lines. Even at rest, DH.98s looked as if they were traveling at HyperSpeed. Graceful beyond mere form, they were specially shaped for high-velocity atmospheric maneuvering as well as incredible speeds in deep space. When he'd flown them during the war, they were among the fastest starships in the known universe. Probably a number of more modern ships were now as fast . . . but not many. And none prettier!

His eye took in the graceful curve of her hull. She was some hundred and fifty feet in length, with huge Drive nacelles—themselves nearly half the size of the main hull—shoulder-mounted on sturdy, fifteen-foot sponsons some quarter of the way back from the bow. Two stubby, ovoid fins in a shallow vee rose an additional thirty feet over the ship's sharply tapered stern. Canby found himself grinning like an imbecile. It was like greeting an old friend after a long, long separation!

Hunching his shoulders, he strode out along the brow to touch the center of the boarding hatch. It was unlocked—though unlubricated—moving back out of its frame with an audible squeak. Giving a practiced shove, Canby moved the hatch sideways into its stored position, then stepped into the tiny boarding corridor that acted as a main air lock. A single EverLamp glowed dully near the ceiling, its dim light just enough for him to find his way inside. Through ports in the inner hatches, he could see that the ship was completely dark inside. Nodding, he closed the outside hatch, then opened the power console. Four neat rows of indicators were dark and lifeless—the ship's two big three-drum delta-fusion reactors were powered down. Only small squares at the bottom right of the panel glowed dimly in the half-light. Two in red were battery-powered thumbprint readers that—could he activate them—would draw control rods from the reactors and begin the process of bringing the ship back to life. The third, a green one, would activate the ship's emergency lighting system. He touched this, then waited while some long-slumbering system tested itself. Presently, a glow came through the inner hatch ports—*that* system, at least, seemed to work.

Stepping to the forward inner hatch, he activated the latch and pushed it open. Cold, stale air hit him like a brick wall. He hadn't been quite prepared for that: pent-up effluvium from sealants and flexible gaskets; the greasy odors of aging lubricants; a sour, decaying stench that could only come from dried-up life-support and waste systems; and the heavy, phenolic redolence of long-unused logics. He sniffed for a few moments, testing. . . . At last, satisfied that the atmosphere was neither poisonous nor life-threatening, he stepped through the hatch and carefully mounted a steep companionway to the bridge. The effect was akin to coming home after a long absence. Overhead, the low arch of Hyperscreens was filthy, admitting only a dull, grayish light, but beneath these, the bridge itself was neat and clean. Two columns of three console pairs on either side of the narrow aisle seemed reasonably intact, although one of the port Navigator stations appeared to have been victim of a parts raid during some period of the ship's storage. He walked forward to where the bridge narrowed, directly beneath the raked Hyperscreen windshield. Here, there was room for only three consoles:

the helmsman's station, flanked by a cohelmsman on the right and a Systems Chief on the left. As if in a dream, he took his accustomed place at the helm, fingers seeking out console controls while his feet settled at the rudder sensors. The latter were located a little too far forward for him; clearly the last person at the helm had been blessed with somewhat longer legs. He grinned; he might not have been able to bring the ship to life, but his own movement beneath the transparent Hyperscreen had at least frightened off the filthy seagulls. Only bloody remains of the misshapen fish remained outside on the ship's nose—that and tons of seagull by-products.

A thousand memories passed his mind's eye as he sat at the helm, his fingers resting comfortably on the cold flight controls. He smiled. One of the few things that had always bothered him was the layout of the helm console. There was that damnable unbroken row of—he looked—nine sensors on the starboard side. How was the helmsman to select the correct one to touch in the dark? He could remember a number of occasions when he'd extinguished the nav lights instead of lighting the landing beams. Had the switches been separated up into mini-rows, as they were on the Norton VT.25, there would have been no problem. . . .

Even with their faults, 98s were lovely starships to fly, though they did have their critics. They tended to swing on both takeoff and landing, and had a terrific landing speed—mostly due to the smallish linear gravity repulsor that provided near-surface lift. Nine degrees of freedom meant phenomenal maneuverability, but within fifty thousand feet of the surface, one had to be on top of the controls every moment, from liftoff to landing.

To his right, the cohelmsman's console was toed-in slightly toward the fore-and-aft line, and this sometimes caused the right cheek of the cohelmsman's backside to go to sleep. This numbness, in turn, gave the impression that the starship was in a slow roll to the right, especially at night or when flying near the surface in dense clouds. It needed firm discipline to believe the instruments, especially below ten thousand feet, when the ship's local gravity was disabled. He remembered a case when a new man was converting to the starship and thought the ship had gotten out of control. Quite a tussle with the helmsman had ensued, which later had caused the new man considerable embarrassment for the remainder of his career.

A glance through the port Hyperscreens—at a departing steam ferry—reminded Canby that he'd dreamed rather longer than he'd planned to. But, as he observed with a smile, he now had another two hours to explore the ship before he'd have to leave—a bit more indulgence for the eight credits he'd invested. Springing to the deck in a most practiced manner, he strode aft toward the machinery spaces. . . .

He missed the next ferry, too, exploring every nook and cranny with increasing fascination. Her maker's plate in the tiny wardroom gave a launch date of December 10, 2679—nearly ten years ago—but she had only 180 hours clocked on her Drive logs. Except for elapsed years, the ship was nearly brand-new. After determining that both Drive rooms and the reactors were complete (at least they *looked* complete), he checked the huge weapons bay and was astounded to find everything intact except for the massive buses that carried energy to the weapons themselves. Of course, he already knew *those* had been removed; while he was still outside, he'd seen hullmetal plates covering the empty holes where once ugly snouts of disruptors poked through. Leaning against a railing on the second-level inspection gallery, he gazed out at the maze of pipes, OptiCables, and wave guides that filled the room. Once they processed wavelengths of energy, then reflected them to the outsized disruptor cannon. Now, their feeds from the reactors had been severed at the aft bulkhead, rendering the complex mechanism useless junk—that could only be removed by destroying the ship's hull. Canby nodded. It explained why the ships were scheduled for the breakers. Nobody wanted them because there was no way to free up cargo space—or any other kind of space, for that matter. DH.98s were purely attack ships; they had no other existence aside from flying and fighting—both of which they did extremely well.

He was in the starboard Drive nacelle when he heard a woman shouting at the far end of the access tube that led through the sponson to the main hull: "Hey, mister, can you hear me? Where the hell are you?"

"Here," Canby shouted, running to peer through the tube, "in the starboard nacelle." At the far end was a female guard, with short, curly hair; jolly eyes; plump, dimpled cheeks; and ample, red lips. A good face, Canby thought—the sort of face that seemed reserved exclusively for chubby women.

"Com'on, guy," she urged. "We've been closed for damn near half an hour. Time to go home!"

"On my way," Canby called back. Buttoning his coat, he hurried through the access tube. It wasn't her fault he hadn't been in a DH.98 for nearly eight years. "Sorry," he said, emerging into the central corridor. "Guess I just lost track of time."

"S'okay," the guard replied. "I've seen your kind here before. You never get 'em out of your system, do you?"

"No," Canby admitted, shaking his head. "They kind of become a part of you."

"Yeah," she said, meeting his eyes. "I know."

Canby grinned. "Sounds as if you might have been in the Fleet yourself."

She nodded. "Eighth Fleet," she said. "I helped keep 'em in space. I was Crew Chief on one of the old Norton 25s."

"Twenty-fives were great ships," Canby said, finding his interest in the woman more than a little piqued.

She met his eyes again. "They're the ones I miss," she said, a faraway look momentarily passing her eyes. "But I know how you feel—at least a little bit."

Canby glanced at his watch again. Nearly half past five

now. "Don't suppose you're off for the day, are you?" he asked, feeling his face flush.

"Thought you'd never ask," she said with a grin. "What did you have in mind?"

"Well—supper, for starters," he said, returning her grin. "After that . . ." he threw up his hands, "who knows?"

"Mister," she said, "you've got yourself a deal."

"Call me Gordon," he said. "Better yet, Gordo. All right, er . . . ?"

"Lela," she said. "Lela Peterson, Gordo. And," she added, indicating her stature with a little grin, "you'll not be surprised if I tell you that I'm hungry."

"Nothing surprises me anymore, Lela," Canby said, "including the fact that I haven't eaten since early this morning myself."

"Com'on, then," she said, starting forward along the corridor. "Let's take care of first things first."

Aboard KV 388 #SW799 • in space

At exactly the same—relative—hour, deep in interstellar space, two of Kobir's KV 388s were closing in on S.S. *Umbrica Maru*, a grimy-looking old livestock transport, ungainly and angular with no atmospheric shielding for surface landing. From a distance, it looked like some great, bloated insect carrying half a dozen large maggots on its back—atmospheric shuttles used to transfer cargo to and from the surface. The ungainly vessel was moving through space at what was clearly its top speed, and just as clearly avoiding the main space routes through the region. In fact, it was the ship's careful avoidance of any established track among so-called "civilized" planets that had attracted the pirates' attention in the first place. Two straining fusion engines, on long outriggers at opposite sides of the elongated box that formed its hull, were befouling space with such terrific light and radiation that the intercept had to be made at an extremely difficult angle.

Kobir himself was at #SW799's helm as he made final preparations for his attack. A bit of intelligence combined with some gut-level guesswork told him that he was looking at an unusual—and valuable—prize indeed. He narrowed his eyes. Whatever it turned out to be, it was probably crewed by a gang of cutthroats just as willing to fight for its cargo as his Kîrskians were to capture it from them. He smiled, imagining its captain, nervously keeping as close a watch outside as possible, but knowing that radiation from his fusion engines blocked much of the view aft. Kobir would take advantage of that, using his small 8.8-mmi disruptors to shoot away the merchantman's HyCOMM antenna *through* the clouding exhaust before the ship could broadcast for help on its little-understood HyperLight communications transmitter whose signals arrived instantaneously throughout the known universe. *If* indeed the merchantman did broadcast for help in the first place, Kobir observed sardonically. Unless he missed his guess, the merchantman and its cargo were just as illegal as his own pirate ships. In fact, probably even *more* illegal.

"The target is now within extreme range, Kapitan," Bernard Frizell announced quietly from the gunnery console.

Kobir nodded. "Your hit probability?" he demanded calmly.

"At the necessary aperture, sixty percent, Kapitan," Frizell replied.

"Very well," Kobir replied. "Notify me when the probability exceeds eight-five."

"Aye, Kapitan."

Kobir glanced through the Hyperscreens at Émil Lippi, flying close formation in #SR642. How many years had he and wingman Émil Lippi flown side by side like this? It seemed like a lifetime. And Dorian Skoda, who calmly occupied the cohelmsman's console at his right—as he had since, it seemed, the beginning of time. Only the most fortunate of commanders fought with men like this at their sides, he thought.

Behind him, someone sneezed, breaking a near silence on the bridge. The mission was a delicate one, as were all operations that required boarding. Since the beginning of their stealthy pursuit, tension on the bridge had become nearly palpable. Warfare aboard a killer ship was much easier, Kobir considered. One either destroyed his enemy or was quickly destroyed himself. The act of capturing was a great deal different—and orders of magnitude more difficult.

"The enemy HyCOMM is quiet, Kapitan," reported Kruger—another rock-solid crewman who had been with Kobir for the last million or so years.

"Thank you, Kruger."

"Aye, Kapitan."

Muffled commotion from the aft bridge companionway manifested that the boarding party had arrived at the main boarding chamber on the deck below. A little early, he observed, but then a bit of nervousness—in small quantities—before a battle never hurt. Brave people, all of them. Once the merchantman's HyCOMM had been blown away—assuming a good hit—there would be no element of surprise. Something made him think about Frizell's glass eye and he grinned in spite of himself. No matter how the man tried, he never managed to match the color of his real eye, and the result was often hilarious, for he must have a huge collection of eyes by now. Thank God the affliction had no effect on his phenomenal gunnery.

Weapons . . . He must concentrate better than that. His own systems-summary board showed all the ship's weapons were activated and ready. Now all he could do was steer a steady course and wait.

"Eighty-six percent probability, Kapitan," Frizell announced presently. "Our enhancers now provide an excellent view through the merchantman's exhaust. She carries two long-range HyCOMM arrays and a single radio antenna. No more than . . . four shots should be required, allowing for one near-miss."

"Very well," Kobir said, then turned to Skoda. "You are ready to take command of the ship, Skoda?" he asked as if he were only stepping aft to relieve himself.

"I am ready, Kapitan," Skoda replied. "But I should be happier if I led the boarding party. What if something were to happen to you?"

"Then you would simply continue in my place, old friend," Kobir replied. He laughed quietly. "However, I am not ready to relinquish command just yet; therefore, I shall come through unscathed. Trust me on that."

"You are an impossible commander, Kapitan."

"And you are insubordinate, Skoda," Kobir countered in a ritual that dated back to one of their first missions together.

"Unfortunately, nothing can be done in either case," Skoda said, turning with a little smile. "Best of fortune, my Kapitan," he said. "I await your safe return."

Kobir reached across the consoles to press the man's fore-arm, then released his seat restraints. "Your ship," he said, vaulting from his recliner. "Steering engine at zero, zero twenty-one."

"Zero, zero twenty-one, Kapitan," Kobir echoed. "I have the con." But Kobir barely heard the man's answer. He was on his way aft. Less than a minute later, he stepped into the main boarding chamber where his ancient valet, Jakob Tancredi, was holding his standard-issue Kîrskian FlexArmor battle suit. A scarred—but highly polished—helmet in matching ebony lay at his feet beside a holstered .09-mmi blaster pistol.

"Good evening, Kapitan," Tancredi said calmly as the twelve-man boarding party came to attention. Slightly shorter than Kobir himself, he appeared old and fragile—as if he could almost float in air. Nevertheless, the wrinkled old man had served Nikolai Kobir as both valet and confidant since the latter was commissioned as an officer in the Deep Space Fleet. Kobir would have no other, carefully modifying the man's duties to keep pace with his advancing age.

"Good evening, Jakob," the Kîrskian replied. He nodded to the others. Already sealed in their battle suits, they could hear him only on voice circuits. Turning his back to the old man, he slipped his arms into the battle suit, then knelt to pull the armored boots over his own. This accomplished, he closed each leg along its inside seam. Standing once more, he sealed the front seam all the way to his neck and locked the collar ring. As he ran a systems test of the suit's environment controls on his left shoulder, Tancredi attached the blaster to his left hip and was ready with the helmet when he turned—with nearly twenty years' practice, their choreography was nearly perfect. "Thank you, Jakob," Kobir said, taking the spherical helmet in both hands and inspecting its armored crystal viewing aperture before lowering it carefully over his head. As he sealed neck ring to collar band, all noise ceased except the muffled hum of the environmental system. Touching his left shoulder again, he ran a checkout of the suit's closures. Presently, a green pinpoint glowed in the lower right quadrant of his helmet aperture. Nodding, he activated the short-range COMM system. "Testing," he said.

In turn, twelve figures in matching battle suits raised their 7.62-mmi blast pikes and repeated, "Ready." Their voices projected stereophonically into his helmet to accurately represent their position relative to him—the system had saved many lives during hand-to-hand combat in space.

Kobir ran one last personal checklist, signaled Tancredi to leave the boarding chamber, then waited while the old man sealed the inner hatch. When the warning light changed from red to green, he switched his voice circuit to the flight bridge. "Skoda," he said quietly. "We are ready. Tell Frizell he may fire at his pleasure."

"Aye, Kapitan," Skoda replied.

Even sealed in his suit—within the boarding chamber—

Kobir could feel the ship kick each time the big disruptor array fired. Once . . . twice . . . three times . . . The fourth shot never came. As always, Frizell was on the mark.

"Direct hits, Kapitan," Skoda reported calmly. "The target ship now has only radio communication."

"My compliments to Mr. Frizell," Kobir said; all had gone extremely well. At nearly a thousand light-years from the nearest receiver, the crew of their quarry could radio for help as much they wanted. Their message would not arrive until the next millennium. "Now, Skoda," he ordered, "take us through the merchantman's exhaust so we can introduce ourselves by short-range HyCOMM."

"Aye, Kapitan."

As he felt the ship accelerate, Kobir visualized Lippi pulling off a thousand yards to starboard so the two 388s approached their target on either side. Lippi's ship would then take up a parallel course with all its heavy armament pointed at the merchantman's bridge while Skoda approached the opposite side to seal hatches for boarding. It was a time-tested strategy, and usually—but not always—averted fights at the boarding hatch. After all, when a captain is about to have the control bridge of his ship demolished, he or she has great incentive to trade cargo for lives. Unfortunately, there were *also* those who were tempted to fight their way out of such a situation. That was why Kobir and his party wore full suits of FlexArmor.

After what seemed to be at least a year, the voice channel crackled with Skoda's voice: "The star barge purser indicates he will submit to boarding, Kapitan. I am pulling alongside to connect our hatches."

"Very well, Skoda," Kobir acknowledged, then nodded to one of the boarding party, a tall, slim figure with a great handlebar mustache that showed clearly through his visor. "You will take charge of the connection process, Tabor," he ordered calmly.

"Aye, Kapitan," a deep bass voice rumbled as Tabor

stepped to the hatch control panel and peered through the view panel. Kobir had installed standard deep-space transfer hatches on three of his KV 388s; so far they had returned the investment a thousand times over. Most space privateers operated by forcing victims to land before carrying out their depredations, a dangerous business at best—that was also the reason many privateers ultimately ended their lives on the gibbet.

In the next moment, the ship decelerated smoothly, then seemed to run free. Gripping handholds on the bulkhead, Kobir attempted to ignore the sensations. Like most modern warships, KV 388s maintained their own internal gravity systems; all were notoriously unreliable during precision maneuvers.

"The merchantman has extended its boarding tube," Tabor reported, his helmet glued to the viewport. He reached for two small control wheels and began to turn them in small increments—above the hatch, a red warning light began to strobe. "I am now extending ours." After what seemed to be a year or more, the deck lurched; a moment later, the strobing red lamp turned to steady green. "Mated and locked, Kapitan," he said.

Kobir said a silent prayer to an old, half-forgotten God of his forefathers, then waited for a final event.

"The merchantman has opened her half of the hatch," Tabor reported presently.

"Very well," Kobir said, stepping to one side of the coaming. Five of the boarding party crowded in behind him. Six others formed on the opposite side. Kobir nodded to himself. He had done everything he could. "Open the hatch," he ordered.

Manhattan Sector, New Washington • Earth

A dark blue guard's jacket lay neatly folded on a chair near the bed. On top of it were a skirt, blouse, hose, crimson briefs, and a stout white bra, each neatly stacked atop the other. Nearby were Canby's shirt, trousers, underwear, and socks lying helter-skelter where he had dropped them on the floor. Atop the bed, Canby relaxed against the pillows watching Peterson mix them a drink in her small bedroom. Completely nude and bent fetchingly over a small table, she smiled over her shoulder. "Best way to really know each other," she said, "is to spend time together in the buff."

"In that case," Canby replied, "we'll have few secrets, you and I." As he admired her large, dimpled bottom, he grinned, feeling a certain stirring in his loins—again. Already! They'd just finished a few minutes previously. An exciting woman, this Peterson, in a number of ways.

Finishing with their drinks, she turned with the glasses in hand, took one glance, then giggled and set them down again. "From the looks of that, you've got more than drinking on your mind, Gordo," she said, returning to the bed with a broad smile. She had ample, wide-spaced breasts, a sizable belly, sturdy legs, small feet, and a great thatch of honey-brown hair. Without uttering a word, she climbed onto the bed, and for the next twenty-odd minutes vigorously performed a number of highly athletic motions that would have put a woman half her size to shame. Afterward, when she went for the drinks, Canby was ready to relax.

"So you're a helmsman," she said later, sitting cross-legged beside him. "I thought that might be the case."

"*Was* a helmsman," Canby said, "a hundred thousand years ago."

She nodded. "A skipper?"

"Yeah," Canby said appreciatively, sipping the bourbon she'd brought him.

"On one of those little Geoffrey ships you were looking at?"

"Right again."

They sat in silence a few moments before she spoke again. "They're going pretty cheap," she said abruptly.

"What're going pretty cheap?" Canby asked, peering up at her pretty face.

"Those little DH.98s," she replied, sipping her drink. "They're going pretty cheap."

Canby grinned. "You don't say."

"I do say," Peterson corrected, looking him directly in the eye.

"Um?" Canby asked, waggling his hand in bemusement.

"Wouldn't that be a dream?" she sighed.

"Wouldn't *what* be a dream?"

"To buy 'em," Peterson said. "To own all four of 'em. God, what a dream."

Canby nodded. "That's some dream, all right," he agreed. "I guess they're off to the boneyard soon unless somebody picks 'em up."

"They are," she assured him. "And they're going for only three hundred eighty thousand—all four of 'em. Wouldn't it be great if you could just go out and buy 'em?"

"Me? Four starships? My God, Lela," Canby spluttered, "you're a heck of a lay, but you're either nuttier than a fruit-cake or you've mistaken me for someone with a *whole* lot more money to spend. Hell, unless I cashed in my Stipend, I couldn't even buy one of the hatch covers, much less a quad of starships."

She looked at him. "But I'll bet your Stipend would easily cover that three hundred eighty thousand if you cashed it in, wouldn't it?"

Canby shrugged. "Well, yeah," he said, "I suppose it would. Except I'd starve to death after that. Maybe you haven't noticed, but there isn't exactly a big demand for helmsmen these days. And the National Soup Kitchens don't serve people who've cashed in."

"So, you'd make money with the ships," Peterson said with a shrug.

Canby smiled. "Not with *those* ships," he said. "There's no cargo space in 'em at all—they were built around the disruptor drivers. Only thing they're good for is flying and fighting."

"So?" Peterson asked with a little smile.

"Well, hell, Lela," Canby said. "I'd have to become a mercenary or a pirate or something. And besides, where would I find four crews . . . assuming the ships are flightworthy in the first place, which they probably aren't?"

"Well, *Skipper,"* Peterson said pointedly, "I've got to assume you put together a few crews when you were in the Fleet. Are they all dead now? Or d'you suppose there might be a few who would like to get back in space as much as you would?"

Canby thought about that for a moment, then smiled. "Yeah," he admitted, "I suppose I might be able to put together a few crews, although they'd have to work for free at first. But what about the ships? I can't believe they're simply ready to fly."

"Oh, probably they're not," Peterson allowed. "I've not looked 'em over carefully myself. But then, I know at least one former Systems Chief who'd take a chance on you—and she's got a few friends around the City who'd just *love* to get out from under the government."

Canby frowned as he looked into the woman's face. "Lela," he said, "you are out of your fucking mind."

"Actually," she said, pointing, "I fuck with *this* end. I thought you'd have noticed that by now."

"I've noticed. I've noticed," Canby grumped. "You know what I mean. Jesus . . ."

"Just a passing idea," Peterson said. "Forget I mentioned it."

"Yeah," Canby said, sitting up in bed and looking her in the eye, "I ought to, except I can't. I've had the same thoughts myself—I've never allowed myself to take 'em seriously. You know, it's *really* illegal to renovate warships as warships."

"Hell," she said with a wicked little smile. "some of the

stuff we've done tonight is illegal, but you didn't seem to have any trouble with that."

"They don't send the V-Pols after you for that," Canby countered.

"No?" Peterson asked. "What about that actor Gray Noland they caught with some bimbo last week? He got executed on the Public Network for it—prime time—and he wasn't doing anything you weren't."

"Yeah, yeah," Canby conceded. "But the only reason they have that kind of law is so they can get you when they want to. The bastards were *after* him. If they hadn't got him on that charge, they'd have nailed him for something else. He was saying too many bad things about the Nobility, and people were beginning to listen."

"Maybe that's the key," Peterson said after a moment. "If you've somebody powerful on your side, maybe everything's all right. You know, at the Yard, I hear a lot of the inside scuttlebutt, and word is that there are at least four groups of mercenaries operating in the galaxy with surplus ships. And Nemil Quinn himself uses his influence to protect 'em—sometimes even funds 'em. I guess he uses 'em when bringing in the Fleet isn't politically . . . 'appropriate,' that's the word they use, I think."

Canby nodded. "Yeah," he said, "I'd heard there were some mercenaries operating out there. One or two ships—not DH.98s. I didn't know Quinn was involved, though . . ." he nodded his head, "I suppose I'm not surprised. He's the only one in the Political Class who seems to be worth his salt in the first place."

Peterson grinned. "Sounds like you're a Quinn person, too," she said.

"Every vet I know is," Canby said. "He's the only hope we have of getting our government back from Nobles."

"So maybe he's the key to getting your four DH.98s," she said.

"*My* DH.98s?" Canby asked. "Where the hell do you get this *my* stuff?"

"Oh, nowhere," Peterson said with an innocent look on her face. "I just thought that maybe a little help from Quinn would keep you from starving to death after you cashed in your Stipend." She shrugged angelically. "You know, until operations started bringing in some money to pay your crews."

Canby raised his eyes to the ceiling. "Sheez," he whispered. "Quinn's a big wheel down there in the Columbia District. How the hell would I even get to see him? He's never heard of me; I'm too small potatoes."

"Yeah, probably," Peterson agreed. "But then, what do you suppose made him back the others? What made him notice them in the first place? Ask yourself. You've got the answer as well as I do. Nobody's small potatoes who risks his life because he believes in something, is he? I mean, Quinn would hear about someone who did that."

"I suppose he might," Canby said. "But even then, what makes you think I'd get in to see him?"

"You wouldn't," Peterson said, looking him in the eye. "He'd damn well know you were going to do something illegal with those ships—and so would everybody else. He'd *never* let you inside his office."

"Then why're we even talking about Quinn?" Canby demanded. "I'd never get to see him, and I'd be stuck with four ships I can't maintain while I starve to death."

"Since it's obvious he couldn't let you contact him, did you ever think that he might just *privately* get in contact with you?" Peterson asked. "He must have contacted the others the same way."

Canby closed his eyes for a moment and took a deep breath. "Yeah," he said after a moment, "I suppose you're right." He shook his head. "But my God, what if he *didn't* call?"

"Then you'd have to do it yourself."

"Yeah," Canby said. "Jesus, what a risk."

"It's what separates the men from the boys," she said quietly. Then she looked slyly at him and lay on her back. "Speaking of men," she said, drawing up her dimpled knees. "I'm going to need *some* rest tonight, and so will you. Could I talk you into one more little workout to relax us before we pop off to sleep?"

"No risk there," Canby said with a grin.

"Yeah," Peterson whispered, "I didn't think so."

Aboard S.S. *Umbrica Maru* • in space

Kobir stood on the dingy bridge of the *Umbrica Maru*, shaking his head. Something was very much amiss aboard the battered old rustbucket, but he hadn't been able to put his finger on it—yet. Oh, he and his boarding party had walked aboard without firing a shot. That was the *easy* part. Finding the captain and first officer in drugged comas—while highly unprofessional—was not at all unusual. But except for the drunken sot who had operated the hatch from the merchantman's side, the whole crew appeared to be hiding. It had taken a cabin-by-cabin search to ferret out the various ratings and officers, who to a man (or woman) refused to talk when they were questioned. Instead, they covered their faces or broke down crying until he had them hauled off and locked away behind the stout doors of the forward mooring room. Clearly, some great, hidden wickedness was under way aboard the barge, ready to be revealed like the wriggling maggots in the gut of a dead rat.

And in this premonition, the Kîrskian leader was more accurate than he could even imagine. His epiphany began with an astonished "Jesus, Mary, and Joseph!" gasped over the voice circuit in the gruff voice of Stella Bremmer, who had led a party below to check out the main holds.

"Bremmer," Canby demanded, opening his holster and starting down the companionway she had taken only minutes before. "We're on our way. Where are you? What have you found?"

"Do not hurry, my Kapitan," Bremmer replied in a weak voice. "We are in no danger."

"Then?" Kobir demanded with growing bewilderment.

"We have found the mysterious cargo, Kapitan," Bremmer said, an obvious inflection of disgust troubling her voice. "The cargo is human. Primitives."

Kobir nearly stopped in his tracks and closed his eyes. Damn! "A slaver?" he demanded, slapping his forehead in disgust. "You mean we've captured a *slaver*?"

"See for yourself, my Kapitan," Bremmer replied. "I doubt if it can be anything else."

A minute later, Kobir rounded a corridor and joined the little group gathered around a hatch that led onto a narrow inspection gallery. The latter was built into the forward bulkhead of a deep cargo hold that was clearly designed to accommodate livestock. During his lifetime, he'd become quite familiar with affliction—suffering and war were old partners; soldiers like himself, their entourage. But nothing in his past had in any way prepared him for this.

Below on the deck were at least a thousand miserable-looking human beings, filthy and crowded together like the animals that normally occupied the space. Some twenty of them lay stacked like cordwood beside a large tank that was clearly fitted out as a latrine. A number of others sprawled here and there on what appeared to be ragged piles of clothing. No question that they would be the next to join the pathetic stack of decaying flesh, waiting to be jettisoned during the next cleaning period—if there was one. "By the beard of my sainted grandmother," Kobir whispered as his gorge rose in his throat. "So *this* is the 'treasure' for which I risked our lives." He shook his head as he looked Bremmer in the eye. "Well," he said with a sigh, "at least no one can say Kobir blunders in a small way."

DECEMBER 2, 2689, EARTH DATE

Manhattan Sector, New Washington • Earth

The following day—all day—Canby's thoughts were consumed by the four DH.98s and the possibilities they promised. But *God*, what he risked making those possibilities come true! His whole future was on the line—or at least the one future he could see clearly, dismal as it might be. What truly astonished him was the fact that he found himself seriously considering anything like buying the four old ships in the first place. Peterson's insistent probing had clearly stoked a mental process that had been smoldering quietly in his subconscious for years.

After he and his newfound friend shared a late breakfast, he'd begun aimlessly walking through the city while his mind ran a furious pace. Now, late in the afternoon, he found himself again at the gate of the Salvage Yard.

"Ain't you the fella was here yesterday to see those old starships?" the guard asked, indicating the DH.98s with a wave of his scrawny thumb.

"Yeah," Canby said, handing over eight credits, "that was me."

"You here for the starships or Peterson?" he inquired with a leer. "I watched you leave with her."

Canby grimaced. "Both," he said.

"Great ass," the guard commented.

"I wouldn't know," Canby lied. Taking the proffered ticket, he made his way quickly toward the quay. He'd only come 'round the warehouse when he noticed the first ship's hatch was open—he clearly remembered closing it when he and Peterson left the night before. He frowned as a feeling of apprehension rippled along his spine. Was someone else interested in the ships, too? The feeling intensified when he mounted the quay itself and discovered all four ships had been opened. Walking rapidly, he was just coming abreast of the second ship when he heard a familiar voice.

"Hey, Canby—up here!" It was Peterson, calling from the flight bridge of the third ship in line.

"Hey, yourself!" Canby yelled, experiencing a perfectly ridiculous sensation of relief. As if he were seriously considering the purchase of four used warships. Ridiculous! Nevertheless, he fairly ran along the dock until he stood beside the old ship, shading his eyes from the late afternoon sun as he peered up at the flight bridge.

Peterson had slid open the starboard Hyperscreen panel and was leaning out as if she were about to back the ship away from the wharf. "Nifty little ships," she allowed with a teasing grin. "No 25s, mind you, but still and all, nifty little ships."

"So glad you like 'em," Canby said. He indicated the other three DH.98s. "You've been in all four?" he asked.

"Checkin' 'em out."

"I thought you were workin' today. When'd you find time?"

"Canby!" Peterson exclaimed with a frown and a smile. "This is a government job. Who said anything about work?"

"I see."

"So do ya want to know what I found?"

"Of course I do," Canby said.

"C'mon up and I'll tell you."

Canby arrived in the flight bridge less than a minute later; Peterson was at the systems console, grinning.

"Figured you'd want to sit center seat," she said.

"Thanks," he said, slipping into the familiar recliner. A quick inspection confirmed that this bridge was as spotlessly clean as the one he'd inspected the day before, although, outside, the hull was the dirtiest of all, if that was possible. "So what shape's she in?"

"Well, she won't run," Peterson said. "Can't seem to power her up."

Canby felt an odd sense of disappointment. "How bad is she?" he asked.

"Can't tell for certain," Peterson said, "but I think the reactor's got problems. Everything else looks pretty good—or as good as I can see without power to run test routines."

"Still, sounds like trouble to me," Canby said. "Reactors are pretty complicated."

"And dangerous to work on, 'less you *really* know what you're doing."

"Yeah," Canby agreed, glancing through the forward Hyperscreens. "What about the other three ships?"

"They seem a lot better," Peterson reported. "I powered up all three soon as I got here this morning, no trouble at all. The flight systems seem to be bollixed a bit, but hell, that's probably normal for ships that've floated in wet storage for ten years. I'm pretty sure they'll taxi—probably go damn near anywhere on the planet if you're patient. After that, it's just a matter of hard work before they fly."

"And this one?" Canby asked, noticing a "W 4050" stamped into the control console.

"Good hangar queen, if nothing else," Peterson said. "She's a lot older than the others; looks like she was painted bright yellow once. I've got a feeling she might even be the prototype. She's got a huge logic system down near the power chambers—and I know it doesn't belong."

"Is it hooked up?" Canby asked.

She shook her head. "No," she said. "But I've never seen anything so carefully disconnected and stored. It's almost as if someone expected to come along and reconnect it someday. Even the cables are stored in a special compartment." She shrugged. "Whatever it is, though, it's not important until we get the reactor fixed."

"If she won't run, what good is she?" Canby protested.

"Like I said, spare parts, if nothin' else," Peterson said. "Besides, they're practically throwing her in free. We'll tow her behind one of the others."

Canby wrinkled his nose. "Where do you get this 'we' business, *Chief* Peterson?" he demanded.

"Well, hell, Canby," Peterson said with a grin, "you can't run ships like this without a Systems Chief—and where are you gonna get somebody who can fix starships *and* fuck like I do?"

Canby nodded sagely. "Nowhere," he replied. "You're a rare combination that way. But, well, don't you think you're taking a little bit for granted? I mean, well . . ."

"Well, hell," Peterson said. Suddenly she had a serious look on her pretty face—the first Canby could remember. "Look, Canby," she said. "Aside from spending some time with these old ships today, I also dug into the government database. I got a good feelin' about you last night, and not just between my legs. You made me feel you were somebody I could trust—hell, somebody I'd follow. So it didn't take me long to find out you commanded the 19th Star Legion—I mean that was available in the government records. That's when I started askin' around—and found out a lot of people think you're the guy who started the Legion . . . Skipper."

"Who the hell said *that*?" Canby demanded in surprise.

"I'll never tell," she said. "But it's nothing you need worry about. I got it from a safe source, believe me. Neither you nor your crazy Legion is in any trouble at all."

"I didn't say *anything* about a Legion—mine or anybody else's," Canby protested, looking uneasily around the empty flight bridge.

"You didn't have to," Peterson said. "I did."

"Sheez . . ."

They sat in silence for a moment, then Peterson grinned. "Anyway, Skipper," she said, "when are you gonna get started recruiting crews? We've only got two weeks or so to get these ships under contract. Otherwise, its the knackers."

"Recruiting?" Canby spluttered. "I never even said anything about the ships and now you're—"

"Okay. Okay, Skipper," Peterson said. "But you just *know*

you're going to do it. Hell, *I* knew even before we had our clothes off. Your eyes were full of stars, and there's no way you can deny it."

"Full of *something*," Canby grouched. "Ye gods, even if I did have four crews, where would I take the damn ships? I mean, they wouldn't fit in m' studio apartment even if I could get 'em there in the first place."

Peterson nodded. "Yeah," she said. "That's the part even *I* don't have figured out . . . yet. But look, Skipper, why don't you just sign up for your Stipend? It'll take most of six weeks till all the paperwork's done, especially with the holidays coming so soon. And by then, if you don't think you can make everything go, just cancel the cashout, and nothing will have changed at all. How does that hit ya?"

"Like a low-flyin' pair of rock tongs." Canby chuckled. Peterson had energy and enthusiasm—and faith—that could literally move mountains. He shrugged. "Last damn time I ever pick up a date at a salvage yard, let me tell you."

"Hey, ya got a good fuckin', didn't ya?"

"That's what I'm afraid of," Canby grumped.

"Now, Skipper . . ."

"Hell, Lela, I don't even know how to initiate the Cashout process. I'll have to start at the Veterans Administration and go on from there—before I can do any recruiting at all."

"No you won't, Skipper," Peterson said. "I know all about the process. Trust me."

"What do you mean you know all about it?" Canby demanded.

"Just that," Peterson said calmly.

"I don't understand."

"Well, on m' way to work this evening, I stopped into the Vet's Administration myself and asked."

"Boy, Peterson, you're damned sure of yourself, aren't you?" Canby said sarcastically.

"No," Peterson said. "It's *you* I'm sure of." She reached inside her tunic and drew out an official-looking envelope.

"Y'see, Skipper, I just put in for my own Cashout. I figured you'd need the extra dough for incidentals I didn't think of. And," she added with a wistful little smile, "since I'm now part of your newest Legion, there'll be no more fucking, either." Then she winked. "After tonight," she added.

Later, just before he fell asleep, Canby decided that once he'd made application for his own Cashout the next morning, he would immediately begin looking up veterans with whom he'd kept in touch—mostly people in his own Legion. If he did manage to find someone else crazy enough to sign up, his (or her) serial number would be "3," following his and Peterson's.

Columbia Sector, New Washington • Earth

That same evening, a few hundred miles south, David Lotember was tidying up a long day by checking the Daily Media Situation Intelligence Report, Global (DMSIRG). It had just arrived from the Fleet's Division of Media-Control and Information Dissemination (HQFDMCID), a quasi-secret organization headquartered only a few miles east in the historic (if moderately decrepit) Pentagon building. Because of much political posturing necessitated by an overnight cabinet embarrassment in London, he was only now getting down to important work. The DMSIRG was a forecast of scheduled media events for the following thirty-day period, updated on a daily basis. Lotember was using it to schedule an important event in his career—his first *personal* dispatch of Fleet units into deep space. It was critical to ensure that no other media events were scheduled elsewhere that might detract from the coverage that he needed in order to keep himself before the public eye. He concentrated, scrolling each page carefully. Every day appeared to have at least one event that could cost him viewers at any given hour of prime time. Then, seven days hence, on December 9, he found a slack period of one hundred twenty minutes that actually bracketed the noon hour! "Eva!" he called into the INTERCOM, "come here, immediately."

In moments, Eva Tolton, a svelte blonde, pranced into the room atop platform shoes that added at least three inches to her height. Wearing a skin-tight jumpsuit, she looked and moved like something from the afternoon PornComs—all emphasis on curves and skin. Only the eyes denied her true essence. They had the brittle look of someone who calculates every move, from the first morning piss to the evening's last squeal of bogus ecstasy beneath a current mentor. "You called, Minister?" she asked.

"Here," Lotember said, pointing to the display on his desk. "See this time slot?"

She squinted. "Yes, Minister," she said presently.

"Make Goddamn certain that nobody—*anywhere*—schedules a media event for these two hours," Lotember ordered, leaning back in his chair to make a conspicuous inspection of her small, firm breasts. "Understand?"

The woman frowned. "B-but, that is a job for HQFDM-CID, isn't it?"

"It's a job for *you*, bimbo," Lotember growled. "I don't care who you get to do it for you—or how. Just get it done. Or by God, you'll be back selling your ass on the streets, not in Parliament. Get that?"

A shadow of fear passed the woman's eyes, and her fingers touched her lips. "You promised you wouldn't put me on the . . . *Dole*. Remember?" she asked in a hoarse whisper.

Lotember laughed derisively. "You stay off the Dole as long as you deliver. Screw up once, and you eat in the Soup Kitchens. The street's full of women who'd give both tits for your job, and you know it. Now get out of here and send for that idiot Jennings—immediately."

"Immediately, Minister Lotember," the woman said, fairly rushing from the room.

Her exit brought a smile to Lotember's handsome face. She had been frightened; no doubt about it. A little thrill rushed through his loins. It was useful to frighten people once in a while—kept them on their toes. He laughed and threw back his head. Frightening people also demonstrated the absolutely *wonderful* power that came with his new job. And power was what it was all about: the great provider—of everything pleasurable! It was like sex—maybe even better. Broadening his smile to reveal a set of perfect teeth, he glanced at an ornate mirror he'd had mounted on the wall to the right of his desk. His right profile was his favorite, not that his left side was anything to criticize. . . .

At that moment, his reverie was interrupted by Tolton's voice on the intercom. "Captain Jennings is here as you ordered, Minister."

"Send him in," Lotember acknowledged.

The captain appeared immediately. "Yes, Minister?" he said, coming to attention.

The man wasn't panting—evidently, he hadn't hurried to his ministerial summons. Lotember decided to remember that—he'd have to show the man where his real priorities lay. But later—tomorrow afternoon, perhaps. Right now, he'd need all his energy for the difficult job of simply communicating. God, no wonder ex-military people rarely made it in the Political Class—they had no subtlety. How Nemil Quinn had managed to overcome such a start was almost beyond comprehension. "Jennings," he said sourly, "try to understand the directions I am about to give you."

"I shall attempt to do that, Minister," Jennings replied in a flat voice.

"Yes," Lotember grumbled sarcastically, "I shall count on that." He pointed at his display once more. "Do you see this time slot?" he asked, as if he were interrogating a five-year-old.

"December ninth, from eleven hundred to thirteen hundred, Minister?" Jennings asked.

Lotember was about to upbraid the Captain for using military time, but thought the better of it. "That is correct,"

Lotember replied, exasperated by the clod's absolute lack of civilian social graces—or animation when he talked. "Remember it well, Jennings," he said. "The time and date are now critical to your existence as a Fleet officer—as I shall presently explain. Are you ready?"

"Ready, Minister."

"Good," Lotember said. "It is now your *personal* responsibility to ensure that a suitably sized and equipped squadron of warships is ready for departure during those hours—on that particular date—to avenge the deep-space piracy recently perpetrated on the liner *Queen Anne*." He looked Jennings in the eye. "You do remember that particular act of piracy, do you not, Jennings? You were the one who reported the crime to me."

"Yes, Minister," Jennings replied in his flat, unemotional voice, "I remember."

"Good again, Jennings," Lotember said. "You show promise, for a military man. Now, the squadron will depart during those hours, but not until *after* a suitable ceremony during which *I* shall inform the people of the planet of that mission. Do you understand *that*, as well?"

"I understand, Minister," Jennings replied.

Even more aggravated by Jennings's continued lack of emotion—but frustrated by his own inability to intimidate—Lotember bit his lip. He'd encountered a number of men and women like this stoical Captain in the service. Clearly intimidated by his decisive and commanding presence, they rarely spoke to him unless compelled. And for the most part, he was just as glad of it. Unfortunately, he needed *this* job done, and done well. The man before him might appear unperturbed, but he'd heard the threat, all right. And no military man he'd met had been happy to go on the Stipend. So the Captain would listen, all right. He, David Lotember, would bet on it, and he was *not* a gambling man. Suddenly, he was anxious that the man and the impenetrable wall he had built around him would leave the office as soon as possible. "Repeat my instructions, Jennings," he ordered, "then get out."

"Yes, Minister," Jennings said, staring straight over Lotember's head with a look so intense it would burn hull-metal. "I am to prepare a suitably sized and armed squadron to seek out the pirates that attacked the starliner E.S.S. *Queen Anne*. That squadron is to lift before thirteen hundred hours ECONUS on December 9 after a ceremony, that you will conduct, which will begin at 1100 hours ECONUS on that same day."

"God almighty, Jennings, don't you ever show any emotion? Do you ever *smile,* at least?"

"Rarely, Minister."

Lotember shook his head. "Isn't that the truth," he commented dryly. He thought for a moment, then shook his head. "All right, Jennings," he said. "You sound as if you understand. Now get out of here and make it happen."

"Minister," Jennings acknowledged. Turning on his heel, he disappeared through the door like a wraith.

For long moments, Lotember sat at his desk, somehow dissatisfied about his encounter with Jennings. Damn military bastards, he pouted. Even though they didn't want it, they had their Goddamn Stipend, and it made them harder to deal with. Well, by God, he'd show them. All of the bastards, from the lowest to the highest, worked for him, David Lotember. A day was coming—and not too far off—when they'd all tremble at his power. And they'd damn well deserve everything they got!

Pouring himself a tumbler of cool, perfumed spring water from a heavy gold container, Lotember sipped until he'd refreshed himself. Then, glancing at his watch, he keyed the intercom. "Tolton," he growled. "Is that Liddle woman out there yet?"

"She is, Minister," Tolton replied. "Shall I send her in?"

"Jesus," Lotember growled sarcastically, "what else did you have in mind, imbecile? Of course send her in."

With that, he sat back at his desk and beamed. Ostila Liddle, the famous procuress, was here to help him with his preparations for Quinn's upcoming divertissement. Of all the whoremongers in the Washington Sector, she could—and did—supply the best: young, old, male, female, and transvestites of either sex. She was expensive, but now he could afford her services. And in *this* divertissement, he meant to be noticed. Finally.

Rising to his feet as she came through the door, he smiled beneficently and bowed from the waist. "Ah, Mrs. Liddle," he said, genially kissing the large diamond ring she wore, "how *kind* of you to visit my modest office."

DECEMBER 6, 2689, EARTH DATE

Aboard KV 388 #SW799, in space • off Torrington/190-Mu

In low orbit above a planet known only as Torrington/190-Mu, Kobir impatiently drummed his fingers on a console and watched what seemed to be the ten millionth rickety livestock shuttle stumble off from the *Umbrica*, bound for the surface. Another fifty primitives repatriated to their home planet (if not reasonably *near* their homes) under the watchful eyes of the Kîrskians. Below was a civilization that had progressed to the early stages of steam technology, so probably two to three hundred years at least remained before the poor, put-upon wretches could report what had befallen them to the proper authorities. But it was quite clear that the primitives were journaling everything they could see—and the advanced technology they recorded would save them at least a hundred years of trial and error in their quest for the stars. "How many more loads to go?" he asked as wingman Émil Lippi strode into the bridge.

Lippi frowned. "Near as I can tell, Nikolai, perhaps twenty more. If all four of the slaver's shuttles continue to operate, we should be able to leave no later than the morning watch. They'd captured some load, those rascals—and from the reaction below, my guess is that they weren't at all discreet about how they did it."

"I take it they were pretty rough," Kobir said flatly.

" 'Rough' is not an accurate description," Lippi replied. "During the trip I took, I saw ruined villages and many areas of great fire damage. The scum had no need to wreak such destruction—horse soldiers and chemical explosives pose little threat to people armed with even small disruptors and blasters." He clenched his fist. "These slavers deserve great punishment, Nikolai."

Kobir closed his eyes and nodded. Unfortunately, those same slavers posed a large operational problem in that they were now his own responsibility, and he had no idea what to do with them. After all, if he tried to turn them over to any of the galactic authorities, he and his crew most assuredly would be arrested with them. "We have few options in this, Émil," he said. "Either we shall let them go . . . or kill them. Probably the latter; otherwise, they will simply return here and perpetrate the same sort of horrors a second time."

"Such scum seems to have little use if civilization is to survive in the galaxy," Lippi said, gazing through the Hyperscreens at the repulsive livestock transport orbiting a hundred yards off their starboard bow.

"Probably it is better that way," Kobir reasoned—Lippi was a man who truly valued his freedom. "But if they must be slaughtered, it is best they generate the least sympathy possible."

"True . . ." Lippi began, then snapped his fingers. "Perhaps," he said, looking Kobir directly in the eye, "just perhaps I have contrived a use for one of them that generates little sympathy."

Kobir raised an eyebrow. "Truly, Émil, you must then be a genius," he said to his old friend. "Tell me."

"Well, Nikolai," Lippi said, "consider this. Slaving is an expensive proposition, with all the bribes that must be involved—not to mention purchase and modification of a merchantman with its numerous shuttles and crews. Am I not correct?"

"One assumes you are correct, Émil," Kobir allowed.

"Such an enterprise is also *ruinously* illegal and almost always fatal for those who are apprehended," Lippi continued. "Is this also not so, Nikolai?"

"This we know to be true," Kobir acknowledged. "I myself have witnessed public executions of people in high places—though not for a long time."

"It still follows, then," Lippi concluded, "that whomever might finance an expedition such as this can raise, and risk, vast sums of money. And therefore is a *perfect* blackmail target. One who can bring vast sums of money into play saving his own skin."

"Aha," Kobir exclaimed with a smile of comprehension. "Now I begin to see where your line of reasoning is directed."

"Does such blackmail interest you, Nikolai?" Lippi asked.

Kobir smiled. "Of course, Émil," he said. "I have no more sympathy for one who issues orders than I have for those who perpetrate those orders. In fact, since we probably will have to slaughter the perpetrators, it seems that blackmail is much too good for whomever originally arranged for the crime." He frowned. "Fascinating. Until now, I have given the ultimate owner very little thought. Do you know who he or she might be?"

"I do not, Nikolai," Lippi said with a little smile. "Like you, I have given little thought lately to anything except the problem we have on our hands."

"Wonder who the big cabbage could be?" Kobir mused with a look of fascination. "Do you suppose one of the slavers would tell us?"

"Perhaps," Lippi replied. "If any of them knows."

Kobir nodded. "I strongly suspect at least one of them does know," he said. "Crimes as risky as slaving are best carried out with as few middlemen as possible."

"A valid point, Nikolai," Lippi agreed. "In which case, one immediately suspects this Georges Cortot, the slaver's captain."

"Makes sense to me," Kobir said. "A tough-looking customer. Somehow, I doubt if he will part with the information willingly. If the owner of that ship has even half a brain, he's holding something over the man's head just so he *won't* talk in case things go amiss."

Lippi smiled. "Let me take care of this, Nikolai," he said. "Your stomach is weak when it comes to torture."

"So is yours, old friend," Kobir said, "unless you have changed substantially in the last few years."

"I have not," Lippi assured him with a chuckle. "However, luckily for us cowards, Rosa Gambini is along on this trip, and she has been known to dabble in such activities."

Kobir's eyebrows rose. "We are indeed fortunate to have such a reputed expert with us," he said with a little smile. "Be he willing or not, eventually the captain will gladly tell us all he knows concerning the matter."

"Somehow," Lippi said grimly, "I hope the bastard resists her—at least long enough to suffer a bit for what's happened to those wretched primitives in his hold."

DECEMBER 7, 2689, EARTH DATE

London • Earth

After nearly a millennium, Marguerite's soaring ascension scene that closes Gonoud's opera *Faust* still could sweep an audience to its feet, including Sadir, First Earl of Renaldo—

especially so when sung by the magnificent French coloratura soprano, Brigette Fauré. Shivering with awe in his private opera box, the corpulent Renaldo struggled out of an ornate chair to join the chorus of "Bravos" and "Huzzahs" that punctuated an almost solid wall of applause. Beside him, a svelte, gloriously costumed courtesan applauded with restrained gusto, matching precisely the reaction of Lord Otto Gaspari and his somewhat shapelier companion, Renaldo's guests for the evening.

The ardent operagoers demanded a dozen footlight calls before the curtain fell a last time and the house lights came on. "Nearly a thousand years old," Renaldo enthused as they filed out of the box, "yet the music has a life of its own and never ages. A gem. An absolute gem."

"A gem, indeed," Lord Gaspari agreed later, pushing through the grandly dressed throng toward the lobby. "And speaking of gems," he added with a puckish look in his eye, "one assumes you have heard about the Giulio Cesare Star-Blaze by now, a fascinating reappearance if ever there was one."

Renaldo gulped inadvertently. "The *Giulio Cesare* Star-Blaze, you say?" he said in a voice barely audible above the crowd. "The great gemstone that disappeared during the last war?"

"The same, my dear Renaldo," Gaspari replied with a smile. "Rather thought you might be interested."

Renaldo felt his heart rate treble and his breathing grow shallow. The Giulio Cesare StarBlaze! He'd lusted after the great jewel since he was old enough to understand the kind of personal influence and patronage ownership of such a treasure could bring.

Discovered entirely by accident during an early interstellar expedition, the magnificent gemstones occurred naturally on only two large asteroids, remnants of some colossal supercomet that raged through the galaxy a billion years in the past. This particular StarBlaze, the Giulio Cesare, was the largest and most perfect of the type ever mined. For more than five hundred years, it had been the jealously guarded property of the Hipólito family, Kîrskian heirs of Lázaro Hipólito, who providentially happened upon the asteroids while leading an expedition sent to discover nothing more exotic than new supplies of iridium. Then, during the war, the stone had mysteriously vanished, its disappearance tied inextricably to a double murder of the eldest Hipólito heirs.

Renaldo was instantly on the alert. "Of course I am interested," he said, nodding absently to the pretentious socialites in the gold-encrusted main lobby—God how they would envy him if he owned the Giulio Cesare. *That* would stop their laughing behind his back. He took a deep breath and looked Gaspari in the eye. "Why haven't I heard of this through my own channels?" he asked suspiciously as they climbed into his limousine.

Gaspari—whose narrow face, goatee, and mustache gave him a rather satanic countenance—shrugged with a Gallic indifference. While the Earl struggled his bulk into the seat, he frowned with a parody of concern. "Who knows, my good Renaldo?" he said. "Perhaps my sources are only faster— perhaps you will hear of it tomorrow . . . or the next day."

"Or never," Renaldo growled impatiently, nearly oblivious to his slender courtesan, who had already slipped out of her gown and opened her legs to the obvious delight of Gaspari's more buxom companion. "Did these, er, *sources* mention a price?" he asked—reminded for the thousandth time that a message from Cortot was five days overdue.

Gaspari smiled as the two women locked in an embrace beside him, breathing in slow, wet hisses. "A *great* deal of money, Renaldo," he said.

"Yes, I thought as much," Renaldo said. "I assume you might put me in contact with the proper parties so I can inquire."

"Ah, my dear Earl," Gaspari said, shifting to a seat beside Renaldo, "you think too much about business all the time.

Watch," he urged, indicating the two women who were noisily making love on the seat across from him. "This is as much for our entertainment as it is theirs. Their passion never crests so sharply after the first time. Enjoy, my friend. Enjoy!"

Renaldo grimaced, but nodded and kept his silence as Gaspari began opening his trousers. The man was clearly on to something concerning the Giulio Cesare, or he never would have mentioned it in the first place. However, pushing the matter now would only cost him more in the long run than the fortune he knew he would eventually pay to possess the gem. He sighed and opened his own trousers. "You are right, Gaspari," he said. "We shall talk of it later, under more appropriate circumstances." Nevertheless, Cortot's failure to report from the slaver continued its intrusion into his exertions. . . .

The sun was lightening London's eastern horizon when Renaldo returned to his great manor house off Belgrave Square. He made straight for the study—this time completely missing the fifteenth-century globe with his hat. Conjuring the workstation from his ravaged desk, he switched on power and stood back while the powerful computers inside initialized. All night, he'd been at odds to concentrate on the revels Gaspari's courtesans provided—even though, in all fairness, the women *had* been spectacular. But more important issues had prevented him from enjoying them to their fullest. Now, at last, he could concentrate on marshaling the finances he would need were he to possess the Giulio Cesare StarBlaze.

Not that he'd learned exactly how much the final price would be. Remaining teasingly coy about details, Gaspari had only revealed one hard fact: that he—and only he—possessed broker's access to the gem. And from long association, Renaldo knew it was the truth. The avaricious Noble *never* claimed anything he could not prove—especially when it had anything to do with large sums of specie.

On the downside, that meant a great deal of cash would necessarily change hands before he, Renaldo, at last gained possession. Fortunately, there appeared to be an up side to the situation as well: It was fairly clear Gaspari had come to him first. Now, all that he needed was money—as long as he could get his hands on it quickly.

He smiled with anticipation as the workstation came to life. Humming a tuneless version of the evening's Chorus of Angels (*"Sauvée! Christ est ressuscité!"*), he perched on the very edge of his chair and scanned his message queues for communication from his "composer."

And scanned . . .

Frowning, he peered fruitlessly into the display, searching every message queue in the remote possibility that the message may have been misfiled.

Again, nothing.

"Damn," Renaldo swore through his teeth. "Goddamn!" In this case, no news was *bad* news! He glanced at his watch. By morning the slaver would be a full six days late. He took a deep breath and once more searched his incoming queue.

Nothing.

Frustration scourged his mind. For each day the slaver remained in transit, a certain number of slaves could be expected to expire. It was simply a matter of statistics. When outfitting such a ship, one was forced to invest in a certain level of life-support facilities: food generation, waste management, atmospherics, and the like. But such facilities were expensive—consider the kind of funding it took to properly outfit a passenger starliner. Slavers, of course, were outfitted with no consideration to creature comforts— only the most basic life support at the lowest possible cost. Therefore, one weighed the alternatives and attempted to come up with a sensible commercial balance. First, one needed to know how much profit, on average, could be expected from an "average" slave; then, an average shipload gross could be calculated. That number divided into the cost of the slaver's hull (plus its new life-support facilities) gave a gross payoff cost—and the greater this number, the more trips it had to make before the investor realized a profit. But that was what slaving was all about: quick profits.

Accordingly, to hasten profits, one most commonly reduced the expensive, onboard life-support accommodations, keeping in mind, however, that for each reduction, a certain percentage of the payload could be expected to expire in transit. It was simply a matter of "what-ifing," raising or lowering either the furnished accommodations—or the quality of the slaves—until a satisfactory economic formula was reached.

The solution Renaldo directed Cortot to implement was one with the least possible investment up front. First, he must purchase a large, flyable livestock carrier at the very lowest price available—something little better than scrap. Then, he should outfit the hulk with minimal life-sustaining systems—regardless of comfort or safety considerations. Finally, on each trip, he should always crowd the holds with enough slaves to offset the extra deaths resulting from such a deadly combination. All in all, it was an effective answer to a most complex problem.

Until now, his investment had produced exceptional returns. Cortot—a cast-off war veteran—had been able to keep the ship running in spite of the very poorest maintenance and care. But now, *five* days overdue! "Incompetent bastards," Renaldo growled. That sort of time could cost him . . . he made a hurried mental calculation . . . as many as two hundred slaves. Wincing, he made the calculation again using his workstation. This time, the figure came to two hundred fifteen.

Slamming the workstation back inside its desk, Renaldo ground his teeth in anger and struggled to his feet. Kicking his antique chair halfway across the room, he stormed out of the study, vowing to make both the composer and the slaver's captain pay dearly for their incompetence. "Find Mrs. Timpton!" he shouted to a servant cowering in the hall. "Tell her to summon Gunter and the Kress woman to my bedchamber *immediately!*"

Manhattan Sector, New Washington • Earth

The previous night, a cold, late-autumn wind had blown in from the east; with it came the season's first snow. It closed all the schools and filled Manhattan's parks with happy, shouting children. But as Canby slogged past Battery Park, he hardly noticed them playing in the fast-graying drifts. He was still flabbergasted—nearly everyone he'd approached about becoming a mercenary with him had been immediately taken with the idea. A number of them, like Peterson, had even pledged their Stipends; many more had "signed up," on the spot, promising to report for duty as soon as Canby gave the word. Before his second day had ended, he had already recruited the remainder of his own crew and was well along toward manning a second ship. He was on his way across Battery Park to see Renfro Gibbons, an excellent helmsman and one of his best ship commanders, when he heard a woman scream.

"Look out!"

At almost precisely the same instant, Canby was overtaken by a blurred shape that hissed out of nowhere and bowled him over like a tenpin. He landed painfully on his back, and for the next few moments watched tiny pinpoints of light dance around like stars in the Hyperscreen during a dogfight. Presently, a woman's face appeared against the gray sky— upside down.

"Are you hurt?" the face asked in a worried voice.

Tentatively, Canby tried his arms and legs while the woman circled until she was rightside up. "I don't think so." He laughed cautiously. "Except for m' dignity, that is." A young boy's face joined the woman's.

"Damian," the woman said in a provoked voice. "I told you to watch where you were sledding with that."

"Sorry, Mom."

"Well don't tell *me* you're sorry, Damian; tell this poor man."

"Um . . . sorry, mister."

Canby sat up slowly, blinking the horizon back into perspective. "'S all right," he chuckled, focusing in on the boy's GravFlyer. "That thing packs a wallop, Damian."

"We're *terribly* sorry," the woman said.

Brushing snow from his arms, Canby got to his feet, only now noticing that the woman was quite an attractive blonde. Slim, and perhaps five feet eight inches, she wore her hair long, framing a heart-shaped face with blond, manicured eyebrows, thoughtful blue eyes, a pert turned-up nose, and a full, sensuous mouth with crimson lips. Carrying a pair of tan, leather gloves, she wore a frayed buff overcoat that—by dint of its vast size—had clearly been purchased secondhand. It almost completely concealed whatever bosom she might have had. Diminutive tan slush boots and a mile-long green-striped scarf completed her outfit. Canby thrust out his hand. "My name's Gordon," he said. "Gordon Canby. And I'm glad to meet you."

The woman smiled—and seemed to light the whole park with it. "I'm Cynthia Tenniel," she said, at the same moment the sun peeked out from a hole in the clouds. It revealed the soft fuzz that blesses the cheeks of many true blondes. "And," she added with that particular look of disbelief managed only by mothers, "this is my son Damian."

Canby offered his hand to the boy. "Glad to meet you, Damian," he said.

"Shake Mr. Canby's hand, Damian," Tenniel urged with a little smile. "You're lucky he isn't ready to bop you in the nose for knocking him down."

Gravely, the boy took Canby's hand. They shook. "Er, g-glad to meet you, Mr. Canby. Sorry again about mowing you down with m' GravFlyer."

Canby laughed. "Those things happen," he said.

"Not to *careful* little boys," Tenniel admonished.

"Sorry, Mom—I'll be careful. Can I go play now?"

Tenniel smiled and nodded. "You're certain you're not hurt, Mr. Canby?" she asked.

"I'm certain," Canby said as Damian retrieved his GravFlyer and skidded off into the park. "And my name's Gordon—in fact, a lot of people call me Gordo. 'Mr. Canby' sounds like I'm a thousand years old."

"I think I like 'Gordon,' " she said, her eyes meeting his. "And you've been very nice about the whole thing."

"Maybe," Canby said, "it's because I feel pretty *lucky* about the whole thing."

"I don't understand," Tenniel said.

"Well," Canby said, feeling his cheeks burn like a school-boy's, "I *did* get to meet you because of it."

"Pretty brutal way to meet someone," she said.

"I take my good luck anywhere I can find it."

"That was nice of you," she said. "Thanks."

"You're welcome," Canby replied, starting to run out of things to say. "I, ah, guess you come here often."

"Whenever I can," she said. "It's difficult raising a little boy in the city. He finds some freedom here." She blushed. "That is, when he's not trying to kill someone."

"He's all right." Canby chuckled. "Do you live here in the city?"

"Er, yes," she said. Pointedly, she added nothing else.

"I, ah, take it you work here, too," Canby offered after a time.

"When I can find it," she said, absently stroking her blond hair as if she were relieved Canby hadn't attempted to learn more. "Odd jobs, mostly—enough to keep us off the Dole. I'm saving up to make Tribute on a permanent position, but it seems as if it's going to take forever." She sighed. "You look as though you're ex-military. I suppose you've got a Stipend."

"Yeah," Canby admitted, feeling a little guilty at how well he lived in comparison—and how much he hated it. "It's easy to forget how lucky I am to have it."

She smiled, glancing off for a moment in Damian's direction. "You didn't have to say that," she said. "I'm not envious. I *could* go on the Dole if I didn't want to work."

"You don't look like someone who could stand living on the Dole," Canby observed.

"And you don't look like someone who can stand living on his Stipend," she added with a twinkle.

Canby laughed. "I'd get rid of it in a moment if I could find work that paid as much," he admitted. "But nobody seems interested in hiring helmsmen these days, especially ones trained in the Fleet, so I haven't given much serious thought to giving it up . . . until recently."

"What's happened recently?" she asked. From the look in her eyes, she was genuinely interested—and Canby would have been glad to talk about anything that might interest this beautiful woman. "Well," he began, "they've got these four starships for sale and . . ."

They talked of starships and Canby's plans for much of the afternoon. He learned that Tenniel had never been off planet and seemed fascinated by descriptions of worlds he had visited during his years in the Fleet. He also discovered that she was a civilian professional who lost her career during the Big Demob. When, in the late afternoon, she told him that she needed to leave for a temporary night job, Canby asked if he might see her again.

"I'd like that a lot, Gordon," she said, taking Damian by the hand. "While this job lasts, we're in the park nearly every afternoon."

"Then, I'll be here, too," Canby said. "At least as often as I can."

"I'll look for you," she said, offering a soft, warm hand that squeezed his in the most compelling way.

Canby watched her until she disappeared into the crowded street, then set out in search of Renfro Gibbons—who accepted immediately, and pledged his Stipend as well.

That took care of crewing *two* ships. Tomorrow, he would contact Olga Confrass at her Frolic House in the Free Zone. But the proposition he would offer the infamous madam would have nothing to do with sex.

DECEMBER 8, 2689, EARTH DATE

In space, aboard S.S. *Umbrica Maru* • off Torrington/190-Mu

Kobir strode into Cortot's cabin with Lippi a few minutes after they received Gambini's call. His stomach turned instantly from the reek of sweat, vomit, feces—and fear.

The large chamber was mostly dark; only a single brilliant lamp illuminated Cortot, slouching naked in a metal chair. His ankles and calves were secured to the legs of the chair by thin plastic straps that had cut cruelly into his flesh. Runnels of drying blood streaked his hairy shanks and puddled around his feet, mixing with a much larger pool of what had to be urine. His hands were out of sight behind his back and a thick plastic strap was secured around his massive, hairy chest, mottled with drying sweat. His bald head lolled on his chest, mouth open and eyes staring silently at his lap. The only sound was a rasping rattle emanating in his slack mouth. Thin driblets of vomit trickled down his matted chest to collect in a puddle around a shrunken sex organ peeking out below his fat, pendant belly. A large clip with serrated teeth was clipped to the head of his penis; an insulated electric cable ran from the clip to the side of a large black box on the floor. Two more insulated wires ran from the side of the box to clips gripping his nipples. Three additional wires led from the box's end and disappeared into the darkness behind the chair.

Beside the captain stood Rosa Gambini with two burly crewmen from Kobir's Drive chamber on either side. Gambini herself was short, slight, and, if one ignored her proclivity for torment, rather attractive, in a fragile sort of way. She had light brown hair—almost blond—an oval face with a prominent nose, thin lips usually devoid of rouge, and deep blue eyes into whose bottomless depths one peered at his (or her) own peril. She was a valuable crew member who attended to her systems console in an expert, professional manner and often volunteered for the most hazardous duty. Despite a modicum of feminine curves, rumor had it that she remained a virgin and could be aroused only by the most base human activities. The men beside her looked as if they were disgusted beyond redemption, and their clothes were bathed in sweat. Gambini looked only slightly spent—as if she had recently experienced a great, lasting orgasm—which Kobir strongly suspected she had. "Captain Cortot will talk to you now, Kapitan," she said with a pleased little smile beneath a slight mustache of sweat.

Kobir swallowed his gorge. Gambini was an animal—but a useful one. Someday, perhaps, he would no longer need her services. At present, however . . . "Thank you, Rosa," he said, forcing himself to look directly into her maniacal eyes.

"It is nothing, Kapitan," she said, but Kobir knew she was only saying what she believed would sound modest—after perfect accomplishment of a difficult job.

Kobir nodded, then stepped in front of the agonized Cortot, who raised a face glistening with sweat. His eyes appeared to be nearly sightless, but they seemed to focus. "Do you know me?" Kobir asked.

With what seemed to be superhuman effort, the man nodded his head slowly.

"And you know what information I seek—the name of your partner as well as the *owner* of this ship?"

Again, the head nodded clumsily.

"Then tell me, Captain. After that, the pain will cease and you can sleep."

As Kobir watched in horror, the mouth opened and started to speak. At first, only animal noises and whimpers came from the swollen lips—along with more drool and vomit. But when Gambini moved into his view, Cortot began bawling incoherently and moved his head clumsily from side to side, his puffed eyes rolling in fear.

"Name the owner of this barge, Captain Cortot," the woman said in a quiet voice. "Name the man for whom you work." It was only necessary for Gambini to reach behind the chair before Cortot began a spasm of dry heaving, but only thick spittle dribbled from his lips.

Kobir could stand no more. He had just placed a restraining hand on Gambini's arm when, with a clearly supreme effort, Cortot managed a great wet groan, followed by a single word, "Renaldo."

Once more, Gambini moved her hand behind the chair. "The *whole* name, please, Captain Cortot," she commanded. Again, the man's eyes rolled in primal fear; then the swollen lips opened again.

"My p-partner, Sadir, F-first Earl of R-renaldo owns this ship," the man gasped, only moments before his head sagged once more to his chest, and this time remained motionless.

The name hardly registered with Kobir. By now, he had seen nearly all he could stand. With his gorge rising, he turned to Gambini. "Is he dead?" he asked.

Gambini looked surprised and a little disappointed. "Of course not, Kapitan Kobir," she said reproachfully. "You desire more information from him?"

With a shiver, Kobir glanced at Lippi—whose forehead was covered by beads of sweat—and shook his head. "No,

Rosa," he said. "Thank you, but I think we've heard all we need to know."

"Shall I finish him, then?" Gambini asked.

Kobir turned his back on the semihuman wreckage in the chair and nodded with a shudder. "Do it quickly, Rosa," he ordered, starting for the door. "The man may be garbage, but he has suffered enough for what he has done." He and Lippi were no more than a few steps down the companionway when an inhuman wail came out of the open door behind them. It went on and on, rising and falling in bloodcurdling arpeggios. Kobir stopped in his tracks, turned, and began to retrace his steps, but the outcry abruptly ended. In the chilling silence that followed, both men stopped again, just short of the door. Their eyes met for only a moment; then, without a word, they reversed direction once more and made straight for the transport's entry port, where a launch waited to take them back to their ships.

Later, after much discussion, Kobir's freebooters unanimously determined that an appropriate fate could only be meted out to the slaver's crew by their intended victims: the hapless aboriginals of Torrington/190-Mu. Accordingly, one final trip in the shuttle—with Kîrskians at the controls—transported the slaver's crew to the surface, screaming and begging for the mercy they had denied their would-be victims. After what the pirates had seen, the pleas fell on deaf ears. With three months' provisions—but no weapons, save for cutlery—Cortot's crew was deposited on a small island in a lake near one of the planet's devastated cities. When the shuttle returned, the crew reported that a number of aboriginal gunboats were already steaming toward the island before the last of the slavers had been forced out of the hold.

After a final search revealed the space barge was completely deserted, the Kîrskians set demolition charges throughout its malodorous hull, then returned to their KV 388s and set course for Khalife and home. Long before the massive explosion in space lit the night sky over Torrington/190-Mu, Kobir had began his research on Sadir, First Earl of Renaldo.

December 9, 2689, Earth Date

Norfolk Sector, New Washington • Earth

At precisely 12:29 P.M. ECONUS, December 9, 2689, David Lotember stepped smartly up three steps to a bunting-draped platform and took his place at a podium emblazoned with the majestic Imperial Seal of New Earth in solid gold. Out on a vast apron of Norfolk Space Fleet Station—specially cleared of the operational gear normally emplaced there—raw wind off the bay nipped his cheeks and swept flurried ghosts of snow from the concrete. The same wind also billowed his elaborate cloak, threatened disaster to his fastidiously coifed hair, and brought with it the scent of polluted water from Willoughby Bay and, beyond, Hampton Roads. Arrayed before him in a tight semicircle, some two hundred of the media—reporters, correspondents, HoloCam journalists, and commentators representing news services from all over the galaxy—jostled each other to see and to be seen.

While flags thundered from hastily erected poles on either side of his platform, the Minister arranged his notes with a practiced eye toward his audience, watching for the most dramatic moment to begin. He smiled with inward satisfaction. Eva Tolton had accomplished her assignments well. For the previous three quarters of an hour, absolutely nothing newsworthy had been scheduled, anywhere. Not only that, but the virtual blackout on newsworthy events would last at least another half hour. He'd rewarded the woman in bed for that—and, of course, permitted her to remain in her job. It was the least he could do.

Jennings—he recalled with a mental scowl—had been another story altogether. Lotember had been on the brink of firing the idiot when he suggested assignment of older Fleet units to the pirate hunt instead of newer, more capable ships that were much more impressive to behold. The man claimed the newer ships were commanded by political appointees. Well, *of course they were!* Welcome to the real world, Jennings. God, what a burden it was working with military people.

He eyed the media again—all eyes were now on him, expectant. It was time; he could sense it. He took a deep breath. "Best wishes to you, my fellow Imperials," he began, chin thrust forward in his best rehearsed pose. "Today marks a special day for our Empire as well as my new ministry." He paused dramatically. "In less than half an hour, these ships lift for deep space," he said, gesturing to a squadron of snow-white starships singled up at bunting-draped wharves behind the podium. "Their mission: to avenge the act of piracy committed against our E.S.S. *Queen Anne* and once again restore interstellar space to the peace you have every right to expect. . . ."

The squadron was composed of eight TA-91 Tarquin-Class heavy cruisers: seven hundred feet of gleaming hull-metal, high-powered Drive units, and murderous disruptors. They were the newest in the Fleet inventory, and—not incidentally—made an imposing background for Lotember's presentation. They were also the most technically advanced warships in the galaxy, each equipped with a battery of eight beta-torqued .50-mmi disruptors with rapid-firing energy feeds. Their crews had been chosen from the best and brightest in the land, young, brilliant, and well educated. The officers—to a person—had been educated in the finest colleges and universities that wealth could provide. Lotember had made certain of that. After dealing with the tedious Jennings, he'd personally ensured that no graduate of the Military Fleet Academy found a berth on the expedition. Originality, cleverness, and a modicum of bravery—that was the kind of stuff needed to deal with pirates. Not plodding military hacks with no imagination.

Precisely ten minutes before the starships were scheduled to lift, Lotember brought his speech to a theatrical conclusion—almost a benediction—that brought impassioned cheers from the shills he'd sprinkled throughout the assembly. Then, with a grand sweep of his arm, he signaled the Captain of I.F.S.S. *Addison* (DD-931), who immediately activated the ship's big 'Gravs in clouds of shimmering gravitons.

One after another, the remaining seven starships thundered into life, each with a powerful rumble that shook the very platform on which Lotember stood. Stifling a wince, he forced himself to smile. He much preferred to hear such harsh clamor from inside a comfortable—heavily insulated—cabin, embellished by a drink in his hand. Military ships were clearly meant for military personalities—all noise, hardness, and polish. People like the dunderhead Jennings. Nevertheless, he reminded himself, such spectacles also seemed to stir the commoners, whose votes everyone needed to stay in office.

Amid much fanfare from the combined Fleet Marching Band and New-Washington Philharmonic Orchestra, the squadron taxied by twos out into the Roads, angled left to the James River opposite ancient Newport News, and stopped, testing their generators in great thundering crescendos. Finally, they turned northeast and began their takeoff runs in soaring cascades of water that gradually diminished until the big ships climbed out over Fort Weel and the Chesapeake, lifting—as carefully instructed—at a point just behind Lotember's platform, where they would provide exciting background for media shots with Lotember himself in the foreground.

Afterward, the Minister remained behind for nearly an hour supplying quote opportunities for the media, until the more well known among the journalists departed to cover a popular vocalist who was making an appearance in the Baltimore Sector, some miles to the north.

All in all, he thought, climbing into one of the luxurious VIP flyers attached to his office, it had been a rather successful day. And he'd gotten through it with a minimum of contact between himself and the awful people who actually ran the base.

"Manhattan," he ordered tersely, as a steward handed him a large brandy to ward off the chills that had been building during more than an hour exposed to the elements. "You know the drill—drop me at the Midtown Executive Verti-Pads, then wait until I return."

The steward bowed. "I shall notify the helmsman," he said.

Within minutes, the Fleet Station and its noisome occupants were far behind in the Chesapeake's perpetual haze. It had been a long, difficult day, and Lotember was on the way to reward himself with the special pleasures of The Square.

DECEMBER 10, 2689, EARTH DATE

Brooklyn Sector, New Washington • Earth

"I'd have a hard time believing it if I hadn't heard it with my own two ears," Canby declared, still a little thunderstruck by the reaction to his call for volunteers. "We've filled manning tables for all four ships plus maintenance and admin groups."

Across the table, Peterson's eyes glanced at him over the top of a large, well-worn menu that attested to the small café's little-advertised excellence. Except for red-and-white-checked tablecloths, the room was more or less dusky inside, with walls and ceiling stained sooty brown by nearly two hundred years of Italian cooking, but the aroma of spicy food from the kitchen mixed with the smells of spirits and brew formed a special kind of sunshine one seldom found in more elegant eateries. "Didn't I tell ya, Skipper?" she said over the hum of conversation that filled the room. "You're not the only one who's anxious to get back into space."

"Yeah," Canby admitted, "but my God, *this* way? I mean, this has got to be the riskiest proposition ever offered. Anywhere."

"Once ya get it in your blood, it kinda takes over. You know that, Skipper."

"What—propositions?"

"Deep space, smart ass."

"Sorry."

Peterson smiled as a grinning, mustachioed waiter appeared with steaming spaghetti-heaped plates, a great brown crock of sauce, a flask of deep red wine, and two goblets. "A good night for celebration, Skipper," she said with a twinkle. "Actually, it's a special night."

Canby grinned waggishly. "It's always a special night with you, Lela," he said.

"Won't do ya any good, Skipper," Peterson quipped in return. "Like I said the other day, my pants are off limits now that I'm workin' for ya."

"Ouch." Canby chuckled. "That was a low blow."

"'S all right," Peterson said. "I meant what I said about it being a special night."

"Oh?" Canby asked with a grin. "What's up?"

"Tell me—what do we need most, now that the ships and the people are in place?"

"You mean like a whole universe worth of luck?" Canby quipped.

"Yeah," Peterson said, "that, too. But seriously, what else do we need before we can really bring this off?"

"Hmm," Canby said. "I can think of a million-odd things we ought to have . . . and some not so odd, too." He frowned and took a deep breath. "I suppose the thing we need most is somewhere to base the damn ships while we bring 'em back to flying condition. I've got use of a couple tumbledown piers at a burned-out refinery in old Secaucus. But until we can get something better than that, things are going to be mighty difficult—maybe impossible."

"How would an abandoned Fleet repair yard hit you?" Peterson asked demurely.

Canby shook his head. "Boy," he said, topping off their wine goblets, "if we could come up with something like *that*, we'd probably be doomed to success. You got one in your hip pocket, maybe?"

"Wouldn't fit," Peterson laughed. "My bottom's too big. But how about one down on the Chesapeake?"

"You're not fooling, are you?" Canby asked, abruptly serious.

"Not at all, Skipper," Peterson said. "I haven't seen the place myself, but I hear it's in pretty good shape. And it's ours, if we want it."

"*Want* it? Jesus, Mary, and Joseph, I'd kill for something like that. But how'd *you* get wind of it?"

"A friend," she replied.

"A friend gives away repair bases?" He frowned for a moment. "My God, Lela," he said. "You're not talking about Nemil Quinn, are you?"

"Maybe."

"It *is* Quinn, isn't it?"

"Do you have to know?"

"Well . . ."

"Oh, what the hell—it's Quinn."

Canby shook his head in amazement. "Of course," he said. "That first night—you talked about him as if you knew him. Lela Peterson, you really get around, don't you?"

She smiled. "*He* gets around," she said, expertly twirling several strands of spaghetti around the end of her fork. "I think he likes to keep his eyes out for people like you,

Gordo. You know, the kind of people who get a vision and then have the guts to go do something about it. Especially people with visions about outfitting old starships for the mercenary trade." She laughed. "Something about him makes me think he doesn't trust the Fleet when he's got, you know, *important* things to do."

"Like important, *illegal* things?"

"Heck, Gordo, I don't know. I get the impression he uses 'em for *semi*legal things, like givin' a bit of help to some of those two-bit dominions that we call 'friendly' because both of us see the same people as enemies. You know. It gets in the media often enough."

"Yeah," Canby said, mopping sauce up with a thick piece of bread. "I suppose that makes about as much sense as anything else." He frowned. "Where did you meet him?"

"At the Salvage Yard," she said. "He drops in every once in a while. Can't think of a better place to find the likes of you, Gordon Canby. Every real space bum eventually finds his way onto the piers there to dream."

"And he just . . . shared these thoughts with you?" Canby asked.

Peterson smiled. "He likes fat bottoms, too, Gordo. You may have noticed I'm not a virgin."

"Yeah," Canby said with a passing taste of invidiousness, "you did look as if you'd been laid a couple of times before."

She smiled. "Anyway," she said, changing the subject, "he asked me to call if I ever met anybody I thought had what it takes. So I called."

"Jesus," Canby whispered, shaking his head in amazement. "How can I ever—"

"By never saying thanks, Gordo. I've had plenty of chances to call Quinn, but never met anybody worthwhile—until you happened along. And it has nothing to do with that thing that stands up between your legs, either. Understand?"

"Understand . . ." Canby felt his cheeks go hot. "Er, what do I have to do to get this repair base?"

"Not much from what he's told me," Peterson said. "Just take a little trip south when he calls. The man wants a talk with you in person. If I'm any judge, all you need do is be yourself."

"Be myself?"

"Yeah, Gordo," she said with a little laugh. "You know, just tell things the way they are. No horse hockey and the like. He's a pretty direct kind of guy." She laughed. "Even when he doesn't have a hard-on."

Canby nodded. "I guess I never was much good at bull-roar," he said.

"That's why you'll get the repair yard," Peterson said. Then she smiled. "And Gordo . . ." she added, looking him directly in the eye.

"Yeah?"

"Well, ah, we *really* aren't started in this thing until we pick up the ships, are we?" she asked, finishing off her goblet of wine.

Canby grinned, feeling a well-known sensation in his loins. "Not the way I look at it."

"How'd you like to play with a fat bottom, then, Gordo Canby? You'll notice, I *didn't* call you 'Skipper.' "

"I'd like that a lot, Lela Peterson—who won't be 'Chief Peterson' again until at least tomorrow morning," Canby replied. For the next few hours, he did very little thinking about either ships or Nemil Quinn.

Book Three

MEETINGS

Monte Carlo-19 • New Belmont

The following Earth day—a number of light-years distant—Flying Fandangle, one of Renaldo's racing griffins, beat a field of nineteen three-year-old stallions on Emperor's Day at the sumptuous Monte Carlo-19 gambling complex on New Belmont, a dominion of Imperial Earth orbiting Alpha Centuri. Out of a famous pride with excellent speed, Fandangle had been a long shot at nearly fifteen to one after finishing a couple of lengths back in his previous two races. Nevertheless, Renaldo quietly bet a small fortune on the young griffin, and as a result nearly broke the casino's bank. He was immediately invited to Philante XXI's private viewing pavilion, floating at twelve hundred feet above the starting pylon of the ten-mile-long, triangular course over which the great winged cats flew. While the Emperor was ceremoniously blessing the beast, Renaldo's launch arrived at the boarding jetty.

As he stepped to the ersatz marble deck, the Earl—dressed today as a Roman senator, complete with toga, golden sandals, and a halo of woven olive branches—experienced a momentary sensation of covetousness at the baroque luxury with which the Emperor surrounded himself. Not that he would for a moment deny The Throne its trappings. Such was all a part of the natural order. Nevertheless, he had never been able to avoid the feeling that he, Renaldo, was better able to appreciate intrinsic beauty. For all his vaunted tutelage, Philante was not a true connoisseur, although he certainly considered himself to be.

Peering around with studied indifference (as if he were quite accustomed to such conspicuous opulence), he keenly drank in Philante's becolumned, Romanesque pergola with requisite golden eagle surmounting its dome, the tiered gardens, the fountains, and the robed servants, all levitated silently on an airborne platform deftly masked as a white, puffy cloud. Such luxury! He felt his upper lip curl involuntarily. He was not accustomed to feelings of . . . well . . . inferiority. Yet the thrice-damned Philante managed to conjure that very emotion at every audience. Renaldo simply *hated* taking second place to anyone, especially when it came to appearances. Of course, when it came to competing with one's Emperor . . .

He watched a page hurry toward him from the royal pergola. The willowy young woman was dressed only in a wide silk ribbon that fluttered from her shoulder. No better looking than his own servants, by God.

"His Imperial Majesty sends his compliments, my lord," the page announced with an agile, liquid bow, "and invites you to his august presence immediately."

"Thank you," Renaldo mumbled, abhorring the necessity of thanking anyone, much less a servant—but acquiescing nonetheless to a suspicion that this seductive young woman might well possess furtive influence with her all-powerful master. Philante's residence wing of old Buckingham Palace was widely touted (in careful whispers) for the nubile pages domiciled there as "special servants." Grinding his teeth, he followed the young woman across a carpet of pillow-soft grass laced with graceful, diaphanous trees and great tracts of flowers in riotous bloom. Nearby, hoofed and horned satyrs—spawned of the same genetic experiments that produced racing griffins—pranced on hairy goat's legs while fat, winged children and young women—all nude save for the occasional bright-hued ribbon—reclined languorously in beds of lilies or danced with equally naked young men. Renaldo mentally laughed with derision—old Philante had been spending too much time studying works by Jean-Honré Fragonard and Piero di Cosimo. But the rococo grandeur also aggravated the sense of inferiority that gnawed away at his well-being, and he became more and more uncomfortable as he approached the throne.

Ahead, Philante carefully plucked from a bunch of cool-looking green grapes as he reclined grotesquely on a grandiose couch upholstered in red velvet. Wrinkled and gray with veins climbing everywhere like hideous blue vines, his gaunt, naked body could only be described as repulsive, at least in comparison with the other occupants of this personalized "cloud." He was nearly bald, with dirty gray tufts of hair over his ears and at the very top of his head. His face, with its long nose, sunken cheeks, massive jaw, and mouth frozen into the rictus of a smile gave the appearance of an imbecile. But his close-set, gray eyes fairly blazed with crafty intelligence that one discounted at his or her uttermost peril. Deftly covering his gray crotch with part of the royal-purple ribbon he wore, he held out his left hand. "You may kiss my ring, Renaldo," he said personally, "We understand that Flying Fandangle was most well disposed toward you today."

Swallowing his pride (and his gorge), Renaldo knelt on

the top step of the pergola and kissed the proffered ring, taking notice—with no little envy—of the huge StarBlaze set in its claws. Goddamn Philante—everything he possessed had to be the biggest or the most expensive! As he rose, he smiled. The Giulio Cesare StarBlaze was larger and yet more beautiful. "Ah, Highness," he purred, wondering if the old blackguard knew the great jewel had been found and was, indeed, being offered for sale, "what a great pleasure to be summoned to this lofty sanctuary. Your kindness overwhelms me."

"As usual, Renaldo," Philante said good-naturedly, "you are full of the ripest shit." He smiled. "But We do like it," he added, "so you may rise."

"Thank you, Majesty," Renaldo purred, desperately squashing a sudden desire for reconfiguring the skinny old man's extra-long nose to a much flatter configuration. Grunting, he pulled himself erect, then took an uncomfortable-looking seat proffered by one of the satyrs, a handsome enough devil, except for those ugly hooves and goat legs.

"So, Renaldo," the Emperor asked, contemplating a new bunch of grapes, "on what will you spend your ill-gotten gains?"

Somehow, Philante's manner suggested much more than surfaced with such an artless question. Renaldo passed a few moments in pseudocontemplation, then frowned. "I have scarce had time to contemplate my winnings, Your Majesty," he replied evasively. "Many excellent causes come to mind—and of course, I am devoted to our contemporary renaissance of classical opera."

"Yes," Philante replied. "We are well aware of your love for opera, and We commend you for it. Imperial Earth is much indebted for your gallant efforts in behalf of the performing arts."

"I thank Your Majesty for his commendation," Renaldo said warily. Something else was coming, and if he was any judge, it had little to do with Flying Fandangle's recent win—or griffin racing—at all.

"But surely, Renaldo, you have other interests aside from opera," Philante continued. "We have personally seen your magnificent gem collection, for example."

Prudently, Renaldo continued to allow the Emperor to steer their rather one-sided conversation in the direction he chose. "I thank Your Majesty for the compliment," he said, noncommittally.

"No compliment meant, my good Renaldo," Philante continued, glancing at his hand. "You must certainly know that except for this StarBlaze We wear on Our finger, your collection would be greater than Ours." After a moment, he returned his gaze to Renaldo. "We trust," he said, "you have heard the rumor that the Giulio Cesare StarBlaze has surfaced once more."

So that was it! With what he hoped was a winning look of innocence, Renaldo raised his eyebrows. "The Giulio Cesare StarBlaze, Your Majesty?" he gasped dramatically. "Where?"

"We do not know," Philante answered with an oblique glance. "We hoped that *you* might have heard."

"Ah, such would be exciting news, indeed," Renaldo said evasively, his mind running now at top speed. If Philante was telling the truth, then Otto Gaspari had indeed kept his word and was offering the Giulio Cesare exclusively. The gem was his! Thanks to the damned missing slaver, he would be nearly insolvent for months to come, but by God, he'd *finally* have a leg up on Philante. And one didn't get such a chance very often at least in this lifetime.

"You seem lost in thought, Renaldo," Philante commented after a few moments' silence. He grinned. "We take it that the Giulio Cesare appeals greatly to your fancy, also."

"But of course, Your Majesty," Renaldo said. "Possession of such a gemstone would satisfy the craving of a lifetime."

"Truly," Philante said. He fixed Renaldo with his gaze, then smiled. "May the best man win, then," he said.

"Win what, Your Majesty?" Renaldo said as innocuously as he could.

"The race for possession of the Giulio Cesare, of course," Philante said. He examined his perfectly manicured fingernails. "You wouldn't consider a small wager, would you?" he asked casually.

"A wager against *you*, Your Majesty?" Renaldo said, sensing an even greater triumph over the skinny nincompoop—who never said anything casually. The Imperial spies must have totally failed to locate the great gemstone. He, Renaldo, had waited a long time for such a victory; soon it would be his— along with an extra reward for his patience and circumspection.

"Of course a wager against Us," Philante remonstrated. "Not many are wealthy enough to make such a bet worthwhile." He smiled. "However, in your case, despite the grandly falsified tax returns you submit, We know you have sufficient resources to risk a worthy amount."

"Your Majesty is too kind," Renaldo purred.

"Say one billion credits?" Philante asked coolly.

In spite of himself, Renaldo felt his heart jump. *Worthy* indeed! Fighting his emotions to a draw, he steadied himself and looked the prelate directly in his eye. "A billion credits will be satisfactory, Your Majesty," he heard himself say.

"You have noted that?" Philante said, as if to thin air.

"Noted and notarized, my Emperor," a voice replied— again, from thin air.

"We like to keep close track of Our wagers," Philante assured Renaldo.

"Yes," the Earl agreed with a shudder, "you, er, do, don't you?"

"We shall expect your billion credits in escrow at the Bank of London, say . . . in one week?"

Renaldo mentally gulped. The Giulio Cesare would cost at least twice that much. To raise that much more money, he would have to mortgage nearly everything he owned. Nevertheless, if the Emperor couldn't be trusted to pay off his gambling debts, then who could? Besides, it was like having the fool Philante help purchase the Giulio Cesare StarBlaze for him! He grinned. "Done," he said.

"Good!" Philante said, glancing at a baroque timepiece suspended from the groined roof of the pergola. He frowned, then peered at a covey of adolescents circling a maypole. "Nearly an hour till the next race, Renaldo," he said. "Do you fancy one of those? They're virgins, you know—all duly certified."

Renaldo felt a familiar sensation in his loins as he peered at the young women. None older than fifteen. "Any of them," he said. "One is more beautiful than the next."

"That one, then," Philante said, pointing to a supple young redhead. "We'll share her—right on this couch. You there, little girl," he called. "Yes, the one in the pink ribbon."

Grinning with pleasure, Renaldo reached for the great, jeweled brooch that closed his toga. Sharing a virgin with the Emperor was a singular honor. It would be the beginning of a *special* afternoon.

Manhattan Sector, New Washington • Earth

At nearly the same instant—10:15 A.M. ECONUS, Earth time—Canby had arrived early in Manhattan. Detouring on his way to the Salvage Yard, he had just sighted Cynthia Tenniel reading on a park bench in old Battery Park. Characteristically for that time of year, the snow of two days ago had completely melted, and cool, autumnal breezes were again blowing from the south. Flat-bottomed clouds promising fair weather cruised the light blue sky, and except for the bare trees, winter seemed a long way off. "May I join you?" he asked.

She looked up from her book and smiled. "Hello, Gordon," she said, sliding to one side of the bench. Today, her buff overcoat was open, revealing a bright yellow sweater over checked slacks. "What brings you to Battery Park this morning?"

"Well," Canby said, watching all his well-rehearsed conversation-starters crumble to dust, "if you want to know the truth, it's *you*."

"Me?" she asked, then laughed. "I know," she said, "you're short a crew member, and you want me to be a disruptor gunner, or something like that."

Canby laughed with her. "How'd you guess? Did I have 'gunner wanted' written all over my face?"

"Well . . ."

In the chilly sunlight, they both laughed again. It was the kind of morning that made Canby glad all over—and evidently Tenniel, too. "Well, *what*, Gordon Canby?" she asked, her blue eyes sparkling in the sunlight.

"Well . . . actually, I've got all the disruptor gunners I need, Cynthia."

"What?" Tenniel demanded with a look of mock consternation. "You expect me to work in the engine room, then— or some horrid place like that? Gordon Canby," she said indignantly, "I'll have you know that it's disruptor gunner or nothing."

"Would you settle for an evening on the town?"

Tenniel raised her eyebrows, then sat in silence for a moment. "Me?" she asked presently.

"Nobody else on this bench I can see," Canby said. "Must be you."

"Gordon," Tenniel said, her expression abruptly sobering, "you don't know anything about me."

"Maybe that's why I'm asking you out," Canby countered as her blush turned into full-fledged crimson. "Is there something the matter?"

"Er, n-no," Tenniel said, putting a hand to her mouth. For a moment, a melancholy little smile passed her lips. "It's just that . . ."

"Just what?" Canby asked warily. "If you don't want to go out with me, it's all right."

"Oh, no, Gordon," Tenniel exclaimed, the melancholy

smile replaced instantly with a look of concern. "Nothing like that. I, er . . ."

Canby could now sense considerable—almost palpable—agitation. "Please," he said, humiliated to his very core. "Let's forget about the whole thing. Just pretend I was never at the park today. Sorry I've caused you so much—"

"You don't understand, Gordon," she said, raising a hand defensively. "I'd *like* to go out with you. It's . . . it's just . . ."

"Just *what*?" Canby asked, a feeling of hopelessness spreading through him. "Is there something wrong?"

Tenniel's eyes dropped while she appeared to give the question considerable thought. At length, she looked up. "I suppose not," she said. "But, well, I simply haven't done a lot of dating, lately, Gordon. I . . ."

"What's *that* got to do with us having an evening together?"

"Well," she answered, while another sad little smile disappeared almost as soon as it materialized, "probably nothing. But I, er, have this night job that, well . . ." She shook her head. "And besides, you really *don't* know anything about me."

"I know I want to go out with you," Canby said. "It won't be anything fancy—I can't afford fancy. But I'll gladly pay for someone to look after Damian. And you did say you'd like to. So, how about it?"

"Well, my job . . ."

Canby smiled. "I can't believe you work every night of the week—do you?"

Almost resignedly, Tenniel took a deep breath. "No," she said. "I have an occasional night off. And," she said with a little grin, "I really would like to go out with you. How about Friday evening?"

Canby's heart soared. "Friday evening is wonderful," he exclaimed. "You name the time."

Tenniel thought for a moment. "Will seven-thirty be too late?" she asked.

"Perfect," Canby answered. He had just settled back to

spend a few relaxing moments in the warming sunlight when his PocketFollower buzzed against his thigh. Frowning, he fished the tiny device from his pocket and keyed in a GoAhead.

A tiny, holographic image of Pete Menderes materialized above the PocketFollower. "Sorry to bother you, Skipper," Menderes said, turning to peer at Tenniel. "Is it okay to talk?"

"I'm with a friend, Pete," Canby said, glancing reassuringly at Tenniel. "What's going on?"

"Call for you, Skipper," Menderes reported, "from that broad Peterson you recruited for the ships. Don't know how she found out about the Legion, but she demanded I use the network to reach you. Life and death, she said. Wants you to call her at the Yard *pronto*, whatever that means. All right?"

Canby frowned. "All right, Pete," he said. "Thanks."

"Anything wrong, Skipper?"

"Not that I know of now," Canby said. "But if there is, I'll call you right back. Otherwise, everything's okay." He rang off, then glanced at Tenniel as Menderes's image faded. "Nothing like a good morning's relaxation, is there?" he said with a mock look of dementia.

"If you say so," Tenniel whispered.

"Sorry," Canby said, keying in Peterson's identifier. Her head and shoulders materialized almost immediately above the PocketFollower.

"Looks like Battery Park," she said, glancing around her. Then she spotted Tenniel. "Oh, hello," she said. "Sorry to interrupt, Skipper. Okay to talk?"

"Sounds important," Canby equivocated. "What's going on?"

Peterson understood; she nodded. "Right, then, Skipper," she said. "You've got a personal appointment with 'The Man' at two-thirty *this afternoon* in the Georgetown Sector. Place called Smokes Tavern. Okay?"

The Man? Of course! He now had his personal appointment with Nemil Quinn! "You bet it's okay, Chief," he said.

"Can you make it *in time*?" Peterson asked with a look of concern. "You only have about three hours."

"I'll make it, all right," Canby assured her. "You were right about where I am. I'll simply catch a train out of Grand Central. Ought to be in Georgetown by three at the latest."

"Figure you can find Smokes, then?" Peterson asked.

"Chief," Canby said, "if it's a tavern, I'll find it. Trust me on that."

Peterson laughed. "Yeah, Skipper. I almost forgot. Okay, then I'll ring off." She turned for a moment to peer at Tenniel. "Terribly sorry to bother you two, lady," she said in a voice that rather belied her words. Then she returned her gaze to Canby. "Let me know what happens, okay?"

"You'll be the first to know," Canby assured her.

"So long, Skipper," Peterson said; her image disappeared.

"I don't think she likes me," Tenniel murmured while the sad little smile returned for an instant to her face.

Canby felt himself grimace. "Really?" he asked in a vain attempt to mollify an unpleasant situation before things got completely out of control. "I didn't notice."

"Perhaps I just imagined it, then," Tenniel said gently. But Canby knew she had lied about the incident just as much as he had.

"One way or another, it doesn't matter much," Canby said. "At least so far as Friday evening is concerned."

Tenniel shook her head and smiled, this time with genuine warmth. "Not at all, Gordon," she said. "Seven-thirty, right?"

"Right," Canby said. "But where?"

She laughed and looked him in the eye—she had a *beautiful* face. "I wondered when you were going to ask . . . but I wouldn't have let you leave until you did." She reached into her worn purse and quickly scribbled on a scrap of paper. "Here," she said. "This ought to get you there. And I've put my identifier on it, in case you need to call."

"Thanks, Cynthia," Canby said, then shook his head. "I'd

sort of hoped to spend a few moments here bothering you. But I guess you heard what I've got to do now."

"Well," Tenniel replied, "I couldn't avoid overhearing that you have a rather important appointment this afternoon. In the Georgetown Sector, is it?"

Canby nodded.

"Then you'd better be on your way," she said, glancing at her watch. "That's nearly a two-hour trip *after* you get to Grand Central."

"I'll be back," Canby said, putting the slip of paper into his battered black wallet. "Friday evening at seven-thirty."

"I'll be waiting," Tenniel said.

Columbia Sector, New Washington • Earth

While Canby hurried uptown toward Grand Central, Nikolai Kobir was already only a few miles from Georgetown, in the Columbia Section of new Washington. Today, he was dressed in the official blue jumpsuit of an Imperial Civil Servant. His counterfeited ID picture badge carried the fictitious name of Quincy Burnside, a Special Records Auditor. Its gold background and encoded identity transmitter—that cost nearly ten thousand credits to counterfeit—gave him access to the Empire's most sensitive document classifications and had taken him through eight sequential checkpoints within the Archive Division of the Imperial Data Authority. During the past hour, he and Casmir Osarian, a slightly built, brilliant Kîrskian, also dressed in an Imperial jumpsuit with phony badge, had culled a remarkable abstract of Renaldo's finances. "There is more, then, Ali?" Kobir asked, using the name printed on Osarian's counterfeit badge.

"Always one can find more data, Mr. Burnside," Osarian answered, still peering into one of the displays they had commandeered, "but of diminishing importance because it ages. Will what we have gleaned so far suffice?"

"A moment, my friend," Kobir said. Rapidly scrolling

through the index, he stopped at certain icons to consider the associated data. At length, he finished and smiled. Accumulating such information firsthand had also required spending a small fortune in the way of bribes and technical operations. Now, however, even the top layers of information indicated that he had made a sound investment. He would presently blackmail this Sadir, First Earl of Renaldo, in a most sophisticated manner, neither demanding so much that the man panicked nor so little that he, Kobir, wasted his time. "This should be sufficient, at least for the time being," he said.

"I shall download it, then, into our cassette," Osarian said, plugging a small DataBattery into the console beside him.

Kobir nodded, and was about to switch off his terminal when he felt something touch his shoulder.

"You will identify yourself," a voice commanded imperiously from behind him.

Though Kobir remained outwardly calm, his mind raced. The pressure he felt on his shoulder probably was a hand; a weapon would have prodded him between his shoulders. Consequently, the person—or persons—behind him were presumably unarmed, or at least had not yet brought weapons to bear. He glanced at Osarian and was comforted to see that years of military training had come instantly into play. The technician had stopped work at his terminal and was warily awaiting orders. Kobir passed a wink of reassurance, then, steeling himself, sat upright; the pressure on his shoulder instantly withdrew. "Who *dares* touch my person?" he demanded, rising slowly from the chair as if he were stiff with anger.

"Silence!" the voice replied. "You will turn around slowly and present your credentials."

Kobir nodded. So it would be a matter of wills. He smiled to himself, then turned carefully until he confronted a pallid, mean-eyed civilian and a rather worried-looking uniformed guard. The civilian—whose badge read, "Hogarth, Fornolt, J."—was clearly some sort of supervisor, and in order to administer such an inner sanctum had to be someone with considerable authority. But here in the government, authority indicated little in the way of job competence; more often, it signaled only high-level political connections. If Kobir was correct, the man's chief strength would be in wielding—and winning—power within a hierarchy, cleverly exercising deception and innuendo to undercut his competitors as well as those whose positions he coveted.

The guard, on the other hand, one Cornold West by his badge, was alert, but ultimately a soldier like Osarian, waiting for orders. No immediate danger here—and a possible, if unsuspecting, ally.

Kobir went on the offensive immediately. "Hogarth," he demanded contemptuously, "you will immediately describe the authority by which you have interrupted an official government audit."

"How dare you question my authority!" Hogarth roared. "I am Supervisor in this section. You have no right of entry without my personal permission. Just who do you think you are? Guard West, seize this man!"

"Er . . ." the guard began, taking a hesitant step forward.

Kobir raised a warning hand that stopped the guard cold in his tracks. Then he casually turned to Hogarth and smiled. The civil servant's very success would prove to be his greatest weakness. For his apparent power would almost surely have given him the bravado to cheat heavily on his income taxes. Everyone did, and the higher one's position, the more one could get away with. Nevertheless, every year a select committee of Nobles randomly picked out a few thousand nonimportant individuals and made their lives miserable with audits that invariably ended in financial ruin, regardless of guilt. Word got around—it kept the hoi polloi in line. "*This* is how I dare," he said sternly. Reaching into his pocket, he withdrew a bright chromium badge in the death's-head emblem of the BIRCE, Bureau of Imperial Revenue Collection Enforcement, dreaded arm of the Political Class responsible for seizing tangible resources from citizens suspected of tax falsification. It had cost him an extra four thousand credits, but it now paid for itself instantly.

Hogarth was taken completely by surprise. He moved back in obvious terror, stepping on the guard's toe and allowing Kobir to bring his commanding height to bear.

"Ali," the Kîrskian commanded, "record the identifier of this Hogarth for charges of suspicion of High Felony Audit Obstruction . . . and perhaps other interesting charges." He chuckled grimly. "The bureau will be most anxious to scrutinize this man's financial dealings as well—after, of course, thoroughly investigating the first charges we shall file."

Wide-eyed, Hogarth put a hand over his mouth and made a choking noise while the guard stepped back farther, in a clear attempt to guard his toe—while looking as if he would like to melt into the floor.

All military now, Osarian stepped in front of Hogarth to record the information encoded on his badge.

"Be accurate," Kobir admonished. "It is usually those who try to interfere who are the most guilty."

"I shall attempt to be most accurate, Commissioner," Osarian replied.

"B-but Commissioner Burnside . . ." Hogarth began, glancing at Kobir's forged badge.

"Silence, miscreant suspect!" Kobir snapped. The civilian appeared to shrivel, but held his silence. Kobir allowed himself to relax slightly. He was now in complete control. He glanced at their DataBattery. "Is the recording of our information complete?" he demanded imperiously.

Osarian frowned and peered at the cassette. "Perhaps another five minutes, Commissioner," he said.

Kobir pursed his lips—he and Osarian were still greatly at risk until they had returned to the surface and departed from the building, but there was no choice. He turned to the guard. "West," he commanded, "this suspect is now in your charge. Make certain he is unable to warn any possible confederates to corrupt this data until we have recorded *all* suspect records."

"Aye, Commissioner Burnside," the guard replied, reinflating like a balloon. "Shall I keep my blaster on him?"

"No," Kobir replied quickly, noting a number of people stopping to peer at the four of them. "To do so might attract attention," he said, "as well as warn confederates that their criminal days are also numbered."

"Oh, yes. Commissioner," West replied. "I should have thought of that."

"I shall overlook it in my report," Kobir promised sternly.

At last, Osarian drew the DataBattery from its receptacle, shined it against his sleeve as if it had been dirtied. then slipped it into the small, official-looking leather carryall attached to his belt. "I am finished, Commissioner," he announced.

"Good," Kobir said. "West," he directed, "you will detain Hogarth here for the next fifteen minutes to ensure he causes no more trouble than he has—"

"B-but *Commissioner*," Hogarth interrupted.

"Silence," Kobir commanded. "Another outburst could easily add years to your sentence."

"B-but—"

"I take it you have years to spare, eh, Hogarth?"

"No, Commissioner."

"As I was saying, West," Kobir continued, "you will detain this suspect in silence here for fifteen minutes, then march him directly to the Security Office for questioning and incarceration. Do you understand?"

"I understand completely," West said, coming to attention. His arm came up in the beginning of a salute, but he dropped it to his side before he completed the salutation.

"Ali," Kobir directed in a raised voice as they started for the elevator bank, "remind me to mention that Guard West in my report."

"Yes, Commissioner," Osarian said. Then, speaking into his wristwatch—which was nothing more than that—he carefully enunciated, "Remind Commissioner Burnside to mention Guard West *favorably* in his report. . . ."

Within thirteen minutes, Kobir and Osarian had safely cleared the building. Another thirty minutes found the two changed into the green overalls and yellow shirts of the local Paperhangers' Guild. Kobir had additionally donned a small, square mustache and Osarian wore a large, black eye patch while they relaxed in a Georgetown tavern called Smokes. In precisely two hours, they boarded a high-speed train for the Manhattan Sector. But they never arrived at Grand Central Station. Instead, as the train surfaced for its required stop in Red Bank to adjust timing tracks, they jumped from their coach using a special door key available only to railway officials and made their way on foot to one Ilviento's Tavern, where they first dined lustily on Italian food unique in all known civilization, then departed Earth aboard one of their trusty KV 72s—through one of the greatest civilian manhunts activated during the past few years.

Georgetown, Columbia Sector • Earth

At exactly 3:21 P.M., Canby strode through the front door of Smokes Tavern in old Georgetown. That time of the afternoon, the tavern was largely empty. A few couples spoke in low voices among the booths that ringed the room, and two relaxed-looking paperhangers—one with an eye patch, one with an odd-looking, square mustache—were drinking beer at a table near the bar. Ordering himself a beer, Canby seated himself in a booth with a good view of the door and waited.

Three-thirty came and went with no sign of Nemil Quinn. So did 3:45. The two paperhangers finished a second beer and departed shortly after 3:50, by which time Canby was experiencing his first pangs of real concern. Then, a few moments before four, a small, angular man appeared in the doorway. Almost completely bald, he was dressed in a brown wool ski sweater, a soft beaked cap, khaki slacks, and boots. And although he was certainly recognizable from the many times he appeared in the media, he was much smaller than Canby had imagined. Peering around the dark interior of the tavern, the man's gaze at last fixed on the booth.

Canby nodded in recognition, whereupon Quinn made his way across the floor to the table.

"I'm looking for Gordon Canby," he said in the scratchy bass so familiar on the media.

Canby stood and offered his hand respectfully. "I am Gordon Canby," he replied.

Quinn grinned. "Sit down, my friend," he said. "I'll get us a couple of brews so we can talk easier. What's that you're drinking?" he asked, nodding toward Canby's half-filled beaker.

"Any draft," Canby said, pleasantly surprised that a Chancellor of the Exchequer would indeed drink such pedestrian stuff as beer—much less buy some for a stranger. He watched the man saunter to the bar, joke with the bartender while the fresh beakers were filled, then return to the booth with a grin on his face. "Here," he said, expertly sliding Canby's fresh beer across the table to within a half inch of the first. "To DH.98s," he said.

Canby raised his beaker and touched it to Quinn's. "To DH.98s," he replied, looking Quinn in the eye, "and the resurrection thereof."

Quinn smiled. "So, Canby," he said with a chuckle, "what do you plan to do with four DH.98s? Perhaps transportation for that gaggle of your ex-starsailors who call themselves 'Canby's Legion'?"

Canby felt his heart race. "I don't know what you're talking about, Chancellor Quinn," he lied, mustering the most convincing frown he could manage.

"Call me Nemil like the rest of my friends," Quinn said. "And cut the bullshit. There's very little I *don't* know about you." He laughed. "And for your further edification—I didn't learn it from our pudgy-assed friend Peterson. As Chancellor, I've got information sources you can't even imagine. So either trust me or let's finish our beers and quit wasting each other's time."

Stunned, Canby sat in silence for a moment, collecting his thoughts. Finally, he nodded and looked Quinn in the eye. "All right . . . Nemil, I'll trust you," he said. Then he grinned. "Doesn't seem as if I have much choice anyway."

"Not a hell of a lot," Quinn said, matching his grin. "Now, tell me what kind of plans you've got for those ships. I know the crews you've recruited are all old military."

Canby frowned. "To tell the truth, I really haven't done a lot of planning beyond securing my Cashout and getting the ships out of the salvage yard before they're scrapped." He sipped his beer thoughtfully. "If you mean what you said to Peterson about the old Fleet repair yard, then you'll certainly solve my biggest problem so far—and that's where to base them. Then, of course, I've got to start worrying about where to get a few disruptors."

"One thing at a time," Quinn said with a chuckle. "And it all depends on what you plan to use the ships for. You still haven't told me about that."

"You mean after I get 'em running?"

"Yeah."

"Oh. Well, I suppose we'll go after the usual mercenary jobs: flying dirty, dangerous missions for people who don't have starships of their own. It's what I promised the crews. They want to be mercenaries, too."

"How about *illegal* missions?" Quinn asked with a hard stare.

"That depends on what you mean by *legal,*" Canby replied.

"What do *you* mean by *legal*?" Quinn demanded.

Canby thought about that for a moment, then smiled. "Anything *you* want us to do, Nemil Quinn, is automatically legal," he said. "Otherwise, *legal* is whatever we can get away with and not embarrass the Empire. Good enough?"

"It's what I wanted to hear, Canby," Quinn said. "And don't worry about those disruptors; they're not all *that* hard to find when you know where to look. We always need some good, reliable mercenaries—unofficially, that is." He smiled and looked up at the grimy, smoke-stained ceiling. " 'These,' " he recited, " 'in the day when heaven was falling/ The hour when Earth's foundations fled. Followed their mercenary calling,/ Took their wages and are dead.' Recognize the words?" he asked.

"No," Canby said. "I don't read much poetry."

Quinn smiled and continued, his eyes still on the ceiling as if the lines were printed there. " 'Their shoulders held the sky suspended:/ They stood and earth's foundations stay./ What God abandoned these defended/ And saved the sum of things for pay.' Never heard it, eh?"

"No."

"Written nearly seven hundred years ago, Canby," Quinn said, "by a poet named A. E. Housman. He called it, 'Epitaph on an Army of Mercenaries.' " He frowned. "Just how much do you know about this business you're going into, Canby?" he demanded.

"Unless I've forgotten a lot about being a military helmsman and a leader of men, Mr. Quinn," Canby said, suddenly very serious, "I think I know enough to do pretty well at it. And," he added, narrowing his eyes, "there are a lot of dead Kîrskians who would testify to it if they could. Plus a very few who are still alive."

"Sorry," Quinn said hastily. "I meant the *history* of the business. People who did the same kind of work in the past. It'll give you a pretty good idea of what *I* expect to get out of our relationship."

Canby took a deep breath. "Aside from some of the really famous ones like Claire Chennault and Norguard Timber, I know little more than what I could pick up at the Academy."

"How about Carl von Rosen?" Quinn asked. "Who's he?"

"You mean *Count* Carl *Gustav* von Rosen?" Canby asked.

"The same," Quinn replied. "One of the greatest mercenary leaders of the twentieth century. Sounds as if you've got some grounding in the trade."

"As the 'trade' has played its role in the political scheme of things," Canby continued, "especially in peacetime."

"And more than once," Quinn said, "they've 'saved the sum of things' for major powers that hired them when involvement of internal military organizations would have offended interdominion law or morality—or when a weak, threatened government couldn't afford its own military forces. That'll be part of the bargain, too."

Canby nodded. "But if I remember correctly, there were also occasions when mercenaries worked to overthrow those in power—as in 'revolutions,'" he added, watching for Quinn's reaction to *that*.

"Of course," Quinn said without batting an eye. "Mercenaries are the heirs to every soldier of fortune who ever lived, and they're impelled by the same motives. Whether they fly or ride or march, in the end, most fight for money, and their loyalty lasts little more than as long as it takes for their 'clients' to pay. That is why," he added pointedly, "the prices are so high. Usually, they operate without long-term contracts."

"One can find a few mercenaries for whom pay is not the main object," Canby maintained. "A number of the twentieth-century Spanish Republicans who flew during the civil war were true idealists; they went into battle for a cause."

"They were also *well-paid* idealists," Quinn reminded him.

"True," Canby allowed. "But that's not what seems to drive the people I've recruited. In point of fact, many of them are putting up their own money; quite a few have even applied for their Cashouts. These people are simply space warriors by trade. I know; I fought side by side with them—against the best the Kîrskians could put into space."

"I know them, too," Quinn said. "They're more than just warriors; they're also people who can't live without space—adventurers, who will happily shoulder any sort of job that calls for daring and unusual skill at a helm. Like you, perhaps, Canby?"

"Perhaps," Canby admitted. "But we've also got misfits, rogues, renegades, ne'er-do-wells, scions of royalty, romantics, frauds, geniuses, and even a couple of psychopaths." He laughed. "Some of them qualify for several of these categories. Including yours truly."

"I certainly hope so," Quinn said, finishing off his beaker and wiping foam from his upper lip. "Your turn to buy. I'm drinking Foster's."

"Wait a minute," Canby said, finishing his own. "You may be Chancellor of the Exchequer with a world of money to spend, but I'm only a has-been starsailor living on the Stipend. Before I invest in something expensive as a Foster's, I want to know. Am I going to get use of that repair base on the Chesapeake?"

Momentarily taken aback, Quinn raised his eyebrows. Then he broke out in a grin. "With that definition of *legal* you've got, you'll be useful to a *number* of Imperial agencies—quietly, of course. And if you do go after something we don't approve of, we can rap your knuckles before you get any of us in trouble. Yeah, Canby," he guffawed, "you've Goddamn well got your repair base."

"In that case, Mr. Chancellor," Canby said, "you've Goddamn well got your beer."

That very evening, Quinn's limousine skimmer took the two men south to the village of Perrin—a ghost town since the great radiation catastrophe of 2219—on the west shore of Chesapeake Bay. Two miles north, at the end of a little-used road, they came to the long-abandoned Perrin Maintenance Station and explored by flashlight until well past midnight. The morning sun was high in the sky before Canby finally made his way back to Staten Island and crawled into bed. But he slept peacefully for the first time in a week—Canby's Legion was on its way back into space.

DECEMBER 15, 2689, EARTH DATE

Gascar • Orion Alpha/1

Four days after Flying Fandangle's auspicious victory at Monte Carlo-19, Renaldo and Gaspari chartered a private starliner to the ancient, sultry trading center of Gascar on Orion Alpha/1, a small satellite orbiting the star historically known as Betelgeuse. After a short drive from the spaceport aboard a creaking wreck billed as a limousine skimmer, they disembarked, sweating, in a crowded, narrow canyon of a street whose stench immediately turned Renaldo's stomach. Mopping his brow—the hot dampness had immediately overwhelmed his suit's London-adjusted air-conditioning—he glared dyspeptically at Gaspari and shook his head. "Was all this truly necessary?" he demanded, hefting a weighty briefcase that was chained to his arm. "I don't feel at all safe, you know, especially with our bodyguards still at the spaceport."

Gaspari merely shrugged as a confusion of absurdly robed—and malodorous—people jostled past them in both directions, some even leading animals at the end of ropes. "I believe you are in the market for a certain rare gemstone, my friend," he said. "Well, this is part of the price."

"With a price like that, you could at least deliver it," Renaldo grumped, mopping his brow with an already soaked handkerchief.

"We have been over that a dozen times already, Renaldo," Gaspari said with more than a hint of exasperation. "This is not my choice, as you well know." Shaking his head, he consulted a small card, then stepped into the crowded street. "Follow me," he ordered, "and we shall get this over with as quickly as possible." Tiers of balconies and riotously painted, carved towers loomed up on either side of the foul-smelling street as the two men pushed their way through the throng to a low, pointed archway in a white plaster wall. Carved directly above the apex was the numeral 9. "Follow me," the Count directed. "Velanti's office should be upstairs . . . on the top floor."

Grinding his teeth, Renaldo followed Gaspari up three endless flights of narrow stairs lighted only by glowing Ever-Lamps before they emerged—at last—in a dingy hall with filthy plaster walls and noisy, worn boards for a floor. Making their way to the far end where a single open door glowed with dim light, they entered a small, windowless chamber lavishly hung with ancient-looking tapestries, golden chains, and soft lamps. Thick carpeting covered the floor, while the heavy air reeked with the fragrance of spiced cigarettes and incense. A large, clearly priceless antique desk, inlaid with intricately carved scenes wrought in an ivorylike substance, commanded the far wall of the room. Three bearded men dressed in white—obviously air-conditioned—robes sat behind it, their backs to the carpeted wall.

The two on the outside were armed with wicked-looking, high-powered blasters. To Renaldo, panting and trembling from his recent exertions, their dark, bearded faces and cold eyes looked more wicked than the weapons they held—if that was possible. Between them, a serene-looking man—Velanti, no doubt—sat with his hands folded over a small, ornate chest perhaps three cubic decimeters in volume. He had a thin face surrounded by long, sable hair plastered to his head with something that still looked damp. Piercing, narrow-set eyes on either side of a long, thin nose contemplated the Earl with the same consideration one might bestow to a griffin on the trading block. He somehow looked like all the exasperating "foreigners" Renaldo had ever cursed for their vexing, non-Earth behavior. "You are Sadir, First Earl of Renaldo?" the Gascarian asked through thin, colorless lips.

Renaldo glanced at Gaspari, shivered in spite of the sweltering air in the room, then swallowed a large lump that had suddenly formed in his throat. "I—I am Renaldo," he said, suddenly feeling very alone.

Velanti regarded him in silence. "You are perspiring,

Sadir, First Earl of Renaldo," he said without emotion, as if he were examining some sort of peculiar animal.

Renaldo ground his teeth. "Of course I'm perspiring, you dunce," he growled as perspiration coursed down his back. "It's too hot in here."

Velanti stroked his chin for a moment as if deep in thought, still with no visible emotion. "You should purchase your suits locally, Sadir," he said after a time. "Clearly, the air-conditioning in yours is not up to the task of cooling your obese body."

Renaldo felt his cheeks burn—over and above what he was experiencing from the heat. "Goddamn your hide, Velanti, get on with it!" he growled.

The Gascarian inspected the fingernails of his right hand. "Your Gods—if indeed you have any—possess no power over me," he said coolly. "However, your poor manners are having their effect."

Renaldo's head throbbed. He opened his mouth to remonstrate when he felt a restraining hand on his arm.

"No more, my friend," he heard Gaspari whisper, "unless you wish to pay even *more* for your gem."

"I do not have to put up with this foreigner's—"

"Renaldo, you idiot," Gaspari snapped through clenched teeth. "Hasn't it registered with you that these so-called 'foreigners' are the only armed persons in this room?"

"And," Velanti added, nodding to Renaldo, "one assumes your briefcase contains the original amount I demanded in cash."

"Oh, Jesus," Renaldo whispered as the man's point struck home. He glanced at the two men on either side of Velanti. Neither moved, but their cold stares said volumes he had no desire to hear. He shuddered—Velanti was already in de facto possession of the money. And it was only by his sufferance that the StarBlaze would be delivered at all. Here in the relatively lawless Orion group, the man could just as easily keep both the gemstone *and* the money, while, he, Renaldo, would simply "disappear." A cold blade of fear stabbed his chest. "Otto Gaspari," he squeaked, throat tight with stress, "are you part of . . . this . . . conspiracy?"

Velanti answered for the aristocrat. "Your friend Gaspari is part of no conspiracy, Sadir. I personally vouch for his integrity." For the first time, he smiled. "However," he continued soberly, "I believe you *have* reached a conclusion that is essentially correct. If I chose to, shall we say, terminate your life here and now, I should possess both the jewel and your payment—in which case, Lord Gaspari will certainly receive his due commission." He smiled. "It is only you, insulting one, who is close to invalidating the agreement."

Renaldo's headache increased until he felt certain his head would split. With nearly superhuman effort, he managed to keep his silence. He would need to derive a great deal of pleasure from Philante's jealousy to make *this* worthwhile.

"Ah, Renaldo," Velanti said at length. "It is gratifying to see that one is never too old—nor too arrogant—to learn." He nodded, and moved the ornate chest to one side. "Your forbearance has already earned you a modicum of my respect. Place the briefcase here on the desk; I shall inspect your money now."

At these words, the men on either side of him raised their blasters, one aimed directly at Renaldo's head, the other at his crotch.

"Oh, don't let these men deter you, my good Earl," Velanti said reassuringly, "unless, of course, you have planned something untoward with the briefcase, in which case, you will be vaporized, beginning with your genitals, of course. Very painful, I am assured."

Renaldo's heart pounded wildly in his chest. "This contains only money," he said, placing the briefcase on the table.

"Of course. Of course," Velanti said with a pained look on his face. "Please open it, then." He smiled pontifically. "I love to gaze at money."

Renaldo placed trembling fingertips over tiny TipReaders securing the looks. A moment later, both catches retracted and he opened the briefcase, packed with large bills—two billion credits in all.

"Ah . . ." Velanti sighed, raising a packet of plastic currency and fanning through it carefully, "beautiful. Some used; some new. Precisely as instructed." He glanced up at Gaspari. "My respect for your client grows by the moment."

Gaspari bowed silently.

For the next hour, while Renaldo and Gaspari stood in the sweltering heat, Velanti inspected—then counted—Renaldo's money, one packet at a time. At last, he lay down the final packet and nodded. "My congratulations, Renaldo, you have lived up to the endorsement of your friend Lord Gaspari." He smiled. "He said you would have it all, and he was correct."

By this time, Renaldo's feet ached excruciatingly in every overburdened bone; never in his memory had he been forced to exist so long without the comfort of a chair. "The S-star-Blaze, Velanti," he groaned, pointing to the chest. "Either give me leave to depart with it or have your men shoot me. I am in *pain*."

Velanti put a hand to his mouth theatrically. "Oh," he exclaimed, "of course, my dear Renaldo. How thoughtless of me." With that, he pushed the chest to the edge of the table. "Here," he said. "You have paid for it; it is yours."

Hands trembling with both rage and expectation, Renaldo lifted the lid of the chest, then gasped. "The Giulio Cesare StarBlaze," he whispered, his eyes widening.

"Beautiful, is it not?" Velanti commented.

"Beautiful," Renaldo repeated, the heat, the fear, and the fierce pain in his feet momentarily forgotten. Placing the gemstone in the palm of his left hand, he inspected each gleaming, radiant facet. Finally, he set it back in its chest.

"Well, Renaldo, was it worth everything?" Velanti asked, peering into Renaldo's eyes.

The Earl ground his teeth. How he wanted to tell the misbegotten foreign devil what he *really* thought. Still, the Giulio Cesare *was* his. And it seemed as if he was actually going to escape with his life, although he swore that somehow, in the years of life remaining to him, he would absolutely *ruin* Lord Otto Gaspari. "Yes," he said.

"Yes, what?" Velanti asked with a little smile.

"Yes, it was worth it."

"Good. Good. Glad to hear of another satisfied client," Velanti said to Renaldo's extreme displeasure. He motioned to the chest. "Take the Giulio Cesare then, Sadir—with my blessings." He turned to Gaspari. "Your commission will be deposited as you requested, my friend."

Gaspari bowed silently again, inciting Renaldo to an even blacker rage. "Until the next time, Zman Velanti, may your Gods be with you."

"And yours with you."

By now, Renaldo was nearly apoplectic. Ears ringing with what he knew was runaway blood pressure, he opened his briefcase—still chained to his arm—and placed the Giulio Cesare inside, then closed and locked the lid. His voice once more reduced to mere squeaks by the strain, he started for the door. "Come, Gaspari," he squealed. As he limped painfully along the hall, he heard Velanti laugh.

"Your friend Sadir," the Gascarian said, "he has no sense of humor, has he?"

Manhattan Sector, New Washington • Earth

Dressed in his best (and only) suit, Gordon Canby stood nervously before the battered metal door of a fourth-floor, walk-up apartment; it was seven twenty-five P.M. The building had once been a fashionable, lower Manhattan address, but burgeoning population—and rampant social engineering—put paid to that more than a hundred years previously. Today, it was just another of a thousand tenements crowding the south tip of the island with wretchedness. Odors of cheap cooking, and worse, filled the hallway, along with the random discord of life in public housing. Canby shuddered. His rooming house on Staten Island was no nicer. But at least it was in a private dwelling where a tough old landlady laid down the law and kept her tenants—all, like Canby, from the low end of the Enfranchised Class—within at least *some* bounds of civilized living. Ignoring the darkened doorbell, he rapped lightly on the door.

A peephole flashed momentarily, then Tenniel's voice called, "Just a moment, Gordon." This was followed by sounds of door chains—a number of them—before finally the door opened and Tenniel stepped into the hall, coat over her arm. Quickly drawing the door closed behind her, she applied an electronic key to two stout-looking locks, then turned and smiled. "I'm ready," she said, handing Canby her ancient-looking buff overcoat. She was dressed in a close-fitting beige dress with short skirt and plunging neckline, high-heeled shoes, and a simple pearl necklace.

While he helped her into the overcoat, Canby couldn't help thinking what a shame it was to hide all the curves she was covering. He was still grinning to himself when she turned and cocked her head.

"What're you snickering at?" she asked with a funny little smile.

"Believe me, I wasn't snickering," Canby said as his cheeks started to burn.

"Then what *were* you doing?" she demanded with a little laugh that was nonetheless topped off with a frown.

"You want to know the truth?" he asked with a sidelong glance.

"Well, of course," she replied.

He found it difficult to tell if she was serious or joking, but decided on the latter. "I was thinking what a shame it was to cover up all those good looks with an overcoat," he said with a grin.

Tenniel's pretty mouth twisted into a sad little smile and her shoulders retracted a bit. "That's nice of you," she said equivocally.

Canby studied her face. "You don't look as if it was nice," he said.

"What was nice?" she asked, as if she'd forgotten that he'd even spoken.

"What I said about . . ."

She shrugged and closed her eyes for a moment. "It was nice, Gordon," she said at length.

Canby decided to pretend he'd never opened his mouth. He'd somehow landed on dangerous ground, but had no idea how—or what—had done it. "Hey," he said, changing the subject, "where's Damian? I thought I was going to pay for someone to look after him while we're out."

"I know you were, Gordon," she said as her smile returned, "and believe me, I appreciate the offer. Don't think I take something like that for granted."

"Then?"

"There's no need for it," she said with a little shrug. "While I'm temporarily employed on night jobs, I lodge him with a nightcare center that I pay for by the week. It's just down the hall."

"Gee," Canby protested. "I *did* promise."

"You let me pay for the nightcare, and I'll let you buy dinner." She laughed. "Besides, if it's the other way around, we'll have the V-Pols chasing us for felony stealing. I didn't bring enough money to pay for a decent supper."

"All right," Canby said grandly, "rather than subject us to the V-Pols, I'll give in on the nightcare."

Tenniel squeezed his arm. "Good!" she said. "I'm due for a night off!"

They dined at Griffin's Café, a tiny, midtown café on the rundown East Side where the lights were dim, the booths small, and the food excellent—as well as inexpensive. Canby was quickly fascinated by the slim, elegant blonde. Her professional life—before the Demob—had been much like his own, having to do with directing teams of people in extremely hazardous work. Except her teams assembled and repaired mobile reactors—like the ones that powered small military attack ships.

And, like Canby, she'd found that losing the job for which—and *at* which— she'd worked so long and diligently had been a traumatic experience, indeed. Especially so because she'd chosen to become pregnant during a weekend relationship with an old school chum who was passing through town—precisely thirteen months before her employment ended permanently.

She found herself on the streets only a few weeks before the Imperial Supreme Court officially legalized the current system of corporate bribes called "Tributes." These protected employers' profits by making jobs so difficult to find that Noble investors and their lieutenants could—and did—make any demands they chose on their employees. Since then, she'd determinedly eked out a living for herself and Damian, saving every fraction of a credit she could in the nearly vain hope of one day amassing sufficient funds to make tribute somewhere—and once again find at least a modicum of permanency.

Long before dessert, Canby knew she was even more special than he'd dreamed.

Georgetown/Columbia Sector, New Washington • Earth

While Canby and Tenniel dined in their tiny Manhattan bistro, Renaldo made a new acquaintance at the Grand Knight's Divertissement hosted that same evening in the Columbia Sector by none other than Nemil Quinn, Chancellor of the Exchequer.

Earlier in the evening, the Earl had obtained first place in the costume competition, extravagantly outfitting himself as a fourteenth-century nobleman—complete with cote-hardie buttoned to the knees, chain mail and plate armor (both of modern light alloy), and extravagantly pointed shoes. However, despite his winning costume, he was only just breaking even at an authentic antique roulette table when a tall, powerfully built stranger appeared at his side. Dressed in the sinister-looking costume of a late-eighteenth-century magistrate, the man wore a huge caped greatcoat and cocked hat turned up front and back with a cockade in front, Napoleonic style. He had the broad forehead, high cheekbones, and flattened nose Renaldo associated with Slavs, but precious few of *those* ever appeared with the Grand Knights—frightening types. usually, and prone to uncivilized acts. It was the man's sardonic, wide-set eyes that set his teeth on edge. They seemed to be staring down—and through him—baring his soul and all its inner secrets.

"Good evening, Sadir, First Earl of Renaldo," the man said in a deep voice that somehow brought visions of large bears to mind. "I trust the Gods of fortune have treated you benevolently tonight."

"Do I know you?" Renaldo demanded, delaying the croupier with a wave of his hand.

A thin smile appeared on the stranger's lips. "Not yet, Sadir," he said quietly. "but you will, soon enough."

"Sadir" indeed! Low-bred riffraff like Slavs were expected to address him as "my lord." Nevertheless, this Slav must represent money and power, else he would never have been invited to the august gathering of the Knights in the first place. And the man's eyes! A shudder of unreasonable dread ran along Renaldo's spine. "Who are you?" he demanded.

"Does the name Nikolai Kobir strike a familiar chord?" the stranger asked with his sardonic little smile.

"None whatsoever," Renaldo said.

"It is my given name," the stranger said.

"Well, it means nothing to me," Renaldo said, dismissing the foreigner as one of those horrid gate-crashers that occasionally bought their way in past the guards. By now, the other players at the table were looking at him, waiting impatiently for his wager. The Tableaux were scheduled to begin in less than an hour, and he was about to place his bet on the table when he heard the deep, quiet voice again.

"Perhaps the name of a mutual acquaintance is more familiar to you, Sadir," the stranger said. "I am certain you have heard of Georges A. Cortot."

Cortot! The words pierced Renaldo almost physically, like an icy bullet. He stiffened, a thousand anxieties racing through his brain, each worse than its predecessor.

"Er, is m'lord feeling well?" the croupier asked with a look of concern.

Grinding his teeth, Renaldo glanced at the inquisitive faces around the table—some were clearly irritated, too. "I, er . . ." he stammered. "Of course I am feeling well."

"You will place your wager, then, m'lord?"

"I can spare only a short time, Sadir," Kobir whispered. "After we talk, you may return to the wagering table— should you still wish to do so."

Heart beating like a trip-hammer, Renaldo cleared his throat. "I . . . I . . . shall withdraw from the game for the present," he stumbled, his voice once more shrill with terror.

"A wise decision," Kobir said as Renaldo picked up his tokens and the two moved from the table toward a quiet corner of the room. "I have a proposition I am certain you will find most interesting."

"How did you get in here?" Renaldo demanded angrily as they walked through the glittering crowd. "Clearly, you are not one of the Grand Knights."

"Clearly," Kobir said with a mordant smile. "But long ago I discovered that money often substitutes well for a membership card."

"I knew it!" Renaldo said with a thrill of triumph. "You are not even a guest—nothing but a foreigner. A Slav, probably."

"A Kîrskian," Kobir replied in an even voice.

"Yes, of course," Renaldo declared sourly, stopping beside an empty divan while he willed his knees to stop their shaking. He narrowed his eyes. "All right," he said, "what news have you concerning this, er, *person* of whom you spoke?"

"Georges A. Cortot," Kobir reminded him. "Surely you remember his name. A professional in your employ, if I am not mistaken."

"Perhaps an acquaintance," Renaldo allowed. "I, er, believe I *knew* a man of that name—once. No importance, of course."

"Ah, too bad," Kobir said sympathetically. "Your name was on his lips shortly before he died."

"Cortot . . . *dead*?" Renaldo demanded, his anxiety returning with a vengeance.

Kobir raised his eyebrows. "A strong reaction concerning someone who has no importance," he observed with sober mien.

Renaldo felt icy tentacles of panic exploring his ribs. Who *was* this man . . . and what did he know? "L-listen, Nikolai Kobir, or whatever your name is," he squeaked, "either come to your point immediately or I shall summon the guards."

Kobir smiled. "I think not, Renaldo," he said, reaching inside his greatcoat for a small golden tube with delicate silver inlays in the form of a grapevine, "either now or in the future. Not after you examine this."

"A pornoscope?" Renaldo demanded. "What do I need this for when the Tableaux are about to begin?"

"It has only the appearance of a pornoscope," Kobir said quietly. "However, if it sadly lacks in prurient content, it will afford the opportunity to look into certain HoloViews my colleagues recorded recently—HoloViews I am certain you will find fascinating." He proffered the pornoscope.

Renaldo frowned, looking this way and that to see if anyone was watching. "What if I don't want to look?" he pouted.

"Sit, Renaldo," he commanded, pointing to the couch, "and view these carefully. Most assuredly, you will find the view interesting."

"Who are you to order me—an Imperial Earl—to—" Renaldo began, his anxiety momentarily overwhelmed by spleen.

"Sit!" Kobir commanded in a whisper, stepping so close that the Earl felt he would smother.

Renaldo's first impulse was to summon the guards—but the very threat of Cortot's name suppressed that instantly. Breathing in short gasps, he collapsed backward, heavily, onto the couch. Then, grasping the pornoscope, he switched off the volume and activated the show—whose animated views soon turned his hands icy. First there were scenes of a livestock transport—*his* transport. Renaldo recognized the old ship immediately; he'd been over Cortot's plans a number of times. "Where was this taken?" he demanded.

Kobir smiled. "In deepest space," he said. "Far from the normal lanes of commerce."

"What makes you think that this . . . derelict means anything to me?" Renaldo asked.

"Perhaps only intuition," Kobir said with a phlegmatic shrug. "But continue to view, Sadir. The presentation has a great deal more to reveal—some of which I am certain will pique your interest."

Frowning, Renaldo activated the pornoscope again. This time, it depicted views of the transport's hold, crowded by wretched slaves and corpses. After these, it changed to low-level views of badly ravaged primitive structures—he could easily guess how *those* came about. Hands shaking in spite of his best efforts, he stopped the motion and looked up at Kobir again.

"I . . . I f-fail to see what these horrid views have to do with me," he gasped, his breathing all out of control.

"Oh?" Kobir said with sardonic amazement. "Well, no matter. The last segment will surely refresh your memory. Please," he said, gesturing to the pornoscope, "continue."

Reluctantly, Renaldo once more placed the viewer to his eye and started the motion again, which abruptly changed to Cortot's darkened cabin—with Gambini and her assistants flanking the ravaged figure of Georges Cortot himself. "Jesus Christ," the Earl gasped while the rank acid of vomit burned his gullet. He'd witnessed enough ritual torture to know what was attached to the man's penis. "Oh, *Jesus Christ.*"

"Shabby content for such a God, one would think," Kobir commented.

Faint from shock, Renaldo took the viewer from his eye—but the freebooter stayed his hand. "To receive the full effect, Renaldo," he said, "you must now turn up the volume so you can hear your *acquaintance's* final words."

"N-no," Renaldo said, feeling himself begin to sweat profusely. "I can't."

"The *volume control,* Renaldo," Kobir whispered vehemently. "Otherwise I shall see to it that everything you have seen so far becomes common knowledge—along with the last few moments, which you have yet to enjoy."

At that moment, a series of chimes sounded in the hall, after which the revelers blatantly began to fondle everyone—and anyone—within reach while they congregated before a stage set up at the far end of the ballroom. "The T-tableaux are about to begin," Renaldo, hoping against hope that something—anything—would distract this huge Slav from God knew what. "They are not to be missed."

"Time enough for your Tableaux," he heard Kobir reply fiercely, "once you have witnessed the last of these HoloViews."

Tears burned Renaldo's eyes; he felt one stream along his cheek. "*No!*" he squeaked again. He let the pornoscope drop to the floor.

Kobir merely shrugged. "I cannot understand why you would desire such embarrassing information to be made public. But if that is your wish, Renaldo, then so be it." Retrieving the pornoscope, he started off toward the stage.

"W-wait!" Renaldo called, fear ultimately conquering his aversion.

"For *what*?" Kobir demanded. "I have already asked you

to view this pornograph, and you have refused. It seems, therefore, that we have no more business with one another, and I shall turn this over to the proper authorities." He shrugged. "Who knows? Perhaps you might have found the remainder most agreeable."

"Please," Renaldo begged, sweat running down his brow into his eyes. "I shall watch it."

Kobir paused, as if considering. He tossed the pornoscope carelessly in his hand while he frowned.

"*Please,*" Renaldo beseeched. As he spoke, the room dimmed and the stage lights came on accompanied by wild applause and cheering. It all seemed a hundred miles away.

Kobir at last handed him the pornoscope. "Don't forget the volume control," he cautioned. "With everyone drawn to the stage, you now have all the privacy you need to listen—except for me, of course. But"—he shrugged indifferently—"as you will see, I was there in person to witness the recording."

Heart in his mouth, Renaldo raised the pornoscope with hands trembling so badly he could hardly focus into it.

"The volume control," Kobir whispered.

Renaldo fumbled the tiny control ring clockwise, just as the image of Kobir strode into the picture. "Y-*you!*" the Earl exclaimed, glancing momentarily at the freebooter.

"Keep your eyes on the pornoscope," Kobir ordered quietly. "We can talk about my presence later."

Almost as if in a dream, Renaldo watched the appalling spectacle play itself out:

"Captain Cortot will talk to you now, Kapitan," a small, demented-looking woman said, making a pleased little smile beneath her mustache of sweat.

"Thank you, Rosa," the Slav said, appearing to look directly into the woman's maniacal eyes.

"It is nothing, Kapitan," she replied with a modest look—apparently quite self-satisfied with the horror she appeared to have effected on Cortot.

The Slav nodded, then stepped in front of Cortot, who raised a face glistening with sweat. His eyes appeared to be nearly sightless, but they seemed to focus. "Do you know me?" the Slav asked.

With what must have been superhuman effort, Cortot nodded his head slowly up and down.

"And you know what information I seek—the name of your partner as well as the owner of this ship?"

Renaldo gasped. The tiny scene had become his only reality. "No!" he cried. "No!" But his pleas went unheard. Suddenly he felt warm liquid spreading through his loins.

Again, the head nodded clumsily.

"Then tell me, Captain," the man named Kobir said. "After that, the pain will cease and you can sleep."

As the Slav watched with obvious distaste, Cortot's mouth opened and tried to speak. At first, only animal noises and whimpers came from the swollen lips—along with more drool and vomit. But when the madwoman moved into his view, Cortot began bawling incoherently and moved his head clumsily from side to side, his puffed eyes rolling in fear.

Abruptly, Renaldo's stomach heaved out of control, filling his mouth with burning vomit, which he swallowed again in his horror. Somewhere a thousand miles away, he could hear the music and cheering of a Tableaux, but now, it had very little importance.

"Name the owner of this barge, Captain Cortot," the madwoman said in a quiet voice. "Name the man for whom you work." She only needed to reach behind the chair before Cortot began a spasm of dry heaving, but only thick spittle dribbled from his lips. Yet somehow, with a

clearly supreme effort, the wreck of a man managed a
great wet groan, followed by a single word, "Renaldo."

Cortot's word slashed into Renaldo like a cold, sharp
sword, finishing off any hopes for some sort of accommoda-
tion with the huge Slav standing before him. Grinding his
teeth, he waited for the horrid view to end.

Once more, the madwoman moved her hand behind the
chair. "The whole name, please, Captain Cortot," she
commanded. Again, Cortot's eyes rolled in primal fear,
and finally the swollen lips opened again.
"My p-partner, Sadir, F-first Earl of R-renaldo owns
this ship," the man gasped. He spoke only moments before
his head sagged once more to his chest, this time remain-
ing motionless.

At this juncture, the view faded.
Totally drained, Renaldo attempted to put the pornoscope
on the couch beside him but his hand was trembling so, he
dropped it on the floor. He bit his lip. Looking up at Kobir,
he suddenly found himself beyond fear and—surprisingly—
in some slight control of himself, although bodily functions
like heart rate and breathing were still completely out of control. "W-what do you want of me?" he panted.
The freebooter smiled like some great death's-head.
"Clearly," he said, "release of such a HoloView could cause
you no end of trouble, Sadir."
"Clearly," Renaldo agreed sourly, his respiration slowing
a bit.
"So, just as clearly, it should be worth a great deal of
money to keep it from publication. Correct?"
"Perhaps," Renaldo answered, unwilling to admit to any-
thing at this juncture.
"Only *perhaps*?" Kobir asked.
"Well," Renaldo said, searching for any sort of defense,

"I, ah . . . have seen little in the way of verification. Perhaps this is all a sham?"

Kobir laughed. "Don't you wish, Sadir," he said. "I have *more* than enough verification—including documents of sale and many authenticated records of funds transfers. Your flunky Cortot kept excellent records." He laughed. "Surely you would not accuse me of lax preparation?"

Renaldo slumped again. Clearly, the game was up; the pornoscope alone was enough to put him in a courtroom battling for his life. "No," he whispered hoarsely, "I believe you."

"Then," Kobir said, "let us discuss how much money this is worth to you."

"It might be worth a great deal if I *had* a great deal to pay," Renaldo said, desperately attempting to at least limit his losses. "However," he continued, "I invested nearly all my extra cash only a few days ago. And believe me, Kobir, that investment cannot quickly be converted to cash." Let the Goddamn Slav stew on *that,* he thought as he glanced toward the music—and the Tableaux, in which more than ten couples appeared to be copulating in different positions as they formed the letter *Q,* probably in honor of their hosts.

"One assumes you refer to the Giulio Cesare StarBlaze," Kobir said dismissively—as Renaldo's heart sank again.

The music and the artful fornicating fled from the Earl's mind on a new wave of fear. "How did you know about the Giulio Cesare?" he demanded.

"I know more about your finances, Renaldo—than do even *you,*" Kobir said.

"But I have *nothing.*" Renaldo wailed. "Believe me."

Kobir sat next to him on the couch, wrinkled his nose, then moved off to the far side. "You have pissed yourself, Renaldo," he said in a disgusted voice.

Face burning with humiliation, Renaldo was about to protest when the Slav stopped him with a glance that would halt a speeding lorry.

"Let me educate you concerning your finances," Kobir ordered in a voice that made Renaldo's blood run cold, "and what your payment schedule will be—starting tonight. . . ."

For the next fifteen minutes, the freebooter lectured about Renaldo's own finances: the worth of his mansions, his investments, his present cash outlays, and his plans for future capital spending—such as the grand ballroom with its Star-Blaze vault he had already contracted for the house on Belgrave Square. When he was finished, he sat back and looked Renaldo in the eye. "Tonight," he said, "you will make your first of twenty weekly payments to me—after which we shall discuss the further disposition of scenes recorded on the pornoscope at your feet."

Renaldo capitulated. Truly, this Slav had a better understanding of the Renaldo family finances than did he. "H-how m-much?" he asked, heart pounding once more in his chest.

"One hundred million Earth credits," Kobir said as if he had quoted the price of a suit of clothes.

"*One hundred million?*" Renaldo gasped. "Good God, man, that comes to two billion in twenty weeks. You will leave me nothing to feed myself?"

Kobir laughed and peered theatrically at Renaldo's great belly. "Such might be to your ultimate benefit," he said with a sardonic laugh. "Fortunately, I know that such a sum will hardly be missed among your weekly transactions. Shall I go through the whole thing again?"

Grinding his teeth, Renaldo shook his head. "No," he conceded. "I shall . . . pay."

"Good," Kobir said, as Renaldo half-heard a great cheer go up from the revelers at the Tableaux stage. "Your first installment is due immediately."

The Earl only shivered. "I c-carry no cash with me," he said, cold fear once again invading his loins.

"Not to worry, Renaldo," Kobir said. "With most revelers at the Tableaux, now is a most propitious time to visit the cashier for more gambling money. Eh?"

"B-but, one hundred million credits . . ."

Kobir only shrugged. "Oh, and by the way, Sadir, First Earl of Renaldo," he added, "should unfortunate circumstances befall me before I safely depart with the money, others in my organization will most certainly release the information where it will do the most good—or *harm*, in your case. One assumes you understand."

"I understand," Renaldo grunted, his head beginning to ache with what he knew was elevated blood pressure. Shaking his head in resignation, he struggled to his feet and led the way to the cashier.

Manhattan Sector, New Washington • Earth

After supper, Canby and Tenniel strolled arm-in-arm through Manhattan's sparkling, holiday-decorated Entertainment District to watch the new HoloDrama, *Soldiers of Fortune*, laughing and talking about every subject under the sun. More than once, they were forced into gutters by wealthy revelers flanked by bodyguards who cleared the sidewalks in their path, but neither bothered to take notice; they were too busy talking. Afterward, it became clear that the night had suddenly become very special—certainly it was for Canby. And from the glow on Tenniel's face, he could tell that it was special for her, too. By the time they reached her apartment, it seemed to Canby as if he had known her most of his life.

Their first kiss was so natural that it happened before Canby had a chance to think about it. Suddenly she was in his arms, her open mouth soft and hungry against his, hands gently pressing the back of his neck. Her very breath was like perfume while her breasts pressed urgently against his chest. Their lips parted for a moment while each took an unsteady breath, then touched for a moment more before Tenniel drew away, breathing shallowly. Opening his eyes, Canby held her a moment more, his own breath coming in shallow gasps while he stared into eyes that had suddenly become large and round—almost as if she were frightened.

"Are you all right?" he asked, releasing her from his embrace, then gently taking her hands—that had suddenly become cold.

At first Tenniel's eyes remained fixed at some point off in space. Then, slowly, as if she were coming out of a trance, she moved back a step. Finally she focused her eyes once more. "What did you say?" she asked.

"I, er, asked if you were all right," Canby replied.

She stood in silence a moment more, then smiled a little and nodded. "Yes, Gordon," she said, her gaze dropping to the pavement. "I'm all right now. Sorry." She remained that way for another long interval.

"Sorry about what?" Canby asked gently.

"About the way I acted just now," she said, once more looking him in the eye. "It's just that, well, I haven't kissed like that for a long time, and—"

"Was it . . . all right, then?" he asked fearfully.

"It was wonderful," she replied to his extreme relief.

"Perhaps you would like to do it again?" he asked gently.

She closed her eyes, shaking her head as if she were suddenly trying to rid her mind of something unpleasant. "No, Gordon," she said. "Not now—not yet."

"I guess it's me who's sorry, then," Canby said.

"No," she replied hastily. "Don't be sorry. It's just that . . ." Her voice trailed off while she seemed to grope for words. Finally she shook her head. "I don't think you'd understand."

"Want to try me?" he asked.

She shook her head. "Not now, Gordon," she said. "Give me time."

"All the time you want," Canby said, taking her hands again. "Just let me know."

"Thanks," she whispered, glancing at her watch. "And I'm afraid it's well past my bedtime." She smiled. "Tomorrow, Damian will want to know all about our evening together. He thinks you're wonderful."

"Me?" Canby asked in surprise. "Cynthia. He's only seen me a few times in his life."

"Yes, I know," Tenniel said, her little laugh returning like a warm breeze. "But I told him you're a starship helmsman, and now he's fascinated."

Canby felt his cheeks flush. "Thanks," he said, "even if it won't be strictly true for a little while."

"I take it the important meeting went well the other day?" she asked.

"The meeting?" Canby asked.

"Yes," she said, "the meeting you had in the Georgetown Sector the day you asked me to go out with you."

Canby smacked his forehead. "Of *course.*" He grinned. "Not very thoughtful of me to make such a big thing about it and not tell you how everything turned out."

"So everything turned out well?" she asked again.

"Extremely well," Canby replied.

"I'm glad for you, Gordon Canby," she said, glancing at her watch.

"Thanks," Canby said, realizing their evening was now over. "May I help you pick up Damian?" he asked.

"I pick him up first thing in the morning," Tenniel replied. "But now I need some sleep—as I imagine you do also, Gordon."

"Perhaps we can do this again?" Canby asked, heart in his mouth.

"Yes. I'd love to," she said. "Call me." With that, she unlocked both locks and keyed the door. But before she opened it, she turned once more to Canby. Suddenly throwing her arms around his neck, she planted a long, wet kiss on his lips. "I could love you, Gordon Canby," she said. Then without a word, she pushed open the door and disappeared inside.

To the end of his days, Canby could not remember how he got home that morning.

Book Four

PERRIN STATION

Manhattan Sector, New Washington • Earth

On February 6, 2690, as always, Manhattan's Fleet Salvage Yard opened for business promptly at 8:00 A.M. That day, however, Gordon Canby and more than one hundred impatient people, most veterans of his 19th Star Legion, were waiting as the gates swung inward. While Canby and Chief Warwick Jones, the Paymaster, made their way to transfer funds at the Commercial Exchange Office, Chief Lela Peterson led the others directly to the four ships, where each set to work on tasks that had been planned days in advance. It was 11:35 A.M. before Canby and Jones completed the long and complicated process of transferring title to the ships from the Imperial government to Canby's Legion, Ltd.—a corporation christened for the *second* time by wild acclaim over the strenuous objections of Gordon Canby.

145

By noon, the names *War, Famine, Death,* and *Plague* were painted over the government serial numbers of the four DH.98s, and *Death,* at the head of the line, was actually ready to run. Canby sat in the helmsman's recliner with sun streaming in through miraculously clean Hyperscreens. Flanking him were Chang O'Connor in the cohelmsman's seat and Lela Peterson at the systems console. Behind them, the flight bridge hummed with terse conversation of technicians and engineers busily checking the ship's controls. Canby took a final glance at his readout panels. With exception of low pressure at the starboard lift enhancer activators—which wouldn't be used for this trip anyway—the ship seemed at least willing to taxi. "Ready to start 'em up, Lela?" he asked, turning to his left. At this, the entire bridge fell silent, as if everyone had been furtively listening for the words.

"Ready, Skipper," Peterson replied tersely, placing her fingers over a glowing red STB. MAIN button on her console.

"Power starboard," Canby ordered.

As Peterson's fingers touched the button, its color changed to yellow for a moment, then green. "Power to starboard," she echoed.

"Clear to starboard," O'Connor reported from the cohelmsman's seat to Canby's right. Quiet, introverted, and highly accomplished at starflight, the bantam helmsman was almost dwarfed by his own drooping beard.

Canby glanced through the Hyperscreens at the wharf beside them; it was empty. "Check," he said, with a rush of exultation he hadn't felt in years. Unsuccessfully wiping a tremendous grin from his face, he activated the starboard SpinGrav controls. When they completed their million and one self-test routines, he moved the graviton/energy control to IDLE CUT-OFF and pressed the direction control to NEUTRAL. Then, from a thousand hours' experience, he opened the right-hand thrust damper about an inch, selected the PRIMARY energy feed and INTERNAL energy source, switched the graviton boost to ON, and touched three of the five primer switches. A glance outside revealed coruscating, ever-changing networks of sparkling electricity beginning to wreathe the waste gates—the 'Grav was ready! Once more satisfying himself that the dock area was clear, he pressed the starter—heart in his throat. Outside on the nacelle, the tensioner strobed once . . . twice . . . three times . . . a fourth . . . then the circle of blow-in doors blurred as the big machine woke, shaking the whole starship and hazing the wharf area in a sparkling, blearing cloud of gravitons.

"Don't see any flames," Peterson called out through an ear-to-ear grin.

"Always a good sign," Canby yelled while the big Napier SpinGrav settled to a smooth, earthy rumble and he resumed something close to normal breathing.

The port SpinGrav thundered to life with nearly the same ease, and all the vehemence. At this point, Canby sat back in his seat to discover his brow was covered in perspiration—though the temperature in the bridge had become quite cold while technicians checked out the environmentals. "Run 'em until you're sure they're all right, then shut 'em down," he told O'Connor, then slipped from his recliner and followed Peterson out onto the wharf—holding his ears—to check the other ships.

Next in line, *War* also started smoothly. With Peterson hunkered beside Chief Rusty Dobbs at the systems console, Canby leaned on the back of the helmsman's recliner while Olga Confrass started both SpinGravs with practiced ease. The capable black madam—dressed today in a lavender silk jumpsuit—was still looking for someone to manage her enormously profitable Frolic House while she flew, but swore she'd close it down before she gave up "The Legion."

Tied up behind *War,* old W4050—*Famine*—was dead in the water. True to Peterson's prediction, her reactor showed only a slight power increase when its damping mechanism was inhibited. Pete Menderes, the ship's commander, had al-

ready run a power back cable from *Death,* and was in the
process of rigging a towline when Canby and Peterson hurried past on their way to *Plague,* last ship in the line. "What
d' we know about this one, Chief?" Canby asked.

"Only one 'Grav was accepting power last time I
checked," she puffed.

"The other?"

"Somethin' about the energy feeds," Peterson said, dodging through the hatch. "I'll duck into the nacelle and ask
Chief Gardner while you talk to the ship's Skipper upstairs."

"Got you," Canby said, bounding up the companionway to
the bridge.

At the forward end, lanky Steve Hatch hovered over the
Systems console like a huge insect contemplating its prey.
Beside him, Renfro Gibbons, the Skipper, watched with obvious concern while a holographic miniature of Chief Gardner spoke with a frown. "All right, Steve," the Chief said,
"hit it."

Carefully, Hatch consulted a handheld display, set a number of lighted switches on the console, checked the settings
with the display, then nodded. "Power starboard," he said.

Canby watched the MAIN button as Hatch carefully touched
its surface. It flickered, slowly changed color from red to or-
ange . . . to yellow, steadied a moment, then quickly returned
to red and stayed that way.

"Shit," Gibbons commented quietly.

"Triple shit," Hatch grumped. Both he and Gibbons
peered at Gardner in the holographic display. "Anything else
you can think of, Chief?" Hatch asked.

"Prayer," Gardner replied with a shrug. "Otherwise, I'll
have to tear into the macrocoupler—"

"And that's not an option," interrupted the holographic
representation of Lela Peterson, who joined Chief Gardner in
the display. "We've got to be off this pier by end of business
today, so we're either going to tow this rustbucket like

Famine, or you make the trip on one 'Grav." She looked at
Gibbons. "What d' you think, Cap'n?"

Gibbons shrugged. "Let you know in a moment," he said.
Glancing at Hatch—who clearly needed no explanation of
what was coming—he placed his fingers over the PT. MAIN
button. "Power to port," he ordered.

"Power to port," Hatch replied.

Canby crossed his fingers as Hatch carefully pressed the
button. Like its opposite, this one flickered, slowly changed
color for a moment, then reverted back to red.

"Oh, WUN-derful," Hatch grumbled.

"Hold on a second," Gardner cautioned, his head dodging
out of the display. Frowning, Peterson's image peered in the
direction in which he'd disappeared. Then she smiled. "All
right," she said, and looked up at Hatch again. "He says try it
now."

This time, Hatch mashed the button—which immediately
turned yellow, then steady green. "Power to port," he reported—almost as if he were surprised. "Hot damn!" Less
than a minute later, the 'Grav was running.

"What did it?" Canby demanded.

"Eight-phase switch down here," Peterson explained from
the display. "Gardner was feeding only six—he'd shunted
the other two to zero while he tested."

Canby nodded, listening to the steady beat of the big
Napier in the port nacelle. "What do you think now?" he
asked Gibbons.

"I'll go on one 'Grav," Gibbons said. "Hell, if she quits,
somebody can always tow us, too."

"Good man!" Canby said, stifling a sigh of relief. He
thumped Gibbons on the shoulder. "How soon can you be
under way?"

Gibbons turned in his recliner. "Corbin," he yelled to his
cohelmsman, a wiry little black with a thoughtful expression
on his face. "How soon ya ready ta help me up here?"

"Gimme ten more at the Nav station?" Corbin said, looking up. "Yo, Canby!" he acknowledged with a grin, then went back to work on a logic board at the end of a snarl of tiny cables.

Gibbons grinned. "He'll be there another fifteen at most, then maybe half an hour more to skew the steering engine. Forty-five tops. All right?"

Canby nodded. "I'll call a Skippers' meeting when we've got the other three sorted out," he said, heading for the aft companionway.

An hour and a half later, Canby called the Skippers and their Navigators to *Death*'s bridge. "Everybody ready to shove off?" he asked, checking his watch. "We ought to clear Long Branch before dark—so that gives us maybe four hours. Olga? How about you?"

"Ready as I can make things," Confrass said, throwing her head and shoulders back in the attitude of children and whores. Her close-fitting jumpsuit did little to hide the svelte curves of her hips or the two great breasts that bobbed freely each time she moved. Her hair—what little she had—was cut short, perhaps a half inch from her scalp. She had dark brown, penetrating eyes, a sharp nose, and wide, sensuous lips.

"I'm ready, too," Menderes reported with a grin, "even if old *Famine*'s got to go at the end of a leash." He was tall, slim, horn-rimmed, with a humorous mouth, gray eyes, and the kind of wavy locks that usually settle down after the first flash of youth. His hadn't, and he'd used it to find his way into more warm beds than he could remember.

"*Plague*'s at least half ready," Gibbons reported, "so what the heck, I'm ready, too." Robust and athletic-looking—though no more than a meter and three-quarters in height—he had a striking handsomeness that was closer to aristocracy than mere good looks. His long, graying mane of hair was the kind that causes its owner to be immediately addressed as maestro among people of Italian descent, and indeed, the term had often been applied during the war when people spoke of his prowess at a helm.

Canby chuckled. "Things will get better," he promised.

"Things are *already* better," Menderes put in. "I sure as hell would rather be in a broken-down starship than sittin' on my dead ass waitin' for m' Stipend."

"Amen," Gibbons added.

"Amen for all of us," Confrass said, eyes rolled toward heaven.

Karen Nargate, Canby's navigator, took her place at the Nav console, then passed out ChartPacks and inserted one into a reader. She was a short, graying woman whose face was customarily picked out as the most striking in any group through sheer intensity of countenance, though her features were indifferent to the point of dullness. "No need to tell you what this is," she said with a grin. "But instead of flying over it, we'll be making like boats most of today and tomorrow, so it'll be worthwhile to talk about it as a group before we leave. Especially since we're heading out into some heavy weather," she added, glancing at Elcott Skarbinski, the Legion's gravitologist—and weatherman when not in deep space. She smiled grimly. "Cott'll talk to you about all that in a few minutes. Meanwhile, I'll let you in on where we're going." As she spoke, the surface of the console became a three-dimensional holographic representation of the ECONUS Seaboard from Montauk Point at the tip of Long Island to Cape Hatteras off the Carolina Coast. "We've got a pretty simple route," she began, "from the standpoint of navigation. It's just that most of us are more accustomed to making a nine-hundred-kilometer trip like this in a matter of minutes—*over* the water. . . ."

For the next half hour, Nargate described a trip that—at the ship's usual surface taxi speed of thirty knots—would *normally* take some twenty-four hours. However, Skarbinski's ensuing weather briefing gave little hope for that sort of speed. Small starships like DH.98s were, after all, designed to taxi and take off in no more than moderate seas. Storms, especially those encountered in open waters, could cut speed to a *very* few knots.

It was late afternoon before the little flotilla was ready to clear the Salvage Yard. At the head of the line, *Death* was moored alongside the pier pointed inward, with her bow only some thirty meters from the seawall. A tight spot, and Canby knew it. He looked beyond the column of ships to the greasy East River, where a cold mist had begun to form over the gray-green water. Mixed rain and snow were already spattering the Hyperscreens—normal dirty weather for the season. It wasn't going to be easy. Pursing his lips, he took one last look at his console, listened to the gentle pulsing of the big Napiers in their nacelles, then ordered mooring parties in the forward and aft cupolas to take in the bowline and the two sets of springs. Moments later, shore parties cast off the lines—which were quickly winched aboard—until only the stern line remained attached to the pier, just aft of a heavy fender. "Take a strain on that stern line," Canby directed the mooring party aft.

"Aye Cap'n," Bennet, the ranking Bosun, replied from the aft docking cupola. Almost immediately, the bow began swinging to port as the ship pivoted against the fender.

When the bow was inclined some seventy degrees from the pier, Canby took a deep breath and nodded. "Cast off and take in that stern line smartly!" he ordered. As soon as the ship was free, he put the helm over a few degrees toward the pier, then nudged both thrust dampers ahead. He grinned, listening to the Napiers growling as if well pleased to be under load again. When he could see daylight between the stern and the pier, he put the helm over hard to port and threw the port 'Grav astern, swiveling the ship around her pivot point, heart in his mouth. *It was going to be close!* A wave of gasps went up all over the bridge when the rapidly swinging stern barely cleared the pier; the gasps returned moments later when the two swept-back fins *nearly* scraped a two-story shed built directly on the seawall. Nonetheless, suddenly they were heading for open water, and the bridge erupted in cheers. Canby felt his cheeks burn while he swallowed a great lump in his throat. "Thanks," he called over his shoulder. "Guess I'm a bit out of practice."

" 'S all right, Skipper," O'Connor guffawed beside him. "Can't say I'd have done any better myself. *Besides,*" he added significantly, "you didn't actually hit anything, did you?"

"Came damn close," Canby said, only now noticing that his hands were shaking. He brought *Death* to a stop and peered aft through the rain to Confrass, who was getting *War* under way in preparation to taking the disabled *Famine* in tow. She had considerably more turning room ahead than he had, but it would still be a tight squeeze—especially since she had to mind the towline as well.

With her stern cable to *Famine*'s bow paid out to its maximum, Confrass made her turn, then stopped with her port side directly abeam of the disabled ship's starboard. While Canby watched through his binoculars, dock workers in yellow rain slickers cast off the bowline and both sets of springs, leaving the stern line attached to its bollard, but ready to drop at a moment's notice. Next, Confrass dropped her two anchors to starboard, then began reeling in the towline, angling *Famine*'s bow away from the pier. When the ship was nearly perpendicular to the pier—and *War*—the dock party cast off her stern line and Confrass weighed both anchors—they came right up in the relatively shallow basin of the Salvage Yard. Finally, Confrass nudged her 'Gravs forward toward open water, with *Famine* swinging around to follow in her wake. "Nice work!" Canby sent as she passed him to port and stood out into the stream—where the mist was rapidly being blown away by a rising wind.

"You better believe!" came the reply from a grinning image of Olga Confrass. "We do good stuff—just ask any of my clients."

With *Famine* clear of the basin, Canby waited while Gibbons cast off and struggled to turn around his one good 'Grav. Even at a distance, it was clear he had a more difficult job of getting *Plague* under way than the one that had faced Confrass. But Gibbons made it, with a minimum of backing and filling, standing out into the now white-capped river with a definite "crab" to port caused by the skewing of his steering engine. Before Canby could offer congratulations, the hard-pressed skipper appeared in a display with a wry smile. "Not bad for a gaggle of antiquated Fleet castoffs," he said.

"Not bad at all," Canby agreed with a mock serious look. "And, hey, if nothing else, we can always operate fishing charters." He followed Gibbons until the ships were clear of the basin, then fed power to his 'Gravs and pulled into the lead, throttling back to the thirty-knot cruising speed on which they'd agreed and leaving a white trail of icy spray in his wake. Down the East River they went, with Manhattan's great towers outlined against—sometimes hidden by—the grayness of the failing day, while flashing, garish city lights struggled with the oncoming night. Dodging piers and the wreckage of ancient, tumbledown bridges, the starships thundered past Brooklyn on their left, lower Manhattan on their right until they rounded Battery Park—Canby pictured Tenniel at a desk somewhere, just beginning her night job. At last, they stood out into upper New York Bay, passing Bedlow's Island and the ancient iron colossus that once stood there. Now, only the stone base remained, although a rusting, metal foot of gigantic proportions still protruded from the river at low tide. The curious old monument—despised by generations of correctness champions as a symbol of inequality—had crumbled into disrepair, then toppled late in the twenty-second century.

A few miles farther on, they skimmed through the Verrezano Narrows, dodging treacherous wreckage from the huge fallen bridge, then set an east-southeast course across lower New York Bay and the long rollers of the Atlantic. By this time, Canby didn't need to track the storm by radio—it was upon them.

Leaving Sandy Hook in their wakes, they turned due south in column, smashing through mounting seas along the New Jersey coast with the lights of Seabright, Monmouth Beach, Long Branch, and Asbury Park almost lost in gales of snow to starboard. By now, their speed was down to eighteen knots, and Confrass was only just managing *Famine*, which, at the end of her towline, was swinging and rolling like a drunken starsailor.

At a point some five kilometers off a point Nargate claimed was Mantoloking, the ClearView picked up the long, low strand of Island Beach, and for the next eleven hours, they fought their way across two hundred stormy kilometers of open ocean to Barnegat Light. There, they were about to shift course once more for the three-hundred-kilometer leg to Cape May when Menderes announced from the heaving *Famine* that *Plague* had begun to fall behind in his ClearView.

Only moments later—at exactly 5:19 A.M. by Canby's panel clock—Gibbons's aristocratic visage appeared in one of the displays with a concerned look. "We just lost all power for a spell," he reported. "Generators—there's a leak in the coupling from the reactor. Whole thing turned red-hot. Gardner got us back at about thirty-five percent, but that's max for now—and he doesn't know how long he can maintain it."

"Which means?" Canby asked, heart in his mouth. But he already knew.

"Only two choices I can see," Gibbons said. "Either I try to beach her north of Barnegat or we may well go down. The leaky Drive doors on this bucket are already startin' to take on water every time she broaches to."

"I've got a third choice," Canby said, thinking furiously. "Get a crew in your forward mooring cupola and we'll try and heave a line across to them. Even with twenty percent power, we'll have an easier time towing *Plague* than Confrass has with *Famine*."

"Hoped you'd say that!" Gibbons hooted. "I'll get some people up there right away." Turning from the display, he started issuing orders.

Canby immediately ordered Bennet to form a mooring crew and deploy the aft mooring cupola, then he opened a channel to Confrass. "I'm going back to pick up *Plague*, Olga," he said, peering back through the Hyperscreens to her tossing navigation lights, nearly lost in the storm. "They're almost dead in the water."

"Figured that's what you'd do," Confrass said. "I'm havin' my own sweet old time keepin' the two of us on course."

"Understand," Canby said. "You keep driving south for Norfolk. Skarbinski says the worst of the storm's about over, so things'll start going easier soon. And you'll have daylight in about an hour."

"Good luck, Skipper," Confrass said. "See you at Norfolk."

"At Norfolk," Canby replied, putting the helm over carefully as Confrass faded from the display. Outside, an endless succession of white surges rose above the heavy rollers and gleamed fitfully in his navigation lights. *Death* tossed like a leaf in a millstream as she turned in a large circle that allowed *War* and her tow to pass safely on course. Canby found himself holding his breath as he finessed the controls with all the skill he could summon—after nearly ten years of inactivity. But beside him in the cohelmsman's station, Chang O'Connor sat placidly seconding his every move. That kind of backup, he considered, was *mighty* important at times like these. Shaking his head, he glanced through the Hyperscreens—then forced his fingers to relax their grip on the controls: a light touch was needed now. He'd been through worse with most of the present crew, and they'd al-

ways come through—but there was always a first time. . . .
"Norma," he said to the display.

Griffith's head appeared immediately. "Skipper?" she
asked from the Engineer's compartment.

"We're going back to pick up *Plague*," he said. "Likely,
we'll be doing some violent surface maneuvering—and I
know you haven't had time to thoroughly check out the
steering engine. So, well . . ."

"You go latch on to *Plague*," she said intently, "I'll keep
things runnin' down here."

"Thanks, Norma," Canby said.

"It's my job," Griffith replied as the display faded.

"Got the aft cupola deployed," Bennet reported. "The
mooring crew's with me here, and we're standing by with a
towline."

"Very well," Canby replied, peering through the
ClearView at *Plague* tossing in the giant combers bearing
landward from the storm. "How long till you can get some
light on the subject, Lela?" he asked.

"Had everythin' set up in advance, Skipper," Peterson reported from the systems console, "just in case. Watch your
eyes, everybody." Instantly, the tossing ocean was illuminated in a blinding glare, that swung through several degrees
of arc before it passed—then returned to—the floundering
starship.

"Lela," Canby muttered in amazement, "you are magnificent."

"So what else is new?" Peterson asked.

Canby was about to answer with his own sly remark when
O'Connor shouted, "Breakers! Breakers, dead astern!"

This appalling announcement had hardly died away when
a second voice cried out from astern, "Breakers to starboard!"

"We're in a bight of the Barnegat shoals," Canby heard
Nargate shriek at the mooring crew. "Throw out the anchors
for God's sake! Now!"

"Belay that, Bennet!" Canby shouted, glaring over his shoulder at the Navigator.

Nargate stood and screamed. "Goddamn you, Canby—isn't it enough that you've run the ship into danger? Now do you want to kill us all?"

Canby ignored the outburst; there was no time for a reply. *Plague* had been rapidly falling off before the wind, and his own crew—still unused to the military discipline that had spared them from hazard in the past—was paralyzed by the woman's outburst. In a voice that thundered above the storm and their own straining 'Gravs, he began to issue orders while delicately moving the *Death*'s stern near enough *Plague*'s forward mooring cupola that a line could be fired across. He gave each command distinctly and with the precision that made him famous years before as an absolute master of spaceflight. Dealing almost from instinct, he kept the helm fast and swung the steering engine hard up against the wind. In a matter of moments, the starship was whirling around on her heel with a retrograde movement, falling off slowly before the gale—but now nearly parallel to *Plague* and only a few yards from her cupola. When *Death* had fallen off dead before the wind, Canby took a moment to compose himself, judged the distance, then yelled, "Fire!" An instant later, the mooring crew fired their line across, striking *Plague*'s cupola with the first shot. But in the confusion, the line slipped back into the tossing water before it could be brought aboard. One of *Plague*'s mooring crew jumped in after it, only to be hauled out moments later when a rogue wave lifted *Death* so high the line was snatched nearly a hundred feet away.

"Once more!" Canby roared, working the thrust dampers by pure instinct—and memory. By now, *Plague* had drifted past *Death* and was nearly into the breakers herself. *Death* was in little better circumstances, but Canby was made of stuff that considered capitulation unacceptable—*any* capitulation. Grinding his teeth, he waited until the mooring crew had the tow rope once more in position, then more as an act of will than expertise, he spun the ship on her axis, threw her into reverse with the furious waves beating violently against her stern, then slacked off the thrust dampers until the two cupolas were nearly perpendicular—and only a few feet apart. "Throw the Goddamn thing by hand, Bennet!" he ordered.

Instantly, the mooring line sailed through a great, perfect arc into the waiting hands of *Plague*'s crew—like Peterson, Bennet had anticipated his next order, too. A moment of breathless astonishment followed, but there was no opportunity for the usual expressions of surprise. The two ships were still far from safety. Canby continued to maneuver as, little by little, he brought *Plague* under tow, all the while maneuvering *Death* only a few scant yards from the breakers and shouting occasional orders above the howling gale whenever prudence or skill required changes in management of the ship. While dawn came and went, he waged a fearful struggle with the storm—and little by little began to gain an edge. Again and again, it seemed as if the two starships were rushing blindly on shoals where the sea was covered by foam— and where destruction would have been as sudden as it was certain. But time and again, *Death* yielded in his steady hand on the controls and the towline held. The ship was recovering from one of these critical tacks when Canby narrowed his eyes. "See the rotating light on the western headland?" he asked, peering through the slackening rain.

"Yeah," O'Connor gasped as if he were out of breath. "I see it."

"And the tower a little north of it—the one that looks like an XmasTide tree?"

"Yeah."

"It's a broadcast tower—WNRG-19, far inland. I remember it from my days in the Fleet. If we can keep the light to the south of the broadcast tower, we'll be okay; if not, I've put both ships on the reef."

"Jesus," O'Connor exclaimed. "Maybe we ought to go 'round again."

"No way," Canby said, shaking his head. "Look at the chart—there's no more going around this night. We've barely room to pass out of the shoals on the course we're on. But if we can weather a rock they call Satan's Snag, we'll clear the outermost point. Otherwise . . ."

"Why didn't we go out the way we went in?" Nargate demanded.

"I would have," Canby said grimly, "if the tide permitted. But with fighting the storm, we simply didn't have enough power on the surface." Suddenly he peered through the Hyperscreens and pursed his lips. It *wasn't* going to be easy, was it? "Griffith," he ordered, "I'll need full liftoff power for a short time."

"Jesus, beggin' the Skipper's pardon," Griffith swore, "but we haven't tested her with that much power yet."

Canby felt himself grin. "No time like the present," he said. "Besides, d' you want to live *forever*?"

" 'Course not," Griffith grumbled. "Couldn't stand old age." Moments later, her image looked Canby in the eye. "You've got it all," she said, "even military overload. Go to it!"

"That's suicide," somebody yelled from aft.

"It's got to be done," returned Canby. "Look," he said, pointing landward, "the two towers are nearly touching now. We're still being forced to leeward. Gibbons!" he yelled into the communicator, "give it all *Plague*'s got—even if her 'Grav goes—and follow me." Then, he pushed the thrust dampers forward past LIFTOFF to MILITARY OVERLOAD, put the helm over, and waited—heart in his mouth. There was an instant when the result was doubtful. Deep threshing from the two unadjusted 'Gravs shook the starship to its very spaceframe. Glancing back, Canby forced himself to breathe. The towline was still holding and both ships were moving forward against the storm. He'd done all he could . . . it would either work or it wouldn't. Around him, he could feel the tension build as the bridge crew sat rapt in breathless anxiety. Waiting . . .

A short distance ahead, the whole ocean was white with foam, and the waves, instead of rolling on in regular succession appeared to be tossing about in wild confusion. Canby could see a single streak of dark billows, not a hundred meters in width, running into this chaos of water, but it was soon lost to his eye. More by feel than anything else, he guided the ships into this channel among the breakers. An utter calm had settled over him, and he steered as if someone else had taken the controls. Again and again, as the foam rolled away to leeward, the bridge crew started to cheer, supposing they were past the danger, but breaker after breaker heaved up before them, following each into the general swirling confusion.

At length, the two ships arrived at a point where they appeared to be rushing directly into the jaws of destruction. Canby had been waiting for this. With all the skill he could muster, he watched the pattern of the waves, spotted the great rock just as a deep trough momentarily unveiled its presence, then curved around the far side of the narrow channel, flicking the steering engine at the last possible moment, and drove both ships safely from the reefs into the heavy waves of open ocean.

Shouts of joy and relief burst from all over the bridge—as well as *Plague*. In the display, Gibbons looked as if he had been at the controls for ten straight years. Canby could understand why. He'd had the harder job, just hanging on and following with no choice but to trust someone else's judgment. Outside, even as they cheered, the storm was quickly breaking up, although the wind—which had come around nearly a hundred degrees—raged on nearly unabated. Clear sea was all around them, and with Barnegat Light nearly down on the horizon, Canby set a south-southwest course and turned the helm over to O'Connor. Just as he was about to make an inspection of the ship, Griffith appeared in a display.

"Ah, Skipper," she started, "about those 'Gravs . . ."

"What about 'em?" Canby demanded warily.

"They're tested, Skipper," she reported with a little grin, "and ready for takeoff anytime you want to test the flight controls. Just thought you'd want to know."

Canby chuckled and settled back in his recliner as he caught sight of his other two ships ahead in the distance. "Many thanks, Griffith, m' friend," he said. "I'd almost been dyin' to know that. But I think we'll put off the flight tests for a while. I've had enough excitement for this morning."

FEBRUARY 7, 2690, EARTH DATE

• Omega-932

While Canby went aft to inspect storm damage to his DH.98, Kobir and four of his KV 388s were more than a million light-years distant on the tossing, liquid-nitrogen surface of Omega-932, a small, dead planet in a remote corner of the galaxy. He and his crews had just finished transferring a valuable cargo of Type 94/A Drive crystals to one of their old KV 72 transports from a merchantman they had captured only the previous morning. Under a cheerless black sky, they were nearly ready to release the vessel after crippling its Hy-COMM communications units. Kîrskian ground crews in FlexArmor were already fussing around the 388s in preparation for the flight home to Khalife when Kobir's helmet speakers picked up the voice of Zerner Petroski, Captain of the KV 72, as he broadcast an alarm: "We are picking up eight heavy attack ships on the long-range proximity alarm. Probably the Imperial TA-91 Tarquins again—and no question they are headed for us this time."

"*Zvolki!*" Kobir swore in Kîrskian. He'd known for weeks the ships were out there looking for him and had made it a point to avoid them. Eventually, however, the inevitable had to be faced. . . . "All Captains—scramble! Immediately!" he ordered, running along the backbone of his ship for the dorsal airlock. "Petroski," he ordered over the short-range radio, "take the 72 to the other side of the planet, then set a reciprocal bearing from home until we can clear this up. Understand?"

"Understand," Petroski replied. It was all that was necessary.

In the corner of his eye, Kobir saw the old starship begin to move forward over the endless waves of liquid nitrogen, then he was inside the air lock and fumbling to seal the hatch. "Hands to battle stations! Close all airtight doors!" he ordered on the ship's blower. "Hands to battle stations. Skoda, take us up—*now!*" Moments later—in ship's gravity—he pushed his way through the confusion of the flight bridge, where Skoda already had the ship moving rapidly over the nitrogen. They lifted at full power as he slipped into his recliner. "That them?" he huffed, pointing through the Hyperscreens to two groups of four sparkling motes racing at an odd angle across the dark sky.

"Such would not surprise me," Skoda said in his unflappable manner.

As he spoke, each of the motes flashed in the blackness and a great glow shot up from the receding surface of the planet. Kobir glanced back at the tossing lake of liquid nitrogen where they had been moored only minutes before. It had suddenly erupted in bright flashes of disruptor fire and towering geysers. "Sweet Mother of God," he swore as one flash burst forth into a great explosion, "they're firing at the merchantman!"

"They're *what?*" Skoda gasped uncharacteristically.

"They're . . . they've *hit* the merchantman we captured!" Kobir cried, feeling his stomach churn. "Good God, the explosions! Must have gotten her square in the power chambers. Nobody could be alive."

"Who would—who *could*—do such a thing?" Skoda asked, glancing back at the flare of radiation fire that marked the grave of the transport.

"They must have been shooting at anything—without even the first attempt at identification."

"Like a whole squadron of . . . of hysterical . . . *recruits* in battle for the first time."

Kobir nodded his head. "My thoughts precisely," he said as Lippi pulled his 388 in close to port. "And yet, can this be the Imperial Fleet that bested us only a few short years ago? It may *also* be possible, my old friend, that they are putting on a show that might lure us into a sense of overconfidence."

"We can find out soon enough, Kapitan," Skoda replied, pulling the ship up and over, with the little star passing through the forward Hyperscreens.

The brightness caused Kobir to momentarily lose sight of the eight Imperials—now below them—as the big warships made a low-level firing run at the glowing wreckage. But at about nineteen thousand meters altitude, Skoda spotted them again. "I see them," he said.

"Where?" Kobir asked.

"There," Skoda said, pointing ahead of the sinking wreckage that was now disappearing rapidly beneath the surface.

Kobir sighed. "I suppose it is time we do something about these Imperials," he said, looking out to starboard, where Quadros and Roualt were pulling into formation. He considered for a moment, but came up with no other alternative. The eight ships had been shadowing them for nearly a week—so amateurish that he found it hardly credible. He switched his suit COMM to short-range radio. "We shall attack them," he said to the other Captains. "Now."

"You will fly the ship?" Skoda asked.

"Enjoy," Kobir said with a smile. "Today I shall luxuriate as a spectator."

"Enjoy, my Kapitan," Skoda replied, putting the helm over into a plummeting dive that closed the distance to the Imperials in a matter of seconds. Outside, the four killer ships were keeping formation as if they were wired in place. The two quads of attackers had now broken off their assault and were climbing steadily on a course that made it clear they had never even spotted Petroski and his lumbering 72 as they escaped around the curve of the planet.

Kobir glanced into the IFF; it was now displaying EIGHT TA-91 TARQUIN-CLASS ATTACK SHIPS. He nodded. "Tarquins," he said. "Powerful starships, those."

Skoda shrugged. "Perhaps," he said. "But only as good as their crews."

The eight Tarquins continued their steady climb, apparently unaware of their imminent danger. "We shall attack the rightmost ship in the right quad," Skoda announced.

"Rightmost ship in the rightmost quad," echoed Frizell. "Weapons systems enabled and tracking."

Still in a shallow dive, the 388s were closing rapidly on their quarry. The new Tarquin cruisers *should* have been able to show the older killer ships a clean set of heels, but it was clear carelessness had prevailed. As Kobir relaxed, the rightmost TA-91 grew larger in the Hyperscreens, then suddenly broke hard to starboard just as Frizell was about to fire. Kobir frowned, momentarily considering that they might actually be up against Imperials who were smart enough to *feign* incompetence, but surprisingly, no more violent evasive action followed, and although the Tarquin was now obviously accelerating, its delta was not enough to escape the 388s' new disruptors. Frizell's first burst caught it directly in the reactor section before its turrets even began to swing aft. Two of its disruptors discharged feebly, then all power seemed to fail, and the nose dropped as the helmsman started toward the surface in a steep glide.

Kobir glanced at his instruments—they were down to less than three thousand meters over the dark ocean of tossing liquid nitrogen. He glanced around: nothing in sight. "The Imperials have no more energy for their disruptors, Dorian," he said. "Follow him down. Perhaps we can save some of the crew."

Skoda smiled and cast Kobir a sidelong glance. "As you wish, my Kapitan," he said. In moments, he had positioned the 388 close off the starboard bow of the crippled starship.

Through his binoculars, Kobir could clearly see the control consoles—and a bridge crew that had sunk into raw chaos and panic. One or two stood beating at the Hyperscreens with their hands, mouths agape in what must have been screams of anguish. A number of bodies sprawled in awkward positions on the deck—*without battle suits!* One pathetic figure seemed to be aiming a HoloCAM at them while only a single helmsman struggled almost futilely with the controls. Kobir grimaced and placed the binoculars on a console. Except for the blackened, torn hole in the reactor section, the gleaming white starship—"I.F.S.S. *Addison*" appeared in gold letters at the bow—appeared to be in perfect condition. Shaking his head, he glanced at the white star superimposed on concentric roundels of red and blue. How could such an amateurish—no, idiotic—gaggle of incompetents have been placed in command of an Imperial starship? At length, the helmsman made an attempt to belly-land on the rolling surface, but a stub fin dug in as he touched down, and the starship cartwheeled in great torrents of nitrogen spray, pieces breaking away and the forward end shearing off at the reactor in a brilliant upwelling of energy and debris. Only Skoda's consummate skill kept them from disaster as the 388 thundered through the explosion. A second pass over the crash site showed little more than fragments of wreckage—and not a single LifeGlobe.

After a third fruitless pass for survivors, they lifted for deep space. Kobir called the others over the HyCOMM, and was delighted to hear his other three Captains had also scored kills—Lippi accounting for *two*. He scratched his head; the Imperial survivors were in full retreat, and according to the HyCOMM channels, on their way back to Earth reporting that they had been attacked by a superior force of at least twenty pirate ships. So much for the contemporary Imperial Fleet.

Columbia Sector, New Washington • Earth

In a deep basement of the old Pentagon building in the Columbia Sector, the Situation Room had suddenly gone stone silent except for bleating calls on the HyCOMM from three surviving TA-91 Tarquin-class cruisers fleeing from what could only be called a disastrous encounter with superior forces. No matter that the superior forces had numbered only four, and the Imperial squadron had started with *eight* of the latest, most powerful ships in the Fleet. David Lotember's mind, though stunned, was already working at top speed on damage control in the media. He glanced at Jennings standing beside him, fists clenched. "What were those pirate ships, again?" he demanded.

"Kvlokovs, I believe, Minister," Jennings replied, "KV 388Ls—some of the finest ships made in Novokîrsk during the war."

Lotember nervously chewed a fingernail. "B-but our . . . our . . ."

"TA-91 Tarquins, Minister."

"Of course, our T-tarquins . . . well, they're so much newer, aren't they? And more powerful."

"Yes, Minister."

"And more heavily armed?"

"Tarquins do have more disruptors, Minister," Jennings replied.

"And . . ." he threw up his hands, "something *torqued*?"

"*Beta-torqued,* Minister."

"Well, then?"

"Minister, the 388 we watched following I.F.S.S. *Addison*

down *also* appeared to be armed with beta-torqued disruptors."

"I was afraid of that," Lotember said with a growing feeling of irritation. "But still—eight against four. Why couldn't eight of them destroy—or at least capture—the pirates, as I ordered? God knows I *personally* sent the most talented and best-educated crews on that mission. It simply doesn't make sense." He pushed back into the cushions of the plush Minister's chair he'd had installed in the room and frowned angrily at Jennings. "It's your Goddamn fault, you know."

"Minister?"

"Don't give me that 'Minister' shit, Jennings," he gulped—frustration was making it difficult to breathe. "It's your fault—yours and all the Goddamn military dunces I let you assign to those ships." He looked up at the emotionless Fleet officer and ground his teeth in ire. "It was . . . sabotage, that's what it was, Jennings," he continued in a low, trembling voice. "I can't prove it this time, but you won't get away with it again. I know damn well you and your Goddamn cocky superiors put the worst men on those ships you could find. What do you have to say to that?"

Outwardly, Jennings seemed to remain calm, though his hands clenched once or twice and his cheeks colored slightly. "I . . . we . . . did nothing of the sort, Minister," he said, his eyes focused somewhere in space, to Lotember's utter irritation. "In fact, Minister," he continued, "I personally assigned some of the finest petty officers I knew to the crews of those ships."

"You did not!"

"Yes, Minister, I did," Jennings said, his eyes closed and his lips formed into a thin slit, "because the officers you assigned were so inexperienced they couldn't have gotten those ships off the water without competent help." He ground his teeth as if he were in physical pain.

"Liar! Liar!" Lotember screeched from the cushions of his great swivel chair. "That's what you are—a dirty *liar!*" His head ached and he felt himself beginning to sweat. Jennings only continued to stand at attention, his eyes focused off into space, his hands still formed into white-knuckled fists. Why wouldn't this concrete statue of a uniformed dunce react? Suddenly an idea came to him. Perhaps all the insolent bastards needed a shakeup. He'd certainly been placed in power to accomplish that sort of thing. Yes. That was it, shake them up—and not a little but a lot. "All right, Jennings," he said with a little smile of satisfaction. "Have you ever heard the word *purge*?"

"I have, Minister."

"Good," Lotember said with what he considered his most withering glance. "Perhaps I should see how you hidebound Fleet types react should I begin winnowing out the true incompetence." He smiled and rose from the chair. "If I do, you and your stone-faced friends might as well begin packing," he said, "because I shall order a purge that will bring your service careers to an end. Got that?"

Jennings stood in silence.

"Well?"

More silence—although, Lotember noticed to his gratification, everyone in the room was staring at them in rapt watchfulness.

"Answer me, Goddamnit!"

"I . . . understand, Minister."

"Good," Lotember said, gathering at least some comfort in having forced the man to react.

"Will that be all, then, Minister?" Jennings said, still staring at a point somewhere above Lotember's head.

The insolent *swine,* Lotember thought—speaking before he had been spoken to. "Not yet," he said, thinking rapidly. Something *did,* after all, have to be done about those pirates. He frowned. Of course . . . He would simply dispatch another squadron against the pirates. This time, however, Jennings and his arrogant cronies would have full control over crew selection—including officers. Should they fail this time, Lotember would simply implement his purge, both absolving his person from all blame *and* giving himself an all-important reputation for action.

Of course, if they *did* succeed, he would take all the credit and still benefit greatly. All in all, he considered, it was a masterful plan, with no risk to himself whatsoever—the finest kind, in his own modest opinion. Smiling, he looked the emotionless Captain in the eye. "For reasons I cannot fathom, Jennings, I am going to provide you with a chance to save your own worthless hide from the Dole. Tomorrow, you will personally organize a new squadron of Tarquins for deployment against those pirates within the week. This time, however, the personnel choices will be all yours—as well as the responsibility for its success. Do you understand what I am telling you?"

"I understand *fully*, Minister," Jennings replied, his stare never wavering.

"Good," Lotember said after a few moments' further consideration. "Now, a second assignment. I want you to ask the Media-Control and Information Dissemination people upstairs—*my* appointees, as I am certain you know—to prepare a news release concerning the heroic stand our tiny squadron made against an overwhelming force of twenty to thirty Kîrskian pirate ships. Without delay. And you'd better get it right—*my* kind of right—if you know what's good for you. Understand?"

"I understand, Minister. Will that be all?"

"No, Goddamnit—I'll tell you when I'm finished. After the crew from MCID finishes with the release, have a team of their best documentary makers report immediately to my office. I'll want them to make an *accurate* historical record of this *unfair* combat. You understand that, too, Jennings?"

"I understand that, also, Minister."

"Then remove your worthless self from my office and get to work. God knows there's little time to lose."

FEBRUARY 7–8, 2690, EARTH DATES

Off the Eastern Seaboard, Atlantic Ocean • Earth

While Lotember planned his next moves, Canby's four ships drove along the Jersey coast, increasing speed as abating wind and waves permitted. With the tumbled, radioactive ruins of Atlantic City in their wake, they arrived at Cape May by noon, then lost sight of land for nearly one hundred kilometers at the mouth of Delaware Bay. Abeam Cape Henlopen by 3:08 P.M., they began the ten-hour run to Cape Charles past Ocean City South, the long Chincoteague strand, and Assateague Island. By midnight, they had entered the lower Chesapeake, where they set a west-northwest course past the lights of Norfolk's sprawling Imperial Fleet Headquarters for the long-abandoned Perrin Maintenance Station on the west shore of the bay. When all four ships were safely at anchor a few hundred feet out from the dark shapes that were the station, Canby sent, "Thanks in advance for the bottle of bourbon each skipper will bring to the brief Captain's meeting aboard this ship ten minutes after all ships are secured for the night." It had been a long trip.

In the half-light of false dawn, Canby, O'Connor, and Peterson took one of *Death*'s small inflatable launches to the shore amid the cries of wakening waterfowl and a myriad of unseen shore creatures. Canby had never observed the station from the water, but in the early morning gloom, it certainly contradicted any impression he'd gotten during his visit with Nemil Quinn. Then, the wharves and maintenance aprons had been empty; now, they appeared to be laden with large, angular shapes. "What's the frown for, Skipper?" O'Connor asked over the threshing of the little outboard 'Grav in the stern.

"Not sure," Canby replied. "But the place looked a lot more empty when I saw it with Quinn."

"Looks like . . . packing crates on the wharves," O'Connor offered. "Big ones."

"Yeah," Peterson agreed. "Covered by tarps. I'm sure of it."

By the time Canby maneuvered the launch against one of the service piers beneath its overhead cranes, it was quite obvious they were correct. "Quinn never said anything about these," he said while the first tendrils of unease began to intrude in his thoughts. Was it possible Quinn had changed his mind? Or maybe the base was about to be activated again, and the man didn't even know about it. After all, who would notify a Chancellor about something as unimportant as that? He ground his teeth. "Let's get up on the wharf and see what's what before we start to worry," he said as confidently as possible. Moments later, all three were standing beside three large, boxlike forms, perhaps four by six by four meters each. They were covered by oily-smelling canvas tarpaulins. Stepping to the nearest box, Canby snapped open a catch that secured a rope around its bottom and lifted a corner of the tarpaulin. "It's a storage crate, all right," he said, peering at the olive-green plastic surface. "Chang, lift the other corner of the tarp; let's see if it's got any markings on it."

O'Connor picked up the other corner, and together the two men wrestled the heavy tarpaulin over the top of the box.

"It does!" Peterson exclaimed, pointing to the center of the box. All three gasped at the same time as Canby read the stenciled letters aloud:

> CRATE, 1 EA. HOIST SLING ASSY. DH.98
> ATTACH @ FORWARD FRAME 91
> I.F. PART NR: AO 309 85 51 REV. 0
> CRATE 1 OF 3 CRATES

"My God," Peterson said in a stunned voice. "It's the forward end of a hoist system to lift DH.98s. I figured we'd have to make our own. Why, this crate'll save us *weeks* of work—" She stopped in midsentence. "How in hell did it *get* here?"

"I've got a few suspicions," Canby said, looking around him. "But first let's see what we've got in the other two crates. Lela, while Chang and I start on this next box, you call the other ships and tell 'em it looks safe to land."

"Will do, Skipper," Peterson said, and started for the raft.

Canby frowned at the large, covered boxes. Beyond, on the station proper, a number of its concrete aprons were also laden with stacks of large crates, all carefully covered by tarpaulins so clean, they might have been delivered only days before. "None of this was around the last time I was here," he said, shaking his head.

"Apparently someone loves us," O'Connor said.

"Apparently," Canby replied. He glanced across at the other five service piers of the station. Two were empty, but three contained boxes wrapped in tarpaulins that appeared to be the same size as the three on the pier where he stood. "D'you suppose . . ." he whispered, more to himself than to anyone else, "that *those* contain . . . ?" He shook his head. First things first. "Let's check these out before we do anything else," he said. "If they're going to blow up, then they'll only get us. Right?"

O'Connor nodded phlegmatically. "A good—if not altogether pleasant—idea," he commented.

In tension-filled silence, he helped O'Connor open the other two crates labeled SLING HOIST ASSY. Except for a rush of air when they lifted the hermetically sealed lids, nothing else happened. The whole hoisting system seemed to be there. Shaking his head in amazement, Canby peered across the other piers through the early morning sunlight. "D'you suppose that's what's on those docks, too?"

"Only one way to find out." Peterson gulped, her voice still hushed with surprise.

Together, the three hurried to check the other piers; sure enough, each was equipped with a complete lift kit. By the time they were finished, people from the other ships had begun to arrive and open the mysterious packing boxes stacked inland on the station's service aprons. At noon, the amazed legionnaires were gathered inside one of the abandoned hangars to consolidate their information. In addition to the sling hoists, their mysterious benefactor—most were unaware of Quinn's involvement—had supplied three sets of special tools, two complete complements of spare parts, and expendables such as gaskets and sealers to last at least a year plus two spare reactors. Wonder of wonders, they even found the manufacturer's simulator on which the original test pilots had trained for the first flight. "The old so-and-so really took care of us. didn't he?" Peterson said that evening as the two stood on a wharf watching the light fade over the Lower Chesapeake. "Damn near everything we need."

"Damn near," Canby said, lost for the moment in his thoughts. "Except . . ."

"Except what?" Peterson demanded. "What in hell *could* we want after all this?"

Almost painfully, Canby returned to reality. He watched a fish ripple the water a few yards off the pier. It all seemed so easy when you had only one part of the puzzle to manage. He turned to Peterson and smiled. "Look behind you," he said, indicating the base with a sweep of his arm. "See all the lit windows and doors?"

Peterson turned around and frowned. "Of course I do," she said presently. "What's missing? We've got everything we need—even the right people. What could be better?"

Canby smiled. "It's those people I'm worried about," he replied.

"I don't understand," Peterson said with a confused look. "They're the best in the business. You picked most of them yourself. So what could go wrong?"

"What's the favorite pastime of those people when they're not out in space?" Canby asked with a grin.

"Fucking?" Peterson asked with a grin.

Canby laughed. "Even more than fucking," he replied.

"Nothin's better than fucking," Peterson protested. "And *you*, Gordon Canby, of all people, know that."

Canby felt his cheeks burn in the fading light. "Yeah," he agreed with a chuckle. "I can't keep *that* from you, now, can I?"

"Not hardly, Skipper," she said.

"But," Canby persisted, "on that first date of ours. What did we do *before* we started fucking? Remember?"

"We, ah . . . went to . . . supper, I suppose."

"You bet," Canby said, putting his hand on her forearm. "That's a big part of our problem."

"Going to supper?"

"Eating," Canby replied with a grimace. "We've got to feed all these people—and that's expensive."

Peterson grimaced. "You mean money?" she asked. "I never thought about . . . our running out of money."

"That's my trouble," Canby said, staring bleakly out over the darkening waters of the Chesapeake. "I was so focused on getting the starships themselves that I didn't either—until just now."

MARCH 13, 2690, EARTH DATE

Columbia Sector, New Washington • Earth

Curious about reports from a Pentagon informer about Lotember's story of an ambush in space, Renaldo found time in his busy social schedule for a surprise visit to the Pentagon. *Twenty* pirate ships—he reasoned as he sat with a number of others in Lotember's briefing room—made for a real ambush, by dangerously large forces that would need dealing with immediately. However, if his informer was correct, and the eight powerful starcruisers had actually been bested—no, savaged—by a mere four ships left over from a war that had ended nearly ten years in the past, then something was *very* wrong with the Fleet. He frowned. If not handled correctly, either situation could easily result in serious embarrassment to his persona as First Patron of the Admiralty.

At a wall-sized Holojector, David Lotember was in full stride presenting his version of the pirate attack, complete with three-dimensional recordings broadcast during the battle. He had just launched into a poignant sequence from the bridge of the doomed I.F.S.S. *Addison* sent during the last moments before it crashed.

It was a scene out of Renaldo's worst dreams. *Addison*'s crew had obviously panicked, and the fool Lotember hadn't even picked up on it. He was expounding on the courage of the young men and women of the crew while in front of his very eyes the bridge had erupted into a shouting, screaming chaos. A number of the dolts lying on the deck weren't even dressed in battle suits—they'd clearly died when the pirates' fire had violated the pressure hull. A single helmsman was struggling with the controls; God only knew where the others were. Some idiot had even taken pictures of the 388 through the Hyperscreens. Jesus! Who were these bunglers, and how had they gotten into his Fleet? He could feel his blood pressure rising and was just about to give Lotember a piece of his mind when the view changed to the pirate ship again, now much closer and on a parallel course. Familiar shape, Renaldo mused through his ire—angular, angry-looking, and powerful. He remembered enemy ships with the same rugged shape from the war. Never one for details, he recalled only that they were considered one of the Kîrskians' most dangerous. As the camera zoomed in, he frowned. Where would twenty of these old ships even come from? Then his attention was drawn to a tall, powerfully built figure on the enemy bridge staring back through . . . old-fashioned binoculars! Familiar, some-how . . . Suddenly he felt his heart miss a beat as the figure put down the glasses, shaking his head in what appeared to be genuine compassion. Tall and powerfully built, the man had the broad forehead and high cheekbones of a Slav, with straight black hair, wide-set eyes, and a countenance he would *never* forget. "Kobir!" he gasped inadvertently.

"My lord?" Lotember asked indulgently.

"Jesus, Mary, and Joseph!" Renaldo groaned as the display disappeared with the starship's impact. "Stop! Play that again!"

"Play what, my lord?" Lotember asked, eyebrows raised.

"The . . . the part that shows the pirate's bridge," Renaldo said in a shaken voice.

"But my lord, I have not finished with the briefing," Lotember protested.

"I don't give a Goddamn for your silly briefing, Lotember," Renaldo growled. "I want to see that pirate ship's bridge again. Understand?"

"B-but—"

"*Now*, Goddamnit!"

"Yes, my lord. Immediately."

Renaldo watched the short sequence again and again. Each time, he became more certain that the man on the pirate's bridge was indeed Kobir. Finally, he held up his hand. "Enough!" he thundered.

"S-shall I continue with my briefing, then?" Lotember asked, clearly confused.

"No," Renaldo said, only just in control of himself.

"T-then . . . ?" Lotember started.

"Silence," Renaldo ordered. "Clear the room. Immediately."

"Y-yes, my lord," Lotember stumbled. "A-all of you. Out! Clear the room. Now!"

Renaldo watched as the others filed past him on their way to the door. Their frightened glances provided some mollification for the situation in which he found himself. Only one—the lone man in uniform—appeared to have an amused expression. But then, military people were a breed all to themselves. . . . At last, the door closed and he was alone with Lotember. "Turn off all your recording devices," he growled. "I'll guarantee you'll want no record of what we are about to discuss. Understand?"

"I t-think so, my lord," Lotember stumbled, touching a number of panels near his lectern.

"Sit down, Lotember."

"Y-yes, my lord."

"First, Lotember, I don't appreciate your cooked briefing. At all."

"Cooked?"

"Bullshit."

"My lord?"

"If there were twenty pirates, I'll eat my hat."

"B-but my lord—"

"Silence, idiot. I know bullshit when I hear it. God knows I've heard enough of it from your predecessors. Now listen and listen well, or you will be the next to depart. The Empire is full of dimbulbs like you who have no talent except passing money around under the table. Even I know more about military matters than you do. Understand?"

"My lord!"

"Do—you—understand, you incompetent little shit?" Renaldo felt his blood pressure rise again.

"I u-understand."

"That's better. Now pay attention, and I may permit you to remain in office. Otherwise . . ."

"Anything, my lord."

"Good. This pirate—it doesn't matter how many ships he had, although I'll bet it's *a lot* fewer than twenty—I want him destroyed immediately. Get that, *immediately*." He ground his teeth as he looked into the other's frightened eyes. "I don't care what it takes. I don't care if you have to send the whole Goddamned Fleet. I don't care what you spend nor what measures you take. But I want that man . . . er, those pirates dead at once, or you're out on the street in the next election. *If* I let you live that long."

"My lord!"

"If that's what it takes to get someone into this office who can obey my orders, then . . . Well, you won't be the first."

"I—I have a squadron scheduled to lift t-tomorrow, my lord," Lotember said in a shaky voice.

"Double it!" Renaldo ordered. "Triple it!"

"A-as you w-wish, my lord. But I have already threatened the crews with a purge of the whole Fleet should they fail in this mission."

"Whatever," Renaldo growled, struggling from the huge, soft recliner. "Just destroy those pirates—to a man. No prisoners. Understand?"

"I understand, my lord."

"Very well," Renaldo said, feeling better about the whole thing. With three times the ships, even a squadron under the guidance of an idiot could eventually wipe out a small group of pirates with antiquated ships. He glanced around the luxurious briefing room, then smiled when he found a large divan at the rear. Every plush briefing room in the Empire had one—for the same purpose. "Your secretary," he said, as anticipation spread through his fat loins. "I didn't catch her name."

"Tolton," Lotember said in surprise. "Eva Tolton, my lord."

Renaldo smiled. The svelte blonde had been half on his mind since she'd served him coffee just before the briefing.

"Is she clean?"

"My lord?"

"Free from disease, idiot."

"T-tolton?"

"Who in hell did you think I meant, idiot, Emperor Philante?"

"Er . . . Tolton? Disease?"

"My God, man! Have you lost your senses? Is she safe to . . . you know . . . ."

"*Oh!* Er, yes, my lord."

"I assume *you've*, ah . . ."

"Of course, my lord."

"Then for Christ's sake," Renaldo roared, opening his trousers and waddling toward the couch, "get out of here and send her to me with her clothes off."

Book Five

FLIGHTS AND
REVELATIONS

Perrin Station • Earth

During the next weeks, work at Perrin Station proceeded at a rate Canby found astonishing—in spite of reduced rations. Clearly, much of the progress was thanks to the government equipment furnished by Nemil Quinn. But much credit also accrued to determined legionnaires who were spurred on by those two most compelling of goads: anxiety and hope—the former engendered by a fast-dwindling money supply, the latter by rumors of lucrative jobs going begging for lack of mercenary teams to accomplish them. When he could spare time from his many administrative duties, Canby spent innumerable hours in the excellent old simulator, sharpening his flying skills and practicing for the billion and one emergencies that could threaten a starship during combat.

However, he'd also found time to catch the tube from nearby Hampton, Virginia, for an occasional evening with Tenniel in the Manhattan Sector—a place in which he found himself only days before *Death*'s scheduled first flight. After a leisurely supper at Griffin's Café—and two bottles of an inexpensive but delicious merlot—they bumped and pushed their way uptown through noisy, gaudy rivers of humanity to take in a HoloDrama, then returned at length to her apartment building, talking about the 'Drama and, as they often did, discussing the Empire's postwar breach of faith with its middle class—and how it had affected them both. Canby tried everything he could think of in an attempt to prolong the evening, but inevitably they were on the fourth floor at her door. In the dim light of the hall, she fumbled for her keys for a moment, then turned to face him with a questioning look and remained that way for a long time, as if she were deliberating.

"Everything all right?" he asked at length.

At that moment, Tenniel seemed to reach some sort of decision and took his hand. "Yes," she said softly, "everything's wonderful." On this springlike, late-winter evening, she was wearing a pullover sweater beneath her down jacket, a short skirt, stockings, and high heels. She smiled at him, a solemn look in her eyes. "You know, Gordon Canby," she continued, "on our first date, I said I could probably love you, and you know, sometimes I think I do. You are one terribly nice guy. I haven't enjoyed anyone's company so much in years—maybe ever."

Surprised, Canby put his arm around her, almost without realizing what he was doing. "I think I love you, too, Tenniel," he whispered, pulling her close and placing his lips on hers. The perfume she wore was strong and stimulating. At first they kissed gently, but in spite of everything Canby could do, his breathing became shallow—and so, he noticed, did hers. Slowly, her mouth opened. He reined in his emotions. Since their first date, he'd been careful not to push this part of their relationship; she'd seemed to appreciate that, although each time at the door, their good-bye kisses had been longer and longer. In control of himself once more, he pulled away. "This could get out of hand, " he gasped.

"Yes," she murmured, her voice urgent and strangely breathless. "It's been a long time, but I think I'm finally ready for that now."

No sooner had he kissed the wet lips again than her tongue darted into his mouth once or twice before thrusting between his lips with an animal urgency while she violently twisted her body toward him, grinding her breasts into his chest until he felt himself losing control. She pulled away for a moment, breathing now as if she had run for miles. "Wait," she huffed. "Let's go inside—I want to take off my clothes for you." Fumbling in her purse for her keys, she opened the first lock immediately, then took three tries for the second. Finally, the door opened, and she stepped inside, flinging her jacket over a chair. "Hurry, Gordon," she said.

Head swimming, Canby stepped into a small living room and closed the door behind him. She was already opening her skirt when he put his hand on her arm. "Could I do that for you?" he asked.

She looked at him for a moment, then smiled. "Would you?" she asked.

"After another kiss," Canby replied, taking her in his arms again. This time everything was slower, deeper—more passionate. When he could wait no more, he slid his hand along her hip, then finished opening her skirt and let it drop to the floor. As he skimmed her briefs over her hips, he felt more than heard a low, animal moan.

"My sweater, Gordon," she breathed into his open lips. "I want to be naked with you. Now."

Canby released her just enough to gently pull her sweater

over her head, then tried to kiss her again, but she grinned and slipped from his embrace.

"First look at me, Gordon," she said, stepping from her shoes, then slipping her briefs and stockings to the floor. As she touched a light switch, she stepped back into the room.

Canby had never encountered such a gorgeous woman. A long blond mane streamed around two small, pointed breasts. Her waist was trim with just a tiny swelling for a belly—and beneath, a furry thatch of darker blond hair centered within ample hips that took his breath away. All this atop long, slim legs and tiny feet.

"Am I beautiful?" she asked, turning slowly to reveal the gorgeous buttocks he'd admired since the day they'd met.

By now, his heart was pounding as if it would burst. "Cynthia, you are the most beautiful woman I have ever seen," he whispered in a trembling voice. He meant it.

"Then come make love with me, Gordon Canby," she said. Gently, she took his hand and led him to an adjoining room.

In the darkness, he sensed more than saw a child-sized couch at the far end of the room, then a larger bed, where she was busily skimming off the spread, and suddenly they were lying together with her leg drawing him inward.

She sighed as her fingers stroked his hardness. "Mmm," she whispered, "that's terribly nice, you know."

He put his hand on her breast. It was firm; her nipple felt almost painfully hard. They kissed again, long, slowly, and passionately.

Presently, she twisted slightly and rolled on her back. "Are you ready for me, Gordon Canby?" she asked.

Trembling, Canby nodded. "Maybe *too* ready," he said.

"Come down here and find out, then," she panted, drawing his face to hers. "Now!"

He did. . . .

Next morning, long before daylight, a dazed Gordon Canby caught the first train south out of Grand Central.

Never—not in a career's worth of bawdy surface leaves throughout an entire galaxy—had he experienced more skillful, more gloriously dissolute sex in so many disparate forms. As he hitched a ride on a farm truck from Hampton to the ruins of Perrin, he shook his head with somber realization—if he hadn't been completely in love with Cynthia Tenniel *before* their night of lovemaking, he certainly was *now*.

MARCH 20, 2690, EARTH DATE

Belgravia Sector, London • Earth

The first explosion nearly bounced Renaldo from his bed. A beautiful young man with whom he'd been spending the night ran squealing from the room, his screams merging with shouts and howls of alarm from the corridor. Struggling from a tangle of silken bedsheets, Renaldo was about to flee the room himself when billows of pungent black smoke came surging through the door, followed by a huge apparition dressed in jet-black FlexArmor that looked as if it were left over from the last war. Of course it looked that way, he thought; it was obviously Kîrskian. Everyone who had lived through the war knew what they looked like! And even in the half-light of his bedroom, Renaldo recognized the grim countenance behind the helmet's visor. "Kobir!" he gasped, feeling his heart begin to pound.

"The same," Kobir's sepulchral voice agreed through the battle suit's external speaker. He crossed his arms, revealing a huge blaster in an open holster at his side, then stood silently, legs slightly open, while screams and explosions came from the still-smoking doorway.

Shrinking backward, the now thoroughly frightened Renaldo touched fingers to his lips. "W-why are you here?" he gulped. But he already knew the answer.

"A small matter," Kobir said almost benevolently, "most likely an oversight. However . . ." He paused during an extended series of explosions, punctuated by more screams and shouts. "I felt the charitable thing to do was to jog your memory in person—and, of course, leave you with a small reminder should you have trouble remembering in the future. It should save us both trouble." Another explosion rattled the windows, as sirens began to wail outside.

"Jesus Christ!" Renaldo gasped. "What's going on out there?"

"My little favor to you," Kobir replied with a smile. "Call it a memory jogger."

"A *what*?"

"A memory jogger, Sadir, old friend," Kobir replied jovially. "My men and I have simply demolished everything in the next wing of this lovely house. Nothing overdone, mind you. But you'll find the job professionally done—we caused a little smoke damage outside the immediate area, unfortunately. But that couldn't be helped. I'm certain you'll understand."

"You've done *what*?"

"Hmm," Kobir muttered, looking at his watch, "I'm afraid I have no time to tell you all about it. Pressing business elsewhere—I trust you understand. But it is all here for you to see. The fires should burn themselves out soon, then it will be safe to inspect. And, of course, I shall expect your payment draft to appear in our joint bank account within the hour. I have made certain that your glorious antique desk is intact and connected to power." He frowned. "Unfortunately, the remainder of the room is . . ." He shrugged as if he were admitting to rather painful embarrassment. "I tell my men to be careful, but when they hurry, they tend toward indifference. One supposes it is only natural."

"M-my study?" Renaldo asked as an icy finger of apprehension stabbed his chest.

"Yes, a pity," Kobir said. "But a loss that will certainly

keep you from forgetting your payments in the future. As I said, it will benefit us both." He glanced at his watch again. "Ah," he said sorrowfully, "unfortunately, I am out of time. Farewell for now, Sadir. I shall expect your payment within the hour." Then he stepped back into the smoky corridor and disappeared in the confusion.

Local police and firemen arrived minutes later—delayed, they said, by a number of highly unusual traffic accidents all over Belgravia. By that time, no trace of Kobir or his crew remained. And no threats—or combination of threats—could make Renaldo's servants speak a word about what they'd seen.

Near the end of the hour, Renaldo had singed his eyebrows and burned his hands in the still-smoldering wreckage of his study. But orders for Kobir's payment went out with five minutes to spare—after which he made a long, noisy call to David Lotember.

MARCH 26, 2690, EARTH DATE

Perrin Station • Earth

Canby awoke minutes before his alarm was to chime at five-thirty A.M.; he was instantly ready for action. It had been exactly forty-eight days since the Legion had departed from Manhattan's Salvage Yard, and *Death* was ready to fly—the first Legion starship to complete her fitting out. Surprisingly enough—to Canby, at least—the others were not far behind. Even *Famine*, oldest ship of the lot, was no more than two weeks from her resurrection. Sitting up in his bunk, Canby switched his communicator to Nargate, who was duty officer in their makeshift operations center near the wharves. "How's the weather out in the bay?" he asked.

"Not good," Nargate reported, "but not all that bad, either.

We've got a ceiling of about a thousand feet, wind from the north at twenty-eight knots, intermittent rain, and swells running between three and four feet."

Canby shrugged. "Could be worse," he said. *Anything* was better than waiting another day to fly. He wanted to be back in space nearly as much as he wanted more time with Cynthia Tenniel—which lately had been almost nonexistent. Throughout the last week, the legionnaires had worked nearly twenty-four hours a day, but *Death* was finally spaceworthy—at least in Lela Peterson's opinion. The ground crews had finished work just before dark and scheduled initial taxi tests for early the next morning. Canby had taken to his bunk almost immediately after a hurried supper in the mess hall and slept like a rock.

Struggling into his battle suit—no telling what might occur after the ship's decade-long layup—he stopped at the crowded mess hall for a quick cup of coffee, then headed through the rain for the wharves at a trot, a full hour prior to schedule. The unique smell of the bay was strong and pleasant in his nostrils. From the crowd gathered on the pier, it looked like he was the last to arrive. "How's she look this morning?" he asked Peterson, who was waiting for him by the boarding hatch.

"Not bad," she said, lifting the rain-streaked visor of her battle suit. "We've got a few minor problems, but nothing so important it needs to be fixed now. I'll fly in her."

"Can't think of a better recommendation," Canby said, looking up at the dripping ship as she hung suspended over the water on her sling hoists, "but we're only going for high-speed taxi tests this morning. All right?"

"Taxi tests . . . that's *all*?"

"Now, Lela."

"Well, she *is* ready to fly, Gordo."

"Maybe *she* is, but I'm not. Okay?"

"Gonna disappoint a lot of people this morning, Gordo."

"Like who?" Canby asked.

Peterson shrugged. "Like *them*, for beginners," she replied, cocking a thumb over her shoulder.

Canby glanced back along the dock where the entire Legion seemed to have materialized under a forest of umbrellas. He raised his eyes to the heavens. "WON-der-ful," he groaned.

"Yeah, I know," she said. "It *is*—isn't it?"

"Well . . ." Canby allowed. "I guess it is." Then he frowned. "But we're still here for high-speed taxi tests only. Understand?"

"Aye, *Captain* Canby," Peterson said.

"I'll give you, 'Captain,' " Canby grumped with a smile. He led the way through the hatch. Inside, *Death* smelled like a live ship again—heated logics and oil, sealants, coffee, people in wet clothes. To Canby, it was the most compelling fragrance in the universe. "Who isn't here yet?" he asked.

"Everybody's here," Peterson replied, wiping her boots. "They've been waiting for you."

"All right. All right," Canby grumped, wiping his own boots carefully. Halfway up the steep bridge companionway, he glanced at his watch—still nearly an hour before their scheduled test. The way everyone had been working themselves, their loss of sleep showed real dedication.

"These guys are really excited," Peterson nudged.

"I *hear* you," he said, pulling himself onto the bridge deck.

"Then we'll fly?"

"No guarantees, damnit, Lela," he said on his way forward, greeting the flight crew with slaps on the shoulders. "When she's ready to fly—in *my* estimation—then I'll fly her; not before." As they took their seats, he turned to look her directly in the eye. "*Understand?*" he asked pointedly.

"Sorry, Gordo," Lela said.

Canby shook his head while he scanned the streams of data flowing across his console. "It's all right," he said without looking up. "I'm probably the least patient one on the ship. But I'm *also* the one whose decisions can kill us all. So . . ." He shrugged and turned to Chang O'Connor. "If everybody's here, then let's get to the checklists."

During the next half hour, they completed what seemed to be the ten-millionth systems preflight, then slowly worked their way through the Engineer's checkout. At last, Canby looked up and peered through the rain-spotted Hyperscreens, then turned again to Peterson. "Looks like we're ready for the water, Lela," he said. "Tell the sling crews to let us down and we'll get to the start checkout."

"Coming down, Skipper," Peterson replied, then busied herself with an image of Jeff Edmonson, the Pier Chief. Presently, the huge sling spindle overhead began to turn and the ship started down toward the water. On either side, handlers stood by with long mooring lines wound once around the bollards, ready to take up slack when the ship was floating free.

Even before they were in the water, Canby began the checklist. "Altimeters?" he asked.

"Set and cross-checked," O'Connor replied, as if he had been ready for a year with the answer.

"G-wave service?"

"Ninety-one and eight hundred, G_O and G_H."

"Takeoff bugs?"

"Ninety-two, one thirty-eight, and one fifty-one," O'Connor said.

"Start pressure?"

"Ninety-one fifty. Subgenerators on and steady."

Canby looked through the Hyperscreens again. The pier crews were only a few feet below the Hyperscreen tracks now. The ship was nearly afloat. "Gravity brake?"

"Set."

"HyCOMM?"

"Energized."

"We're floating," Peterson advised. Outside, the sling wires were no longer taut, while the pier crews cleated in the shore ends. "Look sharp there in the mooring cupolas," she ordered.

"Ready to go, Skipper?" O'Connor asked.

Canby peered out over the nose. The rain had stopped, but the Chesapeake was still dappled with whitecaps. "Power to starboard," he said.

"Power to starboard."

Moments later, both of the big Napier SpinGravs were rumbling slowly at idle, not-so-mute testimony to the care that had been lavished on them during the last few weeks. Canby checked both wharves, where pier crews stood ready to handle the lines. Very professional, he considered with a smile. The Legion had come a long way in a *very* short time—an excellent example of the how much these forgotten warriors wanted—no, *needed*—to change their lives.

He activated the blower, set it for ALL STATIONS. "Seal all airtight doors and hatches," he announced throughout the ship. "Seal all airtight doors and hatches." One by one, green indicators replaced red on his hermetics display until only one remained beside MAIN HATCH. Then that turned green also. The ship was sealed. "Liftoff quarters," he barked next. "Liftoff quarters. All hands man your quarters for liftoff!" For a few moments, he could hear boots sounding from the companionway, then the bridge became silent. He turned to O'Connor. "Anything else?" he asked with a grin.

"Only the gravity switch-over," O'Connor assured him.

Canby nodded. "All hands seal your battle suits," he ordered, bringing his visor down and sealing it. He changed the blower to SUITS ONLY, then twisted in his seat to check each side of the bridge. Everyone's helmet *here* had its visor down. "All hands seal your battle suits," he repeated, then turned his attention outside. It had begun to rain again—hard. "Switching to internal gravity," he announced, touching a sensor that quickly turned from green to yellow. Canby ignored the momentary sensation of vertigo it caused.

"Internal gravity." O'Connor seconded

"Okay," Canby said, "in for a penny . . ." Carefully, he eased the twin thrust dampers forward, conning the ship from its slip with just a slight bias to port in order to compensate for wind that was blowing almost directly down the bay. Off to port, indistinct movement in the rain caught his attention. Imagination? No. He saw a light battling through the sheets of rain.

"Contact bearing two seventy-five degrees true, nineteen hundred meters, on course three fifty-five degrees true; speed twenty-five knots," Tim Thompson, the PI technician, warned from the Proximity console.

Canby nodded unconsciously. "Got you," he acknowledged. "Contact bearing two seventy-five degrees true, nineteen hundred meters, on course three fifty-five degrees true; speed twenty-five knots." Gently, he applied the ship's gravity brakes in cascades of water from under *Death*'s nose, then turned into the wind and held position. Gradually, an angular mass emerged from the grayness to port, then defined itself as an ancient gravity tug pulling a train of three huge barges that, from the clouds of seagulls milling around them, looked particularly like garbage scows.

"Probably have a hard time cleaning up the ship if you hit that one, Skipper," Peterson observed in a sober voice.

"Yeah." Canby chuckled as the great barges crawled past. "I've decided to forgo that pleasure this time." When they were clear, he glanced around the bridge—everyone still looked ready—then headed out onto the bay as the rain began to slacken once more. It had ceased completely by the time they reached the ship channel and turned north, into the wind. When the way ahead appeared clear, Canby advanced the two master thrust dampers all the way and stood on the gravity brakes. The ship churned up huge geysers of spray as the two units fought each other. At length, he eased off on the brakes, and the ship began to move forward, bow high, until he hauled back on the dampers again and the ship settled back, coasting in the water. He immediately noticed that one of the 'Gravs had not returned to idle. "What's wrong with the dampers?" he demanded.

Peterson reset the verniers, and the surging 'Gravs returned to idle. "Sorry," she said.

" 'S all right," Canby mumbled, concentrating on the readouts again. His first excursion up the bay was actually a series of four short taxi runs during which he accelerated to some sixty knots, then decelerated as he tested the steering engine while moving at high speeds in a continuous line. He grinned to himself as he taxied downwind for a second run—the starship had handled well, responding as quickly to her steering engine as the simulator. A good omen, perhaps?

In position for his second run, Canby's right hand advanced the thrust dampers again while his left hand rode easily over the attitude controls. With the two big Napiers thundering at full liftoff power for the first time, the starship surged ahead, climbing rapidly onto the step at sixty knots, then accelerating to seventy . . . eighty . . . eighty-five . . . ninety knots. Her hull was spanking only wave tops as she started into the air, but Canby held her where she was, and after a few kilometers, he closed the thrust dampers with satisfaction. The run had felt good. As the ship turned downwind again, he felt a nudge on his right arm.

"So?" Peterson asked, her voice muffled inside his helmet. "How's she feel?"

"Pretty good," Canby allowed. "In fact, terrific; she had a great run."

"You gonna fly her, then?"

"Jezzus Pezzus!" Canby swore. "Will you get off my back? No. I am *not* going to lift ship today. I want to look at the test data before I take her up. Okay?"

"No comment," Peterson sulked in a low voice.

Canby glanced across at the Systems station—Peterson was sitting stiff as a board. He shook his head. He didn't need to see her face to tell she was angry. So was everyone else, probably. And he couldn't really blame them—it was pretty obvious the ship *was* ready to fly. He took a deep breath. Only his mulishness was keeping them on the surface, and this early in the morning, they were assured of an immediate liftoff slot from nearby Norfolk Control. So . . . Without a word, he set the COMM to GND CONTROL. "MM-seven four eight—request liftoff to solar-local space," he said, looking neither right nor left.

The head and shoulders of a young woman from Norfolk Control appeared in a display. "MM-seven four eight," she replied. "Affirmative. Taxi to liftoff vector four eight left and hold."

"Four eight left and hold," Canby acknowledged, increasing their taxi speed and turning onto the vector.

"Okay. Lift enhancers comin' to twenty," O'Connor said, as though he had been expecting to fly right along—which he probably had, Canby considered cantankerously. "Trim is, ah, two point two."

"Set it," Canby ordered.

"Set," O'Connor echoed.

"EPR and airspeed bugs . . . one ninety-one."

"Set."

". . . And one thirty-three."

"One ninety-one, one thirty-three, and cross-checked."

"Set cross-check."

"One twenty-five and slaving . . . one thirty now and slaving."

"Flight instruments?"

"Check complete."

"Antiskid?"

"Armed."

"Attitude control check," Canby ordered.

O'Connor moved the controls in all directions while Canby watched the limit indicators. "All free," he said presently.

"Pneumatic cross-feeds checked; PA coming down; transponders and HOME indicator on; liftoff checklist complete," Canby said, glancing at Peterson. A cheek-to-cheek grin was evident through her visor.

OH-WHAT-A-GUY, she mouthed.

Canby winked, then turned and stared soberly out over the water. "Ready whenever you are, Chang," he said.

"I'm ready," O'Connor replied.

"Norfolk Control: MM-seven four eight's positioned for liftoff on vector four eight left," Canby announced.

"MM-seven four eight cleared for liftoff to solar-local space," replied Norfolk Control presently.

"Thanks, Norfolk," Canby replied as the display dissolved to nothing. Carefully, he released the gravity brakes, then slid the thrust dampers forward all the way to LIFTOFF MAX. Again the 'Gravs spooled up seamlessly, this time to a thunderous roar. "Let's roll!" he said as the ship began to race over the waves again. Astern, the water a half-kilometer back was flattened in two half-round troughs as the 'Gravs poured out mighty streams of gravitons. Once more, the ship moved easily onto the step, wave tops reverberating like hollow thunder against her bow. A sensation of high exultation filled Canby—a feeling he'd missed for better than ten years. *God* how he'd missed it!

"Power normal," O'Connor reported. "Ninety . . . one hundred . . . vee one."

Canby raised the bow slightly, fighting back surges of emotion.

"Rotate."

A last thump sounded as the wave noise dropped suddenly to silence. "We're off!" Canby yelled as the attitude controls came alive. Like all her skittish sisters, *Death* began a swing to port, but Canby brought it under control immediately with the port 'Grav momentarily at EMERGENCY thrust. In seconds, the ship was thundering through heavy cloud cover, bumping slightly in the turbulence, then suddenly burst out into bright sunlight and pure blue sky. Below, dirty gray billows seemed to extend in every direction as the DH.98 soared through wispy detritus of the storm and into the stratosphere. Quickly, the sky darkened from blue to black while the horizon became a more pronounced curve with every passing second. He switched a display to the LightSpeed indicator. It read point four. "Chang," he ordered, "call out the LSpeeds."

"With pleasure," O'Connor replied. "LSpeed four point five . . . five . . . five point five. . . ."

In the corner of his eye, Canby caught the moon just peeking over a horizon that had nearly become a half circle. He moved both Drive shutter controls to OPEN.

"Six . . . six point five . . ."

"Two green lights—Drive shutters open," Canby announced. "Lela, fire up the Drive."

Instantly, two frames appeared on his readout panel; both were dark. "Power to number one," Peterson said.

A red indicator lighted in Canby's right-hand frame.

"Firing number one."

While status lights on Canby's right Drive display slowly cycled from red to green, the big Rolls-Royce Wizard came to life with a deep rumbling—more felt than heard—shaking the whole spaceframe with its power before it settled down to a deep, satisfying drumbeat from beneath the deck.

"Drive number one firing," Peterson whooped.

Canby could almost *hear* the great smile plastered across her face—he had one like it, maybe bigger. A greenish blue glow aft confirmed her words—as did a series of green lights on his right Drive status display. As they approached Light-Speed, the view forward became a red jumble as photons began to arrive at the Hyperscreens in irregular clumps—the Jinkens Effect, named for the distinguished twentieth-century Alabama researcher who had first predicted the phenomena. Immediately, the Hyperscreens attempted to translate, but below true LSpeed-1, they were somewhat ineffective—and maddening. Canby concentrated on his instruments.

"Point eight LSpeed . . ." O'Connor reported.

"Power to number two," Peterson warned.

Canby watched as a red light appeared on the left-hand Drive status display.

"Point eight five LSpeed," O'Connor announced.

"Firing number two. . . ." In moments, the second Wizard was rumbling beneath the deck, throbbing cyclically with its partner until Peterson synchronized them in a low-pitched thunder that seemed to fill the whole starship.

"Point nine LSpeed . . ."

By now, the straining Napiers were just about played out and the view outside, fore and aft was nothing but a confusion of colors and meaningless shapes. Canby was ready.

"Point nine five LSpeed," O'Connor intoned.

"That's it," Canby gulped in spite of a voice nearly silenced by onrushing emotion. "Half ahead, both crystals." With that, he moved the Drive power vernier halfway open. "Finished with 'Gravs, Lela."

Immediately, both 'Grav quadrants on his readout panel faded from red-yellow to green. " 'Gravs spooling down, Skipper," Peterson affirmed.

"LSpeed-One," O'Connor announced in a choked voice.

Canby looked up through clearing Hyperscreens into deep space for the first time in more than ten years. "Well, I will," he said fervently to himself—tears streaming along his cheeks—"be thoroughly Goddamned." Nobody heard him. The bridge—and he supposed the whole ship—had suddenly erupted in wild cheering.

A few minutes later, Peterson had run a thorough systems check and Canby was setting up a short local course that would take them only around Uranus, then back to the Chesapeake when he felt a tap on his shoulder. It was Frank Conway, the Communications Mate.

"Personal HyCOMM message for you, Skipper," the muscular little man said through his bushy mustache.

Canby frowned. "A HyCOMM for *me*? From whom—somebody back at the station?"

"It was marked 'Personal,' Skipper," Conway said. "I didn't look. It's in your queue under 'Political Ethics.' Figured nobody'd bother it there."

"Thanks, Frank," Canby said with a chuckle. "I appreciate that." He switched a portion of his display to MESSAGES and selected OPEN ALL. Instantly, a single line of characters appeared: "Fast work, Canby. My congratulations.—N. Quinn."

Canby grinned. Canby's Legion, Ltd., was definitely on the move.

Columbia Sector, New Washington • Earth

At just about the same time, Lotember's fast-intensifying pleasure was suddenly interrupted by the chiming of his HoloPhone. Annoyed, he decided to ignore it, but . . . there it went *again*! Carefully disengaging from the uniformed woman crouched beneath his desk—a senior Captain in the Fleet—he straightened his cravat and touched the 'Phone, blood pressure rising by the moment. "Goddamn you, Tolton," he swore when his secretary's image materialized, "how *dare* you disturb me when I am interviewing Fleet officers for the Promotion Board?"

"I'm sorry, Minister," Tolton said with a frightened look. "But, it's the Earl of Renaldo—he, er, demands to speak to you immediately."

Lotember was suddenly alert. "Didn't you tell him I'm in conference?" he demanded.

"I, er, did," Tolton replied.

"And what did he say?"

"He said . . ."

"Well?"

"Er . . ."

"Goddamn it, *what* did he say?"

"He said something about fastening your pants and answering the 'Phone, Minister."

Lotember felt his face redden. "Out," he growled to the Captain as he struggled to close his trousers. "We'll finish the interview, er . . . later."

Without a word, the Captain gathered her undergarments and raced for the door, carrying her shoes. When she was gone, Lotember glared into the 'Phone as if the interruption were Tolton's fault. "All right; all right," he said, straightening his ruffled shirt. "Connect us."

"It's about time, Lotember!" Renaldo growled, even as his image was materializing over the phone. "When I call, I expect you to be *prompt.* Understand?"

"Terribly sorry, my lord," Lotember said in his most servile manner.

"I'll give you 'terribly sorry,' Goddamn your no-account hide," Renaldo snapped. "Don't take advantage of my good nature, or you'll be out of that office and on the streets so fast your head will spin. Got that?"

Lotember felt the frigid claws of anxiety tighten around his throat. "Yes, of *course,* my lord," he whispered. "W-what c-can I do for my lord?"

"That's better," Renaldo said in a slightly mollified tone. "Now, you can begin by telling me why that worthless Fleet of yours has been sitting on their hands for nearly two weeks instead of going after those pirates—*as you assured me they would.*"

"B-but my lord," Lotember protested as he felt sweat beading on his forehead, "we have made excellent progress against the freebooters. Why, just last week, our ships captured a pirate ring off Callat-91/5 in the Ninety-first Sector—destroyed both starships and captured nearly the whole gang. And before that," he added quickly, "there was the

Mannock Clique, with that gun barge they'd built, and before *that*—"

"Three pissant pirate gangs with a couple of small-potatoes ships each, and you call that *progress*?" Renaldo demanded. "If you'd get your head out of your ass, you'd maybe have noticed that none of those minor-leaguers fly Kîrskian ships—like the ones you showed me. Where the hell are *they*?"

Lotember felt the claws tightening around his neck again.

"I . . . ah . . ."

"You Goddamn well don't know, you miserable little fraud."

"But—"

"No 'buts' about it, Lotember," Renaldo roared. "I'm not about to wait much longer for you to produce. I can have you impeached with a snap of my fingers. Understand?"

"Y-yes, my lord," he said. Sweat was now running down his back, soaking his shirtwaist.

"Say the word."

"I-impeached, my lord."

"Wonderful—at least you can understand that. Now," Renaldo continued, "get up off your skinny, worthless ass and get to work. Immediately. Do you understand that, too?"

"Oh, I *understand*, my lord."

"Good," Renaldo said in a gentler tone of voice. "Notify me the moment you have the news I want to hear. Little pirates don't count—I'm after the big boys. Remember that." Suddenly his image dissolved to nothing. He'd hung up.

With shaking hands, Lotember pulled a clean lace handkerchief from a desk drawer and mopped his brow. Then he sat back in his chair and fanned himself with the Captain's forgotten personnel cassette until his fear began to subside. It was quickly replaced by anger until he reached out and smashed at the 'Phone. "Tolton, you worthless whore," he screamed. "Tell Jennings to get his ass in here immediately, or it will go hard on *both* of you!"

APRIL 15, 2690, EARTH DATE

Perrin Station / Manhattan Sector • Earth

"Olga!" Canby called as they exited the simulator hut at the same time. "You heading for Manhattan tonight?"

"Hello there, Skipper," Confrass said with a smile. "You bet I'm headin' north. That business of mine's the only thing that's puttin' any kind of decent food on the tables down here."

"Yeah, I know," Canby said, feeling his cheeks burn. "Wish we didn't need the help."

"Fact is, we do," she said. "But it doesn't matter just as long as I keep those naughty people happy in my little house of ill repute—at least as far as grub and pay are concerned."

Canby grinned ruefully. "That's what I wanted to talk to you about," he said.

"Money, Gordo?" she asked. "How much do you need?"

Canby touched her arm. "Thanks, but no, Olga," he said. "I have enough to get by. But you're the only one here who's got a personal skimmer, and I wonder if I could hitch a ride with you to the Hampton tube when you go tonight. I've, ah, got some, ah, business of my own in Manhattan that I've sort of neglected."

It was the truth. For nearly three weeks after *Death*'s first flight, the effort at Perrin Station had been so intense that Canby hadn't even found time for a night out with Tenniel. And whenever he'd 'Phoned, she was out. Frustrated as he'd become about that, however, he had plenty else for which to be thankful. His crews had retained much of their old military ethic, and quickly formed themselves into efficient teams that completely revised the old Fleet Table of Organization. Even the problem of missing disruptors disappeared when four complete sets of armaments—plus spares—arrived one day aboard a caravan of civilian lorries. The powerful space artillery was wrapped and labeled as a shipment of antique pipe-organ parts.

Only two troubles really nagged him as work progressed on the ships: the Legion's fast-dwindling bank account and Cynthia Tenniel. He intended to do something about the latter this very evening.

"Would that be *female* business?" Confrass asked with a grin.

"Yeah," Canby said with a blush. "How'd you know?"

"Honey," Confrass said with a grin, "since you aren't messin' around here, you *must* be messin' around somewhere else."

"Why, Olga!" Canby exclaimed. "How could you?"

"Easy, Skipper," she said. "Just like it'll be when I'll pick you up right here in about . . . twenty minutes. Be ready by then?"

"Twenty minutes it is," Canby said, and headed for the nearest 'Phone—where he met with no more success getting through to Tenniel than he'd had during the last three weeks. Back in his room, he frowned. Most likely, she'd be at Battery Park; she still took Damian there almost religiously. He looked at his watch. Four o'clock. He'd have a half hour's drive to Hampton (at Confrass's speeds), then—if they caught the 5:00 local to Columbia and connected to the five-thirty Manhattan Express—he'd arrive at Grand Central by 6:15. By that time, Tenniel would be home, getting ready for her latest job—if, of course, she still had one. Then, he needed an additional half hour to the South Manhattan Projects, so that put him at 6:45, earliest. It was doubtful as to whether he'd even see her, but there was always a chance. And besides, he could at least leave a note to tell her he'd tried to get in touch. *That* made up his mind. In the washroom, he splashed some aftershave on his face, combed his hair (wishing he'd had time for a haircut), then rushed for the simulator shack. Ten minutes afterward, he and Confrass were traveling at breakneck speed on the first leg of their visit to Manhattan.

The 5:00 Local to Washington departed eight minutes late—allowing Canby to dive inside the rearmost door and block it with his body until Confrass could scurry aboard, puffing as if she had run a hundred miles from the parking lot. The local—by some electronic miracle—managed to make up its eight minutes of tardiness to arrive at 5:24 and, even though it deposited the two at the far end of the terminal, they managed to board the Manhattan Express with three minutes to spare. That train was on time both leaving Columbia and arriving at Grand Central precisely forty-five minutes later.

Waving a quick good-bye to Confrass—"See you here, one in the morning"—Canby splurged on a HoverHack—whose computer actually worked well enough to locate Tenniel's address for the driver (who, wonder of wonders, spoke comprehensible Imperial!)—and he arrived out of breath at her apartment by 6:35. Straightening his hair with his fingers, he rapped on the door, heart filled with anticipation. Was that movement he heard inside? He waited, growing more excited by the moment. Then he heard the noise again—it was coming from the opposite apartment. Frowning, he rapped again. . . . Nothing. Disappointment set in rapidly. He must have only *just* missed her. He rapped once more, but only in frustration. She wasn't home. If she was, she'd have answered by now—the apartment wasn't that large.

Shaking his head, he stopped by the apartment where she normally boarded Damian while she worked. The boy was there, all right, and the woman verified Canby's guess that Tenniel had dropped him no more than fifteen minutes previously. "Thanks," he said.

"No problem, mister," the woman said. "She'll be real sorry you missed her—she hates to miss clients."

"I'm not a client," Canby said. "And you're not half so sorry as I am." Borrowing a notepad, he hastily scribbled out a few words of disappointment—along with an apology for not getting in touch with her. "Thanks," he said, handing back the notepad and the nub of a pencil.

"You want me to give the note to her?" the woman asked.

Canby smiled. "Much obliged, ma'am, but, well, it's sort of personal. I think I'll just slide it under her door."

"Up to you," the woman said judiciously, then shut the folding gate that barred exit from her apartment and hurried back inside, where at least two infants were well into a wailing match that appeared as if it would end in a world-class draw.

Canby deposited the note under Tenniel's door, then walked slowly out of the apartment, hands in his pockets. It was a lot more disappointment than he'd expected. *A lot.* A beautiful evening in the middle of April and here he was, stuck in Manhattan with at least six hours of time to kill. He shrugged sadly. So what now? His spirits rose slightly; if nothing else, he could still get a decent meal, even if he would have to eat it by himself. Passing up Griffin's Café— that was simply *too* much disappointment—he dined, rather hastily as lonely people often do. Afterward, with more than five hours *still* remaining, he wandered uptown, idly watching people. Beautiful and not so beautiful, obscure and bizarre, they were all there with every shading in between. Short, fat; tall, lean; painted hair, natural hair, no hair; noisy, quiet. Each boulevard a gushing, confused river of humanity pushing in all directions and moving at every speed imaginable—walking, running, hobbling, dancing, staggering, riding. The very atmosphere was rife with endless kinds of noise—even music—sounding at every volume. A kaleidoscope of glistening, colored lights flashed from every storefront and signboard visible. Intimidating. Exciting.

Intoxicating! By no means was it a substitute for Cynthia Tenniel, but, by God, it was exhilarating. And everywhere were placards kicking off Nemil Quinn's long-awaited election campaign for Prime Minister. *That* alone was good news enough to make him happy! He drank in the people around him—the hucksters, the V-Pols, the bums, the workers, the executives, the whores—and there *were* a lot of them tonight. Good-looking ones, too; of course, he was at the Midtown Executive VertiPads, only a few blocks from midtown and The Square where nearly anything was legal. For a moment, his eyes were drawn to a willowy blonde with her back to him. She was clearly engaged in dickering with a slim aristocratic man dressed in expensive clothes—and from the rear, she might have been Tenniel! He frowned and looked again. The man, who was reeling drunk, looked familiar enough, too. Probably a Politician—and from his clothes, a highly placed one, at that. They came here in droves from the Columbia Sector. The two had stepped into the partially shaded doorway of a closed lunchroom. She was leaning back against the door while the mystery man busied one hand under her short shirt. When she shifted slightly, he got a look at her face and . . .

Tenniel!

He ground his teeth during endless moments he needed to acknowledge that the woman was . . . *indeed* . . . Tenniel. The long, slim leg that arched out of the doorway, the tiny foot, the mane of blond hair. It *had* to be her. Heart pounding against his chest, he turned his head. At last, they stepped from the doorway, the woman—Tenniel. almost certainly— adjusting her skirt, the mystery man reaching clumsily into his pocket to peel a number of bills from a large roll. Smiling, she folded each bill with care as he counted it off with fuzzy-headed precision, then placed it into her purse—Canby recognized *that* now. too. Finally, arm-in-arm, they half-staggered up the street toward The Square. Tenniel obviously helping him along.

In morbid shock, Canby followed, jaw locked in stunned rictus. Nearing The Square, the streets became bawdier—and the mystery man less and less cautious with his hands. It soon became clear that Tenniel was wearing little beneath her skirt, but by that time, most of the whores—of either persuasion—were baring a great deal more than that as they hawked their sundry talents on the street. One reached out to grab the mystery man, but Tenniel raked the woman's face with her nails, then continued along the street as if nothing unusual had occurred.

Soon, Canby found he had a difficult time keeping up because of the insistent offers coming from every side. Some clutched for his genitals while others caught his hand and tried to guide it into . . . He was ultimately reduced to stiff-arming his way through the milling chaos while he watched the two stumble into one of The Square's infamous Temporary Houses. By the time he fought his way into the lobby, they had already taken one of the rooms.

"Peephole ticket, mister?" a pockmarked crone squawked from behind a thick glass ticket window. "Fifty credits for all peeps; five for singles."

"A blonde," Canby gasped. "Just came in with a . . . skinny guy. Which one?"

"Find 'em yourself," the crone cackled. "Don't think I'd remember, do ya?"

Numb, Canby reached zombielike into his pocket and peeled off fifty credits—half of what he had with him.

The crone took the bills, counted them carefully, then handed him a plastic key. "This'll open any of the peeps," she assured him, following the key with a small stack of tissues. "Just don't dirty the walls or the floors, understand?"

Canby felt his cheeks flush. He hadn't been in a place like this since he was a schoolboy awash in hormones. Shaking his head, he grabbed the key and started into the first-floor hallway, a noisy, foul-smelling confusion of men and women squealing and laughing as they peered into peepholes. Grinding his teeth, he activated an empty peep in room one. An orgy. He pushed through a rank miasma of stale cigarette smoke, cheap perfume, and sweat to room two. All peeps there were filled, so he moved on to room three. Two men. Room four was filled with squirming, muscular women doing things in acrobatic positions. He returned to room two, only to find it empty. Rooms five through ten contained other scenes of no interest, so with increasing anxiety, he moved up a narrow stairway to the second floor. Nothing there. Eventually, however, he found what he was looking for in room five of the third floor—and his first glimpse erased all hopes that he might be mistaken. Tenniel was kneeling on top of the mystery man, doing that *very* special thing Canby thought she only did with him. And it was clearly having the same effect!

Stunned beyond movement, Canby dumbly stayed after the others moved on to other peeps, watching the mystery man count out *a lot* more credits, while Tenniel lay back and smiled appreciatively for her tip. Before the two could dress and exit the room, Canby finally summoned the strength to stumble blindly along the noisy, swarming hallway and down two staircases to the lobby. There, he threw the key to the crone, then ran pell-mell out into the street and around the corner, where he vomited his supper into the gutter, heaving violently, again and again until only long strings of thick saliva remained. Picking himself up from the sidewalk at last, he blindly made his way to Grand Central, where he met Olga Confrass in shivering, stony silence that prewarned the painful consequences of asking questions. Returning to the shipyard in deep depression, he buried himself in his work. Days later, he had no recollection of the journey home.

Book Six

THE LEGION

Perrin Station • Earth

By May sixteenth, all four of the Legion's ships were both spaceworthy and armed, and the legionnaires—watching their funds quickly run to nothing—had become nearly desperate seeking that most difficult of all enterprise effects, the first client. It was not as if there were a dearth of jobs. Mercenaries were in constant demand throughout the galaxy, as the hundred-odd Lilliputian domains—by-products of many wars past—settled out, coalesced, and re-formed under a whole subculture of would-be, twenty-seventh-century Bonapartes. However, when calls went out, usually they went directly to the half dozen best-known mercenary groups. Recently formed or unknown groups trying to break into the business—like the legionnaires—found work only when every *known* group with any kind of reputation was already employed a half year in advance. It wasn't a begrudging or hostile exclusion, by any means, but tasks to which mercenaries typically were called always came with disastrous penalties for failure. People used mercenaries as surrogate fists to allegorically punch other people in the nose—it was natural they wanted to be reasonably certain the receiver of that punch was in no shape to return it.

Canby had sent out word at the end of June that the legionnaires were ready for action. It was the day he donated the remainder of his savings to the Legion's dwindling coffers. They were only *barely* ready at the time, but they all knew the situation they were up against, and decided on an early start, gambling that if they were called, they'd somehow be able to carry through. They needn't have worried. Six weeks later, they were still looking for a first inquiry— by now with a certain desperation.

Their first stroke of luck arrived almost by accident when a strangely familiar-looking man strolled into the Legion's shabby headquarters one muggy, overcast morning, as if he owned the building. He had an imposing frame and wore conspicuously expensive, though casual clothes. His face was large and fleshy, with a strong jaw, shrewd but friendly eyes, a tiny mustache that ended in sharp waxed points, and a small mouth filled with large teeth. "Who's in charge here?" he demanded.

"Guess that's me," Canby said cautiously, trying to place the man's face—in the half-legal world of mercenaries, *everyone* was suspect at first. He extended his hand. "What can we do for you?"

"Leon Cowper," the man said, handing Canby a flashy, animated business card. "I do HoloDramas." When he spoke, his brow wrinkled and he peered back at Canby as if *he*, too, were trying to place a half-forgotten face. "And I didn't catch the name."

Canby smiled and got to his feet. "Sorry," he said. "The name's Canby. Gordon Canby."

At this, Cowper's eyebrows raised nearly to his scalp line. "Jesus H. Christ," he whispered. "Not *the* Gordon Canby who commanded the old 19th Star Legion back during the war? You sure as hell look like him."

"Probably a good reason for that," Canby replied with a chuckle. "That's who I am—or at least *was*."

"Well, I will be absolutely Goddamned," Cowper exclaimed. "Canby, I used to fly for you."

Canby snapped his fingers. "*Leo* Cowper!" he exclaimed suddenly. "Lieutenant Leo Cowper. Yes . . . that's *right*. I'd heard you'd gone into the entertainment business, now that I think about it. But, Lord, I never connected you with . . . well, the big time, I guess." He pointed a finger at the grinning figure before him. "Why, you must have done *Soldiers of Fortune* then, didn't you? It was great."

"Hell, Canby," Cowper said facetiously, "everything I do is great."

Canby grinned. "Damned straight," he agreed.

Cowper peered around the shabby little office and ran his fingers through his hair. "So you're the guy with the DH.98s, eh? What's the deal?"

Canby thought for a moment. "Well," he said guardedly, "they're for hire."

"I saw you had one of 'em flying when I came into camp," Cowper said. "Any of the others spaceworthy?"

"All four," Canby said, enjoying a certain rush of pride.

"With crews?"

"You bet—most of 'em people you know, Leo."

"Yeah," Cowper said with a grin, "that makes sense. So, you say they're for hire, eh?"

"Absolutely," Canby assured him.

"And the ships fly?"

"Better than new."

Cowper grinned for a moment. "Yeah," he said. "From what I remember about you and the old outfit, I'd say that was pretty reasonable." He nodded. "Well, just so happens

I'm looking to hire a couple of DH.98s for the HoloDrama I'm making—*Suicide Squadron,* it's called. About the war, of course. Not a big gig, but what the hell, it's a couple of credits on the table."

"Credits always sound good to me," Canby replied, hoping he didn't look as anxious as he really was. "Where'd you hear about us?"

"Called up ol' Nemil Quinn," Cowper said. "He's into all that old-timey war shit—no offense meant to present company—an' he suggested I come down here and talk to you guys." He looked around the office again. "Looks like you're just gettin' set up."

"That's probably a good way to put things," Canby said judiciously.

"So, you interested?"

"When do we start and where do you want us?"

Cowper grinned. "It's a two-week gig," he said. "Couple of little planets off Alpha Centuri; I'll give you the coordinates. And we'd like to start soon as we can. How about this coming Monday, Earth Standard Time?"

Canby thought about it for only a moment. "We can make that," he said. "What's it pay?"

"We start the crews off at scale; standard lease rates for the ships."

"I don't have any idea what that means," Canby said.

"You'll like the rates," Cowper promised. "You got a Paymaster?"

"Yeah," Canby replied, "old Warwick Jones. Remember him?"

"Good man," Cowper declared with a grin. "The guy could dig up credits at places where other Legions were waitin' a week for payroll." He smiled. "I've got a couple of my bean counters outside with me. Let's put 'em together with ol' Jones an' let *him* tell you what a good deal you've got. Okay?"

"Okay," Canby agreed, picking up a 'Phone. "I'll get Jones up here."

Within two hours, the deal was concluded, Canby's Legion had its first client, and financial peril was once again forestalled at the last possible moment. Canby's Legion was now on the march, albeit to a considerably different drummer than any of its legionnaires had expected.

MAY 16, 2690, EARTH DATE

London • Earth

Only a few hours later, nearly halfway around the world, Renaldo presented another brandied chocolate to his fat lips, then smiled in satisfaction as the thick, sweet liquid flooded his tongue with cloying goo. The Mid-Spring's Divertissement, he considered sadly. May was already half over, and time seemed to pass so quickly anymore. No matter. This was an event worth his presence! Everyone who really counted in the Empire was on the guest list tonight. Even Emperor Philante had scheduled an appearance.

Hosted this year by Imperial Prime Minister, the Right Honorable Lord Sterling, Baron of Battersea, in his magnificent London estate on the Thames, the event marked the glittering height of the season. More importantly, however, the revelry also served to introduce the latest, gaudy display of mendicants. These were the fresh courtesans of both sexes who—in the course of the following year—would contribute their services to Knight-Revelers when the latter presented Tableaux they had authored in competition for the society's many awards.

With his own Tableau nearly through casting and scheduled in little more than a year, Renaldo had been more careful about his costume than ever. He was dressed as a late eighteenth-century *Incroyable,* complete with long, striped trousers hugging his thick legs, a white coat with a very high collar, wide and exaggerated lapels, high waistline (which he felt served to distract attention from his stomach), and tails that extended to his calf. His crisp linen neckcloth was so high it enveloped both his chin and mouth, and he wore a red, white, and blue rosette to show "Revolutionary" sympathies. Even his wig was authentic, worn straight and stringy, brushed forward from the nape of his neck to a ferocious-looking mass over his forehead.

This evening, Battersea's lofty, picture-windowed Thames Concert Hall was crowded with costumed revelers—in addition to an exquisite, nineteen-piece chamber orchestra, at least two hundred bustling servants, and a row of serving tables—awash with opulent refreshments—extending all the way from the stage to the rear doors. Invitations had gone out to important members throughout the Empire; consequently London's huge Gatwick Starport had been crowded for days by elegant private and corporate starships from all over the galaxy.

It was Arrival Hours—the stimulating interval preceding the Great Supper and The Tableaux—when powerful guests exchanged pleasantries (and often business propositions). Renaldo, in fact, had just moments ago closed profitable deals with two promising business executives in the market for a political mentor; he was rewarding himself with the *superb* chocolate-covered cherries. Suddenly he felt a hand on his shoulder. Turning, he confronted none other than the blockhead Lotember, perfectly dressed in a cut-away frock coat with tails, low-cut dress vest, shirt with ascot tie, and striped trousers—the perfect duplicate of a late-nineteenth-century diplomat. A dismal surprise, to say the least. On his arm, however, was a rather exceptional-looking blonde dressed in a costume that had clearly been created to match his, Renaldo's, 1795 French costume—to the month. Extraordinary!

"M'lord," the handsome Minister said, dismounting his monocle and bowing low, "how I have looked forward to the pleasure of seeing you in person this evening."

Renaldo was about to say something to indicate how he felt about Lotember's continuing failure to apprehend the Kîrskian pirates, as he now referred to them, but found himself loath to appear so abrasive before the woman. Dressed in the style of a 1775 nymph, epitome of licentiousness in that "new" era, she wore a long, diaphanous clinging gown—slit halfway to her crotch in imitation of the Doric *chiton*—and very obviously no underwear. The gown had a high waist-line—just below her small, lovely-looking bosom—and a very low neckline. The latter might have been terribly reveal-ing except her rouged nipples showed clearly through the translucent material, making such décolleté seem almost un-necessary. Her hair was done in pseudo-Greek fashion, with ribbons wound about a glorious blond coiffure that appeared to be quite real. The woman—whomever she was—magnifi-cently represented the epitome of an era dedicated to bare-faced, unconfined license; she was magnificent! "Er," Renaldo said, starting himself from what must have been a long period of staring blankly, "delighted to see you, Lotem-ber." He felt himself smile. "And who is the absolute god-dess on your arm?"

"Ah, m'lord," Lotember effused, bowing reverently, "you have such exquisite taste!" He stepped aside, taking the woman's hand while she made a deep curtsey that provided an unhindered view of the small, pointed breasts. "This lovely woman is a *very* special friend I recently made in Manhattan," he continued. "I included her myself among the apprentice disciples tonight especially for *your* pleasure, my lord. May I present the lovely Reveler Mendicant, Cynthia Tenniel?"

"Oh, by *all means,* Lotember," Renaldo said, taking the woman's soft hand and kissing it during a low, stomach-squeezing bow. "Cynthia Tenniel," he purred, savoring the sounds, "such a lovely name." She smelled of expensive perfume, and when she shyly lifted her gaze to meet his, Renaldo knew on the instant that he'd been enslaved. As he stared in complete enchantment, she languidly closed one eye in a wink so lascivious and suggestive that, during the Tableaux, Renaldo ignored all but the most spectacular performances, dreaming about her lithe body. And during the early hours of the next morning, she *far* exceeded his wildest, most erotic desire. . . .

JULY 1, 2690, EARTH DATE

Perrin Station • Earth

By the first of July, *Suicide Squadron* had become a smash hit throughout the civilized galaxy. Something about Cowper's production touched psyches in great cities and backwater asteroids alike. It was drama in the old-fashioned sense of the word, and people who hadn't seen a HoloDrama for years spent considerable credits to see it *a number* of times. Even music written for the 'Drama was considered a master stroke, especially a concerto, "Dangerous Moonlight," written for the male lead to play on an ancient instrument called a piano.

The 'Drama was good to nearly everyone concerned with it. Cowper, who was already wealthy, now became famous as well—and assured of first-refusal rights of first-rate plots for the remainder of his life. All three romantic leads joined the rarefied pantheon of performers awarded the Diamond Comet (publicly known as "The DiCom"); the music director (who had laboriously written all the original themes) immediately published a symphony he had been unable to peddle for eighteen years; and many of the bit players found major roles in 'Dramas that previously had been far beyond their reach.

Even Canby and his legionnaires shared in the 'Drama's unexpected largesse. Indeed, so quickly did profits begin to accumulate that before the production company had completed paying normal payroll and ship-lease monies to the legionnaires, actual royalties began to accumulate, and Paymaster Warwick Jones suddenly had ledgers with positive balances—at least temporarily. The 'Drama monies were certainly not enough to end the Legion's shoestring budgeting, but they did put things on a solid financial footing and removed much of the stress from day-to-day operations.

But *Squadron*'s real payoff came—like the 'Drama itself—almost as if it were an accident. A four A.M. ECONUS, HyCOMM call some three weeks following the initial releases brought Canby to the Operations Shack at a run. Originating in the Berniaga Cluster, nearly halfway across the galaxy, it was a *personal* call from one Al'Empat Onak-Ganas, Emperor of the minuscule fiefdom of Genap. Was this, he asked, the commander of the magnificent starships he had seen in *Suicide Squadron*?

"Er, yes . . ." Canby fumbled, struggling to put his sleep-numbed mind into gear.

"Normally, We are addressed as 'Your Most Eminent Worship,'" Onak-Ganas prompted. "But in honor of your role as the heroic starship Commander Canby, *you* may shorten Our title to 'Your Eminence.'"

"Thank you . . . Your Eminence," Canby replied, grateful that HyCOMM transmitted voice only. In the middle of the night, he looked anything but heroic—unless it was heroically sleepy.

"You are most welcome, Canby," Onak-Ganas said grandly. "Tell Us, was it you who flew the bright yellow DH.98?"

Canby thought for a moment. "I flew them all at one time or another, Your Eminence," he said. "We helmsmen traded off frequently because the 'Drama was made on such a tight schedule."

"By the Gods!" Onak-Ganas swore in a surprised voice. "The story took place over three Earth years' time, did it not?"

"I believe you are right, Your Eminence," Canby said (he *still* hadn't found time to view the HoloDrama himself). "But in reality, we recorded the whole thing in a little more than two Standard Weeks."

"We see," Onak-Ganas said. "Such wonders one views these days."

"Er . . . yes, 'wonders,' " Canby stumbled in agreement. Then he waited for the Emperor to continue, sipping from a mug of scalding coffee the Duty Officer had mercifully brought around.

Presently, Onak-Ganas belched. At the going rates for Hy-COMM transmissions, the belch might have been one of the most expensive in history. "Yes," he observed a few moments later.

Canby kept his silence, waiting. At last, the coffee was doing its job.

"We have chosen," Onak-Ganas continued at length, "to bestow a singular honor upon your heroic person, Canby." He spoke in princely voice, as if he were just about to confer some great military honor—Canby already had a chest full of those. "In a few moments," he continued, "you and your ships will be given the opportunity to actually find employment with Ourself—*personally*. One assumes such an opportunity is of great interest to you."

So *that* was what the call was about! "Of course, Your Eminence," Canby replied immediately. "A *great* honor. What is it we can do to serve?"

"Alas," Onak-Ganas pronounced after a few moments, "Asin Batik, one of Our neighboring domains—and a pariah among the Galactic Nations—has seen fit to detain a number of the starships that fly Our sacred flag."

"No!" whispered Canby dramatically.

"Yes!" replied Onak-Ganas. "They must be punished—and their miserable warships purged from space once and for all. We rule a peace-loving domain, Canby," he asserted. "We have no fleet to protect us. Therefore, we search for a hero to take up our standard in retribution. *Suicide Squadron* leads Us to believe that you and your Legion are the correct persons for the job."

While Canby listened, a wry grin spread across his face. Onak-Ganas's long-winded balderdash meant only that he was looking for an outfit that could do a small job for a *very* low price. "My esteemed legionnaires would be delighted to take up the glorious banner of Genap," he said.

"Excellent, Canby," Onak-Ganas said. "Excellent. We shall make you a national hero, along with Ourself and the other heroic men and women who conferred their efforts on the commonwealth."

"A dream come true, Your Eminence," Canby enthused, now getting into the flowery swing of things, "but lamentably, in spite of our great skills, we are only poor mercenaries, and require funds to mount such an offensive. I am certain Your Eminence understand. . . ."

This was followed by a long, rather dramatic—*very* expensive—pause at the far end of the interstellar connection. Finally, Onak-Ganas spoke again, this time all business. "Your Enterprise Manager is available?" he demanded.

"We have a Paymaster," Canby said. "And yes, he's available."

"Our representatives are on their way to your encampment as we speak," Onak-Ganas said. "They will meet with this 'Pay . . . Master' of yours within the hour. Should they successfully forge an alliance, Canby, you may well become a most honored warrior in our pantheon of national heroes."

"What an *honor*!" Canby exclaimed.

"It is," Onak-Ganas declared soberly. "We can only imagine the joy you must feel. Farewell for now, Canby. We shall look forward to meeting you in person one day." With that, the connection went dead.

Onak-Ganas's representatives had clearly been waiting for their Emperor's call. They arrived at Operations within fifteen minutes, and by ten o'clock that morning, Canby's Legion, Ltd., had signed its first client—and accepted a badly needed down payment.

That afternoon at lunchtime, Canby placed a call to Tenniel. He'd discovered she could be counted on to be home with Damian at that hour, and today was no exception. Since his star-crossed evening in Manhattan, he'd only 'Phoned—though he hadn't been able to mouth anything but meaningless platitudes. Today, buoyed by the Legion's good fortune, he was determined—somehow—to clear the fouled air between them.

"Gordon," her image exclaimed when the 'Phone connected. "I was hoping it might be you—it's been a *long* time. When are you coming to see me?"

If anything, she was even more desirable than Canby remembered. "Er," he started, at a loss for words as usual, "I, ah . . . would you *like* me to come see you?"

"Of course I would, Gordon," she said a little indignantly. She looked about her, then frowned. "You don't think . . . well"—she shrugged—"that I would . . . you know . . . "

Canby ground his teeth as painful visions flashed before his eyes. He struggled to make them go away, but they refused.

"Gordon?"

"Er, y-yes," Canby stumbled—he'd been off in a bad part of space. "Sorry. We've been so busy down here, that, well . . . "

Tenniel smiled. "It's all right," she said in a soft voice. "I know what it's like to work hard, believe me."

"Thanks," Canby said, trying to forget angry words that

kept surfacing in his mind. He steeled himself. "I . . . I really do want to see you," he blurted out.

"I'd hoped so," Tenniel said. "When—tonight? I'll take tonight off, if you'll come."

Canby took a deep breath—he'd been hoping for a few days to prepare himself. "Y-*yes*," he heard himself say. "Yes." He glanced at his watch—nearly one o'clock. "I can be there by . . . five. We'll have supper at Griffin's. Will that be all right?"

"It will be wonderful," Tenniel purred. "I'll be ready."

I wonder if I will, Canby thought. "Good," he said. "See you at five."

"At five," she echoed. He waited until she broke the connection, then he switched off the phone and headed for his room to spruce up. Somehow, he wasn't looking forward to *this* Manhattan visit—at all.

Aboard I.S.S. *Princess Dominique* • in space

While Canby made his way by HyperTube to Manhattan, nearly two million light years distant, the Kîrskian freebooters were nearly finished ransacking I.S.S. *Princess Dominique,* a magnificent starliner of Imperial Earth's prestigious White Star Line. Presently, Kobir himself was searching through a safe built into the starliner's huge, temporarily vacated bridge. It was a place where the most precious riches were typically stored.

"You Godless Kîrskian renegade," bellowed Captain (HRH) Sir Hubert Vorlander, Duke of Bedford and fiery young son of Emperor Philante. He ground his teeth audibly while Kobir delicately placed a tiny nineteenth-century statuette in a large sack with the other treasures he had selected so far.

The freebooter paused, turning to look politely through the faceplate of his battle suit. "Yes, Captain?" he replied patiently.

"You will never get away with this, Kîrskian," Vorlander spit angrily, his eyes sliding nervously sideways as he attempted to see the huge blaster Dorian Skoda held against his temple. The Captain looked young—perhaps twenty-five, at the outside. He was tall and good-looking, with the narrow face and nose that practically shouted gentility. His gold-braided uniform appeared as if it had been tailored only that morning, and he looked every inch the part of a *very* important officer with the galaxy's premier starship line.

Kobir smiled wistfully, listening to the deep, nearly imperceptible thunder of the ship's great power chambers, although for the moment, she was coasting in space with all means of propulsion shut down. For a moment, he wondered what life might be like as captain of such a magnificent vessel—and a lawful man as well, admired by a whole civilization. Such had been *his* dreams once . . . until the disastrous war. Now . . . He shrugged mentally. Through the port Hyperscreens, he could see two of his KV 388s against the starry background of space. Bow on, the ships seemed to be training their powerful disruptors directly at his face—a powerful token of reality. "Such is always possible, Captain," he replied, carefully placed a matching trio of diamond bracelets and tiara into the bottom of his bag. "But," he added without looking up, "were I you, I should be extremely careful about moving my head—even to speak." He discarded a long string of T'yén pearls onto the deck—too gaudy for the elegant tastes of the discriminating fences who ultimately disposed of his booty. "My colleague Dorian, who holds the blaster to your head, often complains about the sensitivity of the trigger. Is that not true, Dorian?"

"Sadly," Skoda replied with the kind of somber inflection that only Kîrskians manage to achieve, "it is true, my Kapitan." He sighed. "If there were only time for such niceties as maintenance."

Kobir watched the young Captain's face grow *very* red, then resumed his task—which he finished with no further interruptions. Eventually, he summoned a rating to remove the bag to his 388, then he handcuffed Vorlander to a nearby bulkhead and started off through the forest of consoles to the boarding chamber.

"God will punish you for this dastardly crime!" Vorlander called after them with loathing. "You Kîrskians were never anything more than a cheap gang of worthless riffraff."

Kobir paused beside a navigation station that was strobing urgent queries to an officer presently locked in the starliner's brig with the rest of the ship's crew. Somehow, the young man's furious words nettled him—not that he hadn't heard the same from others whose ships he had plundered. And who could blame them? Yet, *this* man . . . He turned to face the angry Imperial. "Did it ever occur to you, Captain," he asked patiently, "that perhaps Kîrskians such as myself and my colleagues did not choose this profession willingly? Defeat has not been kind to our people."

"You lost the Goddamn war," Vorlander growled. "So you take what you get. And you can go to Hell!"

Kobir shook his head. The misbegotten Imperial had finally managed to arouse his ire. "This 'Hell' you speak of, Captain Vorlander," he asked, "does your religion believe in an antithetical dwelling place?"

"Of course it does," the Captain proclaimed loftily. "We call it Heaven."

"And you—personally—expect one day to inhabit this . . . Heaven?" Kobir asked.

"Absolutely."

"Heaven, then, will be filled with men and women like yourself, one supposes."

"*Only* persons like myself," Vorlander assured him in a haughty voice.

Kobir nodded reflectively and moved off through the consoles again. "Thank you, Captain," he called over his shoulder soberly. "I shall then assuredly look forward to Hell."

During the next two hours, the Kîrskians completed their

plundering before carefully destroying the ship's HyCOMM suite and its all-important antennas. Afterward, Kobir himself placed a small timed charge on the hatch sealing the ship's brig. It would detonate some six hours later, releasing the ship's officers to liberate the passengers from their locked staterooms and resume safe transit to Earth. Then, with the great Imperial liner coasting along well below LightSpeed, Kobir's little squadron of KV 388s took its leave, disappearing into the starry firmament as if they were merely ghosts.

Manhattan Sector, New Washington • Earth

While the passengers and crew of *Princess Dominique* coasted through space awaiting release of the officers, Canby stepped from a tube train near Tenniel's apartment in lower Manhattan. By now, he was filled with foreboding and wished he'd never 'Phoned in the first place. But he was also committed to resolve—in one way or another—his troubles with Tenniel. And Gordon Canby did not renege on commitments. Especially this one; life was too painful while he allowed it to fester in his mind. Striding purposefully into the walkup, he made his way to the fourth floor and rapped purposefully.

"Gordon?" came a familiar voice from behind the door.

Canby ground his teeth in apprehension and excitement. "Y-yes," he stammered. "It's me."

Tonight, she seemed to take hours opening her locks, but at last the door opened and she stood smiling before him, even more beautiful than he'd remembered. Smartly dressed in a navy blazer over a light blue sweater, she wore a short navy skirt, black, high-heeled shoes, and a conspicuous lack of stockings. In spite of himself, Canby felt his pulse take off with pure animal titillation when—without a word—she hugged him, pressing her breasts into his chest while she kissed him lightly on the lips. Cheeks burning, he fought himself under control while she locked the door, then offered his arm and started down the hall toward the stairs.

"You're quiet tonight, Gordon," she said as they descended to the street. "Anything wrong?"

Canby shook his head. "Er . . . no—nothing's wrong, Cynthia. It's just been a difficult couple of weeks."

"Maybe I can do something about relaxing you later," she suggested with a shy little smile.

Canby managed to squeeze her arm and smile back, but all his mind's eye could see was his view through the peep in the Temporary House. "Yeah," he said, achingly torn between anger and lust. "Later . . ."

In Griffin's, he had no luck whatsoever summoning any kind of appetite; despite the bistro's magnificent ambience, nothing appealed but the wine. Tenniel, on the other hand, wolfed down a large plate of spaghetti and clams with obvious gusto. It was only toward the end of the meal that she began to peer across the table with increasingly concerned looks. Finally, she blotted her lips and pushed the nearly empty plate aside. "Gordon Canby," she said with a great frown, "you've hardly touched your food or spoken a word. What in the name of heaven is wrong with you tonight? Is it something *I've* said or done?"

Instinctively, Canby started to protest, then allowed the nightmare of the peep to capture his mind once more. Bracing himself grimly, he nodded. "Yes," he said in a small, tired voice.

"Yes, what?" she asked with a stricken look.

Canby shook his head and stared at his plate, not daring to even glance at her face. "I don't know how to say it," he choked.

"Say *what*, Gordon?" Tenniel asked. "Is this some kind of joke?"

"Wish it were," Canby said, looking up. "*God* how I wish it were. But . . ."

"But, I guess it isn't," Tenniel finished for him. "Gordon, what in the name of heaven have I done to you?"

"You haven't done anything *to* me, specifically," Canby said. "It's . . . well . . ." He took a deep breath. "It all started back in the middle of June—on a Saturday night. . . ." With that, he launched into a hurried, chaotic description of his lonely evening in Manhattan.

When he came to the part about the closed lunchroom, Tenniel slumped in her chair and put a hand over her eyes. "I was afraid that might have been you," she whispered. "Jesus, Mary, and Joseph—talk about bad luck. I thought of sending the guy off, but the next time I looked, you were gone—and he already had his hand in my briefs." She smiled wanly. "Besides, when you get a good-looking, clean trick like that, well, you set the hook right away. Most of the johns around The Square are pretty raunchy." Glancing momentarily at her hands as if they were unclean, she stared Canby directly in the eye. "What else did you see?" she asked.

"Everything," Canby whispered hoarsely, as if the word burned his throat.

"You followed us to the Temporary House?"

"Yeah."

Tenniel closed her eyes. "Oh, God—you *didn't* buy a peep key, did you?"

Canby nodded. "I did," he admitted, suddenly on the defensive.

"Bastard!" she swore. "Did you like what you saw? How was I . . . or, for that matter, how was *he*? Did you get off watching us?"

Canby closed his eyes. "No. *No!*" he protested. "I didn't."

"Then why in hell were you at the peep?"

"Because," Canby replied shakily, "I had to know if it was *really* you. I didn't get close enough to be certain until the peep."

Tenniel laughed sarcastically. "Which end of me did you finally recognize?" she demanded.

"Doesn't much matter," Canby said, recovering himself somewhat. "The important thing is that it *was* you."

"What's important about watching me get laid?"

"Nothing," Canby said weakly, "except you were doing it for *pay*! I saw him give that roll of bills to you."

"Any amount they want to tip is fine with me," Tenniel said. She frowned for a moment. "As I recall, the guy's roll of bills was a lot bigger than what he had to play with."

"Jesus!" Canby swore. "You sound just like a whore, talking that way."

"Well, Gordon," Tenniel said with a chuckle, "probably that's because I *am* a whore."

"You *admit* it?"

"Of course I admit it. And a damn good whore, too. I managed to give you a night to remember, didn't I?"

"B-but, my God," Canby protested, "that was different. I was *making love*."

"You think I wasn't?" Tenniel asked, her brows furled. "I hadn't opened that door for years. *Years.* And let me tell you, the noises I made were real—every time."

"Were they?" Canby asked, taken aback. "I thought whores didn't—"

"Think again, my friend," she said. "Sure, when I'm selling, I turn it all off; I don't feel a thing. Its easier to concentrate on what the customers want—and satisfied tricks not only tip well, they also come back. Business, Canby. *Business.* But not with you."

Canby put his hands to his ears. "My God, Tenniel," he gasped, afraid to believe what he heard. "How could a woman like you sink so low?"

"Low? Is that what you said?"

"H-how could you?"

Tenniel's eyes narrowed. "Don't you *dare* judge me, Mister Big Fucking Deal Moralizer," she lashed out in a low growl. "Have you ever slept under a bridge in the middle of winter—when you *had* to because you hadn't money to sleep anywhere else?"

"Well . . . "

"Goddamn right you haven't," Tenniel continued in a searing voice. "You don't have a clue about what it's like to be poor—to hear your *own* baby crying because he's cold. Sure, if you're *really* desperate, you can get a meal in the Soup Kitchens—along with enough tranquilizers to knock a horse on its ass. Damian and I only ate that drugged shit when we couldn't beg or scrounge enough to keep us alive. And without a place to live, things started downhill fast. Pretty soon, we didn't look so nice anymore—there was no place where we could clean up or take care of the few clothes we carried around." She shuddered while her eyes glazed momentarily. "People don't give a damn for you when they think you're down and out—they don't even want to see you."

"Jesus," Canby groaned. "What'd you do?"

"You mean, how did I become a whore?"

Canby made an embarrassed nod. "Yeah," he said. "I guess that *was* what I asked."

She laughed cynically. "Don't blush, Gordon. Every guy who crawls between my legs eventually asks—must be testosterone or something."

"Sorry," Canby said. "It must have been tough."

"Actually," Tenniel said, "it was *easy,* now that I look back on that day. I was scared, Gordon. Damn scared. Terrified." She shuddered again. "There were no jobs anywhere, and, well, I caught a look at the two of us in a mirror one cold afternoon after we ate in a Soup Kitchen. Things were bad. I was groggy, and so was Damian—and we had nowhere to go. I mean, *nowhere.* Then I saw this drunk—staring at me. You know, the way guys do when they want something. Until then, I'd kind of brushed them off, but *this* one had a five-credit bill in his hand." She smiled somberly. "I had nothing else to sell, but I was damn well going to have those five credits. So I sent Damian back to wait in the Soup Kitchen and then . . . well, I simply walked up and asked him if he'd pay five credits for me. As bad as I looked, he said yes—he must have been *real* drunk. We did it standing up in an alley—with me bent over a garbage can that I *still* smell sometimes. It didn't make me feel very good about myself, but afterward, Damian and I slept under a roof for the first time in a month, and bought a good breakfast in the morning." She paused to look Canby in the eye. "That next day, I did it again—actually a number of times. Five credits each trick. I looked so bad that all I could get were down-and-out bums like myself, but I ended up with money enough to clean up and buy some new clothes. After that, I could charge a little more for my services, and . . . " She turned her hands palm up. "That's the story. Sorry you had to find out the way you did."

"So am I," Canby whispered. "But, God, there's *got* to be some way you can quit."

"Are you serious?" Tenniel demanded. "For someone like me, Gordon, there is no Stipend—nor 'nice' employment, at least until I've saved enough to make some company's Tribute. And believe me, there's no way I'll take Damian back to live on the streets." Suddenly she narrowed her eyes. "I don't know whether you've noticed or not, Gordon Canby—my friend and sometimes lover—but wealth, and only wealth, means *anything* in this wretched Empire of ours. I intend to get as much of it as I can, as quickly as I can—and in *any* way I can."

Canby folded his hands on the table and stared at them for long moments, a bit stunned. He'd learned a lot about life in a very short time. At length, he looked up. "I've pretty much made a fool of myself, haven't I?"

Tenniel shook her head. "No more than most people," she said. "And, well, it *was* a pretty tough way to find out about me."

"Yeah," Canby said. "It *was* that, all right."

She looked down at his supper. "I'll bet the waiter can heat that up for you."

Canby smiled. "Yeah," he said. "I guess I am a little hungry now."

Afterward, the two strolled uptown hand in hand to see *Suicide Squadron*, then spent the remainder of the evening making gentle love at Tenniel's apartment. In the morning, it was a much happier—and wiser—Gordon Canby who caught the tube south for Washington.

JULY 3, 2690, EARTH DATE

Columbia Sector, New Washington • Earth

"Bloody hell," a perspiring David Lotember mumbled under his breath. The huge, three-dimensional display that fronted his luxurious command chair had just gone dark after manifesting the contents of HRH Captain Vorlander's recording cartridge—the one that showed members of the Kîrskian pirate band who plundered the great White Star liner *Princess Dominique* only two days in the past.

Vorlander had stormed directly to the Pentagon from his ship's bridge only six hours after making landfall. Presently, he, too, was seated in the Situation Room—to Lotember's left. Sadir, First Earl of Renaldo occupied a third plush chair at Lotember's right. Neither of the Minister's visitors seemed any too pleased.

"An Imperial scandal, that's what it is!" Vorlander growled. "An Imperial *scandal!*" His thin young face was twisted with rage.

"A scandal indeed, Your Grace," Lotember echoed with great deference. Philante must have been *very* upset about his son. It didn't take a drive scientist to understand the kind of power that could summon a big name like Renaldo to Washington on six hours' notice.

The First Earl himself sat on a hastily fetched chair like a great bloated toad. Lotember noticed with an odd mixture of dread and mirth that the crimson-faced Renaldo was actually squatting uncomfortably on the edge of the cushion; he was too fat to squeeze between the padded arms. It boded poorly, he thought, for the man's temperament—and his own future prosperity. He waited prudently in silence.

And waited . . .

"Well?" Renaldo queried at length, peering dyspeptically across the few meters that separated them.

"Er, my lord?"

"I have seen these Kîrskian pirates so often that some have become familiar," Renaldo grumbled. "What happened to that squadron you were supposed to send after them? As I remember, you promised they would destroy the Kîrskians to a man—with no prisoners."

"I, ah . . . " Lotember stammered in confusion.

"You what?"

At last, Lotember's mind shifted into lower gear. What to do? Of course! Obfuscate until there was time to calculate something better. It rarely failed. "Ah . . . " he began, his mind searching feverishly for the means of escape he *knew* existed somewhere, "as you must know, my lord," he started, "the Fleet has indeed captured another three pirate gangs since we last spoke, and—"

"Pissants again!" Renaldo growled in a most terrifying voice. "Little fish—the three of them. I want to know what you have done about the Kîrskian pirates. You *do* remember them, do you not?"

Lotember ground his teeth—*that* approach bought very little time. "Oh, I do, Your Grace," he said. "I *do!*"

"Wonderful," Renaldo said, voice dripping with venom. "Then, I repeat my question for Captain Vorlander's benefit.

Why have you not destroyed them as you promised you would?"

"Er . . . I have done what I can, my lord," Lotember said, casting about in near panic for some new course of action. *Anything* to deflect the two fiends who were assailing his comfortable position in life.

"Couldn't have done very much, Lotember," Vorlander grumbled. "They plundered my ship, you know—took everything. *Chained me to a bulkhead!*"

"Yes, my lord," Lotember repeated. "Chained—"

"I am certain Captain Vorlander appreciates how well you can parrot words, Lotember," Renaldo snapped. "But what he—and *I*—want to know primarily is *what you have done about them.*"

"Actually," Vorlander interceded to Lotember's great assuagement, "it seems patently obvious we already have our answer to that question. I think what we really want to know is what Minister Lotember plans to do about the pirates *now*. Am I correct, my good Earl?"

Renaldo paused to consider this. "You are correct, Captain," he agreed at length.

As he spoke, Lotember nearly swooned with relief. Now, *that* was an opening through which even the least alert Politician in the Empire could easily wriggle.

"All right, Lotember," Renaldo growled. "What *are* you going to do about those Goddamn Kîrskian pirates now?"

Lotember almost purred as he stood and turned to face the two angry men. Clearly, young Vorlander had the *real* power, so . . . "My lords," he began in the soft, certain voice he used when briefing *very* important visitors, "I had already made contingency plans for such a happpenstance." He frowned theatrically and turned to address Renaldo. "Even when I dispatched this latest squadron with three times the number of ships necessary for such an elementary mission, I harbored grave doubts as to the ability of the ships and officers."

"You did?" Vorlander asked.

"Oh, I did, Your Grace," Lotember assured him, launching comfortably into his best theatrical manner. "In point of fact," he continued liquidly, "the makeup of our Fleet has concerned me since I took office. Too many of the officers and ratings are superannuated veterans of the last war. What of value can the elderly bring to modern Fleet tactics and strategy? Both of you, my lords, know the answer."

"Well, what about *experience*?" Vorlander asked cautiously. "That's got to count for something."

Lotember sniffed. "Your Grace, what this Fleet badly needs now—and *has* needed for some time—are crews of fresh young intellects, able to act and react at lightning-fast speed." He shrugged deprecatingly, watching a smile of recognition spread across the young man's lips. "Experience can easily be taught in classroom situations, without—I might add—bogging down the mind as it does with most of these hopelessly outdated veterans."

"By Jove," Vorlander exclaimed, "that *is* impressive, Lotember. Come to think of it," he said, "very few of our White Star officers and ratings are youngish." He frowned. "It shows, I fear. We're a rather frumpy line, when one considers things in a clear light." At this, he nodded sagely—as if he were forming a complex abstraction. "Lotember," he said, reaching across to pump the Minister's hand, "I think you're on to something. One assumes you have a scheme to rectify the situation."

"Indeed I have such a plan, Your Grace," Lotember said, glancing at Renaldo—who appeared to have become considerably more at ease than he was only a few minutes before. "For a number of weeks now, I have been devising a plan to purge our Fleet of its ancient deadwood, replacing this human offal with young, contemporarily educated men and women. I shall especially concentrate on populating the Officer Class with scions of the Empire's best families—the cream of the crop, so to speak: best educated, healthiest, most confident. When I am finished, the old Fleet will sparkle with youth, energy, and exuberance. And soon after that, our Kîrskian pirates will cease to exist. What could be simpler?"

By this time, Lotember was at considerable pains to stifle a smile of—well-deserved—satisfaction and Vorlander had a look of total subjugation on his handsome young face. "By God, Renaldo," he exclaimed, turning to face the Earl, "it's easy to see why you backed *this* fellow to be Minister of the Fleet. My compliments, old fellow. I shall certainly pass this along to Father."

The Earl half rose from his perch and bowed—or at least *attempted* to bend his great stomach. "Ah, Captain," he exuded unctuously, "I can take only small credit. Minister Lotember was easy to select, standing as he did head and shoulders above his so-called contemporaries. . . ."

The cultivated drivel lasted only a few minutes before Vorlander glanced at his watch. "Ah, well, good gentlemen," he said, "I should love to continue our discussions, but . . . duty calls, as we say at White Star." Soberly, he shook Renaldo's hand, then turned to Lotember. "Minister," he said with great emotion, "you have honored me with a glimpse of your vision, and I have understood it. Perhaps I can best voice my gratitude—and admiration—by attempting to implement the same grand concept within White Star."

Lotember bowed so low he nearly lost his balance. "My lord," he whispered, mixing just the *hint* of a tremor with his voice, "I am *most* honored."

After a few more flowery words, the young Duke *cum* Captain departed. Smiling, Lotember turned toward his corpulent mentor and prepared for the praise he so richly warranted. Instead . . .

"Lotember," Renaldo ordered in a voice that brooked no question, "have your men clear the office immediately."

"My lord?"

Renaldo closed his eyes for a moment, then opened them

and fixed Lotember with a look that could have stopped a train in midtube. "Clear . . . the . . . room," he said, pronouncing each word slowly and distinctly, as if he were speaking to a dull-witted child. "I want a word with you."

Lotember gulped with anxiety. "C-clear the room," he ordered, his voice suddenly tight with stress. "Secret meeting—clear the room."

When the last of the analysts and COMM officers was gone, Renaldo turned to Lotember and grabbed the man's lapels. "Lotember, you shitty little weasel," he snarled. "You have just saved your worthless balls—but only temporarily. Understand?"

"I . . . m-my lord?" Lotember stammered at this unexpected turn.

"You heard me, Goddamnit, Lotember," Renaldo snarled. "If you think you've gotten yourself off the hook about those Kîrskian pirates, you are in for a real disappointment. Now listen and listen well, because this is your last chance. Muck things up again and you can forget any support from me in the next election. I want those Kîrskians wiped out—to a man. Understand?"

"Er, of course, my lord," Lotember replied, heart thudding in his chest.

"Say it, then."

"S-say what, my lord?" Lotember stuttered in tongue-tied confusion.

"What I want."

"Er . . . "

"Lotember, you worthless dimbulb," Renaldo growled in a voice that sent icy tentacles of dread exploring the Minister's rib cage, "what is it you need to do to keep me from backing someone else in the next election—or better yet, from having you impeached for downright incompetence?"

Lotember managed to surface partially from his confused funk. "T-the Kîrskians—" he stammered, "I've got to g-get rid of them."

"Don't forget it," Renaldo growled, starting for the door, "unless you're awfully Goddamn anxious to join those peons in the Soup Kitchens."

After the door slammed, Lotember slumped back in his chair, panting and exhausted, his sweat-soaked suit chilly in the air-conditioning. He sat that way for nearly a half hour before his breathing and heart rate returned to normal, then he called his limousine and returned directly to his suite of offices.

While he spruced up in his private washroom—carefully applying fresh makeup to hide any traces of his recent discomfiture—he ordered Tolton to summon his closest followers from Media-Control and Information Dissemination. When they had all assembled around the long table in his largest conference chamber, he entered the room theatrically. "Gentlemen," he announced, "you will immediately cease all your department's normal operations." That got their attention! He seated himself when the room had quieted again. "Tomorrow morning," he continued, "we—you and I together—begin a task that will prove our worth to the whole Empire once and for all." He paused dramatically, looking each of his lieutenants in the eye. "Soon, I shall send you to your homes—perhaps it will be the last time you will see family and friends for weeks. When you return to your offices in the morning, I shall expect a supreme effort from each of you—and every soul who works within your purview." He narrowed his eyes and set his shoulders in a heroic pose. "From tomorrow, you will eat, sleep, and labor in your offices until the task is complete."

By this time, the room had hushed so completely that the air-conditioning sounded like a heavy wind.

"And the task?" he demanded dramatically. "Gentlemen, in the next few months, I intend that we will devise and implement a plan that will completely purge the Fleet Officer Corps, expelling its present cast of ancient military incompetence and replacing each individual by a younger, better-educated person of good breeding."

JULY 19, 2690, EARTH DATE

• Menphosa

Dawn on steamy, verdant Menphosa had just begun when Stevens, the Duty Officer, rushed onto the dark wooden pier with a scrap of plastic in his hand. "The mission's on, Skipper," he called breathlessly.

From his perch atop *Death*'s fuselage, where he was adjusting one of the radio antennas by flashlight, Canby nodded. "What's the drill?" he asked.

Stevens peered at the note in his hand. " 'Desir-Oming starbase on Batik/3,' " he read, " 'reference V-2275, N-3285-980, T-297A. Eight large transport starships loaded on beach or at anchor. Some killer ship–activity possible. Attack at once.' Signed: Grand Field Marshal Mannri OObjidd for His Eminence, Emperor Al'Empat Onak-Ganas."

So, Canby considered, the day had finally arrived. "Did you check what kind of weather we have over the target?" he asked.

"I did," Stevens reported proudly. "According to Onak-Ganas's spy there on Batik/3, it's pretty well blocked from all directions—lightning-spiked clouds, with showers up to thirty thousand meters."

Canby conjured a map of the target from his simulator runs. Desir-Oming was some one hundred twenty kilometers from the enemy capital, so it naturally would be heavily defended—at least to the extent that the shabby little domain could afford. "All right," he called down. "Let's get everyone awake immediately. We'll lift at . . . " he glanced at his watch—it read 3:19 P.M. ECONUS, "in two hours." Grinning, he watched Stevens rush off toward the little tent village they'd called home since arriving on the planet. Then, after one final test of the antenna, he carefully made his way forward along the ship's rounded spine, popped down into the bridge, and sealed the hatch behind him. Minutes later, he, too, was in tent city, climbing into his battle suit—and reflecting how odd it seemed returning to active operations after ten long years of relative idleness.

As things had turned out, His Eminence, Emperor Al'Empat Onak-Ganas really had been threatened. No more than ninety parsecs distant, a grasping, self-proclaimed "Grand Imperiator" named Zeried 'Alli despotically ruled a dimly lighted, three-planet domain named Asin Batik that orbited a small, reddish star named Iota-73/0185-n. The latter provided so little energy that Asin Batik was forced to import nearly all its food, save mushrooms and other low-light crops—although its exports of the latter were nothing less than phenomenal. In contrast, Genap, Onak-Ganas's diminutive empire orbited Alpha-Neeko, a bright little star that provided plenty of energy to its two planets, Korlanda and Menphosa, each of which could outproduce all three of the Batik satellites. Hence, 'Alli was about to annex them by invasion.

As Canby struggled into his battle suit, sweating in spite of the tent's air-conditioning, he experienced the old, familiar sinking feeling—fear, really—that always occurred before he lifted on a combat mission. Would he achieve goals—or make it home afterward, for that matter? After more than a thousand operational flights and God knew how many close calls, he was this time returning to mortal danger with neither the zest of a young helmsman newly hatched from the Academy nor the self-confidence that he once got from his long experience. Somehow, going back after being completely away from everything for ten years seemed not only risky but practically insane. But here he was. Minutes later, he was on *Death*'s flight bridge, starting the checkout routines.

Boots drummed on the deck. He looked out over the four piers jutting into the unnamed tropical lake where they were based. The legionnaires were beginning to arrive now, carrying steaming mugs of coffee and munching improvised sandwiches.

When the ships were fully manned, Canby quickly broadcast the situation. He couldn't then and there provide exact details as to how the strike would be carried out because the situation at Desir-Oming was extremely fluid. It seemed to be more of a question of what turned out to be advisable at the time rather than following an effort carefully programmed around mere guesswork; therefore he would provide necessary orders over the radio when they got there. "Synchronizing clocks," he warned, slaving clocks on the other three ships to *Death*'s. "I've got 1707 hours. We'll do 'Grav startup at 1715 hours. I shall lift off as Number One: *War* will fly my wing as Number Two; *Famine* will fly as Number Three and *Plague* will fly wing on *Famine* as Number Four. I shall set course on the target at 1725 hours. Any questions? All right, then let's get this show on the road."

At 1715 hours, *Death* was ready. The 'Gravs were already ticking over and the ground crew on the dock did a thumbs-up to show that everything looked ready from the outside. The long, jungle-lined lake was nearly still, although great cumulus masses building in the deep blue sky presaged the afternoon's thunderstorms. As Canby strapped himself in, he looked around. Mooring lines were singled up, and the other ships were starting the 'Gravs, too, giving off shimmering clouds of gravitons as they spun up. Here and there, crew members rushed along the wharves with maps or blasters forgotten at the last moment. Through the Hyperscreens, he could see bridge crews in the other ships settling into their consoles. They looked ready.

"Cast off all lines," Canby ordered, and started out onto the lake. Precisely on schedule at 1725, with tropical storms forming nearly everywhere and heavy cloud banks rolling toward the lake, *Death* thundered up from the water and set course for Desir-Oming, followed by *War*, *Famine*, and *Plague*.

They approached Batik/3 at high speed, nearly grazing the huge asteroid belt that ringed the orbits of all three Asin Batik planets, then dove wildly through roiling, lightning-filled storm clouds for the surface in a trajectory designed to bring them in over the port of Desir-Oming at ground level, from what on Earth would be southwest to northeast. Leveling out, they bumped and juddered through driving rain that dragged down the clouds lower still until Canby could only just see *War* bouncing along abaft his starboard beam. They were scarcely thirty kilometers from the target when a black, rolling barrier of cloud blocked the way. Plunging heedlessly into the storm, Canby immediately lost sight of almost everything outside while he concentrated on his instruments and kept an occasional eye for his companions. Desir-Oming was somewhere, quite close, in the muck ahead. Suddenly, the weather cleared, their target dead ahead. The sky, under a very high vault of absolutely smooth cloud, was that clear, luminous gray that one finds only in very cold air. In spite of everything, all four DH.98s were flying in near-perfect formation. Off to the left, Canby spotted a regiment of soldiers hastily attempting to drag camouflage over two NovoGascony-built GGM-33 killer ships left over from the war. Immediately, the air filled with ground fire. Glowing coals rippled toward the little squadron for a moment, then the entire surface of the spaceport seemed to light up with 20-mmi and 37-mmi disruptor beams. Bright yellow staccato flashes from the 20s, regular strings of eight in bright red from the 37s. Canby's heart leaped to his mouth, his clenched toes swam in his boots—no better than ten years ago. Combat was the most frightening—and exhilarating—activity man could experience. *Death* was nearly flipped over by a close burst of crimson. Sudden, bright flashes from *Plague* and *Famine* cloaked three of the big emplacements in great, roiling explosions of green and yellow energy.

Now Kellerwand was firing the powerful Hispano 20-mmi disruptors in *Death*'s nose, forming a ribbon of explosions worming its way among the enemy defenses and climbing over disruptor emplacements in a haze of broken metal, dirt, and debris. To port, *War* unloosed a burst of fire that smashed into an elevated disruptor emplacement, cutting it in two beneath the platform. The heavy plastic frame flew into the air; a cluster of soldiers hanging on to the disruptor itself collapsed into flaming space. The legionnaires were now almost through to the harbor. Canby lowered his head instinctively, then laughed at himself—a lot of shielding those few inches of hullmetal and Hyperscreen would do! Salvos of 37-mmi burst so close that he got only the flashes, not the smoke or the concussion. *Death* jumped a number of times as near misses jarred the hullmetal, then—almost unbelievably—they were past the ring of fortifications.

Below, to the right, was the port of Desir-Oming. Within its curved strand was a calm sea with eight massive troop-carrying liners, desperately trying to get under way. Above, a dozen or so of the GGMs orbited the harbor. They had been good killer ships years ago at the beginning of the war—and were still effective fighters *if* they were manned by decent crews. But in no way were they a ship-for-ship match with the likes of a DH.98.

Now was the time for decisions! Canby made them in the instant. Menderes in *Famine* and Gibbons in *Plague* would engage the antiquated killer ships above; meanwhile, he and Confrass would separate to independently shoot up the primary target. He passed this over the radio, then hauled *Death* around in a near-vertical turn toward the strand, straightening out into a shallow dive to ground level through scattered disruptor fire. The radio altimeter read only thirty-five meters when he reached the edge of the water. White lines of foam marked the wake of three big Reinrod 24 starships that had just taken off. Ahead, two hulking Ssov & Mholb troop transports on wheeled cradles were lined up on the launching ramps. Kellerwand opened up on the nearest one, hitting it with his first discharges. The moorings of its cradle snapped and *Death* passed over the enormous, smoking mass just after it tipped over on the slope and fell into the sea, taking what must have been at least a thousand Batik soldiers to a watery grave. At once, every disruptor in sight seemed to aim for his faceplate. He veered to the right so fast, he couldn't fire at the second Ssov & Mholb, but it brought him out over the water once more—and directly behind still another one that had just left the water and was already growing alarmingly large in the Hyperscreens. Kellerwand fired one long, continuous burst from the Hispano 20s until Canby broke away just before they collided. He glanced in the aft display as the big star-ship—its drive chambers ablaze and its whole stern section sheered off—bounced into the harbor and exploded.

Out on the harbor, a flaming Reinrod 24 crashed in a shower of spray behind Confrass, who was now hot on the tail of its partner.

The Batik disruptor fire from shore redoubled in fury. By this time, *Death*'s speed had swept Canby far out over the water—straight for a crude floating disruptor barge that was spitting away with everything that would fire. He passed within ten meters of her blunt bows, just above the water and the thousand spouts raised by her disruptors. He caught a glimpse of battle-suited shapes rushing about the barge's decks and blinding shafts of energy from her armaments. The entire camouflaged superstructure seemed to be alive with them. A wild burst mowed down a flock of sea fowl that fell into the tossing water in clouds of feathers. Then, at last, *Death* was out of range.

Canby found himself sweating all over, his throat so con-stricted he couldn't speak. He soon realized that he'd held his breath through the whole attack and his heart was thump-ing as if it were about to burst. He gained height in a wide climbing turn to starboard, attempting to comprehend what was happening. Off to starboard, Confrass was just splash-ing still another Reinrod, while above, a small but heated dogfight appeared to be in progress. Three starships were coming down in flames—all easily discernible as GGM-34s—along with a veritable shower of LifeGlobes. Another ship—identity unknown—was burning on the ground near an outcropping of low buildings.

Should he try to join the dogfight above or try a second run over the Batik harbor? At least half the transports were still intact, including the three he'd seen taking off during his first run over the strand. Unwillingly, he decided on the second course—the transports, after all, were what they were being paid to destroy. Diving to sea level again, he started back at full speed when he suddenly spotted the three fleeing Reinrod transports again.

When he had recovered from his surprise, he sheered off to keep outside their defensive fire, opened the thrust dampers wide, and zigzagged back toward them—finally remembering to turn on the recorders so he'd have something to show Onak-Ganas when the time came to demand payment. Then, keeping out of range of their small disruptors, he waited until Kellerwand drew a deliberate bead on the first one. After a few bursts from the four Hispanos, two of the starships three 'Gravs were on fire. The helmsman attempted a forced landing, but this far outside the harbor, the water was rough and he capsized, his hull breaking in half, spilling hundreds of thrashing soldiers in the heavy seas.

Immediately, Canby made for the other two that were skimming the waves and attempting to get away. Long trails of gravitons from their wide-open 'Gravs blurred the view of the water aft. For a moment, Canby almost felt sorry for them. With his great margin of speed and four powerful disruptors, they had no chance at all. He lined up with the right one, which seemed to be extra heavily laden and lagged slightly behind the other. Whoever handled the controls on this ship was a good helmsman. At the last moment, he—or she—turned sharply. Carried forward by his speed, Canby found himself, like a fool, having to turn within point-blank range of the Reinrod's aft turret. The enemy gunner scored a number of clanging hits with his small, blaster-sized 7.7-mmi disruptors, but to little avail. A side slip brought *Death* into firing position again, and Kellerwand ravaged the big ship at less than a hundred meters' range. The Reinrod's starboard 'Grav caught fire;

its aft turret stopped firing abruptly, and within moments, the entire hull was engulfed in flames. The helmsman attempted to gain height and turn back toward shore, but he was too low. His big machine was nothing but a ball of fire rolling a few meters above the wave crests in a thick trail of black smoke. Seconds later, it exploded and disappeared.

Canby looked for the third ship and found it moments later. It was also going down in flames, with Confrass riding herd off to starboard. Destruction of the last two victims had brought *Death* around and once more heading inland for Desir-Oming just off the wave tops, his powerful 'Gravs leaving twin rooster tails like an old-fashioned racing boat. This time, he took the Batik gunners by surprise. By now, they were firing in a rather desultory manner in the general direction of the dogfight. The DH.98 swept in off the harbor between two large buildings and emerged over the starbase at nearly five hundred knots. There were all manner of small transports—so many that Canby didn't know which to choose. Directly ahead, however, were two enormous Odara 232 transports with their curious fuselages, five decked cabins, and twenty-four-wheeled undercarts for use on land. Kellerwand made the decision, his big Hispanos stitching a column of blazing craters that marched at an angle across each of the hulls.

A clanging hit somewhere aft from a hidden disruptor battery shook the DH.98, but produced no change in *Death*'s flying characteristics—Canby ignored it. When he was safely out of range, he broke away in a climbing spiral, only to find himself in the midst of the dogfight, which—with six of the twelve GGMs in ruins below—was quickly beginning to slacken. A thousand feet above, Gibbons in *Plague* appeared to be in difficulties; one of the ship's 'Gravs was trailing a fine ribbon of smoke. He had engaged a GGM that was fighting very cleverly—and beginning to get the upper hand. Canby climbed toward the Batik ship immediately and Kellerwand caught it with at least two disruptor blasts near the tail section. Taken by surprise, the GGM's helmsman instinctively reversed direction—thereby placing Gibbons in position to fire again—which he did, scoring another two or three solid hits. Clearly flummoxed, the GGM reversed again, and Kellerwand fired—more hits; another reverse and *Plague* fired. This time, the GGM seemed to hang in the air for a moment, then his fuselage cracked in half. Two or three LifeGlobes popped out of the flames, but one of these was already alight and plummeted to the bay, where it exploded only a few meters from the wreckage of its GGM host.

By now, Confrass had joined up, and Canby checked for damages. Everyone had taken a few hits, but with the exception of *Plague*, no real damage had been done. At this, he gave the order to withdraw—after assurances from Gibbons that *Plague* was indeed capable of making the journey in spite of its damage. One by one, the few GGMs that remained in the sky began to turn back toward Desir-Oming, from which a considerable number of smoke columns rose into the clear, cold air. Below on the surface, the dim little star Iota-73/0185-n would be sliding close to the horizon; already the outlines of the landscape were becoming blurred. Canby re-formed the legionnaires and they accelerated through Light-Speed toward Menphosa with running lights burning, their mission a clear success. Somehow, being a mercenary didn't seem quite so insane as it had at the beginning of the day.

SEPTEMBER 21, 2690, EARTH DATE

Calabria • Khalife

It was the first day of autumn in London and New Washington, but merely one of the three annual—delightful—warm periods in the "southern" hemisphere of Khalife. Outside Corte-Michael, a small tavern in the ancient city of Calabria, Kobir and Émil Lippi sipped sweet Vannal with bitters beneath an umbrella that, earlier in the day, would have shaded them from the rays of Sa'anto. Now, in the late afternoon, their accustomed public house was shaded by intricately carved walls of whitewashed buildings constructed a thousand years before Earth's first interplanetary flights. The street before them was still crowded by a polyglot mixture of shoppers and merchants from all over the galaxy. During the years since Khalife had become his home, Kobir had taken to spending free afternoons here, meeting with one or another of his Kîrskian freebooters in an atmosphere free of occupational stresses. For an inveterate people-watcher like Kobir, it was a restful place for keeping in closer touch between missions. The two men had just ordered a second round of sweet Vannals ("very easy on the bitters") when Dorian Skoda hurried out of the crowd and drew up a chair. "Did you hear about the purge?" he asked.

"Who could miss it?" Lippi countered.

Kobir nodded and smiled; he and Lippi had been discussing the momentous occasion since they had arrived together nearly a local hour ago. "Who could even *believe*?" He chuckled, pressing a small button that ignited the aromatic cavendish leaves in the clay bowl of his long-stemmed pipe. He took a satisfying draft and exhaled luxuriously. Pipes were one luxury that sadly remained behind on space missions.

"Such a purge in the Fleet that destroyed our own?" Skoda whispered, signaling for his own Vannal and shaking his head in obvious consternation.

"Well," Lippi said, wrinkling his nose, "lately they haven't exactly covered themselves in glory. During our last encounter, they acted as if their crews had never been in action before, and since then, they have been incapable of even finding us."

"Indeed," Kobir said, the cavendish deliciously spicy in his nostrils. "Those Tarquins off Omega-932 appeared to be commanded for the most part by raw graduates from the Imperial academies. But such made no sense . . . until now."

"Yes," Lippi agreed, "at least in the light of this David Lotember's apparent agenda."

"I don't understand," Skoda protested. "None of it makes any sense whatsoever to me."

"First, Dorian, ask yourself in *whose* milieu does it make no sense?" Kobir imposed.

"My Kapitan?"

Kobir smiled, sipping Vannal thoughtfully. "One often attempts to make sense of events in terms of one's own system of logic," he explained, "when in reality, those events are solely rational within another's purview." He peered over his glasses. "Only in the harsh light of putting them to practice do events—and the reasoning that caused them—prove to be rational otherwise."

Lippi nodded agreement. "What Nikolai means is that the Imperial purge may not make sense to you or me, but it probably makes *great* sense to someone like David Lotember."

"Lotember . . . " Skoda mused. "Oh, yes, the Imperial Minister of the Admiralty. Can he *be* such a dunce?"

"Depends," Lippi replied, "whether you are judging him as a Politician or a Commander. In the former category, he is a genius."

"But in the latter," Kobir said, pointing at Skoda with the long, curved stem of his pipe, "he may well prove to be an idiot."

"My God," Skoda whispered, his eyes opening wide. "Do you suppose that the poor youngsters commanding those Tarquins might have been selected by Lotember himself?"

Kobir nodded soberly. "When one considers known details of the Imperial purge," he said, "such becomes a *distinct* possibility."

"Think of it this way," Lippi said, lighting a much shorter, squatter pipe made from wood. "Lotember has been a Politician of one sort or another all his life—even during the war. Because of it, he has always lived a life of relative privilege—"

"And earned no grounding in reality at all," Skoda finished for him.

"Exactly," Kobir continued. "And for true Politicians,

nothing worthwhile exists at all unless it has direct ties to power of one sort or another, especially political power—which usually reduces to money."

"So in Lotember's eyes," Skoda said, "the only competent people in the universe are those with ties to wealth or power—or better still, *both*." He frowned. "That explains the strange new Imperial rosters: Admiral, the *Duke* of this, Commander, the *Baroness* of that, Lieutenant, the *Baronet* of something else. I wondered about all that."

"Another trip to your workstation," Lippi declared, "will reveal that all the new officers without an actual title are scions of families with other kinds of power—industry, transport, politics, crime."

Kobir nodded in a cloud of spiced smoke. "If such is true," he said, peering at his pipe, "then it *does* explain those Tarquins off Omega-932, except . . . "

"Except what?"

"Well, when they failed so miserably, why on Earth would this Lotember subject his whole fleet to the same nonsense?"

"My guess," offered Lippi, "is that the man simply blames his crews." He laughed. "You'll notice that only the officers have been purged."

Kobir nodded. "Of course," he exclaimed. "I noticed, but failed to make the connection. Very good, Émil! Clearly, my mind has begun to deteriorate after so many years in deep space."

"Not only yours, my friend," Lippi chuckled, "but mine as well, for I *still* cannot fathom why all these new, highborn officers are mostly children."

"That," Skoda said with a chuckle, "makes sense to me. Wealthy people are usually too busy becoming—or staying—wealthy to be in the military. Only their children can afford such luxury."

"Joking aside," Kobir interjected in a cloud of smoke, "this emphasis on extreme youth is a wrinkle that puzzles me as well. Perhaps it is fortuitous—but we cannot be certain.

Lotember's purge was not accomplished on the spur of the moment; therefore, we shall suspect all such obvious trends."

"For now, however," Skoda said, "one must applaud Minister Lotember's actions, for he appears to have deprived his fleet of the experienced hands that kept it in space."

"Not exactly," Kobir cautioned. "In his fleet as well as in our little squadron, it is still the enlisted crews that *actually* keep the ships in space. Officers may guide them, but even then, ratings set and maintain the machines by which the ships are navigated."

"True, my friend," Lippi agreed. "Only during combat do officers *really* take command of warships."

"Fortunately," Skoda said with a little grin, "during combat is the only time we have much interest in the Imperial Fleet. Is that not so?"

"It is so," Kobir declared soberly. He raised his goblet. "A toast, gentlemen. Let us drink to the health of David Lotember, special benefactor to freebooters."

DECEMBER 2690–JUNE 2691, EARTH DATES

By the XmasTide season, Canby and his legionnaires had earned an excellent reputation for themselves, contesting successfully against an abundance of capable "enemies" and amassing considerable wealth from appreciative patrons—including Nemil Quinn, who not only quietly recommended their services to prospective clients but also made personal contact with Canby from time to time. Granted, they incurred the casualties inevitable with their dangerous vocation—including loss of *Plague* and most of her crew in an ambush by nine marauding starships. But all in all, the surviving legionnaires considered the risks far inferior to their rewards.

Canby himself bestowed much from his first three "draws" on Tenniel, providing sufficient corporate Tribute for her to acquire full-time employment at any number of large enter-

prises. To his immense relief, she accepted gratefully, re-
nouncing her previous calling soon after purchasing a position as Human Resources Director for Interstellar
Amalgamated Reagents, a huge Manhattan-based chemical
firm. However, she warned Canby from the first that no
amount of money would allow her to turn down one of her
old clients—a Noble so powerful he would crush her and her
son if he was refused. By this time, Canby had become suffi-
ciently urbane to accept this fact while refraining from attempts to discover who the Noble was, and their relationship
continued.

For the remainder of the winter, success endured as the legionnaires achieved victory after victory. Each time Canby returned home, he watched Tenniel prospering in her new
occupation. Their romance appeared to prosper as well, at least
in his eyes. They no longer mentioned the mysterious Noble—
and she was only seldom "busy" on evenings when Canby
'Phoned for a visit. Additionally, he found himself becoming
even closer to Damian—who would talk about nothing but
starships, especially after a short ride around a nearby star in
Death. Life was not perfect, Canby reflected one evening as he
traveled to Tenniel's impressive Manhattan apartment. But it
certainly beat anything life had to offer on the Stipend.

By early summer, the legionnaires had purchased three
more DH.98s and lavishly refurbished the three surviving
originals to better-than-new condition, then equipped each
with the latest propulsion systems and beta-torqued disruptors. When the work was finished, their six veteran ships had
few equals anywhere—and wasted no time proving their
worth to the next four clients. Word spread quickly.

Book Seven

TREACHERY

London • Earth

Battersea Manor's Great Concert Hall resounded with tumultuous applause, interspersed with extravagant shouts of "Huzzah!" and "*Bravissimo!*" Naked and drenched in perspiration, Sadir, First Earl of Renaldo, stood center stage, hands raised in acknowledgment amid a flurry of tossed bouquets and flowers. The whore Tenniel still knelt at his feet, wearing only a superb StarBlaze ring he had given her after their last, triumphant dress rehearsal. Behind the Earl, a comely young man—also naked and drenched in sweat—backed away with a spent look on his angelic countenance, while thirteen groups of various composition began to bow as one by one they extricated themselves from remarkable positions they had assumed. Only moments ago, all thirty performers had reached climax at the very same instant, a feat unequaled in the archives of the Tableaux. Some would claim it was a miracle, but Renaldo knew the achievement to be a result of hard, dedicated work; he and the performers had practiced diligently for nearly a year to perfect the performance.

Reveling as much in his triumph as in Tenniel's most recent ministrations, Renaldo bowed as low as his protruding belly would permit, then, with a sweeping gesture, bade his blond costar to stand. Smiling jubilantly, she turned and rose to her feet, lifting her own hands in acknowledgment of the renewed applause. It was a moment of triumph—one that Renaldo knew he would relish for the remainder of his life. No other audience in the galactic civilization could fully appreciate what they had just accomplished.

Later, as three buff-bare "nymphs" gently sponged his great bulk in a perfumed bath, he allowed himself to relax, enjoying the glow of his hard-won victory. Today, he mused, had *nearly* been enough to make him forget the Goddamned pirate Kobir—except lately, nothing had been able to do that. He grimaced at the very thought of the huge Kîrskian. The cheerless fact was that he found himself slowly going insolvent with obligatory payments—to pirates, to projects like today's magnificent Tableau, and to contractors for building the great, domed ballroom and gem house near his newly renovated mansion in Belgravia.

He shivered as one of the nymphs brushed a portion of his body that was still tender from Tenniel's expert-but-prolonged ministrations. Ah, Tenniel. Mere thoughts of the elegant blonde brought a rare smile. There seemed to be nothing she wouldn't do—or try. She even kept a mercenary as a lover—and a famous one at that. He shook his head in wonderment. She'd rather proudly told him about the man herself, but Renaldo had heard of him previously—from Nemil Quinn, of all people. Remembering *that* brought a glower to his face! The upstart Chancellor had boasted, in his—*Renaldo's*—own presence, that this Canby and his followers were the equal of any squadron in the Fleet. He claimed they'd even purchased beta-torqued disruptors recently. . . .

At that very moment, an idea struck like a bolt of lightning. Of course! The fellow Canby. Who better to send against the Kîrskian devils? He sat bolt upright in the tub, accidentally sending one of the nymphs sprawling to the wet, soapy floor. What an opportunity. Why . . . he wouldn't even need to dirty his own hands. Tenniel could handle the whole transaction as intermediary while he needed only to transfer funds. A smile of genuine pleasure formed on his face—the more he thought about it, the more he smiled. Yes! The fellow Canby.

And—as an added bonus—it would provide a well-deserved goad for the idiot Lotember! That turned his smile into a grin. What a *wonderful* way to show his displeasure while ridding himself of the Kîrskian pirates once and for all!

Beaming like a schoolboy, he patted one of the nymphs on her dimpled behind. "My dear," he said, "go fetch the whore Tenniel to me here—immediately."

July 20, 2691, Earth Date

Admiral Phillips Sector, Singapore • Earth

Canby nodded as a waiter poured *precisely* the correct amount of chilled dessert white wine into his goblet. Waiters with perfect demeanor who dressed in nineteenth-century formal gear often put him off; this one was no exception. But then, restaurants that charged as much for a meal as many people got from the Dole in half a year tended to put him off, too—even though now he could afford them easily. Through a great picture window, he watched the sun setting over Singapore Bay to the strains of some half-remembered melody played on a huge, golden harp. Beside him, Tenniel delicately finished a heroic chocolate soufflé the size of an ancient top hat. It was a very different world in which they rendezvoused since she'd gone to work for Interstellar Amalgamated Reagents.

From her earliest assignments, she had risen rapidly in the hierarchy, due in large part to an uncanny ability to pick—and back—eventual winners in the struggles she laughingly referred to as "corporate combat." She'd introduced Canby to some of her new colleagues on their sleek star yachts and in their tony resorts. And while they treated him nicely enough—some even seemed mildly interested in what he did—they clearly preferred bragging among themselves about crushing rivals, coercing more effort from fewer workers, and planning for the next thrust upward on some corporate ladder. For a while, Canby had actually tried to understand these skirmishes, but he never quite got past questions of who actually accomplished any useful work on these corporate jousting grounds. Clearly, it was not the executives whom Tenniel called friend—their only concerns seemed to be garnering and preserving personal power. He glanced at her as she stared out the window, poised and beautiful. "Earth to Tenniel," he said with a little grin.

"Sorry," she said. "Guess I was somewhere else."

"Anywhere I've been?" he asked.

"*Everywhere* you've been," she replied.

"I don't understand," he said.

She stared through the window at the twilight for a moment, then smiled a little wistfully. "I've got a job for you, Gordon," she said.

"You've got a *what*?"

"A job, Gordon," she repeated, "for you and your legionnaires."

"I see," Canby joked with a grin. "So the corporate wars have really turned hot, eh?"

"No," she said with a strange, nervous little laugh. "This

job doesn't have anything to do with Amalgamated Reagents."

Canby frowned. "You're serious, aren't you?" he said.

She nodded.

"Who?" Canby asked.

Pressing the palms of her hands together, she touched her fingertips to her mouth. "Do you have to know?" she asked with an anxious look.

Canby waved off the hovering waiter. "Do we have to know—is that what you just asked?"

She nodded again, avoiding his eyes in a troubling manner.

"Tenniel," Canby protested, "of *course* we have to know who we're working for. For starters, we've got to find out what it is we're being hired to do. And then we have to negotiate a contract. And after that, we've got to set up some way for us to be paid—both *before* and after we do our job." He shrugged. "I mean, how else would we do things?"

To Canby's surprise, Tenniel only pursed her lips and frowned, toying with the last of her soufflé. "How about *this*?" she asked at length. "How about if I tell you what you're being hired to do—and handle all the money transactions as well?"

Canby thought about this for a moment. "Well," he allowed, "I suppose the first part is all right—you can give me mission instructions as well as anybody else. But what about payment?"

"I already said I'd handle the money," Tenniel said. "And you can practically name your price."

"Do you have any idea what we charge?" Canby asked.

Tenniel shook her head. "Just tell me; I'll pass it on."

"We also require half payment up front as a retainer," Canby added.

"I doubt if he'll find that much of a problem," Tenniel assured him. "I'll see you get paid in any form you choose."

Canby nodded. "Yeah," he said, "the retainer part would

be fine. But *after* the mission—when you go to collect the second half of our money—what would you do if this mysterious person decided he didn't want to pay?" He frowned a moment. She didn't much like violence; that was the reason they seldom discussed his new profession. Then he simply gave up. There was no other way. "Look, Cynthia," he explained, "our second client tried that, and we had to blow up his palace piece by piece before he gave in."

Tenniel's eyes widened. "I didn't know that," she said with a pained look. "You had to attack his palace until he paid up?"

"Actually," Canby said, deciding she might as well know the whole thing, "his *successor* ended up paying to save what was left of the palace. We accidentally killed our original client himself when we destroyed the throne room." He laughed. "Had to shoot down half his four-starship space force before we did. Then . . . " He shrugged: it was enough. "That's why we need some sort of . . . well, *hostage,* I suppose. I'm certainly not going to blow up your apartment building if this guy doesn't come through."

"Nice of you," Tenniel said with a theatrical grimace.

Canby shrugged. "Look," he said, "let me put this friend of yours in touch with Warwick Jones, our Paymaster. They can work out the details, and you won't even have to be involved."

Tenniel smiled ironically. "Unfortunately, Gordon," she said, "this *friend,* as you call him, doesn't want to be involved, either. That's why he asked *me* to set things up."

"That Noble you still see?" Canby asked with a twinge of envy. "Who is he, anyway?"

"Gordon—*please,*" she said, looking around the room fearfully. "I wouldn't dare tell you. He wields too much power to defy, believe me."

"Would I know him?" Canby asked.

"You've heard of him," she said.

"Does he live in Manhattan?"

"Gordon!"

"All right," Gordon conceded, "but if I don't know who
the client is, I won't be able to get the legionnaires signed up
to do a job for him. They don't work unless they've got a
good shot at getting *all* the money promised them, and I
won't, either. The job's just too dangerous, Cynthia. We've
lost sixteen people since we started—that's more than half a
crew."

Tenniel nodded and pursed her lips. "Yes," she said at
some length, "I guess I understand that."

"So let's drop the whole thing," Canby said breezily. "Tell
your john we're all tied up with advanced contracts and he'll
have to go find himself another team of mercenaries."

Tenniel gently took his hand. "Thanks, Gordon Canby,"
she whispered, "that's an awfully nice gesture."

"It's not a gesture," Canby said. "We really don't need the
work right now."

Tenniel shook her head. "It's a gesture, Gordon," she said,
"believe me. When this . . . er, john, gives an order, it gets
carried out. Period. He's *big* game."

"Big game, eh?" Canby repeated.

Tenniel nodded. "Big enough that we'd better try to work
something out. Otherwise . . . well, neither of us needs that
kind of trouble."

Canby was about to remonstrate when she raised her hand.
"Wait a minute," she said, staring off into an idea. "How
about if this person gave *me* the second half to put in some
sort of an escrow account for safekeeping?"

"At a bank, you mean?"

"Yes," she said. "Then you'd *both* have some protection.
And I could give you a copy of the deposit certificate to
show your legionnaires—along with a cash retainer. Would
that work?"

Canby thought for a moment. "Yeah," he said at length. "I
think it would."

"All right, then," she said, "will you have *time* to do a job?"

"Depends on the job—and of course the price your john's willing to pay," Canby said.

Tenniel smiled. "I said you can probably name your price." She laughed. "As long as it's *somewhere* within reason."

"And the job?"

"I don't know much about it," Tenniel said. "It has something to do with wiping out a band of pirates. Those Kîrskians you keep hearing about, I think. The man said that was all you needed to know up front."

Canby nodded. "He's right," he said. "It'll be an extra tough job, and it's going to cost."

"Funny," Tenniel said, "that's pretty much what he guessed your reaction would be. He said to tell you he'll pay top credits for the kind of work you do."

Canby felt his eyebrows rise. "All right," he said, making up his mind, "here's our price. . . ."

AUGUST 20, 2691, EARTH DATE

Columbia Sector, New Washington • Earth

Fierce summer sun beat down on Renaldo's bare head like beamed fire while Columbia's dreaded heat and humidity threatened to overwhelm the high-powered air conditioner in his custom-made Admiralty Cape. An atmospheric low— with its associated warm front—had stalled over the village of Mercersburg, some one hundred twenty kilometers to the north, and the resulting atmosphere for this year's Fleet review was best described as appalling.

Renaldo ground his teeth—at least the ordeal was nearly over. No more than a hundred yards to his left, the final marching band approached. *Thumpa, thumpa, thumpa.* He rolled his eyes to the glaring heavens—only one more braying—*blaring*—cacophonic nightmare from the long-dead (and deservedly so) J. P. Sousa to endure, then closing ceremonies and many cool drinks before a boring, but bearable, reception and a state banquet. He glanced to his left where the nincompoop Lotember saluted and waved to marching ranks of starsailors as if he actually knew something about running a space fleet.

Renaldo laughed to himself. At least the nitwit *did* understand politics; he was *wonderful* at that. Unfortunately, he also occupied one of the few offices that required results, not the normal Politician's output of hedged promises and balderdash. That thought brought a surly smile to the Earl's face. Today, at some appropriate moment of his, Renaldo's, own choosing, he had a surprise for the overweening dimbulb.

Much later, following cessation of the receiving line, where he held the honored position, the Earl circulated among a hodgepodge of officers from Lotember's new Fleet (they looked like a bloody *kindergarten!*) as well as the customary military harlots: Politicians, weapons makers, starship builders, contractors, lobbyists, consultants, and other military/industrial residue without whom no high-level soldierly function would be complete. He loved these moments, airily passing out indulgences (and receiving benevolences) like a God—which, in all fairness, he actually considered himself to be, so far as these craven lackeys were concerned.

Afterward, some hundred of the top movers and shakers in the Empire's military peerage retired to the ancient White House, where Lotember hosted a lavish, private banquet that spanned a full thirty-one separate courses. Then many of the guests retired to the historic Oval Office for brandy and tobacco. By this time most of them were well in their cups, including Renaldo, who was also logy and out of sorts from stuffing himself, although he'd visited the lavatory a number of times during the banquet to vomit. Dressed in his navy blue First Patron of the Fleet uniform, complete with gold epaulettes, sword, and cocaded tricorn hat, he had just accepted another brandy from a formally dressed waiter and was busily fingering the plump bottom of a well-endowed, giggling Admiral when Lotember appeared at his side, drink in hand. "Well, my lord," the Minister said in an expansive tone, "it has been a *fine* day, in my perception."

Renaldo peered at Lotember from the corner of his eye with a certain grudging respect—the man simply *ought* to be drunk, yet he appeared to be completely in charge of his faculties. A consummate Politician if ever there was one. "Later," he whispered to the Admiral, who giggled off into the crowd, adjusting her skirt. Then he turned to skewer the Minister with an ill-tempered scowl. "Perhaps it has been a fine day for *you,* Lotember," he growled, "but for me, it has been nothing but business as usual."

"My lord," Lotember said in surprise. "I don't understand."

"Seems there's a lot you don't understand," Renaldo said, "such as capturing pirates and the like—or did I miss seeing a number of Kîrskians swinging in gibbets somewhere outside?"

Lotember's facade appeared to droop a little, but he continued with his oily smile. "Ah, never fear, my lord," he said as if Renaldo had spoken words of praise instead of sarcasm, "I shall soon have that little problem cleared up. My newly purged and reorganized Fleet will soon lift on a mission to—"

"*Little problem?*" Renaldo exploded. "Jesus, Mary, and Joseph, man, those Kîrskians have been jacking us around for years now, and you call them *little*? Where's your fucking head?"

"But they *are* a small problem now," Lotember continued in his smooth-as-silk voice. "As soon as the Fleet—"

"I can't wait for your silly-assed Fleet anymore," Renaldo

snarled. "I want something done *now,* so I've hired a band of mercenaries to do the job."

Abruptly, Lotember's facade collapsed. "M-mercenaries?" he asked, looking as if he'd just been hit by a brick.

"You're Goddamn right, Lotember." Renaldo smirked, enjoying himself immensely—feelings of power like this heightened his pleasure in everything. He waited eagerly for the man's next helpless bleat.

Instead—to his utter astonishment—Lotember's eyes narrowed and he squared his shoulders. "That, my lord," he said quietly, "will be a serious mistake."

Thunderstruck, Renaldo felt his blood pressure skyrocket. He looked wildly around the noisy room—no one seemed to be listening in. "How *dare* you even imply I am mistaken?" he demanded under suddenly heaving breath.

"Because, my lord," Lotember said in apparent serenity, "you *are* mistaken."

Renaldo ground his teeth while he wrestled his runaway ire to a wary armistice. The slimy, lickspittle Politician was actually getting the best of him—but not for long. He knew from years of experience that the greasy little bastard would eventually hang himself if he was given enough rope. "Tell me about it," he said through closed jaws. "Tell me all about my mistake."

Lotember opened his hands. "If you insist, my lord," he said, as if it pained him to even *think* of such a thing.

"I . . . fucking . . . insist—"

Lotember bowed. "My lord," he said in his most mellifluous tone, "your mistake is one of omission."

"Well?"

"You have, my lord, failed to take into consideration your exalted position as First Patron of the Admiralty. Because of it, the good name of Renaldo is now closely bound to the reputation of the Fleet—*your* Fleet, my lord, as well as mine." He raised his eyebrows theatrically. "Should you denigrate its good name in favor of a mere band of mercenaries, think how you will *concurrently* harm your own reputation."

Renaldo scowled as the Minister's words hit home. He bit his lip. In his desperation to rid himself of the infernal Kîrskian pirate, he had begun to neglect details—*important* details. In the corner of his eye, he caught the approach of a powerful—and presently hungry—Managing Director of a large starship building yard. He grimaced. Clearly, the woman wanted to talk—and with the kind of money she controlled, not even God could deny her. "You have a point, Lotember," he whispered. "Tomorrow we will discuss this further. I shall summon you in the morning."

August 21, 2691, Earth Date

ArlingtonVa Sector, New Washington • Earth

David Lotember found himself rousted to the side of his great, canopied bed at the ungodly hour of five o'clock A.M. At first, he was simply bewildered. Why? He *never* rose before nine-thirty, and most mornings he slept till eleven. Then, quickly, he was angry. "Who *dares* disturb my rest at this hour?" he growled at an orderly cowering near the doorway.

"Sadir, F-first Earl of R-renaldo, Minister," the orderly stuttered. "He requests your presence at the hotel at six o'clock."

Lotember closed his eyes again and shook his head, recalling the fat Noble's words from the night before. But at six A.M.? Beside him, a skinny, long-haired redhead he'd picked up on the way home sat up and rubbed her eyes uncertainly. Meager breasts and prominent ribs held little fascination for him this morning, and he pushed her roughly onto the floor with his foot. "Get out of here," he ordered. "Someone downstairs will feed you and give you some money." He wrinkled his nose in the wake of cheap perfume she trailed while she wordlessly retrieved her clothes, then scurried off like an emaciated rodent. "Why this early?" he demanded. "Nobles with Renaldo's power don't get up at dawn."

"I don't know, Minister," the orderly said. "I didn't take the call."

Lotember snapped his fingers. Of course. Renaldo's home was in a time zone six hours later than ECONUS. In London—as registered by the Earl's biological clock—it would be just after eleven A.M. That explained it. "Send a servant to dress me—and be quick about it!" he ordered. "I have less than an hour to make my appointment."

At precisely 5:58 A.M., the Minister arrived at Renaldo's suite atop the staid old Washington Hotel on historic Pennsylvania Avenue. He was immediately shown to a huge, marble-and-mirror lavatory where the Earl—still in rumpled, silken nightclothes—squatted regally on a great porcelain flush toilet that was elaborately ornamented with baroque bas-reliefs of cherubs and mythological gods.

Disgusted beyond belief, Lotember initially attempted to hold his breath, but soon abandoned that idea and settled for surreptitiously breathing through his mouth. "My lord," he said, desperately attempting to keep his hurried breakfast where it was.

Renaldo looked up sullenly; his face reddened momentarily, and he seemed to strain, then he indicated a chair placed on the tile floor directly before him. "Sit down, Lotember," he said, reaching behind himself to flush the toilet.

Grinding his teeth, Lotember sat, trying desperately to keep his eyes from the great, hairy roll of dead-white fat that emerged from under the Earl's nightshirt and bulged over the front of the toilet. He was actually feeling faint.

"I have been considering what you said yesterday," Renaldo grunted over the muffled sound of rushing water, "about the reputation of the Fleet."

Despite the nausea he felt, Lotember forced himself to nod with an expression of cheerful interest. If nothing else, the interest was genuine. "My lord?" he prompted.

"I still don't trust . . . your . . . Goddamned Fleet," Renaldo said, straining again.

"But, my lord," Lotember cried. "I have only just completed the most extensive reengineering of the Officer Corps in Fleet history. Why I have gone so far as to—"

"From what I can see," Renaldo interrupted, "all you've done is beggar all the officers with even an ounce of experience, then put a pack of children in their places."

"My lord," Lotember protested, "the *children* you denigrate are the scions of the Empire's greatest, most powerful families—the very cream of the crop. No brighter, more idea-filled group of leaders exists in civilization anywhere."

Renaldo strained for a *long* time before he reached behind him to flush. "Perhaps, Lotember," he said, his face still crimson, "and perhaps not."

Lotember's spirits dropped like a rock. Last night, he'd thought he had the problem resolved. Now . . . "My *lord,* surely not the mercenaries!" he protested. "What of your reputation?"

"Oh, shut up," Renaldo grumbled. "For the sake of my own reputation, I shall let you send your flying kindergarten after the pirates," he said. "But since I am still extremely interested in ridding space of the Kîrskian pirates, I am *also* sending the mercenaries."

Lotember felt himself stiffen as the Earl resumed his red-faced straining. "But my lord," he remonstrated, "what if the mercenaries get to the pirates first?"

"Forget the word *if,*" Lotember said over still another surge of gushing water. "The Fleet will make *no* attack on the Kîrskians. Its only job will be to *stealthily* track the mercenaries until after *they* attack the pirates.

"B-but . . . " Lotember began.

"Lotember," Renaldo said, fixing the Minister with a malignant glare, "instead of an affront, consider those mercenaries to be free insurance on your worthless balls. I want those pirates out of the way, and another failure on the part of *your* Fleet will cost you dearly. You know what 'the Dole' means, don't you?"

Lotember nodded. "W-what if the mercenaries f-fail?" he asked wretchedly.

"Should the mercenaries fail—which in light of their reputation seems improbable—then your vaunted fleet has my permission to attack the pirates, too," Renaldo answered with a sarcastic chuckle.

"A-and if they are successful?"

"Which they most assuredly *will* be," Renaldo finished for him, "then I have another, *more important* task for you and your Fleet. One that will enhance their reputation as well as mine—if you can manage to bring it off."

Frowning at this unexpected turn of events. Lotember forgot for a moment to breathe through his mouth. He corrected immediately. "Er . . . what is it you want us to do?" he asked, forcing his gorge back where it belonged.

Renaldo smiled. "I have little doubt that after their battle with the pirates, my mercenaries will be greatly weakened," he said. "It will *then* be the job of your squadron—that has until now only tracked the mercenaries—to attack and destroy *them*."

Lotember needed a few moments before *this* information sank in. "Destroy the mercenaries?" he asked in disbelief. "B-but *why*?"

"Well," Renaldo said, straining once more until his face was red, "for one thing, to save me from paying what I will owe them by that time."

That sort of reasoning Lotember recognized at once. "E-excellent plan, my lord," he mumbled as Renaldo reached behind him to flush again.

"Couldn't hear you," Renaldo said.

"Excellent plan, my lord," Lotember repeated, "except for one thing," he added, heart in his mouth.

Renaldo looked up with a frown. "Except for *what?*" he demanded.

"Well," Lotember said, "I assume the mercenaries you hired operate within Imperial laws."

"Of course," Renaldo assured him.

"Then," Lotember asked with a shrug, "on what grounds will our Fleet attack them?"

Renaldo laughed derisively. "Lotember," he brayed, "certainly you have more faith in my abilities than to imagine I would overlook something like a legal pretext."

Lotember grimaced. "Of course not, my lord," he said. "I was only, er, checking on your, er . . . safety. B-but—"

"You would like to know the pretext, Lotember?" Renaldo asked overweeningly.

"If you please," the Minister said, grinding his teeth—how he *hated* the fat, sickening bastard!

Renaldo laughed. "You have heard of beta-torqued disruptors, of course?" he asked.

"Of course," Lotember replied with a shudder. "*They* have such equipment?"

"So I understand," Renaldo assured him.

"How did they come by it?" Lotember asked breathlessly.

"Who cares?" Renaldo said. "The important thing is that they *do*—and are therefore illegal under Imperial law. Your people will have every right in the galaxy to attack them—when the proper time comes." Suddenly he fixed Lotember with a malignant glance. "But *not* until the proper time. Understand?"

Lotember gulped in spite of himself. "I understand," Lotember said.

"Understand *what?*"

"Er . . . t-the proper time, my lord."

"And what *is* the proper time, Lotember?"

"Only when the mercenaries and pirates have ceased to fight, my lord."

Renaldo nodded, shifting his great bulk on the toilet seat. "Excellent," he grunted, reaching for a chocolate from a lace-festooned box on the sink beside him. "Now," he said, biting into the gooey confection, "before I dismiss you, what can I provide that will more fully assure the success of your mission?"

At first, Lotember was tempted to simply thank the Earl and run as fast as he could for the nearest fresh air. Then the Politician in him took charge and he thought better of it. He could only profit from remaining a few more minutes, especially if he did come up with something that enhanced the chances of his new Officer Corps. As he watched the Earl stuff chocolates in one end, then strain and flush at the other—simultaneously—he considered distractedly that perhaps the two orifices might be directly connected, with no digestion process in the middle. Then decided immediately that *something* had to account for the great rolls of fat from which Renaldo seemed to be entirely constructed. He concentrated on the job at hand— where was the Fleet most at risk? Well, they *were* admittedly weak at gunnery, but that weakness could be passably countered simply by sending a *lot* of disruptors, and the Earl had already given orders that the squadron be a large one. He forced himself to think farther afield. Could someone perhaps sabotage the mercenary's ships or poison the mercenaries themselves before they started fighting? Not very likely in the first place; besides, they—and their ships—had to be healthy enough to take on the pirates first.

Think, Lotember! Where was the Fleet most likely to slip up? Helmsmanship? Tactics? Navigation? *Navigation!* Of course—he should have thought of that first! The *real* trick would be to successfully shadow the mercenaries until the time came to attack, a task requiring much finesse. It was a property seldom required of civilization's largest Fleet, which was more at home smashing what little opposition it encountered by unadulterated weight of arms. Pursing his lips, Lotember attempted to fathom what kind of help Renaldo could come up with for *this* sort of demand. From the corner of his eye, he watched the corpulent scoundrel stuff *two* of the huge bonbons into his maw. Lotember ground his teeth. He simply couldn't—and *wouldn't*—remain in this nauseating hell much longer. He was just about to get to his feet when it came to him. "My lord," he said, "there *is* one small assistance you might render."

Renaldo flushed, then nodded. "Yes?" he asked sagaciously.

"The mercenaries' operational plan," Lotember explained. "Were there some way my commanders might obtain information concerning strategy, possible course plots, and the like, we would have a *much* better likelihood of obtaining our objective."

Renaldo frowned. "The mercenaries' *operational* plan?" he asked in amazement. "Do you have any idea what you are asking for?" He shook his head in clear rejection. "Of course you don't," he said, answering his own question. "You don't have a clue about anything except politics." Suddenly he brightened. "But you would understand *this*. How well do you protect the tactics you plan to use against opponents before election time?"

Lotember grimaced and looked Renaldo in the eye. "With my life," he admitted.

"Well," Renaldo said, "then you understand what sort of activity would be necessary to pry such information out of a fully armed mercenary organization." He laughed. "Why, it would take . . . " He paused a moment, one obese finger to the stubble on his chin. "Yes," he said. "A lover—a certain type of lover—might just turn the trick, so to speak." Smiling at what seemed to be some sort of personal joke, he turned to Lotember. "Just how important would this information actually be?" he asked. "Would it be *critical* to your success?"

Lotember considered only a moment. "It might well be critical, my lord," he said.

"Critical enough to put me deeply into someone's debt?"

"That would be my lord's decision entirely," Lotember hedged. "However, should you *genuinely* wish to ensure the success of our mission, such a debt might be of great benefit in the long run."

Renaldo nodded. "Then perhaps . . . just perhaps, Lotember," he said, "I may be able to fulfill your wish."

SEPTEMBER 6, 2691, EARTH DATE

Perrin Station • Earth

"All right, that takes care of crew rosters for the mission," Canby said, scrolling his notebook to the next item on the agenda. "What's the word on our decoy ship?"

At the end of the table, Steve Long, mission coordinator in charge of vehicles checked his own notebook. "Lela Peterson's just reported in from the asteroid camp," he said, looking up. "Claims the whole crew might die from boredom before they get the old rustbucket ready to go. Otherwise, things are going well. She's ready with the bridge armor and will install it when she gets the word."

"No problems, eh?"

"We picked out a good ship," Long said. "But those old ED-3 transports were all built to last. She'll do the job and then some."

"Good," Canby said, glancing at the other ten members of the Operations Committee for Mission X, as everybody called the operation. "Any showstoppers before Lela installs that expensive armor? How about the finances, Warwick?" he asked.

"Your friend Cynthia Tenniel transferred every credit of

the retainer to our account this morning," Chief Jones said, "and I checked with the bank for the remainder. It's in a joint account I share with Ms. Tenniel and an unnamed copartner."

"Sounds good to me," Canby said. "Chief Harper, what about the new electronics?"

"The DH.98s are all ready to go," Harper said, with the nearsighted look of a man who had been peering at tiny items most of his life.

"How about the new extended-range proximity detectors we picked up on Rayno Talphor last week?" Canby asked. "They installed?"

Harper nodded. "They are," he said with a frown. "We don't have them fully adjusted yet. But from the initial tests, those 2HD/19s ought to make it a *lot* easier for us to spot the Kîrskians before they spot us. Maybe even while they're still shadowing the decoy."

Canby nodded. "Thanks, Don," he said, turning to the other side of the table. "How about you guys from Intelligence?"

"We're ready to release the cover story soon as this meeting's over," Sam Young, the Legion's Intelligence Officer, reported. He smiled for a moment with a look of someone who enjoys the rare professional surprise. "Just for the record," he added, "our little scam has more than just the ring of truth to it. When we got to digging into things, we found there actually *was* a big collection of StarBlazes lost during the war. Belonged to some wealthy Kîrskian named Ambronovsky, and reputed to be *quite* the treasure. Its principal stone—set into some sort of scepter—was the second largest ever found. The biggest one is called the Giulio Cesare, or something like that. One of our Nobles, the fat guy who's now Fleet Patron, just bought it—right under the nose of the Emperor, who also wanted it pretty badly."

Canby grinned; jewels were things *other* people wore.

"The Ambronovsky Collection, eh? Well, if it helps the mission, I'm all for it."

"Ought to," Young said. "I can't imagine a bunch of Kîrskian pirates who wouldn't damn near kill themselves to get even part of something like that. If it really existed, it would be easily worth a couple of planets."

"All right, people, anything else?" Canby asked. "Looks like we're GO status, then—for both the armor and the fake media release. We'll leak details of the ED-3s' route on September 15, then start the ship herself toward Earth a couple of days later. With any sort of luck, it'll draw the Kîrskians right away. Afterward, all we've got to do is put 'em out of business and collect the rest of our money. Doesn't get much simpler than that, does it?" He laughed grimly. "Wish it were as *easy* as that."

SEPTEMBER 10, 2691, EARTH DATE

Gould's Rainbow Grand • Rainbow Swarm

Gould's Rainbow Grand was arguably the most opulent—assuredly the most *expensive*—casino in the galaxy. Located nearly eight hundred parsecs from Earth in the midst of the Rainbow Swarm (a spectacular kaleidoscope of multicolored planetary rubble illuminated by swirling reefs of bright, variegated protostars) the Grand was a principal watering spot for kings, potentates, royalty, and the most privileged of the super-rich.

Beneath the colossal transparent dome of the Rainbow dining pavilion, a toga-clad Renaldo inhaled spice-scented fragrance and gazed with satisfaction across his table at the lovely whore Tenniel. Dressed tonight in a tight silken gown of deep blue accented by a single diamond brooch, she contended well with the slowly swirling kaleidoscope in space behind her.

And—as he had planned—she clearly felt obliged to be here with him. No sooner had they been shown their suite of rooms than she'd entertained him with a spectacular display of her appreciation, even while the titillated servants were still unpacking their luggage. He'd almost asked her then. . . .

Now, at the close of an elaborate supper, she was relaxed in her chair, sipping fine brandy from a huge crystal goblet and staring at the kaleidoscope outside. Wherever she might look, the galaxy's most powerful citizens were dining and otherwise entertaining themselves in the same ornate splendor as herself. The ambience itself could make a poor lower-class whore beholden to her sponsor—and that, precisely, was why he had brought her. "A credit for your thoughts," he said agreeably.

"Why, Renaldo," she exclaimed, smiling through a sham expression of surprise, "only a credit here at the Grand? Certainly, one would expect to be offered *millions*."

Renaldo smiled to himself. "Indeed I would, my dear," he said, "had I that kind of wealth to dispense. But alas, I am only a poor Earl and can pay no more than a single credit."

"Perhaps for my *thoughts*, Renaldo," she said, sipping her brandy through a little smile. "But how much would you offer for something more tangible?"

Renaldo widened his eyes theatrically. "That depends," he said, inwardly amused.

"On what?"

"On what that *something* might be, of course," he answered.

"Oh, and must it be tangible?" she asked, cocking her head to one side. Her soft blond hair followed in a golden billow.

"Well . . . " Renaldo hedged, "*possibly* not."

"Renaldo," she demanded with a little smile, "just what is it you want? I can't imagine it has much to do with the kind of services you usually summon me for."

Renaldo smiled and peered meaningfully through the crystal table at her primly crossed legs. "Mmm," he mused, "maybe yes and maybe no."

She took his hint, peered around the room for a moment, then moved slightly, causing the long gown to fall open and expose her slender legs nearly to the thigh. In the dimly lighted room they looked stunningly white. "Is this what you had in mind?" she asked, looking up with a little grin.

"Well, of course." Renaldo laughed. "But not entirely."

She nodded. "Then I can finish my brandy before we go back to the suite?" she asked.

Renaldo laughed in appreciation. "Finish all the brandies you like, my dear," he said. "For the nonce, I am quite satisfied ogling your magnificent legs. What *also* interests me, however, is talking about this mercenary of yours. Canby, is his name?"

At the mention of the man's name, a frown came over Tenniel's face. "Yes," she said warily. "Gordon Canby . . . Is something wrong with the job you've contracted with him?"

Renaldo shook his head. "First things first, my dear," he said, looking pointedly through the table again.

Tenniel slid the gown higher. "What about Gord . . . er, Canby?" she asked.

"Pull the skirt higher like a good girl," he said petulantly. "Then we shall talk."

Taking a deep breath, Tenniel deftly moved to the edge of her chair and adjusted the skirt so he could see she wore no undergarments.

"That's better," he said, licking his lips. God, she was a good-looking woman—he liked to show her off. "Now, this Canby of yours," he said, "let us talk about him."

She nodded—with clear reluctance.

"Do you love him?" he asked.

"I don't know what you mean," she said in a low voice.

"Love," Renaldo repeated, "as in 'beloved,' one supposes. . . . Do you love this man?" He opened his hands. "It has nothing to do with *us,* of course. I love no one—only fucking, which you do magnificently."

The woman seemed nonplussed at the question—as if she had never considered it before. "I don't know," she said, looking off into the scintillating colors whirling outside the casino. Finally she returned her gaze to Renaldo. "I suppose I do love him," she said at length. "Certainly more than I've loved anyone else. Why?"

"No particular reason," Renaldo replied airily.

Tenniel smiled. "My dear Renaldo," she whispered across the table. "You *never* ask anything without *some* reason."

"True," he admitted grudgingly—the woman had indeed gotten to know him.

"Then why do you want to know about him?" Tenniel persisted.

"Not specifically about *him,*" Renaldo said, taking the plunge. "It's his plan that interests me."

"Plan?"

"Yes, my dear. One assumes he has a plan for carrying out the contract he has with me."

Tenniel set her brandy down carefully. "I don't really know," she said, staring into his eyes with a look of wary interest. "We hardly ever discuss his business."

Renaldo laughed. "I'll bet I know what you *do* discuss," he said.

Tenniel ignored him pointedly—he let it go.

"You mean you don't discuss what he does?" Renaldo asked in the uncomfortable silence that followed. "Everybody does that."

"We don't," Tenniel replied. "And I'm getting a little uncomfortable sitting in this position."

Renaldo felt his eyebrows raise. The whore was certainly presumptuous today. He thought about slapping her, but she *did* have something he wanted. He took a final gaze, then nodded. "You may sit back, then," he said grumpily.

"Thank you," she said stiffly, sliding back onto the cushion—and covering her legs to the ankles.

Renaldo ground his teeth. The bitch! "So you and this Canby don't talk about business, eh?" he demanded.

"Not about his business as a mercenary," she said. "I can't stand all that killing and violence."

Renaldo felt his stomach squirm; neither could he—especially when it might become focused on himself! He swallowed a lump that had just materialized in his throat. "I'll bet you'd talk to him about his business *for a price,*" he said, his voice lowered to a gentle whisper.

Tenniel narrowed her eyes. "Just what do you have in mind, Sadir?" she demanded quietly.

Renaldo blanched—whores were permitted to use his surname *only* when they were actively servicing his needs—which she definitely was not accomplishing at the time. Glaring, he opened his mouth to remonstrate . . . only to shut it again a moment later. He needed what *only* she could give him. Unfortunately, from the look in her eyes, it was clear that she'd used his name as her own test—and now knew that she had some control over the situation. "Er," he stumbled, now on *very* unfamiliar ground, "what I mean is—"

"You want something from me, don't you, Renaldo?" she asked, a hard smile forming on her lips. "Something only I can provide. Right?"

Renaldo ground his teeth. So many things these days seemed to be running out of his control: Kobir, the Fleet, and now this . . . *magnificent* . . . whore. "Perhaps," he equivocated—to no apparent avail.

"What is it you want, aside from a good fucking tonight?" she demanded with a little grin of triumph—the same little grin she always got when she brought him to fulfillment.

"This Canby," Renaldo began, suddenly at a loss for words, "I need to know his plans for performing the services I contracted."

The woman's brow wrinkled. "Canby's plan?" she asked. "You mean his operational plan?"

"Y-yes. His operational plan," Renaldo stuttered.

"Why?" she asked coldly.

"I c-can't tell you," Renaldo said, his mind whirling. "I just need it."

"*You* need it?" she asked in a sarcastic tone. "What would *you* do with an operational plan?"

"Silence, woman!" Renaldo screeched in spite of himself, then shut his eyes. "Does it matter?"

Tenniel smiled. "Depends," she said, leaning forward in her chair with that *horrible* little smile again.

"On what?" Renaldo asked.

"On how much you are willing to pay," Tenniel answered. "And let me warn you, my corpulent friend, for information about *this* man, the price will be high."

Renaldo felt a thrill of relief flood through him. Tenniel was a true whore, after all. He smiled, too spent for haggling. "A Directorship," he panted, "on the board of Amalgamated Reagents. It's my best offer; take it or leave it."

"A *Directorship*?" she demanded.

"In Amalgamated Reagents," he answered. "I own most of it."

She looked at him for a long moment, then smiled and allowed her skirt to fall open again. "Renaldo," she said, "you have yourself a deal."

SEPTEMBER 15, 2691, EARTH DATE

Manhattan Sector, New Washington • Earth

For Canby, mid-September was perhaps the most beautiful time of the year in Battery Park. Summer's heat—if not the humidity—had departed for another year, and the days seemed just right, both in length and in comfort, for bolstering the human mechanism. Today, he sat on a bench with his arm around Tenniel, watching Damian happily playing in a small, noisy crowd of boys and girls.

"He might *live* uptown," Tenniel said, with a shrug, "but his real friends are still here in Battery Park."

"*Are* there any kids in those uptown palaces where you live?" Canby asked, half in jest.

Tenniel nodded. "Yes," she said, "a few. And he *does* play with them sometimes. He just seems happier with the children down here. Look at them," she said, pointing to the children who were now playing follow-the-leader along a narrow curb, "they don't have any toys, yet they seem to be having all sorts of fun without them." She shrugged. "Damian's got a whole room full of the expensive playthings I was never able to buy for him before, but when we come down here, he won't bring any. Says they get in the way."

"I suppose his friends uptown have a lot of toys, too," Canby commented.

"My God, yes," Tenniel said. "Some of them have even *more* than Damian."

Canby shrugged. "Maybe pretend toys are more fun— after all, at any given time, they're *exactly* what's needed." He laughed. "See that kid with the stick, there. Right now, I think it's probably a laser rifle, but it could instantly become a thirteenth-century blunderbuss—or even a disruptor. Try to find something that'll do *that* in your uptown toy stores."

Tenniel looked at him in a peculiar way, then shook her head—almost sadly.

"That's a strange look," Canby said. "Something on your mind?"

"Yes," she said, looking him directly in the eye as if she were seeing him for the first time. She frowned. "I've never met anybody like you, Gordon," she said, shaking her head. "You're different. It's probably why I love you—but why do *you* love me?"

Canby felt his eyebrows raise. "I just *do,* that's all," he said. "Isn't that what love's all about?"

Tenniel nodded sadly. "I suppose you're right, Gordon," she said, "at least that's the way things should be."

"They're not?" Canby asked.

"Maybe in a perfect world," Tenniel said, then shut her eyes and shook her head slowly. "Unfortunately," she added, "this one isn't it."

"Maybe we can make this one perfect," Canby said, pulling her closer.

She turned and looked into his eyes soberly. "I'm not counting on it," she said.

"Hey," Canby complained. "This is supposed to be a *happy* afternoon. Why all the gloom and doom?"

Tenniel took a deep breath. "You're right again, Gordon," she said, looking out over the East River. "Let's talk about something else . . . something interesting." She pursed her lips for a few moments, then smiled. "I know—tell me how you're going to catch those pirates."

"What?" Canby asked in surprise.

"Tell me how you'll catch those pirates," she said. "I think that would be interesting."

Canby smiled and raised his eyebrows. "*You,* who never discusses violence, want to know how I'm going to get rid of a bunch of pirates? I don't believe it."

Tenniel smiled. "Well," she said, "it *is* about time I got some understanding of what you do. I mean, we are pretty friendly these days."

Canby frowned. "Yeah," he allowed, "we are *that.* But . . . " he hesitated, fumbling for the proper words, "well, ops plans are sort of secret. Only those legionnaires who are directly involved in the mission know anything about the projected operations, and *they* have access to no more than their *particular* activities. Maybe six of us know the whole plan, but that's all."

Tenniel raised an eyebrow. "Sounds as if you don't trust me, Gordon," she said.

"Of course I trust you," Canby said, somehow disturbed by this unexpected tack. "It's just that . . . "

"It's just *what*?" she demanded. "What could there be about your mission you can't tell me, for pity's sake? Who would I go tell about it in the first place—Damian?"

"Well," Canby said, feeling *really* uncomfortable now, "there *is* that client of yours."

Tenniel laughed. "Nonsense," she said. "Why would I tell him anything? Besides, even if I did, what do you think *he* would do with it, spread the word so your mission fails? That's patently ridiculous."

By this time, Canby was genuinely troubled. "Tenniel," he protested, "I've given my word. I can't just, well . . . you know."

"No, Gordon Canby, I do *not* know," she said, pulling away from his arm. "If I'm no more special to you than that, then maybe I'm not special enough to sleep with, either. You know, for a while there I *thought* you were pretty much in love with me."

"I *am*," Canby protested. "Lord knows I am. It's just that . . . " He shook his head. "You *really* want to know, don't you?"

"Yes," she said, "*now* I really do. There for a long time, I thought I was pretty special to you."

"You are," Canby assured her.

"Then prove it," she said. "Show me that you trust me."

Canby nodded. "All right," he said reluctantly. "The plan's simplicity itself. About two weeks ago, we started this false rumor about discovery of a missing StarBlaze collection. . . . "

SEPTEMBER 16, 2691, EARTH DATE

Columbia Sector, New Washington • Earth

The following afternoon Lotember was napping on the couch in his office—as he was wont to do after a large lunch with a bottle of fine wine—when chimes from the Holo-Phone intercom woke him. "Goddamn you, Tolton," he bellowed, eyes still closed. "You know better than to—" His tongue felt as if it had grown a shaggy coat of hair, and his head ached unmercifully. Why hadn't she stopped him? "Goddamn you!" he howled again, opening his eyes to the darkened office. It didn't do any good—and Tolton didn't answer. She'd been getting uppity, lately; requiring him to calm down before she answered. Cheap bitch! But what if it was Renaldo who was waiting for him—or somebody else important? Sliding his feet sideways to the floor, he sat up, carefully, holding on to the couch as the room began to spin. "Tolton, you Goddamn whore-bitch," he roared, "I'll have your head for waking me. Now Goddammit, what do you want?"

Still nothing from Tolton.

Lotember stumbled to the HoloPhone, switched off the video, and mashed RCV. "All right, what?" he demanded in as civil a tone as he could muster.

"A special messenger from the Earl of Renaldo, Minister," Tolton said calmly as if he had answered the 'Phone at once.

Lotember frowned. "What does he have?" he demanded.

"*She* won't say, Minister," Tolton replied. "It's in some sort of sealed pouch chained to her arm, and she says she won't give it to anyone but you, Minister."

"Does it look like a bomb?" Lotember asked.

"It looks like an envelope, Minister."

"Well . . . send her in," Lotember relented, returning the office lights to their normal brilliance.

Moments later, a svelte woman dressed in a business suit entered his office. "Minister Lotember?" she asked.

"Well, who else?" Lotember demanded, regarding her large breasts and long legs with interest.

She held out an attractive needlework purse that was unobtrusively chained to a silver wrist bracelet. "Please press your right thumb in the center of the embroidered flower, Minister, and hold it there," she said.

Lotember did as she directed. After a few moments, the flower grew warm, then the chain fell loose and one end of the purse opened. "Any words from Renaldo?" he asked.

The woman nodded. "He said, 'Enjoy,' Minister."

"That's all?"

"That is all, Minister."

Lotember shrugged. "All right," he said, unblushingly ogling the woman's breasts. "You may take off your clothes now."

She laughed and started for the door. "In that case, there *are* other words Renaldo asked me to relate," she said.

"And?" Lotember demanded, reaching for her arm.

"He also directed you to keep your hands off me and, as he put it, 'Get busy with the envelope, dimbulb.' "

Lotember stopped in midstride with a surge of anger that turned to instant fear. Without a doubt, those *were* words from Renaldo. He gulped. Probably one of his own women. "Er . . . my best to the Earl," he said as the door closed in his face. He ground his teeth while laughter erupted on the other side. Well, he might not be able to do anything about the bitch of a messenger, but he'd certainly see to it that Tolton suffered for *her* part of it. Meanwhile, the message . . .

He carried the purse back to his desk, where he turned up his security sound curtain (it also blotted out the continuing laughter from Tolton's anteroom) and withdrew six sheets of plastic stationery. Reaching for the spectacles he never wore outside the office, he began. A title at the top read "Confidential Operations Plan," and, as he read with growing amazement, the document contained a reasonably detailed operations plan for the mercenaries' upcoming campaign against the Kîrskian pirates—which was to begin with the dispatch of a decoy treasure ship on September 22, less than six days away. He grinned, forgetting the slight that had been handed him by Renaldo's messenger. This was *important*! He had recently doubled the size of the Imperial task force he intended to send against the pirates; it now consisted of nineteen powerful warships—and it was ready to lift for space within two days' notice. "Tolton," he ordered, "summon the commanders of Task Force Eleven to my office immediately!" This time, he *couldn't* lose!

Book Eight

SURPRISES AND TURNABOUTS

Aboard KV 388 #SW 799 • in space

Kobir fed a course change into the AutoHelm, checked it against instructions he had just received from the navigators aft, then selected ENTER. Moments later, as the onrushing stars swung smoothly to the right and downward, a glance through the Hyperscreens assured him the other three 388s had likewise changed course. If his calculations—and the target's departure announcement—were correct, they would intercept within an hour and a half.

For the ten millionth time, he checked the flight controls—everything was as it should be. A glance at his proximity sensors showed that they were also operating normally; for the past hour, they had been reporting large ships moving high on a parallel course some ninety kilometers abaft the port beam. Big ships were common occurrences on this heavily traveled space route. All seemed to be well, yet in a remote corner of his mind, a small voice warned of something amiss—and he couldn't place it to save his long-lost soul.

Forcing himself to relax, he listened to the steady beat of the Drive crystals rumbling two decks below. The ship bounced and juddered occasionally in the unstable gravity that was normal for this portion of the galaxy. He nodded to himself—whoever navigated the old transport seemed to have chosen his course well: instead of a direct, least-time-in-transit passage to Earth, he had chosen to extend the passage by a day or so to pick up the Eertx Vector, one of the more heavily traveled routes between the Imperial capital and the densely populated Canton Domains. Heavy traffic on that spaceway could make pirating much more difficult, but he had taken that into consideration when he planned the mission. Oddly discontented still, he ran yet another test of the flight instruments.

"Kapitan," Skoda remarked from the alternate helm, "one senses an unusual tenseness in yourself today. Is something amiss?"

Kobir shook his head. "Not that I can put a finger on," he said. "Yet . . . " he pursed his lips.

Skoda smiled. "You made it clear that you were not overly happy with the mission even before we planned it," he commented.

"True," Kobir admitted, "but, well, the Ambronovsky Collection . . . " He shook his head. "National pride won over logic. Who can say?"

"Then *that* is what still troubles you?" Skoda asked.

"At this point," Kobir said with a frown, "I have no idea. All I know is that something seems to be out of kilter, as the Imperials put things. But since I am unable to reckon what that something is, I cannot take steps to protect us from it.

Nor can I abort the mission because of a mere premonition."
He shrugged.

Skoda nodded. "As we have succeeded in the past," he
said, "we will assuredly succeed this time, also, my Kapitan." He glanced at his watch and unstrapped his restraints.
"Action stations are in little more than three hours," he
added. "Before we don our battle suits, will you join me
below in the galley and put your troubled mind to a mug of
coffee?"

"Dorian," Kobir said, "yours is the best offer I have had
since we departed Khalife. One supposes *you* are buying?"

Skoda nodded. "But of course, my Kapitan," he replied.

Aboard *Death* • in space

At the same time, Canby sat at *Death*'s controls, keeping
the ED-3 in "sight" some thousand kilometers to starboard
according to his new 2HD/19 proximity sensors. He wasn't
very happy with the new instruments; Harper had done all he
could to tune them, but they simply were not right. They kept
indicating a large collection of heavy starships astern at
about thirteen hundred kilometers high.

Canby had expected traffic like that in the busy corridor—
it helped cover his *own* presence. However, this particular
manifestation on the instruments indicated a contingent of
large ships—a number of them the size of battle cruisers.
And had any Fleet units of that size lifted for space, he
would have heard. Lately, capital ships never lifted without
lots of fanfare.

With no indication of trouble in the immediate future, he
turned the controls over to O'Connor and went aft for a mug
of coffee. Already they'd shadowed the old ship for two
days—with no sign of the pirates—and the boredom was
nearly unbearable.

Aboard KV 388 #SW 799 • in space

"We have a definite fix on the target ship, Kapitan," a rating advised Kobir. "It is approximately nine hundred kilometers off the bow, and the icon on your display is now validated."

Kobir nodded, more to himself than anyone else. "Thank you, Erika," he said, glancing through the Hyperscreens at the other three ships. They had already taken up the positions worked out for this particular attack. He looked down at the annunciator for a long moment, then punched ALL SPACES. "Action stations!" he announced. "All hands to action stations. Boarding party to the main hatch, immediately!" Then he turned to Skoda. "Well, old friend," he said, "the helm is yours. For me, it is once more into the breach, as the saying goes—or went several hundred years ago. Steering engine is at zero four zero—and the ship is yours."

Skoda nodded, symbolically placing his hands on the flight controls, although the ship was still on AutoHelm. "May Dame Fortune dog your steps, my Kapitan," he said with a little smile.

Minutes later, with the Drive thundering at high speed beneath the deck, Kobir stood with the boarding party in the ship's main boarding chamber, exchanging greetings with old Tancredi and donning his Kîrskian FlexArmor.

Aboard *Death* • in space

Canby hunched over the Proximity Indicator, staring into the display. There were four blips about nine hundred kilometers behind the ED-3 and closing rapidly. He nodded. "I think that's our pirates," he said briskly to Thompson, the PI Technician. "Let's get 'em!" Striding rapidly to the helm, he set the blower for ALL STATIONS, then winked at O'Connor. "General quarters! General quarters!" he shouted. "All hands, man your battle stations! Close all airtight doors and man your battle stations!" As the ship filled with the confusion of thudding boots and slamming hatches, he thought about Peterson for a moment, some hundred kilometers away in the armored cabin of the ED-3. For some reason, she didn't fly with him much anymore. She was always volunteering for special duty in other ships. *Women,* he thought— *no understanding them at all.*

"You want the helm, Skipper?" O'Connor asked.

Canby smiled. "Thanks, Chang," he said.

"I'll get plenty of center-chair combat time when *you're* tired of it," O'Connor said with a grin, "if either one of us lives that long."

"Don't hold your breath." Canby chuckled, concentrating on his readouts. A copy of the proximity indicator display shone in the bottom left quadrant of his situation screen. The pirates—or alleged pirates, at any rate—had by this time closed to about eighty-five kilometers behind the ED-3. Normally, his crew aboard the old ship would have no idea of this. The pursuers appeared to be flying well within the "cone of silence" produced by ED-3's Drive wake, but *Death*'s HyCOMM operator had been sending coded reports to the transport since the blips began to appear. Canby glanced through the Hyperscreens. Outside another five DH.98s flew in close formation. Confrass in *War* was tucked in to port no more than fifty meters away. Some hundred meters higher and slightly aft, old *Famine* sped along to port as if she had only come off a production line that morning; beside her and slightly aft was *Plague II,* one of the three new ships purchased earlier in the year. *Calamity* and *Revenge,* the other new ships, flew approximately a hundred meters to *Death*'s starboard. In a few moments, Canby would give the order to attack, using the phenomenal speed of the DH.98s to arrive at the targets before the pirates had a chance to properly react. He had taken no chances on this mission, employing even his reserve ships in an attempt to surprise and overpower the pirates in the first moments of combat, forcing them on the defensive before they could bring their own offensive tactics to bear. It was a strategy that had worked well against other Kîrskians during the war. He keyed his low-power HyCOMM to the planned frequency, then pressed BROADCAST. "Everyone ready?" he asked.

Moments later, five "Yes" answers sounded simultaneously in his battle helmet.

"Countdown from three, then," Canby broadcast. "Three . . . two . . . one . . . *zero*!" With that, he kicked the rudder to starboard and moved the thrust dampers all the way forward. "The game's afoot!" he bellowed.

Aboard KV 388 #SW 799 • in space

Tancredi had sealed the boarding chamber hatch; now Kobir and his party waited in taut silence for Frizell's request to blast the target ship's HyCOMM antenna. It never came. Instead, without warning, the smooth rumble of the Drive suddenly bellowed into a thunderous roar and the ship turned so sharply that even in their artificial gravity, everyone was swept into a tangled huddle in one corner of the chamber.

"Skoda!" Kobir bellowed into his microphone. "What is happening? Where is the target ship?"

"Kapitan!" Skoda answered in a tight voice. "The target ship has . . . *escaped*! We are now under attack! Six fast starships . . . heavily armed!"

In the next moment, the ship veered again, then juddered violently as the lights pulsed—near misses by incoming disruptor fire; Kobir had felt shocks like that a million times in his long career. Seconds afterward, Frizell fired their own disruptors, violently shaking the deck a second time. Scrambling to his feet, Kobir unsealed the boarding chamber and made his way back to the bridge companionway, ricocheting off bulkheads from the ship's violent maneuvers and the silent-but-deadly near misses. It seemed a million years before he fought his way to the helms. "Who are they?" he demanded, struggling into his restraint system.

"Don't know," Skoda grunted, cranking the starship into a tight turn. "But look!" In the Hyperscreens sprang the surface of a stub wing with a huge nacelle, the outline of a maintenance hatch, and the rounded belly of what could.only be . . .

"It's a *Geoffrey*!" Kobir gasped in surprise. "A DH.98!" Just then, Frizell fired, and the whole ship shook from the discharge of two 30-mmi MK 108 disruptors, two 20-mmi MG 151 disruptors, and two 7.9-mmi MG 81 disruptors—all beta-torqued. A large metal plate went spinning off the speeding Geoffrey just before it did two flick rolls, then vomited a sheet of flame, debris, but no LifeGlobes. Threshing like some wounded fish, its vee-tail passed less than five meters from the freebooter's tail before it spun away to burst like a great, incandescent puffball.

As the 388 slammed violently through the shock waves, Skoda attempted to complete his turn, but he'd been carried away by his own reflexes, and the starship tumbled into a spin, the most vulnerable of all positions with its fly-by-wire logics in a state of total confusion.

A blinding explosion in front of Kobir's eyes smashed him painfully backward till his seat hit its recoil stops with a stunning jolt that even a battle suit could not cushion. The ship's gravity pulsed again and again and he let go of everything, instinctively covering his faceplate with his arms. Beside him, Skoda lolled weakly at his helm, clearly unconscious—or worse. Heart in his mouth, the stunned Kobir dragged his chair forward so he could reach the controls. One of his smashed instruments hung on the end of its feeds, and he could see blue sparks flashing deep within the panel. Panting, he mechanically brought the 388 back under control, cleared his tail, and . . .

Again they were hit!

This time, it was aft. He felt the impact like a hammer

blow through his seat back while the intercom erupted with screams and shouting. Frantically, with both hands, he put the ship into the steepest possible turn. Another DH.98—vivid white against the darkness—flashed before the Hyperscreens, its drive doors glowering like green eyes, then pulled away vertically as if it were headed around for another shot. Perhaps five kilometers away, another ship, God knew whose, was being consumed by bright, pulsing radiation fires as its hullmetal, a collapsium, began to violently uncollapse.

Kobir hesitated only a moment. In spite of the damage, the Drive was still thundering smoothly beneath his feet while the ship responded to its controls. But the people who flew those DH.98s *had* to be stopped! He slid the thrust damper all the way forward, waiting for his ship to explode or accelerate; either would do. Somewhat to his amazement, it did the former—at once. And although there was no chance his ship could outspeed a DH.98, he found another enemy, this one in a tight turn, so he might at least come abreast for some telling shots. Over the thunder of the wide-open Drive, he listened to Frizell calling off the deflections. By God, they'd get a piece of *this* one!

Suddenly, a salvo of huge explosions erupted between the DH.98 and himself—intense, dazzling beams of raw energy a hundred meters across, at least, that—that passed on either side of his 388. But who was firing now? None of his ships mounted disruptors that big—nor, he proved by a glance around, were any nearby. Kobir concentrated on keeping the DH.98 in sight while, for a moment, the huge explosions appeared to double in intensity. There came a tremendous clang of a near miss that must have knocked the ship a hundred meters up from its course, and abruptly he realized that the shots weren't meant just for the DH.98, they were meant for *him* too!

A glance to the rear explained this curious phenomenon. Flying on Kobir's tail were five huge battlecruisers in perfect close echelon formation—perfectly backlit by throbbing, bright green spheres of their Drive units firing at what must be maximum rate. Off to his left and right—as well as from overhead and . . . he rolled the ship quickly . . . beneath, other big ships were closing in from forward. The huge Fleet units could match neither his speed nor that of the DH.98, but the range of their disruptors made this a nonissue. "Good God!" he yelled aloud as realization struck home. "They're after us *both*!"

By this time, he and the DH.98 were jinking through a tremendous barrage, with the latter making use of its astonishing top speed to lengthen the distance between them. But they'd all been "globed," as the term went, and even though the forward end of the globe was open, mathematically neither the mysterious DH.98s nor his 388s could reach it before they were destroyed. The only way out was to shoot a hole in the globe—but nobody had that kind of firepower alone. However . . . grinding his teeth as he jinked in every direction, he checked for other ships. High to starboard was at least one of his own; another was limping along to port. Aft, two more DH.98s were pulling alongside their sister ship. That made up his mind. He glanced at the HyCOMM, selected ALL-CHANNEL BROADCAST, then FULL POWER, and touched the switch at his throat to link his helmet output. "KV 388 to DH.98 attackers," he broadcast in broken Imperial, "KV 388 to DH.98 attackers. Come in, please."

Aboard *Death* • in space

Canby had achieved the surprise he'd sought, and then some. His DH.98s tore into the four pirate ships with a vengeance, scattering them before they had a chance to use their disruptors on the ED-3. But before he could take any real advantage of the situation, an angular shape appeared in his forward Hyperscreens and a beam of disruptor fire came straight toward him, missing the bridge by no more than a few meters. Instinctively, he pushed the nose down and felt the pirate's Drive wake against his two fins. Turning back into the fray, he was just in time to see a 388 chasing another DH.98. The latter was pulling away handily, but not without collecting three or four hits along the way. Canby engaged the pirate, who turned so tightly that the ships almost collided—and provided no chance for a shot. These Kîrskians knew the ropes!

"Hello—legionnaires, *Calamity* here. Please help; we've had it."

It was Felton, the ship's Captain, shouting for help.

The 388 came back in a vicious turn, and Canby had to break so violently that he tumbled his logics and only brought the ship under control by a recklessly hazardous snap roll. Heart in his mouth, he fired on the pirate in turn, but the blackguard cleverly skidded out of the way on its short Drive axis and he missed again—the engagement had lasted maybe sixty seconds. Another snap roll—this one in full control—brought him back toward *Calamity,* in time to see the ship careen into a long curve, trailing a long cloud of radiation fire and debris—no LifeGlobes. Moments later, it burst in a great blaze of light and energy, winking out into a swarm of glowing comets that quickly fell behind and were lost. No survivors.

Grinding his teeth in horror, Canby rolled again, this time fixing on another 388—perhaps the one that got *Calamity*. Kellerwand had a clear shot, but . . . before he could fire, the pirate spotted them, fell off to starboard, and rolled into an incredibly steep turn. Suddenly he pulled up onto his back with such violence that momentum carried him all the way over and into *Death*'s cone of fire. Within range at last! Canby felt the deck shudder as the big disruptors in the nose discharged, then "walked" along the pirate's hull toward the bridge. The pirate was now so close, every detail was clear. It was one of the latest 388s—he'd only seen a few of them at the end of the war, but they were *deadly*. He could see the green glow of the Drive exhausts, the oxide trail left by the

Drive plume along the aft hull, the ebony back and dark blue belly. Suddenly the sharp, clear picture shook, disintegrated. The bridge exploded into a mist of Hyperscreen shards and internal atmosphere that glittered wildly in the Drive plume, then disappeared aft. More disruptor beams tore into him, retreating aft toward the Drive section in a series of explosions and sparks that danced on the hullmetal. Then a spurt of radiation flame, followed by particles of debris. Canby flicked off out of the way with a last vision of the pirate erupting into a white-hot comet that exploded on the instant and disappeared aft like a child's pyrotechnic toy.

In the next moment, Canby spotted a 388 closing in on *Revenge*. He was about to send a warning when his own HyCOMM blared, "Look out, *Death*—break! Break!"

Before he even had time to realize the warning was meant for him, he hauled the nose up—but too late. His DH.98 took a near miss aft near the Drive section by what could only be a perfectly colossal disruptor. The impact was so violent his hands and feet were jarred from the controls and the gravity pulsed sickeningly. Glancing aft, he could see a 388 on his tail, with another pulling into formation beside it—but neither ship's disruptors were firing! Another great explosion aft—between himself and the pirate. Then another . . . and still another. In moments, space was filled with gigantic explosions that seemed to come from every direction. *And whomever was firing was also after the pirates!* Jinking desperately he managed to give himself a better view aft and . . . sweet Jesus! Behind both the pirates and himself were five huge battlecruisers, firing for all they were worth. Luckily, they had no more accuracy than one would expect from the Pentagon-savaged Fleet, but with all those disruptors in action, someone was bound to get lucky. As *War* and *Famine* pulled into formation beside him, he glanced around for others that might have survived. Below and to port, *Plague II* and *Revenge* were both limping along as if they were damaged, but had little chance of surviving the explosive holocaust around them.

Why in the name of God would the Fleet be trying to get both the pirates *and* his ships? After all, he and the legionnaires were mostly legal—they'd gone to some pains to be that way.

The ship lurched violently as a near miss blasted the ship sideways with energy shock. He bit his lip. Clearly, both he and the pirates were in real trouble. Just as clearly, however, they'd escaped the worst of the Fleet's violence thanks mainly to someone aboard the battlecruisers who'd opened fire much too early, providing a few seconds' warning before everyone began to fire.

But *why* were they firing in the first place?

Jinking randomly here and there, he had just sent coded evacuation orders to the people remaining at Perrin Station and commanded the ED-3 to execute emergency plans when, abruptly, his HyCOMM alert sounded in emergency mode.

"KV 388 to DH.98 attackers," someone with a deep voice broadcast in broken Imperial, "KV 388 to DH.98 attackers. Come in, please."

Dumbfounded, Canby shook his head, then shrugged to himself. Why not? Everything *else* seemed to be going mad. He mashed the ALL CHANNELS, then SEND. "DH.98 attacker to KV 388," he broadcast. "We read you."

"DH.98 attackers," came an immediate, and somewhat breathless, answer, "we are both under assault by large squadron of apparent incompetents—who might yet score lucky hit by mathematical probability. I have two sound ships; you perhaps have three—can we work together?"

Canby instantly grasped the other's point. "KV 388: We'd better," he sent, his mind whirling at top speed. "If you two merged on us, we could make a Fire Point on one of the battlecruisers," he barked, referring to a last-ditch maneuver used by both sides during the last war. "You know it?"

"DH.98," the deep voice said. "Fire Point is good—on *center* battlecruiser, where leaders probably ride. Okay?"

"Yeah," Canby said. "Good idea."

"Good," the pirate said again. "We will form on you. Cripples on both sides can follow. Please slow your speed so we can catch up."

Heart in his mouth, Canby called in his damaged ships, then retarded the thrust dampers until the two angular pirate ships arrived, jinking in perfect harmony with his own three—damn fine helmsmen there, he thought to himself. At a glance, the KV 388s themselves appeared in remarkably good condition, except for a number of jagged holes burned into their hulls. They'd taken a few casualties from those, all right—but then, so had his legionnaires. "We'll count down to zero," Canby said, his voice bouncing with the near misses, "from five."

"On zero," came the answer.

"Five . . . four . . . three . . . two . . . one . . . *zero!*"

It was as if they had practiced the maneuver for years, which in fact they had—separately and a decade in the past. The five starships quickly pulled into line abreast, then rolled into position forming a pentagon with their bellies toward the inside—and an awesome array of tightly packed firepower concentrated forward. "All right," Canby broadcast, glancing aft as his two damaged DH.98s and a badly holed 388 limped into position aft, "either way you look at it, this gets us out of our predicament. Let's go beat up a battlecruiser!" With that, he moved the thrust dampers forward and led his odd little formation directly for the bridge of the center battlecruiser.

The Pentagon, Columbia Sector, New Washington • Earth

During the initial moments of Canby's attack on the pirates, an exultant David Lotember sat with a large smile plastered across his face on the edge of his wing-backed chair in the Pentagon's great, underground Situation Room. He was about to be vindicated for all the criticism he had taken since he'd brought such drastic improvement to the Fleet. In a room filled with winking, flickering windows that watched locations throughout the galaxy, all eyes were glued to a large three-dimensional display that duplicated the view forward through the bridge Hyperscreens of I.F.S. *Glorious*. The great battlecruiser was racing ahead at top speed toward what *might* have been an inconsequential space battle between starships left over from a war that had been finished for more than a decade. *This* particular battle, however, was anything but inconsequential. One of the most powerful and influential individuals in civilization had a deep, personal interest in it—and, in a way, Lotember's own job depended on it.

With his hand control, he zoomed his view into the distance. But the battle itself was still too far distant to detect with equipment designed for human eyesight—all he got was onrushing stars. Minutes ago, he'd watched icons racing around a long-distance proximity display, but they'd meant little—except that already one of the ships had been destroyed. He wondered if it was one of the abominable pirates, but then, it really didn't matter. Only a few minutes more before that little battle would be over, and then . . .

Abruptly, the Hyperscreens flashed and the view jiggled, as if something had hit the ship or . . . *much* too early, someone had *fired a salvo*!

"Oh, *no!*" he cried out, bringing startled looks from all over the room. A number of flunkies rushed to his side. He ignored them, watching with horror as the view swung ninety degrees to a bridge wing where the squadron's Admiral-in-Command—daughter of a powerful, prominent politician—was sitting in a huge command chair, smashing her fists on the armrests and stamping her boots on the deck. "It's not my fault!" she screamed angrily, her image wavering as the ship's main battery blasted out again, then commenced rapid firing. "It's not my fault!"

Grinding his teeth, Lotember switched the display to view the battlecruisers on either side of the *Glorious*. They were firing, too! He closed his eyes and fell back into his great chair—at this distance, *everybody* could get away! Long-range gunnery was definitely *not* the Fleet's forte.

Numbly, he returned the display to *Glorious*'s bridge wing, where the Admiral had launched into a tirade against other officers on the ship, especially one who seemed to have snubbed her during a recent social function somewhere in London. Slapping his hand to his forehead, he ignored her angry babbling while he attempted to swallow his gorge, then sat bolt upright in terror as five distant motes in space rapidly formed themselves into a pentagon, then grew rapidly in the Hyperscreens behind the shrieking woman. Moments before his display abruptly went dark, he recognized them as starships flying in a peculiar formation. Two looked strangely familiar, and he started to call for Jennings to identify them. But he'd personally fired the impertinent officer at the very beginning of the purge.

At the last moment, he remembered: the ships were *Kvlokovs,* the kind flown by Renaldo's pirates! But by then, it didn't really matter.

Aboard *Death* • in space

Canby glanced back while the Imperial squadron—its ships now milling in apparent disarray—shrank rapidly into the distance. I.F.S. *Glorious* was a devastated mass of radiation fire, with half her bow buried in the side of a sister ship after she'd veered out of control at flank speed. Miraculously, the age-old Fire Point maneuver had come through once more, opening the Imperial "globe" by disabling its flagship—and permitting all survivors of the original dog-fight to escape but one. *Revenge* had taken a direct hit as she passed one of the battlecruisers. In all likelihood the shot had been accidental, Canby thought ruefully. At least Peterson and the crew of the ED-3 were unharmed; they'd made a clean getaway and had reported in a few minutes ago from a safe distance, waiting for orders.

With the hammering, hissing noises of emergency repair work flooding the bridge, he glanced through his Hyper-screens at the improbable squadron that had formed in the last few minutes: four DH.98s and three KV 388s—venerable arch-enemies flying in close formation after putting paid to *two* Imperial capital ships. He shrugged. If nothing else, they had common ground in that. But even more important, both factions of the strange alliance badly needed an immediate place to hide. The whole sector of the galaxy would soon be alive with Imperial ships that would eventually score more hits—as the saying went, even blind squirrels occasionally find an acorn. He shrugged. Nothing ventured, nothing gained. "DH.98 leader to KV 388 leader," he broadcast on short-range HyCOMM, "got any ideas about where we can sit this out?"

After a short pause, the deep voice replied with a little chuckle. "DH.98: We were thinking same thoughts. I was about to call. You are finished with shooting at us? Yes?"

Canby had been waiting for something like that—Lord knew the pirate had every reason to ask. "KV 388: We're definitely finished shooting," he said emphatically, "at least at you. Hope you understand there wasn't anything personal about the attack."

"DH.98: We surmised someone took out a contract on us," the deep voice replied.

"You're right about that, KV 388," Canby admitted. "And I'm sorry the whole thing happened, especially the ship you lost. But we lost two ourselves, and—" He stopped. *That* part was beyond words. "In this business," he finished, "you take your chances."

"As in our business," the deep voice replied.

"Anyway, KV 388," Canby said, checking his proximity indicators as well as the Hyperscreens, "we *all* need to make ourselves scarce for a while. Do you know where we can hide?"

"We have used an asteroid shoal not far from here," the deep voice said. "You will follow me there?"

"We will gladly follow," Canby assured him, watching suspicious shadows form at the edges of the proximity indicator.

"Good," the deep voice said. "That way, you won't outrun us so easily."

Canby chuckled and turned the controls over to O'Connor. "We're going to follow the 388s," Canby broadcast to the other four DH.98s. "Can everybody's ship maintain three quarters Drive cruise?"

As the lead pirate ship raised its nose and began a gentle turn, Canby got four nearly simultaneous replies of "Yes."

"Okay, guys," he said, "then let's look sharp. Close up on me: *War* on my wing, *Plague II* and *Famine* to starboard. We'll fly to starboard of the KVs. And if the Fleet attacks again, remember, those 388s are on *our* side, now."

Some three hours later, *Death* was tethered to a huge asteroid beside a KV 388 that carried the symbols SW 799 stenciled on either side of its nose—her captain, the deep-voiced pirate chief. *War, Plague II,* and old *Famine* were moored nearby, separated by two KV 388s. All looked somewhat the worse for wear. Still stunned, Canby sat alone on the bridge racking his brain to discover some plausible reasons the Imperial fleet had attacked him. For that matter, he wondered why a squadron of capital ships was in the area in the first place—and *unannounced*, as well.

Grimacing, he was forced to conclude that the attack could hardly be an accident; interstellar space was *much* too large and empty for that kind of coincidence. Besides, the big ships were firing at *both* himself and the pirates. He could understand they might be after the pirates. But who—aside from some of his recent "enemies"—wanted his legionnaires out of the way as well? And how did someone get the Fleet to do his or her bidding in the first place?

Then there was the little matter of how the Fleet knew *where* to attack. Who let *them* in on his plan—hell, who outside the Legion even knew about it? He'd told no one outside the legion except Tenniel, and she would never, in a million years—

Canby's discomfiting thoughts were interrupted by sounds of the pirate ship sealing its transfer tube to *Death*'s boarding hatch. He ground his teeth. More trouble, perhaps? The pirates would have to be awfully magnanimous to condone his attack. Who could predict what they'd do? Clearly, they'd already teamed with him against a common enemy, but . . . At last, he simply yielded to fate. If the pirate had anything up his sleeve in the way of trouble, all seven ships would doubtlessly end up firing in reflex at their nearest neighbors, and everyone would go up in a single flare.

Abruptly, heavy footsteps issued from the bridge companionway. "Commander Gordon Canby," the deep voice boomed, "I bring a little peace offering!"

SEPTEMBER 23, 2691, EARTH DATE

Belgravia, London • Earth

In London, Renaldo had just returned from an excellent revival of Philip Glass's ancient twentieth-century opera *Einstein On The Beach*, when Mrs. Timpton appeared at his chamber with a HoloPhone. "For you, my lord," she said.

Renaldo took the phone, peered at her perfunctorily for a moment, then motioned her inside with a cocked thumb. "Get your clothes off," he ordered, activating the display to the holographic likeness of . . . Eva Tolton? He'd been looking forward to a call from David Lotember with great expectation—so much, in fact, that he'd missed some of the best parts of the opera. But Tolton? He frowned, the first shadows of doubt beginning to form in his mind. "Well?" he demanded.

The woman seemed frightened, looking everywhere but at him. "Er . . . " she stammered.

"Goddamnit, Tolton," he roared, indicating Timpton, who was undressing behind him, "can't you see I'm busy?"

"Er . . . yes, my lord," she said, her cheeks reddening as she glanced past his shoulder. "I can see that you are . . . b-busy," she stammered.

"Then don't waste my time. What about the pirates? Did the Fleet get them all? And why isn't that idiot Lotember on the phone?"

"Er, Minister Lotember was . . . er, summoned to a h-high-level meeting, my lord. H-he asked m-me to call."

"For that asshole Lotember, no meeting is as high-level as I," Renaldo growled as doubts began to intrude on his expectations. "Now, Goddamnit, what about the pirates? Are they gone?"

"S-some of them are g-gone," Tolton stammered.

"*Some* of them," Renaldo repeated, closing his eyes and angrily pursing his lips. He took a deep breath. "What about the mercenaries? Did they get any of them?"

"Some . . ."

"Jesus, Joseph, and Mary," Renaldo whispered as the situation began to sink in. *That* was why Lotember wasn't making the call—his "improved" Fleet had again failed in this latest mission, and he was *afraid*. Calming himself as much as possible, he fixed Tolton's image with an angry glare. "Give me the numbers," he demanded. "First, how many pirates were there?"

"Four pirate ships, my lord," Tolton said, avoiding his eyes.

"And how many were destroyed?"

"O-one, my lord," she answered, "and one damaged."

Renaldo bit his lip. "I take it all three escaped?"

"That is the general consensus, my lord."

"General *consensus*?" Renaldo exploded. "Doesn't anybody *know*?" He ground his teeth in rage. "Goddamnit, put me through to that Admiral in charge of the squadron. She'd damn well better be able to tell me!"

Tolton only stared at him like a deer caught in the headlights of a skimmer.

"Well?"

"M-my lord," Tolton stammered, "it is no longer possible for you to contact Admiral Volpé."

"What's *she* done, run off with that shithead Lotember?" Renaldo demanded sarcastically.

"Er, not *quite,* my lord," Tolton gulped as if she were trying to talk while she swallowed something very large. "Admiral Volpé was . . . well . . . killed in the destruction of the two battlecruisers."

Renaldo shut his eyes, attempting to comprehend the scope of his Fleet's latest disaster. "You mean to tell me," he asked as calmly as his rising blood pressure would permit, "that not only did most of the pirates get away, but they also destroyed two of the new battlecruisers?"

"Er, not exactly, my lord," Tolton said, her voice little more than a whisper. "It took *both* the pirates and the mercenaries to destroy the battlecruisers."

"It took *what*?"

"Both the pirates and the mercenaries, my lord."

"You mean . . . they *got together* . . . as in 'acted jointly'?" Renaldo asked, apprehension descending over him like a great, cold cloud.

"That is what I have been told," Tolton explained.

"Mother of Jesus!" Renaldo exclaimed. "And how many mercenaries got away?" he demanded.

"F-four, altogether, my lord."

Stunned, Renaldo could only shake his head. Four out of

six—and teamed up with the three Kîrskian devils! Roaring like some raging beast, he smashed the HoloPhone against the wall. Suddenly glancing at Timpton, he found himself sickened by her gray hair and sagging breasts. "Get out of here, you ugly hag!" he screeched. "Out!"

When she was gone, he settled into an overstuffed chair and retrieved a handful of sweet chocolate chunks from the nightstand. Cramming them into his mouth, he began to perspire with a mixture of rage and fear. As soon as the Kîrskians and mercenaries had a chance to talk things over, it wouldn't take them long to determine who was responsible for their troubles. He mopped his head with a handkerchief. And now, where once he had *only* the pirates to contend with, he had provoked Tenniel's extremely capable mercenaries as well! And they would surely want revenge—as would the pirates. Tears of frustration began to run down his cheeks while he stuffed another load of chocolate into his mouth. It was starting out as a *bad* day, indeed.

Aboard *Death* • in space

Heart in his mouth, Kobir stepped into the mercenary ship's bridge, his left hand grasping a liter bottle of vodka and two small tumblers. He'd never been inside a DH.88 before, but he'd diced with enough of them to build a healthy respect for both the ships and the people who operated them. At the forward end, a solitary crewman had just risen from the principal helm and was making his way aft—*without* a blaster in his hand, Kobir noted with relief.

He was a stocky fellow whose deep blue eyes had an honest look of determination to them. Kobir strode forward to meet the man, his right hand outstretched. "I am Nikolai," he said, gripping the mercenary's proffered hand and looking deep into his eyes, "a Kîrskian—or at least I *was* when that domain was permitted to exist. Probably you and I have met on other occasions—in other lives."

"In other lives to be certain, Nikolai Kobir," the mercenary replied, returning the pirate's smile. "My name's Gordon Canby—and I'm certain we've met before. Perhaps out by Megiddo during the last days?"

Kobir nodded. He'd been right. "Koris-19, perhaps?" he asked as sounds of merriment came from the companionway—Kîrskians arriving with more vodka.

"We ran into *warriors* there," the fellow Canby said. "A number of us hoped you people would get away somehow!"

Kobir nodded; the compliment was appreciated. "We escaped," he said, "but only by the skin of our teeth—to use an ancient 'Imperialism.' "

The mercenary shook his head in clear amazement. "To think we'd meet this way," he said as sounds of laughter, strange music, and glassware grew louder from below. "What's going on down there?" he inquired with a frown.

Kobir laughed. "My crews," he said. "They thought it might be an excellent time for us to meet in person."

"And this?" Canby asked, pointing to the bottle.

Kobir placed the two tumblers on a navigation console and filled them from the bottle. "Vodka," he explained. "It is the great enemy of hate." Lifting one of the tumblers, he drained it in one draft, then handed the other to Canby. "Here," he said, hoping against hope. "Soon we must both ascertain if former enemies can also be friends."

"To the Kîrskian's great relief, Canby smiled, then drained his tumbler.

During the next hours Kobir lost all track of time, sharing the excellent Calabrian vodka he had brought with him and discovering that he and the Canby fellow had a great deal in common. It wasn't long before they also began to scour their minds to discover some rational motive for the Fleet's unprovoked—but *certainly* well-planned—attack. Both agreed immediately that the Fleet vessels did not stumble on their dogfight by coincidence, especially since Canby's new, long-range proximity devices indicated vague targets for hours before he attacked. It was clear someone who wanted both the pirates *and* Canby out of the way had used the latter's mission as a stalking horse. But to accomplish such deception, that someone had almost certainly ferreted out Canby's operational plan. How?

"Try to remember, Gordon," Kobir said, refilling both tumblers, "how many of your legionnaires—who didn't actually *fly* the mission—knew enough of the plan to compromise it to such an extent?"

The mercenary nodded and scratched his balding head. "God knows I've been asking that question myself, Nikolai," he said. "And I come up with no one. The job was so weird, I didn't want to trust anybody—even myself. So I made sure everyone who knew enough to get us in trouble would end up on one of the ships." He laughed mordantly. "It's the best kind of security I've been able to come up with."

Kobir nodded. "We agree on that, then," he said morosely, filling their tumblers. "People just don't compromise missions when it's themselves who will be put at jeopardy." He frowned, looking Canby in his eye. "I never even thought to ask, but . . . who hired you, anyway?"

Canby shook his head. "Crazy as it sounds," he said, "I don't have any idea."

Kobir felt his brows knit. Perhaps he had misjudged this man. Only an idiot would attempt such a bald-faced lie. "Really?" he asked. "I find that . . . *amazing.*"

"You mean, 'bullshit,' " Canby replied with an embarrassed little grin. "I know that's what I would say. But it *is* true, nonetheless." He shrugged. "A lady I've been seeing handled the whole thing as an intermediary to a man who insists on remaining anonymous."

"So you never saw your actual client," Kobir reiterated. "This is correct?"

"Correct," Canby said, looking uncomfortable. "She handled the down payment and the instructions. She's even got the balance in an escrow account."

Kobir nodded. *That* part was believable. But the man's troubled eyes fairly shouted that the whole story was yet to be told. He rubbed his chin thoughtfully as continuing sounds of revelry assured him that the mercenaries meant him and his ships no more harm. "This man," he said slowly, "do you have any information about him at all?"

"Not much," Canby said, sipping his vodka. "Except that Cynthia—she's the lady—talks about him being *very* powerful. My guess is he's a Noble, but I can't be sure. She claims if he found out she compromised him in any way, he'd crush us *both*."

"Hmm," Kobir said, as an idea formed. "A treacherous rascal, eh?"

"Seems so," Canby replied. "He's sure got her scared."

Kobir nodded. "I believe," he said, "I may know who your client is. And if I am correct, he is, indeed, a treacherous rascal."

"Who?" Canby demanded.

"In my view," Kobir said, "your client is none other than Sadir, First Earl of Renaldo. A powerful, corrupt, and *most* venal individual."

At this, Canby grimaced as if the words pained him somehow.

Kobir considered that. Was it significant? He pondered a moment. If nothing else, Canby's grimace served as fair indication that this Cynthia woman must mean a great deal to him. He would naturally be pained to learn that she was keeping company with a blackguard like Renaldo. But what *else* did it indicate? Kobir decided the facts would eventually come out as they talked.

After a long silence, Canby frowned and fixed Kobir with a questioning look. "Why?" he asked. "What makes you think it's Renaldo who called out the Fleet?"

"Fair question," Kobir replied, opening a second bottle of vodka that had been delivered by one of his stewards, "and one I should have answered earlier." He poured both tumblers full, handed one to Canby, then relaxed at the cohelmsman's station. "First," he explained, "I have been blackmailing Renaldo for some time, now. *Painfully* blackmailing, to be more accurate. We first studied his finances to ensure that we demanded the maximum amount he could pay without actually going bankrupt."

Canby nodded. "Sounds like good reasoning to me," he said. "But what did you have on him that made him pay like that?" His voice was slurring a little now. The vodka was clearly having its effect on *both* of them, Kobir thought.

"Slaving," he said, feeling his lip wrinkle with distaste. "The misbegotten scoundrel deserves a lot worse than just blackmailing, believe me."

"Jesus," Canby whispered. "No wonder he pays. A charge like that could get him the death penalty."

"It is not the only reason I suspect the Earl, my friend," Kobir said, gesturing with the tumbler. "The blackmail only provides a motive. How many people do you know who can call out the Imperial Fleet?"

Canby snapped his fingers. "Of course," he said. "He's also First Patron of the Admiralty, and that guy, er . . . Low Timber, or something, has gotta please *him* before anybody else."

"Exactly," Kobir said, "otherwise, come elections, the Earl's money will back someone else's campaign."

"The question, then," Canby said with a stricken look, "is who told Renaldo." He closed his eyes as if he were deep in pain. "I'm afraid," he continued after a long time, "that I know exactly who it is." Then he simply fell asleep in his recliner.

Kobir smiled. "Vodka," he whispered to himself, "the great enemy of hate. Makes people so trustful, they share darkest fears with onetime enemies." With that, he fell asleep too.

SEPTEMBER 24, 2691, EARTH DATE

Aboard *Death* • in space

Next "morning," by the ship's clock, Canby awakened in his recliner with a terrific headache and a tongue that felt as if it had grown a shaggy coat of fur. Worse, steamy thoughts of Tenniel had disturbed his dreams. In the shaky transition between sleep and wakefulness, he could not escape the dread feeling that it was she who betrayed the mission to Renaldo—her mysterious client. No one else knew the operational plans—at least no one who didn't plan to participate in the mission. He grimaced—even with all the evidence, his heart rebelled at the heresy. Forcing the thought aside, he opened his eyes.

Across the aisle, Kobir reclined at a Navigator's station with a towel around his neck while an old man—clearly a personal valet—was shaving him with an old-fashioned straight razor. The pirate was staring through the overhead Hyperscreens with a reflective frown on his brow. From the looks of him, he'd been awake for a considerable time. As the old valet changed position, he glanced at Canby, then whispered to Kobir.

"Good morning, Gordon Canby," the pirate said. "One trusts you slept undisturbed."

"One trusts, Nikolai," Canby replied, sitting up ever so carefully so as not to aggravate the headache. "With all the vodka I drank last night, not even the Big Bang could have disturbed me." He shook his head gingerly. "Is that what powers your 'Gravs?"

"Vodka?" the pirate asked with a circumspect chuckle—the valet was shaving his neck. "It is too noble a liquid to use as fuel."

"Glad to hear that," Canby said. "Otherwise, I may have drunk one of your ships out of commission all by myself."

They kept their silence until the valet completed Kobir's tonsure, then the pirate turned in his chair. "This is Jakob Tancredi," he said, placing his hand on the old man's arm, "who has managed to keep me alive for more than twenty years—in spite of my best efforts."

Canby started to get up, when both Kîrskians held up warning hands. "Please stay as you are," Kobir said with a grin. "Jakob understands hangovers, also."

"Many thanks," Canby said, sinking back in his seat. "Don't *you* have a hangover, Nikolai?"

Kobir laughed. "In old Novokîrosk," he said, "vodka once replaced mother's milk at the age of four months. None of us ancients remember what a hangover is."

Canby grinned and shook his head, wondering how Politicians had managed to bollix things enough to start a war with people like this. "No wonder you guys are so tough." He chuckled.

"Not tough anymore," Kobir said. "These days, we are neighborly. Remember, vodka is the great enemy of hate." He smiled. "In fact," he added, "Jakob has offered to shave you also. For free."

The offer took a few moments to sink in. "Shave *me*?" Canby asked, almost in horror. "Why . . . I've never been shaved by someone else in my life."

"A not-to-be-missed opportunity," Kobir said.

The very thought of anyone—especially a Kîrskian—running a razor over his Adam's apple gave Canby serious goose bumps. His mind flew off in all directions until he forcibly reined himself in. *The war was over*—and had been for nearly ten years. Not only that, but right now, these Kîrskians were the only certain friends he had in the galaxy. He'd already trusted them with his life—and they'd done the same with him. Frowning, he almost apologized for his thoughts. "I'm certain of that, Nikolai," he said, then looked the old man in the eye and smiled. "Jakob," he said, "I would be *most* honored if you would shave me."

As the old man began—Canby was amazed at how gently he worked—Kobir began to pace in the aisle. "This scoundrel Renaldo has made fools of us both," he mused aloud, "no matter *how* he got the information he needed. Not only have we been deprived of the income we might have gained by raiding another ship, we have also incurred grievous damages in casualties and ships. The situation is intolerable."

Canby kept his mouth shut and his face immobile. Having someone shave him was a new and rather intimidating experience. Luckily, the man Kobir seemed to understand this and went right on as if Canby had already agreed.

"You, Gordon, have suffered similar losses," the pirate declared—as if that weren't obvious. "Therefore, I shall for the nonce assume that you are as irritated at the man as am I."

Irritated wasn't the word for it, Canby thought.

"The way I see things," the pirate continued, lifting a tutorial finger, "we must devise a plan whereby we not only recoup our losses, but our *profits* as well." He looked down at Canby. "And," he added, "the beginnings of such a plan are already beginning to jell in my alleged mind."

Canby wanted to cheer; however, since the valet was now shaving his neck, he winked instead.

"Actually," Kobir continued, "you—or the ruse you employed to lure me—are the basis of the whole concept." He looked down into Canby's eyes. "The Ambronovsky Collection—it *was* a fabrication, was it not?"

Canby nodded. The valet had finished shaving him and was applying hot towels to his face from some sort of a bottomless hamper.

"My congratulations, friend," the pirate continued. "Yours was a clever plan—executed with ingenuity. I was completely taken in." He smiled sadly. "No Kîrskian worth his salt could have passed up such an opportunity. The Ambronovsky Collection is, or *was*, a national treasure." For a moment, his eyes seemed to stare off into another time and place, then he shook his head. "No matter," he said, fixing Canby with a purposeful stare. "The only important Star-Blaze now is the Giulio Cesare."

"The *what*?" Canby asked from within the towels.

"The Giulio Cesare," Kobir replied, "a StarBlaze. You have heard of it?"

Canby laughed. "I'm usually too busy scaring up rent money to keep close track of baubles like StarBlazes," he said.

"You will soon, Gordon Canby," Kobir assured him with a wink. "That I can promise. If you approve, a certain Star-Blaze will be the object of our first *joint* mission—to relieve Renaldo of his most prized possession." He paused while Tancredi removed the towels and bowed. "Well," he asked, "did Jakob live up to his reputation for the best shaves in the known universe?"

Canby sat up and felt his face in wonderment. "Truly, Jakob," he said with a grin of pleasure, "I have never experienced such a close, nor more comfortable shave. You *are* the best in the universe."

Jakob silently smiled, bowed, then looked at Kobir.

"Thank you, Jakob," the pirate said. "As usual, you are magnificent."

Again Tancredi bowed silently. Then, gathering his accoutrements, he made his way aft with the dignity of a prince.

To Canby, the old valet's proud demeanor said much about Kobir himself. "Thanks, Nikolai," he said quietly. "That was an experience I shall cherish. I am most honored."

"You are welcome, my friend," Kobir said, placing his hands behind his back. "And your shaving experience is much more than that to me."

Canby raised an eyebrow.

"It is a good indicator of how well we can work together, Gordon Canby," Kobir said. "You are a brave man to have risked your neck—literally—with my valet. I shall do everything in my power to deserve that trust you just placed in me." He smiled. "Now, before we further discuss my ideas for reversing our recent defeat, may I first offer you safe haven in the part of the galaxy I call home?"

"Is that offer for *all* the legionnaires?" Canby asked in surprise.

"All who will come," Kobir promised, "including those who presently remain on Earth. After yesterday, I strongly suspect we have common cause in a number of matters."

Canby thought about that for a long moment, while a thousand random concerns blazed through his mind. He rubbed his smooth chin and nodded thoughtfully. Nothing was more important than getting the legionnaires to some sort of safe haven—and the pirate's invitation was by far the best (as well as the only) one his legionnaires had in hand. "Nikolai," he said at length, "we'll be proud to accept your offer. Then," he added grimly, "once everybody's safe, I really want to talk about repaying this fellow Renaldo for his troubles. And the sooner, the better."

Kobir smiled. "Let us call a navigators' conference immediately," he said. "The sooner we begin to seriously plan for our joint mission, the sooner Sadir will feel our retribution—and unwillingly line our pockets."

Book Nine

THE GIULIO CESARE

Belgravia, London • Earth

Following a night's debauch at the Belgravia House to mollify his troubled mind, Renaldo sat on the side of his great canopied bed frowning as a beautiful young man darted from the silken sheets and pranced for the bathroom. Expensive enough! But high price was preferable to constant thoughts about blackmail or, worse, revenge. Even construction of his elaborate gem room and anticipation of Philante's upcoming reaction to seeing the Giulio Cesare failed to keep his mind from the fact that both Kobir and Canby were probably coming for him now—*together*. He'd tripled the number of guards in his mansion, but the devil Kobir had already shown himself well nigh immune from guards or police . . . or the Fleet, for that matter. He ground his teeth.

The young man pranced back from the bathroom, all powder and perfume—*very* obviously ready for more of what he'd been hired to do, but Renaldo waved him off. "That will be enough for tonight," he growled. "Pick up your clothes and go. Someone downstairs will give you money."

"But my lord—" the man protested.

"Enough!" Renaldo growled, sending the youth flying with a backhand to the mouth. He ignored the whimpering as he waddled to the bathroom and squatted on his custom-built commode. Immediately his mind returned to the dilemma that had dogged him for days: what to do about the accursed pair whose very existence threatened his sanity—and probably his life. What *was* he to do? No question that they would eventually strike, and he needed some warning before they did. Perhaps with a little advance notice, he could alert the police—quadruple his bodyguard. Something . . .

But how to get that advance notice?

Reaching into the box of chocolates, he retrieved two huge liquid-filled confections and crammed them both into his mouth, savoring the thick, healing syrup as it glided soothingly over his lips and tongue. There—that was better. Then Kobir's face passed before his mind's eye, followed by the mercenary's. Another chocolate—but this one didn't help. What *was* he going to do?

Suddenly he snapped his fingers. Tenniel again—of course! She'd be maintaining contact with the damned legionnaire. Certainly she'd be under some suspicion—anyone with whom Canby had shared his operational plan would be. But Renaldo slyly guessed her ministrations to the mercenary were at least as professional as the ones she supplied to him—probably even better, since she professed to love him. So at worst the man would probably be in a state of strong denial—even honest disbelief. Hence he would almost certainly be counted upon to keep in touch—men tended to make poor decisions when their balls were involved. Renaldo chuckled as the cloud of worry dissipated considerably. "Mrs. Timpton," he shouted, "get the whore Tenniel on the HoloPhone—immediately!"

Minutes later, Timpton appeared at the lavatory door with a 'Phone in her hand, clearly breathing through her mouth (why did they all *do* that?). Tenniel's sleepy face and torso were already materialized fetchingly in the globular display.

Renaldo took the 'Phone and smiled into its camera. "Cynthia, my dear," he simpered, "I require a tiny, *tiny* favor. . . ."

She reported back within two days. "He 'Phoned today," she said, this time appearing in the display outfitted in her most severe business apparel.

"Well?" Sadir demanded.

"What do you want to know, Renaldo?" she asked.

"Everything," he growled. "Tell me everything."

"Well," she began, "I've got to assume his commission to you failed, because he said something about an 'accident' that not only wrecked his mission but cost him two ships and many casualties."

"I'd heard something about that," Sadir commented. "You'll notice your escrow account has disappeared. Was he hurt?"

"No," Tenniel replied with a troubled look. "But I couldn't actually *see* him. His call came on the Nekní-HyCOMM network. I had the source traced, as you asked; that's all the farther they got. The network's so old it doesn't carry source *or* video. And it only serves remote areas."

Renaldo ground his teeth. He was not surprised. Though stupid, neither Canby nor Kobir was an utter fool. "Did he *say* anything that might indicate where he is or where he called from?"

"I recorded our conversation for you," Tenniel said. "But I didn't catch anything myself—it was almost as if he were being careful with me." She narrowed her eyes. "Sadir," she demanded with a frown, "did *you* have anything to do with that 'accident' of his?"

Renaldo raised his eyebrows. "I?" he asked in a hurt voice. "Of course not, my dear," he said placatingly. "If you had any idea the trouble those pirates were causing me . . . In any case, how could *I* affect a battle far in space?"

"You *did* have Canby's operational plans," she reminded him.

The Earl raised his hands in supplication. "Tenniel, words such as those cut me deeply. Besides, he's *only* a mercenary, after all."

"Keep in mind that I love him," she warned.

Renaldo laughed. "As much," he asked, "as you love that Directorship you purchased with his secret plans? Don't forget, harlot," he said, fixing her with a cold stare, "that I could have you out of that job in a moment."

Tenniel clamped her eyes shut a moment. "Yes," she said, presently, "I have that in mind, Renaldo."

"Good," Renaldo said. "See that you *keep* it in mind." He frowned. "Now," he continued, "I want to be notified the moment he appears at any location you can trace. Understand?"

Tenniel never opened her eyes; she only nodded. "Yes, Renaldo," she said, "I understand."

"*What* do you understand, whore?" Renaldo demanded.

"T-that you are to be notified as soon as Gordon calls me from any 'Phone that can be traced."

Renaldo felt himself grin while the old thrill of subjugation began to titillate his ego. As always, he felt the sensation most strongly in his loins. "Take off your clothes, whore," he commanded. "I want to see. . . ."

Afterward, his worries soon returned and he fretfully consumed a whole box of chocolates while contemplating the distinct probability that—under the devil Kobir's tutelage—Tenniel's mercenary friend had just become a great deal more perceptive than he was before his failed raid. The very thought made him shudder.

Calabria • Khalife

Throughout much of Earth's late summer and autumn, the surviving legionnaires made sanctuary with Kobir in the ancient, exotic city of Calabria. Canby himself continued to be in touch with Tenniel, but only by Nekní-HyCOMM. His passion for her endured; however, a slow-burning mistrust prevented him from revealing where he was hiding when she asked—and he dared not return to the Empire. Helplessly, he sensed their relationship beginning to unravel.

By mid-October, Kobir and Canby completed plans for relieving Renaldo of his prized Giulio Cesare StarBlaze. At no little cost, Kobir had covertly obtained detailed, highly confidential architectural drawings of Renaldo's huge new ballroom and its sophisticated gem vault. Then, after careful study, teams of Kîrskian technicians jointly devised a scheme for defeating its security devices.

Now Canby and the pirate waited eagerly for word that the magnificent addition to his Belgravia Mansion was complete and the famous gem had been installed in its display crypt.

DECEMBER 9, 2691, EARTH DATE

Belgravia, London • Earth

With the approaching XmasTide season—and coincidentally with completion of his grand ballroom and gem house—Renaldo finalized plans for his greatest triumph. This year, as he hosted the Grand Knight's XmasDay Masquerade in the Belgravia Mansion, he would accomplish *two* long-sought-after goals—in addition to gratifying his fellow

Knights. First, it would serve as a fitting inaugural for the new ballroom, designed specifically to exceed—by a wide margin—excesses built into Lord Sterling's Battersea Concert Hall. But it would also provide an appropriate event for unveiling the colossal Giulio Cesare StarBlaze—as well as its elegantly impressive security vault, which the builder and architect had certified to be impregnable.

Today, as he sat in his study, ignoring the faint, sour odor of charred wood (it simply *would* not go away!), preparations for the gala event offered scant assistance in deflecting the awful concerns that dogged him night and day. For months, his every waking moment had been fraught with the promise of sudden violence—and it *still* hadn't happened. Sometimes, late at night, in his darkest, most sweaty sleeplessness, he even wished they'd get it over with. Out there *somewhere,* he knew Kobir and Canby were biding their time until they did something perfectly horrible. . . .

Forcing his labored breathing under control, he smashed his fists on the antique wood of his workstation. That *thrice*-damned Lotember! Even thoughts of the man made him almost physically ill. Renaldo had sponsored an incompetence declaration in the House, but the measure was killed by opposition from powerful families who owed Lotember the high-level appointments their sons and daughters enjoyed in the Fleet. After that, Renaldo had simply withdrawn all financial support for the utter nincompoop. With elections scheduled for early the following year, the man faced almost certain defeat at the polls. *That* brought a smile to the Earl's bloated lips. If anyone *ever* deserved ruin, it was Lotember!

But revenge contributed little to solving his problems—and nothing to easing his fears. Stuffing three chocolates into his mouth, he swallowed them almost whole, then mashed the intercom HOUSE BROADCAST key with a sticky thumb. "Mrs. Timpton," he cried at the top of his voice, "bring a new woman here to me immediately!"

DECEMBER 20, 2691, EARTH DATE

Near Calabria • Khalife

Preparation for the Belgravia raid had been complete for more than a week now; it was time to execute the plan. Canby's old ED-3 was moored alongside a boarding quay, singled up, and ready to lift for space. Around it, Kobir's great pirate cave echoed with the rumbling generators, slamming hatches, shouts of farewell, thudding space boots, squeaking lifts, and other sounds of imminent departure. The two leaders waited near the quay end, ready to deal with last-minute contingencies while a group of legionnaires and pirates—outfitted in traveling clothes from sundry economic and cultural denominations—marched over a short brow to the ship's hatch. Inside, they then would step directly into a comfortably outfitted container disguised to appear as if it accommodated only freight. "Wonder what we've forgotten," Canby remarked, rubbing his chin.

Kobir grinned. "Nothing, I think." He chuckled. "That magnificent woman of yours, Lela, would not permit such a thing. She even sent old Zerner Petroski on ahead in the KV 72 to wait in Southampton, just in case we need a backup once we arrive."

Glancing up to the bridge, Canby watched Peterson at her station beside the right quarter window, juggling the ten million details that became her responsibility before any mission in space. "I don't think we could get along without her," he agreed. "She's one hell of a trooper."

"In many ways, one suspects," Kobir added with a frown. "You two were . . . shall we say, *close* at one time?"

"Yeah," Canby acknowledged over the shriek of a loading crane. "But after we started the Legion, we . . . " he shrugged, "well, you know what shipboard romances can do to a ship's morale. Actually, it was *her* idea to break things off."

"Sad," Kobir declared, pursing his lips. "I have little experience with the ways of Imperial women, but my heart tells me that she still feels deeply for you."

For more than a year, Canby had been denying the same conviction. "Hmm," he mumbled noncommittally.

"Only an observation," Kobir said with a little shrug, "and certainly none of my business." He pointed to the starboard boarding hatch, where a few stragglers were hurrying over the short brow. "Observe," he said. "The last of our joint assault team. Have *you* forgotten anything?"

Canby smiled, glad to change the subject. "Everything that goes with me is either *on* my back or packed on the bridge. I'm ready."

"Then let us take our places for liftoff, my friend," Kobir said, placing an arm around Canby's shoulders. "I find myself anxious to be on the way."

The last commandos aboard were followed by strings of well-worn luggage similar, at least in appearance, to those that might follow any of the million-odd tourists traipsing across intragalactic space at any given hour. Once the old ship had cleared Imperial Customs at the Starship Terminal on London's historic Greenland Dock, she would taxi to a nearby wharf where the container would be off loaded into a warehouse. From here, the "tourists" could, one by one, scatter and mix with normal denizens of the streets to spend the night on their own. They would gather the next day to ready their equipment in the crypt of St. John's Hall, Smiths Square, not far from the House of Nobles. From there, they would mount their assault on the Earl's Belgravia mansion.

DECEMBER 23, 2691, EARTH DATE

Belgravia, London • Earth

As corps of valets prepared Renaldo for a holiday revival of Massenet's sumptuous, but incoherent, *Hérodiade* (with dazzling soprano Idlabet Ataner singing the title role), a servant appeared at the door with a 'Phone in his hand. He bowed. "For you, my lord," he announced quietly.

Renaldo was about to rebuke the idiot for interrupting his toilet—the twelfth-century knight's costume was difficult enough to don without interruptions—but he noticed Tenniel's head and shoulders already materialized in the holographic display. He took the 'Phone and completed its connection. "Good day, whore," he said with all the amicability he could muster within the comfortless strictures of his corset. "What do you want that you couldn't ask for when you arrive tomorrow?"

"It's Canby," she said with a strange, almost triumphant expression in her eyes. "He's called—from here on Earth."

Renaldo froze. "Where?" he demanded.

"Oh," she said breezily, "that's *my* business at present—but probably he's close enough to you this very instant to put your life in danger."

"Goddamnit, woman!" he screamed into the 'Phone, his blood pressure mounting. "Tell me immediately, or I'll terminate that job of yours faster than you can blink! Understand me, you filthy slut?"

Tenniel appeared to ignore his words. "You won't do anything like that, *Sadir*," she said, a wicked little smile forming on her lips. "Otherwise I may not tell you a little secret."

So *that* was her game! Renaldo sank into a chair. "What kind of secret?" he asked suspiciously.

"Oh, you *may* find out," she assured him, "if you are especially good to me."

"Goddamnit," Renaldo demanded in a voice tight with anger, *"where is he?"*

"That," she said firmly, "is a secret that I *may* share with you tomorrow—after the masquerade." She smiled and cooed happily. "You do remember the masquerade, don't you?" she asked solicitously.

Renaldo bit his lip. "Of *course* I remember the masquerade," he growled. "But this Canby—"

"Ta!" she interrupted with a little wave of her hand. "Send a limousine skimmer to the first-class lounge of Victoria Station. My HyperTube arrives at noon." With that, the 'Phone's display disappeared.

Renaldo slumped in the chair, awash with perspiration. He had a sick feeling that the price for this "secret" of Tenniel's was going to make even blackmail payments to Kobir seem insignificant in comparison. An even *sicker* feeling warned him that he'd pay.

DECEMBER 25, 2691

Smiths Square, London • Earth

XmasDay, Imperial Earth's most commercially important bank holiday, had long ago lost its devout trappings. But throughout the Empire shrewd merchandisers nevertheless kept it alive for their own purposes. Outside St. John's Hall, Smiths Square fairly rang from carolers in gaudy, varicolored finery, chanting the latest popular mantras of sex and violence at the top of their lungs and trampling the remains of once-perfect snow that had gently fallen overnight. Their noisome clamor made it that much easier for the commandos to gather unobserved in the ancient, vaulted crypt where the full company now worked diligently preparing their weapons.

By 6:45 P.M., the commandos were outfitted and ready. Canby and Kobir inspected each man and woman, checking for flaws in their camouflage: long, multihued wigs, garish sports hoods, huge shirts, and voluminous trousers covered their battle suits. The costumes produced a rather odd appearance of persons seriously challenged by upper-torso birth defects, but amid the crowds of revelers Canby had encountered on his way to the square, they would attract little notice at all.

To Canby's way of thinking, the most conspicuous of all was Kobir, who stood nearly a head taller than the rest. His fashionably obtrusive disguise made him look like some terrifying vision of ancient Harlequin—a costume absolutely perfect for encounters in dark alleyways. On the other hand, Canby himself—already somewhat thickset—appeared in the mirror as the one most seriously in need of a weight-loss program.

At 6:55 Kobir stood and held his hand in the air. "We shall synchronize our watches on local time," he announced as the vaulted room fell attentively quiet. "I have eighteen fifty-six hours . . . now! We leave for Belgravia at precisely nineteen hundred. Each of you will follow your team leader and travel so that everyone reaches Grosvenor Square and Halkin Street at twenty-one thirty hours. Any questions?" he asked, glancing around the room. Only the sound of camouflaged battle packs being hoisted broke the silence. "All right, then," he said, starting for the winding staircase that led to the street. "If all proceeds according to plan, we will soon entertain Renaldo and his guests with some unscheduled diversion."

Belgravia House, Belgravia, London • Earth

Nine o'clock P.M. GMT—the traditional XmasDay Moment of Unveiling. Standing naked at the center of the dance floor, Renaldo had disrobed with more exuberance than he had managed for years. In turn, the whore Tenniel—already

out of her exquisite, early-twentieth-century ball gown repro-
duction—was languidly sliding down her briefs to wild applause from the encircling guests. Nearby, Targas, Ninth
Baron of Manchester and next in sequence to undress, was
grinning like an idiot while he fidgeted impatiently in his authentic twenty-first-century jumpsuit.

The Earl sighed happily, accepting a cocktail from a servant dressed as a first-century Roman tribune. Even though
Tenniel had yet to reveal her "secret," so far his XmasDay
Masquerade appeared to be an even greater success than he
had dared to dream. The new ballroom was a triumph in itself, with guests—including skinny Emperor Philante—beside themselves with envy. He could tell from their sneering
remarks—and awestruck eyes.

But the surprise unveiling of the Giulio Cesare had so far
crowned the evening. As the great gem vault rose majesti-
cally from the ballroom floor, banks of ceiling-mounted
lasers had kindled its many facets with coherent light of all
colors, filling the great room with almost painful splendor.
The look in Philante's eyes alone was worth everything! A
complete triumph!

As one by one the guests disrobed, Renaldo's thoughts
continued to return to Tenniel's "secret." She had steadfastly
refused even to discuss the matter until *after* the masquerade,
and now there was no further opportunity to question her, for
the night's zenith—the Great Union—was about to begin. . . .

Grovsner Crescent at Hawking Street, Belgravia, London • Earth

Under a lowering sky, the commandos dodged purposely
through inebriated throngs in the Belgravia streets. Canby
was in front, followed closely by Kobir and Rosa Gambini.
No one seemed to notice the fast-moving group in the
drunken holiday confusion. Ahead, Renaldo's huge Belgravia House stood head and shoulders above its neighbors,

blazing with lights, an oversized grotesquerie in the midst of an otherwise elegant neighborhood.

Canby led because he was least likely to be recognized during the critical opening operations. Leaving the others just beyond the mansion's heavily guarded main portico, the three made their way to a nearby mews, where more than a hundred chauffeurs were drinking themselves insensible beside the arrogant limousine skimmers they drove. Breaking left between two enormous Daimlers, Canby made swiftly for a brick-walled, windowless blockhouse at the back of the lot, then stopped in deep shadows, just short of the door. "Everyone set?" he asked.

Gambini nodded while Kobir spoke quietly over a small communicator. He raised a momentary warning hand, then nodded. "Dorian reports everyone is in place," he whispered.

Canby nodded, then snapped a fresh power pack into his blaster. When its tiny neon glowed OK, he flipped off the safety and stuffed the weapon behind his coat, then removed a half-filled bottle of gin from his battle pack and threw away the cork. Next, he retrieved a gaudy credit card with his picture on it, pinning the latter onto his belt as if it were a security pass. Finally, keeping his hooded battle helmet turned from view, he lowered the visor, paused to compose himself, then stumbled into the dim light, boldly rapping on the door as if he belonged there.

Inside, a guard dressed in an imposing gold uniform opened the door a crack with his hand outstretched for the shadowed badge. Canby reckoned he was as new as the security system—and, from his fixed smile and poorly focused eyes, more than slightly drunk. Instead of the "security badge," he proffered the gin with a jovial but slurred, "Happy XmasDay!"

The guard affably opened the door wider and reached for the bottle, but Canby pretended to slip on the narrow stairs and fumbled it. The guard bent down for an attempted save, but never got his fingers close. The butt of Canby's blaster was the last thing he felt—a crackling blow to the back of the head that crushed his brain stem and killed him instantly.

Motioning the others to follow, Canby awkwardly dragged the body back into the guard room, placing it slumped over the desk, head on its arms and already smelling strongly of feces. Beside him, Kobir and Gambini ran system checks on their silenced ZJ-36 assault blasters—both passed.

Kobir checked his watch, then paused a moment, and nodded. "It is time," he whispered.

With his blaster ready to fire, Canby took the electronic access keys from the guard's body and unbolted the first inner door. It opened flawlessly—with no audible alarm, though he knew there would be some sort of indication within the security control room ahead. The second door also opened easily. At the third, however, a peephole was already in use as he approached. Immediately, he blanked it with his credit card while inserting the third card key and yanking the big steel door outward with all his might. The suspicious guard who had been using the keyhole came out with it— sprawling head first in the open doorway.

Even as Kobir shot off the back of his head, Gambini used the body as a carpet, leaping into the control room with her assault blaster snuffling through its silencer like some slavering beast.

Inside, nine gold-uniformed security technicians—wearing party hats and clearly into the holiday spirit—had been monitoring systems in the security control room. Jumping from their consoles in fright, they were literally blasted apart while Gambini and Kobir patiently worked their way around the room. Only four managed to draw their weapons, and of those, one managed to make a dash for the door. Canby stopped him with a shot directly between the eyes. The assault was over so quickly, none of the technicians had a chance even to touch the consoles.

Afterward, Kobir grimly made the rounds of the room, shooting each body directly in the base of the brain. "It is over," he said, looking up with a certain distaste. "Now, Rosa," he said gently, "we look to you for dealing with the security systems."

Gambini nodded, a strangely fulfilled look in her eyes.

Canby swore she'd just had an orgasm.

Seating herself at the central console, she retrieved an envelope of scribbled notes from her battle kit, then began operating the controls as if she had worked in the building for years. Less than five minutes later, she pushed back her chair and smiled proudly. "My Kapitans," she said, swinging her gaze from Canby to Kobir, "the ballroom doors are no longer alarmed. And," she added with a little smile, "the gem vault has already been raised and is open for display in the center of the ballroom floor. I have made certain that it can no longer be closed—or lowered."

Kobir nodded. "Thank you, Rosa," he said. "As always, you have executed your duties commendably." He turned to Canby. "Well, my friend," he said, "are you ready for the next phase?"

Canby glanced around the bloody, corpse-littered control room and nodded. "Let's get to work," he said, opening the door. "Be a damn shame if we went to all this trouble for nothing."

Grinning appreciatively, Kobir put the communicator to his ear. "Dorian," he said, "let us now execute phase two." With that, he shouldered his weapon and jogged into the corridor, Gambini and Canby sprinting in his wake.

Belgravia House, Belgravia, London • Earth

Heart pounding, Kobir joined a small group of commandos poised outside the steel fire doors of Renaldo's new ballroom and lifted his visor, savoring the cold, fresh air. He'd outrun his two partners and felt rather good about it. The other commando groups had already reported they were in place and listening for his signal. In retrospect, he'd been pleasantly surprised at the fellow Canby, who'd proven himself to be a tough, able soldier as well as an excellent helmsman. At first, the mercenary hadn't seemed like a very promising commando, but then, he, Kobir, had been wrong before—and he was certain he would be wrong again. He frowned as the two approached, panting to catch their breath. "Émil," he whispered, turning to Lippi, who held a detonator aimed at the small charge that would open the ballroom doors, "you are ready?"

"Ready, my Kapitan," Lippi said calmly.

Kobir spoke into the 'Phone, "Dorian . . . Olga," he whispered. "You are ready?"

"Ready, Kapitan," Skoda reported.

"Rarin' to go," came Confrass's reply, bringing a smile to the Kîrskian's lips in spite of the grim situation.

"O'Connor," Kobir broadcast, "you have your charges in place?"

"They're in place, Captain," he reported in the strange dialect he called "New York accent."

"Feliks Dzerezhinsky—your charges?"

"My charges are in place as well," an elderly Kîrskian intelligence officer replied from a rooftop skylight.

"And yours, Commander Gibbons?"

"In place," Gibbons reported from the mansion's electrical room.

Kobir nodded to himself. "All right, my friends," he said, pronouncing the words slowly into his communicator. "Fire your charges!"

In the next moment, blinding flashes lit the immediate area, then faded. "Door's open," he heard Canby announce as he turned. Shutting his visor once more, he raised his ZJ-36 and made for the colorful brightness beyond the door where frightened screams and shouts of terror were just beginning to ring out.

The Ballroom, Belgravia House, London • Earth

Ecstatic groans and squeals of the Great Union were just beginning to fill the ballroom as a panting Renaldo settled to his back on one of the many couches scattered throughout the ballroom. During the last half hour, he'd been aroused to a positive frenzy by Tenniel's practiced ministrations. Now—at last!—he was watching deliriously as she settled over his haunches, twisting and turning as she descended. She had just begun the singular pelvic motions for which she had become deservedly famous when the world erupted in a paroxysm of mind-numbing explosions, blaster fire, shouts, screams, and pounding boots. Huge, misshapen figures thudded past their couch while the shrieking whore threw her hands over her head and dove for the floor, disengaging at a *most* excruciating angle and leaving him to scramble from the couch with no assistance whatsoever.

Unintentionally, he landed atop the screaming woman, and immediately rolled off in an attempt to scuttle beneath the couch as others were doing nearby. He soon discovered, however, that there was simply too much of him to fit. Frantically extricating his head—directly into her bottom (which only heightened the screaming)—he shoved her aside violently. Then, his heart racing with apprehension, he struggled to his knees, peered over the couch . . . and groaned.

In seconds, his beautiful new ballroom had been turned to a shambles; the Grand Entranceway and stairs were only a smoldering tangle of metal formers; three of the eight Doric columns had been tumbled; and another two rested uneasily at odd angles. Beyond, in the vaulted promenade that led to his lofty Grand Refectory, he could see at least five sprawled bodies—dressed in the new gold livery he'd only just purchased for the event. He gasped. Their uniforms would be *ruined*! The fire doors had been blown from their hinges and one of the two grand chandeliers lay in a glittering heap, a hundred thousand crystals hiding (to some extent) the unfortunate revelers that had been underneath it when it fell—and all that blood could *never* be cleaned from the blond mahogany dance floor. Everywhere, confusion reigned supreme. Stark-naked people were frantically running in circles through the smoke-filled air, screaming, shouting, and trying to cover themselves with scraps of the clothing that had been strewn over the floor. And herding them toward an exitless corner were some of the most outlandishly dressed XmasDay carousers he'd ever seen—strange, misshapen people with huge heads and shoulders . . . *what were they doing here*?

Suddenly Renaldo's heart stopped. The StarBlaze! Spinning about violently—and sending the whimpering whore Tenniel into an adjoining couch—he was just in time to see a gigantic form dressed as some demonized Harlequin step, unharmed, into the dazzling circle of laser beams. "Don't!" he screamed with a nauseated sensation of absolute helplessness. "Oh, my God—NO! Not the Giulio Cesare! It's *mine*! Guards! Guards! Hel-l-l-p!" His voice was swept away in the swirling confusion. He struggled to his feet just as Harlequin dropped the great stone into a large, fashionable backpack and stormed back onto the ballroom floor. His menacing appearance alone was enough to scatter the shocked revelers.

Screaming for help at the top of his air-starved lungs, Renaldo watched in near paralysis while the giant was joined by another of the oddly shaped intruders, this one much shorter. As the pair stormed toward the ruined fire exit, he found himself directly in their path. Then he realized for the first time why the intruders looked so misshapen. Under those ludicrous XmasDay costumes, they were wearing battle suits. And as the two horrible apparitions drew near, he fell back onto the couch in dread. The tall one—whose ebony FlexArmor now showed through his costume—could only be the Goddamned Kîrskian pirate Kobir!

"My God!" Canby swore, catching up with Kobir near the center of the huge orgy into which they'd blundered. "Did you ever see anything like this?" Everywhere he looked, naked people were shrinking from their path, slithering beneath the myriad couches, or covering themselves with parts of what appeared to be a thousand fantastic-looking costumes that littered the floor.

"Only in my wildest dreams," the pirate replied with a chuckle. "Not bad when you consider everything—good smut show like this *and* the Giulio Cesare!"

Ahead, a screaming fat man had just fallen backward onto a couch in their path while a slim blonde cowered on her hands and knees beside him. "Yeah," Canby agreed. "Some mighty attractive horseflesh here." Suddenly he stopped in his tracks while the whole insane universe seemed to crumble from beneath his boots. The woman had been crying, and her long hair was in total disarray—but there could be no mistake. "Cynthia!" he gasped while she screamed in terror at him, eyes wide in fright and arms covering her head.

"What?" he heard Kobir ask. He felt a hand on his arm. "Gordon, my friend, now is *not* the time to sample the merchandise!"

"Oh, my God!" Canby gasped while reality hit him like a runaway lorry. With shaking hands, he inadvertently reached out to her, but she only screamed louder, then fell backward in a paroxysm of raw fear—convulsively wetting herself and his boot. Horrified, he was about to open his visor when he heard Kobir's voice.

"Renaldo!" the pirate called out jovially. "What a coincidence!"

Shock mixing instantly with anger, Canby turned from the shrieking Tenniel. *"This* is the Earl of Renaldo?" he asked, shakily peering down at an obese, rather repulsive little fellow cowering on the couch. The man's eyes were wide as saucers and his thick, open lips dribbled a long thread of spittle. His enormous white paunch barely covered the huge, flaccid organ that lolled between his skinny legs, and his hands were clenched as though he expected to die any second.

"The same, my friend," Kobir assured him.

Canby glanced at Tenniel, then returned his gaze to Renaldo. He shut his eyes for a moment. So this was the man who . . .

Kobir's hand on his arm became more insistent. "Come, my friend!" the Kîrskian urged. "We have been at work for nearly ten minutes—and as you said, it would be a shame to go to all this trouble . . . "

Canby nodded with a heavy heart. There was nothing he could do here. Taking one last glance at Tenniel—she was beautiful, even in the midst of chaos—he kicked Renaldo's couch to one side and followed Kobir toward the exit. But the exultation that *should* have filled his spirit was now replaced by a numbing sense of despair.

Recovering somewhat as the intruders disappeared, Renaldo struggled shakily to his feet, fear quickly turning to rage. "Guards!" he screamed. *"Guards!* H-e-e-l-l-p!" No one came, although the shouts and screams of panic from his terrorized guests were abating by the moment—and the fires were nearly out already, tribute to careful fireproofing he'd specified after the Kîrskians' previous raid. He continued to yell, futilely, for several minutes more until he realized that his guards were either dead or incapacitated—and no one else was interested in risking his or her neck in an attempt to help.

Beside him, a squatting Tenniel furiously toweled her bottom with someone's expensive-looking silk shirt . . . *his*! Presently, she glanced up at him, got to her feet, and tossed the shirt over a couch. Then she retrieved a discarded cape, pulled it around most of her nakedness with a flourish, and placed her hands on her hips. "The tall one—" she said after a moment, "he is your pirate Kobir?"

"Yes, the wicked, wicked . . . *foreigner*!" Renaldo spit

hoarsely, feeling silly, angry, and helpless all at the same time.

She peered at him for a moment, then wrinkled her nose. "Here," she said, retrieving the shirt. "Cover yourself up."

"This is damp!" he complained, stuffing the garment beneath his belly.

"You'll have something dry in a moment," she said in a soothing voice. "But tell me—you're *certain* that big man was the pirate?"

"He could have been no one else," Renaldo assured her, breathing a sigh of relief as servants and chauffeurs *finally* began to arrive. Among them were a few members of Philante's vaunted Praetorian Guard; many appeared to be wounded—some gravely.

"Would you like to know who the short one was?" she asked with a little smile.

"W-who do you mean?" Renaldo asked, suddenly irritated by the whole contemptible world. "The other pirate with Kobir?"

"Yes," Tenniel replied. "Except he wasn't a pirate."

"Well, who *was* he?" Renaldo demanded.

"Gordon Canby," she declared. "I recognized him only at the last moment."

"That mercenary of yours?" Renaldo gasped as he glanced around the room at his half-addled guests. It was *bad* out there on the dance floor.

"The same," she said, a strange gleam forming in her eyes. "I *could* produce him for you tomorrow evening," she said. "But my price will be *very* high."

Renaldo ground his teeth. "You think he knows where my Giulio Cesare is?"

"He was with your pirate, wasn't he?" she asked.

Renaldo nodded.

"Then it's a good bet he knows."

Renaldo rubbed his hands with glee. "I have people who would *love* to make him talk," he said, smiling for the first time since the attack. He placed his free arm around Tenniel's waist. "And what is your price this time?" he asked, drawing her to his side.

Tenniel smiled. "As I recall," she said as he felt her hand slide caressingly beneath the shirt, "we *first* have business to complete."

"Mm-m," he mumbled happily, momentarily oblivious to the destruction and carnage around him.

"Come, my fat lover," she urged, her fingers launching into the deft ministrations he so loved, "let us retire to your bedchamber where we can *also* privately discuss a replacement for David Lotember in the coming elections."

Book Ten

UNFINISHED BUSINESS

St. John's Hall, Smiths Square, London • Earth

In the early hours of a new day, Kobir relaxed, sipping vodka in the crypt of St. John's Hall and watching his jubilant raiders celebrate the success of a lifetime. He patted the great gem, safe and secure in a leather bag secured at his waist. When it was sold—already three agents had forwarded offers via certain "protected" networks—every pirate and legionnaire would be seriously rich, no matter what his or her share of the take. He grinned, overhearing random snatches of conversation recounting a thousand glimpses of Imperial Earth's most influential citizens interrupted at sport. It was a good morning to be alive!

Not everyone seemed to be happy, however. In an alcove

to Kobir's right, Canby slumped alone on the stone floor, head in his hands, complaining of a stomach virus. Kobir didn't believe a word. At first he'd thought the man was merely suffering from the odd letdown that often affects soldiers after risky action. Usually, however, a little vodka could snap them back after only an hour or so. Not so Canby; he'd been safe in St. John's Hall for nearly four hours now, with no signs of improvement whatsoever.

Kobir frowned, trying to recall when it was he'd last heard the man speak. Back at the ballroom, perhaps? Sipping his vodka, he closed his eyes, visualizing the strange scene they'd encountered there. He remembered Canby catching up with him near the gem vault, just before they blundered into Renaldo.

He shook his head and laughed, remembering *that*. If nothing else, it proved the almighty power of money. The gross rascal's evident partner for the . . . orgy, he supposed . . . had been an extraordinary blonde, slim and beautiful—one of the most elegant women he could remember, dressed *or* undressed.

Then it came to him. Canby *had* cried a name aloud. Something like . . . He scratched his head. Cynthia! That's what he called her—just about the time he'd reached out and she lost control of her bladder. He frowned. He'd never seen a woman do that before—at least not *up*. "My God!" he suddenly whispered. *She* must have been the one to whom Canby had revealed their plans—the one with the powerful lover. He nodded to himself. Few were more powerful than Renaldo!

He peered at Canby, who had hardly moved during the past hour—there could be no doubt. Nodding sadly, he knew full well that the man was very probably suffering a most grievous anguish. He, Kobir, had been in love once himself. His precious Dåna had been killed in an air raid nearly fifteen years ago—and he still yearned for her, no matter how many women had shared his life since her passing. Even now, the thought of a woman like Dåna cavorting with an evil, loathsome toad like Renaldo was enough to make his stomach turn. He could *well* imagine Canby's pain. Grimly, he refilled his tumbler and walked slowly across the floor to seat himself at the mercenary's side. "A penny for your thoughts, my friend," he said. "If, indeed, pennies still exist in this tired old world."

Canby looked up with a sad smile. "My thoughts?" he asked. "They're free—not that they're worth as much as a credit in the first place, mind you."

"I'll take that chance," Kobir said.

"Very well," Canby said. "Probably the most important thing on my mind is that I won't be going back to Khalife with you tomorrow."

"You won't be *what*?" Kobir demanded, both in surprise and concern.

"I'm not going back in the ED-3 tomorrow," Canby said. "I've got unfinished business here on Earth." He gripped Kobir's knee. "Don't worry, my friend," he added. "Eventually I'll make my own way back to Calabria. I'm not about to miss my share of the spoils."

"Glad to hear *that*," Kobir said with real concern. He rubbed his chin, debating whether or not to bring up the subject of the blonde. Then he shrugged. Better a live friend than a dead acquaintance. "This, er, 'unfinished business,' " he asked as carefully as he could. "Does it, perhaps, have something to do with the slim blonde we, er, *encountered* at Renaldo's mansion earlier this evening?"

"What blonde?" Canby asked with an expression of innocent puzzlement. "I saw a lot of good-looking blondes there."

"The one who peed on your boot," Kobir said judiciously.

"Oh, yeah," Canby said without meeting his eyes. "I do remember her. A real knockout."

"I suppose you don't remember calling her something like Cynthia," Kobir inquired, narrowing his eyes.

Canby gulped, but said nothing.

"Can it be possible," Kobir asked presently, "that this gorgeous blonde is the same woman who represented an anonymous Noble so powerful he could not be denied?" he asked. "Clearly, she was Renaldo's partner for the evening—painful as that might be to grasp."

Canby opened his mouth as if he were about to protest, then abruptly buried his face in his hands. "Yeah," he mumbled. "It's her."

"Did you *also,*" Kobir asked, "share your operational plan with this lovely woman?"

"Right before the mission," Canby admitted. "But that doesn't mean she was the one who . . . " He couldn't seem to finish the assertion.

Kobir shook his head. "I suppose it goes without saying that you love her."

Canby nodded. "God, how I love her," he swore in a tormented whisper.

By force of sheer will, Kobir unclenched his teeth. He took a deep breath, then a slow sip of vodka. "What have you told her about our hiding place here in Smiths Square?" he asked, as calmly as possible.

"Nothing," Canby said, looking him directly in the eye for the first time. "I've told her nothing since the battle last summer. And we only talked by Nekní-HyCOMM, since. Until I arrived here a day ago, that is."

"You mean she knew you were in London yesterday?" Kobir asked in amazement.

"It's a big city, Nikolai," Canby replied. "I could have been anywhere within a couple hundred miles."

"True," Kobir said, offering a silent prayer for the nameless gods who had prevented this lovesick idiot's presence in London from . . . God knew what. At length, he let the matter pass. No harm had been done, after all. But until Canby had managed to purge himself of this clearly treacherous blonde, he, Kobir, would think twice before trusting the

Earthman with operational plans again. He shook his head in bewilderment. He *ought* to be angry enough to kill the blithering idiot. But he wasn't. Something about the man—perhaps his very *humanity*—prevented that. "So, my friend," he said, "one assumes you two have arranged a rendezvous?"

Canby nodded. "Tomorrow evening at Waterloo Station," he said, "after you and the others are well on your way back to Khalife."

Kobir nodded. "I hate to even suggest such a thing, but,"—he raised his hands palm up—"isn't it possible that she might, well, betray you to Renaldo again?"

"Maybe," Canby said, dropping his eyes, "but maybe not. I still don't know for certain it was she who gave us away last summer." He shrugged. "And, yeah, I damn well saw who she was with at that orgy yesterday—but . . . " he shrugged. "You have no idea what she's been through. Without going into details, she deserves some pretty special compassion."

Kobir nodded noncommittally—they all did, he supposed. "I don't suppose I could talk you out of this rendezvous, could I?" he asked solicitously.

"You know me better than that," Canby said.

Kobir pursed his lips. In point of fact, he did. "Very well, my friend," he said tossing off the remainder of his vodka in one stinging draft, "then I shall leave you to your 'stomach virus.' " He laughed grimly. "You might wish to avail yourself of more vodka, however. For the kind of virus *you* have, it is one of the *only* specific cures."

Rotherhithe, London • Earth

Some two hours after bidding Kobir and the last of the raiders farewell, Canby caught the Underground at Blackfriars and rode to Rotherhithe near the south bank of the Thames. There, he found a pub near the water's edge where he could kill time until the ED-3's departure. He bought coffee and a hot roll, then settled at a corner table, oblivious to the dockyard characters who filled the tavern. In spite of everything, Kobir's doubts had managed to rekindle his own suspicions concerning Tenniel. But he *still* couldn't bring himself to abandon her completely. What if she really *did* love him? What if she *really* was casting about for some way to escape Renaldo's evil influence—God, wouldn't that be a fine time to let her down?

He shook his head grimly. Even if she did want his help, though, what could *he* do about things anyway? He had little power to protect her—or himself, for that matter. He'd *really* wanted to take her back to Khalife on the ED-3, but that was simply too risky for his comrades. So he'd let them go, and Godspeed, as the old saying went.

Power to help . . . He frowned and stared into his rapidly emptying pint. Certainly *he* had little power, himself, but . . . Suddenly it came to him. Of course! He knew someone who *did*!

Nemil Quinn!

Wondering where his head had been, he reached for his wallet. Did he still have that number the man had given him years ago? He fumbled through a worn collection of the—mostly useless—documents (large and small) he never found time to throw away, and . . .

Yes. There it was!

He smiled to himself. He wouldn't go to Quinn empty-handed, either. In point of fact, he had something that could be important to the man, as well—critical information he could use to secure Renaldo's powerful support in the upcoming election. Information that could also weaken the evil Noble's hold on Tenniel. If nothing else, the Earl could at least be blackmailed into granting the woman's release from his "service." There and then, he decided to 'Phone.

At 11:45 A.M. local time—5:45 that morning in New Washington—he placed his call.

"Hello, Quinn here," the Minister answered, with a towel

around his neck, as if he had only just finished his daily workout.

"Hello, er, Nemil? Gordon Canby here. Sorry to bother you so early this morning."

"No problem, Gordo!" Quinn exclaimed. "Haven't heard from you in a long time. What's going on—everything all right?"

Canby frowned. One thing he hated himself was a whiner, and guessed Quinn was the same way. But hadn't the man heard about last summer's shoot-out? "I'm fine," he lied, putting as much hardiness into his voice as he could. "The legionnaires and I were in a little scrape a few months ago, but that's mostly over. Probably you heard about it."

"Yeah." Quinn laughed adroitly. "Something about a battlecruiser or two, wasn't it?"

"Something like that," Canby said.

"Some '*little* scrape,' " Quinn offered.

Canby shrugged. "Well, maybe not little, but manageable," he said, forcing a grin that he hoped looked real. "Anyway, that's only *related* to why I called."

"So, what's on your mind, my friend?"

"What's on my alleged mind, Nemil," Canby said, "is that as a result of that little scrape, I got the goods on one of our Imperial Nobles who could go a long way to paying the rest of your way at the polls—whether he wants to or not."

"You're serious?" Quinn said, leaning forward in the display. He smiled as if he could hardly believe his ears. "I guess you didn't know my campaign's nearly out of funds."

Canby shook his head. "No, sir, I didn't," he said. "But you probably won't have to worry much longer about that."

Quinn didn't just look interested, he appeared to be *fascinated*. He glanced from one side to the other, then frowned. "Wait till I close the door," he said, then disappeared from the display. Moments later, when he returned, he had a personal note taker. "Who is it?" he asked.

"Sadir," Canby said. "First Earl of Renaldo."

"Renaldo!" Quinn spluttered in surprise. "Jesus, Canby, you don't go for the little ones, do you?"

"I didn't 'go' for anyone," Canby protested. "I happened on the information by, er, accident." He looked Quinn's image directly in its eyes. "Everything is *verifiable*," he continued. "Renaldo's been paying heavy blackmail because of it for more than two years!"

"I believe you," Quinn said quickly. "Don't say anything more over the 'Phone. I'll need to hear it from you in person—with a lawyer to record your testimony." He frowned. "Listen, fella," he said, "if I'm any judge, you're in a bit of trouble right now. Right?"

Canby shrugged as casually as he could. "Nothing I can't handle," he said.

"Bullshit," Quinn said. "What can I do to help *you*?"

Canby had been listening for *that*. "I need some protection till I can get away from Earth," he said, "with a friend. That's all."

"Hell, that's no problem," Quinn said. "I can give you all the protection you need." He pursed his lips. "I know you're too smart to call from a private 'Phone, so where can I get in touch with you?"

"You're coming to London?"

"You bet I'm coming to London." He glanced at his watch. "I can be there by . . . how about if I catch the eleven forty-five HyperTube this morning? It'll get me there at a quarter of six this afternoon—your time."

Canby nodded. "It's perfect, Nemil," he said. "I'll be at Waterloo Station . . ." he checked a scrap of paper in his pocket, "Tunnel Gate Thirty-four, seven o'clock sharp. Meet me there."

"Tonight."

"Tonight," Canby assured him.

"Are you expecting, er, trouble?" Quinn suddenly asked with a serious mien.

"I don't know, Nemil," Canby said. "Maybe."

Quinn nodded. "I'll have some persuasive types with me, just in case," he said. "Anything else?"

Suddenly feeling very obliged, Canby nodded. "I don't know how to thank you, Nemil Quinn," he said. "You're a real friend—and have been for a long time."

Quinn laughed modestly. "Don't mention it, my friend," he said. "Besides, you've helped me in a lot of ways you don't even know about."

Canby started to thank him again, but Quinn held up his hand.

"See you soon, Gordo," he said. "Waterloo Station, Tunnel Gate Thirty-four, seven o'clock—your time—sharp." With that, the display went blank.

It was a much-relieved Gordon Canby who ordered wedges of Stilton cheese with some crusty bread for lunch. Later, he'd go elsewhere to watch the ED-3 lift off. Then, a few hours after that, it would be time to head to Waterloo Station—and a date with both Cynthia Tenniel and Nemil Quinn.

Greenland Dock, London • Earth

Kobir was the last to arrive at the warehouse. When he entered through the small personnel door, it was eleven A.M.; the container had already been loaded aboard the ED-3, and liftoff was less than an hour away—as soon as the Customs inspectors had been paid off. Peterson was waiting just inside.

"Where's Canby?" she demanded.

Kobir flinched, completely unprepared for the question. "Er . . . I don't know, Lela," he said.

"When's he coming, then?" she asked, glancing at her watch.

Kobir bit his lip. Canby *wasn't* coming, and there was no way around it. "He's not," he said, looking into her worried eyes. "He said he's got . . . unfinished business here."

"Like that skinny blonde whore he's been running around after?" she demanded.

"He didn't er . . . " Kobir began, then shook his head. Lying was no good, not in this situation. "You mean the Tenniel woman, don't you?" he asked.

"Yeah," Peterson said.

"Indeed, she seems to be his unfinished business," Kobir admitted.

"Christ on a crutch," Peterson swore, closing her eyes for a moment. "The bastard's brains must be dangling between his legs." She looked at Kobir with a worried frown. "Everybody *knows* she's the one who sold us out last summer. How could he do something that asinine?"

"Perhaps *he* doesn't know," Kobir said, putting his hand on her arm.

Peterson shook her head. "Doesn't matter," she said. "We still can't just leave him here. When's he meeting her—and where?"

"I don't know the exact time," Kobir said. "Sometime tonight—at Waterloo Station."

Peterson grimaced. "I'd be willing to bet my share of that big StarBlaze that she'll be there with a couple dozen of her fat boyfriend's strongmen, just waiting to make him lead them to *us*."

"I imagine that is why Canby scheduled the meeting *after* we're safe in space," Kobir offered.

"*See?*" Peterson said. "He *doesn't* trust her." She clenched her fists. "But he's so much in lust with the skinny slut that he's willing to risk everything—except us." Suddenly her eyes opened wide. "We've got to *do* something, Nikolai," she said. "He's too good of a guy to just . . . leave behind."

Kobir took a deep breath—he'd been thinking the same sort of thing since he and Canby had parted company just outside Smiths Square. "I agree," he said presently. "But what? He said he would be somewhere watching our liftoff from the

Thames, so we've got to leave on schedule, no matter what else we plan to do, or he'll simply meet her another time."

Peterson nodded. "Yeah," she said. "And when you get right down to it, we're really obligated to get the StarBlaze safely back to Khalife. I mean, it doesn't just belong to a few of us."

Kobir nodded. He hadn't thought of *that* little point. "So whatever we do must be done after the ED-3 has truly departed—with the stone safely aboard."

"Yeah," Peterson said. "Still interested?"

Kobir laughed. "That man means a great deal to you, doesn't he?" he asked.

"Of course not," she said, averting her eyes for a moment and scratching her nose. "He's just a . . . good leader. Hell, without him, we wouldn't have the Legion or anything."

"Yes, certainly," Kobir said hastily retreating from *that*.

"So," she demanded, "you still interested in trying to do something for Canby?"

"Of course," Kobir said emphatically, "if there is anything to be done."

Peterson nodded gravely. "Yeah, I know what you mean, Nikolai," she said, squeezing her eyes shut. "But there's gotta be *something* we can do. Think, Lela. For God's sake *think*!"

Waterloo Station, London • Earth

Turning up his collar, Canby rounded the corner of Exton Street, crossed Waterloo Road, and strode into the colossal station at 6:55 by the concourse clock. Nothing remained to be done before his rendezvous with Tenniel and . . .

He didn't *need* to think of the possibilities anymore; everyone else was now safely in space and on their way to Khalife. He smiled to himself as he strode toward the Tunnel concourse—if nothing else, he was certain about that.

He'd been seated at a riverside pub on Dog's Island at about 3:15 when the ED-3 appeared at the mouth of a canal and started out into the choppy water, throwing great sheets of spray to either side. He'd quickly stepped into the chill dampness to watch from the street, emotions tugging almost painfully at his heart as he pictured his comrades celebrating their hard-won victory inside the starship's "freight container." Two of the raiders wouldn't be going back—ever; that was part of the game. The third vacant seat would have been his, but . . . He shrugged. Too late for that now.

From habit, his eyes had swept the southern approaches, searching for other starships—clear, save for a couple of passenger liners following one another on final into the colossal terminus at Gatwick. Then he'd spied graviton streams from the ship's superb old R-1820 'Gravs swirl rapidly backward like great streamers that scoured the river's surface flat for a hundred meters aft.

The bass thunder had reached him moments later, climbing to a great bellow as the starship moved slowly downriver, pushing high, ruffling sheets of greenish water to either side. Then the wake subsided as the ship gradually gained speed until her shadow skidded off to starboard and clear air appeared beneath her racing keel. In seconds, she'd taken up an easterly climb over the ragged metropolitan skyline and disappeared into lowering clouds not so much as a minute later.

At that moment, he remembered, loneliness had descended around him like a heavy shroud, while damp gusts off the water ignored his old flight jacket and chilled him to the bone. He'd shivered and checked his watch, then shoved his hands in his pockets and returned to the pub. Only a few more hours to wait.

And worry . . .

Dodging a score of children and their teachers returning from some kind of field trip, he skittered down a flight of worn marble stairs, then descended what appeared to be a mile-long escalator, taking the grooved treads two at a time.

At the bottom, a sign directed him left to the TUNNEL CON-COURSE.

Pushing his way among beggars, whores, hard-looking loi-terers, and occasional late-evening travelers, he entered the vaulted promenade at precisely seven o'clock—a hall of por-tals, with entrances to HyperTube terminals spaced every thirty meters. About a quarter of the way along the worn marble floor, one of the portals was identified by a single worn sign with 34 painted on its filthy surface. A ramshackle gate across the arch was decorated with a crooked tile that read OUT OF SERVICE. And before the gate stood Tenniel, gor-geous in a severe blue business suit. Damian was at her side.

Canby breathed a sigh of relief. Were she planning some-thing untoward, she wouldn't have risked bringing Damian. Not for anything in the world. As he hurried along the con-course, their eyes met. She smiled—a strange smile, with no warmth or emotion. "Tenniel," he whispered. "God, how I've missed you." They embraced, but her lips were cold; the kiss rushed—almost perfunctory—and . . . nervous. When he crouched to greet Damian, the child moved away—as did Tenniel.

Suddenly he glimpsed movement in the corner of his eye and turned to see at least ten armed men—rough-looking thugs every one of them—coming from the other portals. At the same time, Tenniel was scurrying off along the con-course, dragging Damian behind her.

God, what a fool he'd been—she *had* sold him out!

He started to draw his blaster, but instantly realized how futile that would be. Turning to flee, he spotted Quinn, com-ing from the other direction. The little man had a crowd of burly, conservatively dressed companions with him—more than a match for the pursuing gunmen. "Nemil, thank God you came!" he shouted as he arrived at their front ranks—only to be grabbed and roughly forced backward into another out-of-service portal, where his blaster was violently ripped from his jacket. "Nemil!" he shouted in absolute stupefaction, "it's me, Gordon! No-o-o!"

In the next seconds, he felt the stinging bite of hypo guns firing through his jacket. Coldness spread rapidly from each shoulder until he lost control of his limbs and collapsed backward onto the stone floor with a blow to the back of his head that nearly knocked him out.

Able to move only his eyes, Canby glanced helplessly about the dirty plaster ceiling while confusion around him began to subside. Presently, he heard Quinn's voice ask, "Is he under control?"

"Absolutely, Mr. Chancellor," another voice said. "He'll be paralyzed for hours."

"Leave us a moment," Quinn's voice commanded. "I want to question him myself."

"As you wish, Mr. Chancellor."

Moments later—when the stirring and scraping ceased—Quinn's face appeared overhead, shaking back and forth sadly. "Sorry, Canby," he said with what appeared to be genuine sorrow, "we simply couldn't let you get away—not after what you and your pirate friend did last night in Belgravia."

"But why?" Canby demanded, his speech slurred and twisted by numbed lips. "I can hand you Renaldo on a silver platter—he's a slaver, and I can prove it."

"Unfortunately," Quinn said, dropping to his hunkers with a pained look, "I don't want to know."

"What?" Canby asked with a feeling of dread. "That kind of information would guarantee that every credit he has will go to your campaign. And not only that, it's your chance to start some of those reforms among the Nobility you've talked about in your campaign. My God, Nemil, we're all counting on you to—"

"You poor fool," Quinn interrupted. "I didn't think *anyone* believed that garbage anymore—at least anyone with half a mind." He shrugged. "The *real* truth is that political campaigns exist only to give the half-witted masses like yourself enough hope that they'll stay under control until the next elections, when we hoodwink them again." He laughed sadly. "I had no idea that you didn't know that—but then, you're going to die for that kind of ignorance."

"But *why*?" Canby demanded in growing anger—as well as dread. "What'd I ever do to you?"

"Nothing," Quinn said. "Like I said on the 'Phone, your little Legion provided me a lot of valuable service. It's just that, well, you got unlucky. That Kîrskian friend of yours—Kobir, I think—told you too much, and now *you've* got to die, just as he will when they finally catch him."

"So you're owned by the Nobles just like everyone else in the Political Class," Canby spluttered in helpless anger.

"Only till I purchase a peership," Quinn said. "When I agreed to do this election, Philante promised to knock off nearly thirty percent." His eyebrows rose. "That's a hell of a lot of money, I'll have you know. Peerages don't come cheaply."

"Then I guess the Empire's never going to change," Canby said, feeling drool starting down along his cheek.

"*Nothing's* going to change, Canby—anywhere," Quinn explained as if he were lecturing a schoolchild. "It's all rigged. It has been through most of history, and it will continue to be, just so long as people—the little people—vote their *wants* instead of their beliefs. Sorry, fella," he said. "You just managed to get in the way of the whole thing—like a lot of others have down through time." He patted Canby's cheek gently. "Too bad, in a way. I kind of liked you." Abruptly, he rose to his feet. "Good-bye, Canby," he said, moving out of sight. "You'd be well served to tell 'em everything they want to know right away. Then they'll kill you clean. Otherwise . . . "

By this time, Canby was so filled with loathing, he hardly had any feeling for life at all. Moments later, his view overhead was filled by two huge, tough-looking men who looked down indifferently, as if he were already a corpse. Helpless, but appallingly conscious, he felt his head loll clumsily while they boosted his arms over their shoulders as if he were a drunk. Toes dragging on the pavement, he tried to call out, but a fist smashed into his solar plexus and left him in a paroxysm of agony, gasping and retching for his very breath. After a confused torment of escalators, elevators, and stairs, the light faded and he could feel cold outside air on his face. His shoulders seemed as if they were about to leave their sockets when he heard the door of a skimmer open. Moments later, he was thrown onto a sumptuous leather bench seat, then propped upright, head lolling on his chest, with two enormous men on either side—neither of whom smelled as if he had bathed in years. After a few minutes, doors slammed and a 'Grav whirred into life. Then the skimmer began to move, whizzing off into the night with Canby staring helplessly at moving patterns of light and shadow on the floor.

DECEMBER 26, 2691, EARTH DATE

Belgravia House, London • Earth

As Renaldo transferred a large portfolio of stocks to Quinn's campaign headquarters in New Washington, his 'Phone chimed in the stillness of the great study. Dressed in white breeches, green polka-dotted stockings, yellow dancing slippers, and a white silk shirt, he'd been waiting anxiously for the call and mashed VOICE ONLY with more than a little enthusiasm. "Yes?" he growled in anticipation.

"Kendall here," a rough voice on the other end announced. "We've got your man."

Renaldo sat back and smiled gratefully. Tenniel—what a *marvelous* woman . . . so long as she was paid! He chuckled happily. At last, the beginning of the end—both for the Goddamn Kîrskian *and* his troublesome mercenary accomplice. "I take it he's alive?" he asked.

"He is," the voice assured him. "They've just put 'im in the limo. Not even knocked about much."

"Very well," Renaldo said. "You know what to do with him, then. Right?"

"Right, Gov," the voice asserted. "Down the M3 to Southampton. Nine Goncard Street, Bursledon."

"Correct," Renaldo assured him—he certainly didn't want the fellow brought to Belgravia! "Make no mistakes," he added on the spur of the moment, "and I shall double your fee. Understand?"

"You'll have no mistakes, Gov," the man promised.

"Be sure of that," Renaldo growled, then broke the connection. He sat back and folded his hands over the enormous flowered brocade vest he wore. He'd recently employed an Intelligence officer dismissed by the Admiralty for excessive cruelty—interesting chap, to say the least. And if anybody could extract information from this Canby, *he* could. Renaldo envisioned him at work in the old house on Goncard Street whose stone walls could contain *any* amount of screaming.

He frowned. Unfortunate that tonight's concert at Royal Festival Hall would prevent him from watching, but one had only so much time. . . . Besides, he could watch torture whenever he pleased. The *really* important thing about this Canby fellow was his knowledge of the Kîrskian hideaway. Once he'd screamed *that* out, they could kill him—or do whatever else they pleased.

Wrestling his great bulk to his feet, he stopped to put a drop of perfume—exquisite!—behind each ear, then called for one of his chauffeurs. A symphony by the ancient Ludeslowski tonight. An occasion *not* to be missed!

Near Basingstoke • Earth

The limousine's 'Grav whirred quietly as Canby languished in the backseat, head lolling in time to the road, hands and feet prickly as his circulation slowed. The rapid succession of light and darkness at his feet had subsided nearly an hour ago, as far as he could estimate without seeing his wristwatch, which was twisted out of sight. Now there was more dark than light on the carpeted floor, although the big skimmer seemed to be moving at extremely high speed. He guessed they were traveling along one of the major roads out of London, but had no idea in which direction.

Suddenly someone up front gasped excitedly, "M'God—a great hulkin' lorry's smashed the lookout car behind us! I thought 'e was catchin' up awful fast." He gasped a second time. "An'—Jesus Christ!—our second one's just smashed into the wreck, too! I knew Lenny was followin' too close!"

"Keep going," another, darker voice commanded. "Dead men cannot collect their share of the payoff."

Before long, the sound of the 'Grav increased along with the speed with which the few lights on the floor came and went. "What's the matter?" the dark voice demanded.

"I think . . . we're bein' followed," the first voice said with a clear tenor of anxiety. "Watch 'im, Benbo—see if 'e's catchin' up!"

As he spoke, Canby heard a fast-moving VertiFlyer pass low overhead, flying in the same direction.

"He is catchin' up," Benbo said, his dark voice reduced to an anxious whisper. "Go faster."

"It won't go no faster," the first driver said. "I told you we shoulda used a smaller one."

"Warder, Trevol," Benbo commanded. "Take care of 'em."

Heart in his mouth, Canby felt the thugs on either side of him move as if they were wrestling blasters from their clothes—little room remained in the backseat. Abruptly, he was pushed awkwardly onto the floor, facedown. What felt like a shoe scraped the back of his head and planted itself on his neck. Something similar crushed his shoulder. He heard breaking glass, as if the back window had been broken— then the sharp reports of blasters set at full power. Could it be?

Suddenly what sounded like a huge explosion erupted somewhere ahead. The big limousine skimmer jumped and skidded violently before the driver wrestled it back under control. "Someone's blown the bridge ahead of us!" a new voice shouted from the backseat—just as a second tremendous explosion seemed to come from behind. Instantly, whoever was driving applied the brakes, jouncing Canby's two guards on top of him, as the limousine yawed to the right, then spun violently and came to a shuddering halt.

As the two men struggled to their feet, Canby heard the distinct snuffle of silenced blasters, then two screams, and something—or someone—crumpled heavily against his legs and lay still. "Don't shoot!" the dark voice screamed. "F' Chrissake, don't shoot!"

"Throw out your weapons," Kobir's deep voice commanded—nobody else sounded like that.

Canby heard three metallic objects strike the pavement . . . then a fourth. In the silence that followed, he also heard the VertiFlyer again, then another familiar voice. It was Peterson!

"Come out with your hands up," she ordered. "And you bastards better pray Canby's still alive!"

Canby heard doors open—the one beside his head first. This time, the thug was extremely careful where he put his feet when he exited. In the next moment, gentle hands touched his neck.

"He's alive, at least," Peterson said.

"I won't last much longer crumpled up like this," Canby

managed. In the background, he could hear the VertiFlyer landing.

"Gordo—thank God!" Peterson exclaimed. "Guys," she shouted, "help me get him out of here!"

Moments later, Canby found himself being carried rapidly but carefully toward the VertiFlyer. Close by, he could see Peterson's small boots directing the operation. Presently, shouts and scuffling sounded to one side, punctuated by more snuffling of blasters and the sound of falling bodies. Then Kobir's boots appeared and he felt a hand on his back.

"All is now under control, my friend," Kobir's deep voice assured him.

"Thanks, Nikolai," Canby said weakly as he felt himself propped up in the VertiFlyer's cabin.

"You are most welcome," Kobir replied, climbing in behind him. "But you will need more *special* thanks for your friend Lela, I think."

Canby closed his eyes. "Yeah," he said. "I've got a *lot* of thanking to do, I guess." In the next moments, two men climbed in beside him, the flyer's door slammed shut, and he felt the deck begin to rise.

"These will bring you around in a few minutes," the voice of Chaplain Amps declared as two more hypo guns stung his shoulders. "Just relax, my friend."

He did. . . .

DECEMBER 27, 2691, EARTH DATE

Columbia Sector, New Washington • Earth

Just before one A.M., David Lotember sat in his office while a gaunt young woman took off her shabby clothing. As he waited, he idly browsed a seconded police report of a triple murder on a dark stretch of Greater London's M3 highway between exits six and seven, just south of Basingstoke. Under normal circumstances, the Admiralty didn't receive police reports, but because two huge bombs had been detonated nearby—and destroyed two bridges that shut down the highway for what was estimated to be a minimum of two full months—a possibility of terrorism existed.

With a vitriolic laugh, Lotember discarded the message—he no longer cared for *anything* related to his office. Just the previous afternoon, he had been informed that Renaldo's support was withdrawn for Lotember's reelection campaign. The Earl's new protégé: none other than the beautiful whore, Cynthia Tenniel. Good as she'd been at the time, he wished he'd never picked her up that night in Manhattan. But then, who could predict the future?

Shrugging pragmatically, he left a message for Tolton, directing her to arrange an appointment with a colleague at the Ministry of State, then pushed away from his desk and opened his trousers. True members of the Political Class were never discouraged by a little partisan intrigue. One won and one lost—it was all part of a game he loved as much as he loved his life.

Wharton Dock, Southampton • Earth

To Kobir, it seemed that *quite* a bit of life had flowed back into Canby's shoulders by just after two A.M., when the VertiFlyer reached the Southampton docks and landed near the old KV 72 that Peterson had sent ahead a week previously. "Think you can make it to the ship on your own, friend?" Kobir asked.

Canby grinned at him. "I think I'll lean on Lela's shoulders," he said. "Just to be certain."

Kobir smiled. "Those shoulders look as if they might be quite comfortable, indeed," he said, musing for a moment on what sort of future the two had in store.

Lippi interrupted his reverie with a salute. "We have paid off Customs, my Kapitan," he reported.

"Very well, Émil," Kobir said, placing an arm on his old friend's shoulder. "The ship is ready to lift?"

"Immediately," Lippi assured him.

"Then let us be on our way home," Kobir said, watching Canby and the rather amazing Peterson step through the old transport's boarding hatch. He smiled. The two of them would have a lot to work out—Canby had, after all, made a perfect fool of himself. But they'd *all* learned a few lessons for their pains—as well as a share in what he was certain would become civilization's largest transaction to date—the upcoming sale of the Giulio Cesare. *To whom,* he wasn't yet certain. But one thing he did know for sure—when the sale was final, he or she was going to pay a *lot* of money. Smiling, he stepped over the coaming and pulled the hatch shut behind him.

An hour later, he was sipping vodka with Petroski and Skoda on the bridge as the old ship passed the limits of w.hat was called the Solar System—headed home.

DECEMBER 28, 2691

Belgravia House, London • Earth

Renaldo blanked the HoloPhone and turned, frowning, to Tenniel, who lay in bed beside him. "I cannot believe it!" he fumed, rolling his eyes to the baroque ceiling that surrounded the mirror above them. "It seems this Canby person of yours has gotten away—again."

Tenniel smiled and stared at the satin bedsheets for a moment. "He's not mine anymore," she said quietly, "but I suppose I'm glad, if you want to know the truth."

"Tenniel, my little whore," Renaldo exclaimed in mock

approbation, "how could you be glad? After all, you recently sold him like a piece of meat—just to become Minister of the Admiralty."

"Everything and anything has a price, Renaldo," she said, looking him directly in the eye. "Especially me, my corpulent lover. Don't *ever* forget that I would sell you just as quickly, should the occasion ever arise."

Renaldo raised his eyebrows and grinned. "I *could* have you killed first," he said. "Or I might even give you back to that Canby fellow. What then?"

"But you won't, my dear Renaldo," she purred.

"And why not?" he demanded.

Without a word, she shifted slightly and unfastened his silken robe. He watched the mane of blond hair fall forward from her head to shroud his great shuddering belly, then lay back, and sighed with pleasure. Really, he considered, he should have gotten rid of Lotember long ago.

July 14, 2692, Earth Date

Villa Kîrskia • Khalife

Little more than six Earth weeks following the combined raid in London, Kobir's business arm safely fenced the Giulio Cesare to a surprise buyer—Emperor Philante XXI— for nearly triple what Renaldo had paid. As an incentive to close the deal quickly, as well as *quietly,* all members of Kobir's pirate band and Canby's Legion were immediately granted pardons throughout the Empire. Additionally, the Kîrskians were offered full citizenship after only a year's residence on any Imperial planet. When, some weeks later, the monies were actually distributed, Kobir's prediction came true. No matter how small the individual share, each member became wealthy beyond his or her wildest dreams.

In the weeks and months that followed, so many Kîrskians and legionnaires availed themselves of the Empire's proposition that Kobir eventually was forced to lay up his ships and retire, leaving Canby and his remaining stalwarts to contemplate their futures under *greatly* altered circumstances.

But inasmuch as the Kîrskians had spent their last decade somberly peering *in* at a civilization that in fact repudiated their affiliation, most of the legionnaires had spent virtually the same interval desperately searching for some way *out*. It was that dichotomy that eventually found Canby and Kobir on the porch of the latter's elegant lakeside villa one early evening, sipping sweet Vannal with bitters and rocking in two of the wicker chairs that the Kîrskian had "liberated" from a transport carrying antiques back to Earth.

"I shall miss you, my friend," Canby said, raising his glass by way of a toast.

"That signifies there is no last-minute reasoning to dissuade you from this plan of Peterson's, eh, Gordon?" Kobir replied with a twinkle in his eye.

"None, Nikolai," Canby said with a certain anticipation. "I think we're all ready for the next galaxy—this one is too full of Earth. When we tested *War*'s intergalactic Drive last week, it operated perfectly—carried us damn near to Sector Nineteen before we could shut it down."

Kobir nodded. "Quicker work than last time, too," he said. "Many of us were concerned because of the troubles you previously encountered during *Death*'s conversion."

"*Much* quicker," Canby agreed. "Replicating old *Famine*'s special logic was a bear the first time—but we learned a lot while we worked, and applied the knowledge when we made the modifications to *War*." He laughed. "Would you like us to make you an intergalactic KV 388? I think we could do it now!"

Kobir grinned appreciatively, but shook his head. "I think I shall remain behind in this old galaxy of ours for a while," he said. "Unlike you and your legionnaires, I have not yet had the opportunity to form a lasting . . . how shall I put it? . . . *appreciation* for Imperial Earth's brand of government—although I must admit to hoping for a few changes."

Canby looked at the pirate and shrugged somberly. "You already know what I learned from that little shyster Quinn. And after thinking about the Empire for a couple of months, I've become a believer. Nothing's going to change because *they* won't let it change."

"To whom does your 'they' refer?" Kobir asked with a little smile.

Canby sipped his Vannal. "Yeah, I know," he admitted. " 'They' is everyone—both the 'little people,' as Quinn called us, *and* the big shots, like Quinn himself. The first group votes with short-range, selfish goals in mind; the second panders to them on the surface and ignores them when the chips are down. It's a self-sustaining process so far as I can see—one that's already lasted a couple thousand years."

"Well, yes," Kobir conceded, "but there *have* been periods in which the people managed to wrest power from their oppressors. How about late-eighteenth-century France, or twentieth-century Russia, or, for that matter, the Nelson Cluster just a few hundred years ago?"

"Did any of them *last*?" Canby asked. "That's the real question."

Kobir shook his head. "No," he admitted, "but maybe it's because they took on too much of a job in too little time. Sooner or later, poor planning and hasty action catch up with everybody. Perhaps it's best to go in and try to bring about just a *few* changes at a time—then let them take hold before stirring things up again."

Canby tossed down his drink and walked to the porch rail. Thoughtfully, he looked out over the little harbor below where his four remaining DH.98s were drawn up to Kobir's fishing pier, ready for a morning liftoff. "Maybe . . . " he said, getting to his feet, "maybe even 'probably,' but I'm not going to be around to see it."

"Certainly not if you're in the next galaxy," Kobir agreed, standing to join him at the porch rail. "But once more imagine what the two of us could accomplish with the information we now *legally* possess. No matter *how* poorly you feel toward this Empire of yours, think how much good we could do by simply bringing Renaldo to the gallows—a fate he *richly* deserves—then unseating the Ministers he controls. Such a thing would be a good start toward cleaning up your whole government."

"But *only* a start," Canby said, placing a hand on Kobir's shoulder. "Then, you'd have to fight off all the other Nobles and Ministers and . . . hell, the Managers, too—everybody with a vested interest in the system." He smiled as dock lights came on below, illuminating the waiting starships. "I think your idea of nibbling the problem to death is a much better idea. Unfortunately, to do things that way, you've got to live within it, and that's something I—*we,* the ones of us who are leaving—simply aren't willing to endure anymore." He shrugged. "I guess when it comes right down to a bottom line, we don't think the old Empire is worth saving anymore. There are a lot of good things we'll miss—like *you,* my friend—but for me and the people in those ships down there, it's time to move on."

Later, when Canby returned to *Death,* at the head of the pier, most of her crew were already turned in for the night. The graceful ship seemed restless as it floated on the dark lake, testing its moorings in the light breeze. Behind her, *War, Plague II,* and *Famine* were dark, familiar silhouettes against the shore. At the top of the bridge companionway, he checked the bridge, where two consoles were still manned by technicians running last-minute logic checks. Hands in his pockets, he retraced his steps to the main deck, then quietly entered the tiny captain's cabin, where he crawled into his bunk—content. Tomorrow began a new future. What could be better than that?

July 15, 2692, Earth Date

Villa Kîrskia • Khalife

Kobir stood, arms folded, at his empty fishing pier, watching old *Famine*, the last of Canby's ships, thunder past on its takeoff along the glassy, dawn-lit lake. In the distance, its wake diminished, then ceased completely as light appeared beneath the streamlined hull and the starship soared effortlessly into the dark, crisp morning air to join its three sisters. A short time later, spent waves sighed against the shore, even while the velvet rumble of 'Gravs faded in the distance. In less than a minute, he could no longer distinguish running lights from the pale morning stars.

Turning slowly, he returned to his villa and breakfast, with a strange discontent chafing his mood. He smiled. For himself, as for Canby, much unfinished business remained. Perhaps after a little rest, he thought . . . who knows?

EPILOGUE

Supported by the veteran's movement, Nemil Quinn handily won his election bid for Prime Minister. Unfortunately, none of his reform promises ever came to pass, but he managed to shift blame elsewhere in the corrupt government. After winning reelection twice, he retired as a national hero to purchase a Dukedom from Philante XXI, then lived a long and respected life as a member of the House of Nobles.

Nine years following the legionnaires' departure, Kobir relocated his household to London, Earth, where he purchased quite an expensive—and powerful—title, entering the House of Nobles as First Earl of Koris. Before slipping into a cheerful and still-productive old age, he bequeathed to his adopted domain many rich and enduring gifts in the form of libraries and educational institutes that were largely credited with initiating major portions of Imperial Earth's renaissance nearly two hundred years later.

As for Sadir, First Earl of Renaldo, he was eventually apprehended in his slave trading—no thanks to Kobir or any of his Kîrskian colleagues—and denounced openly throughout the civilized worlds. But he was never brought to trial. Though thoroughly disgraced by the scandal, he not only sustained his control over the Admiralty for many subsequent years, but also preserved Cynthia Tenniel in her office as its Minister. The latter's management of the Fleet—or mismanagement, as many pronounced openly—led eventually to wholesale corruption that nearly bankrupted the Imperial government. Notwithstanding, feebleminded Philante XXI awarded Renaldo the Empire's highest honor for "Service to Mankind" during his centennial birthday festivities on Earth in 2700. On his deathbed, the Earl puzzled his physicians by gasping "Damn you, Gordon Canby" as his last words. Most of the learned doctors had no idea to whom he referred.

David Lotember lived a long and—in his own eyes—productive life, the high points of which were supporting nearly every bad bill that managed to limp through Parliament. He became the worst Chancellor of the Exchequer in recorded history. Later in life, having coauthored still another rewriting of the *Book of Common Prayer,* he became a Bishop in the Revised Imperial Church & Spiritual Authority, passing away peacefully in the very odor of sanctity.

Cynthia Tenniel outlived both her scandalous handling of the Admiralty and Renaldo himself, with whom she lived until his death—many whispered only for his estate. She passed away seventy-three years later after a long reign as the feared queen of London society. Her son, Damian, attended Annapolis and joined the Fleet, in due time rising to the position of Grand Admiral, then Minister of the Admiralty, and ultimately restoring the so-called "Senior Service" to its former glory. One of his first acts after taking ministerial office was naming a new classroom complex in Annapolis "Canby Hall."

And what of Gordon Canby himself? As is the case with most who fly beyond the boundaries of the home galaxy, he was never heard from again—at least by anyone who records such information. One can only hope that he and his legionnaires found their "new future" out among the stars—and that it was a good one.

BILL BALDWIN, the author of *The Helmsman* series, is a graduate of the Mercerburg Academy and the University of Pittsburgh, where he earned a B.A. in journalism and a Masters of Letters degree. He served in the U. S. Air Force at Cape Canaveral supporting Project Mercury. He also managed astronaut public relations during the Gemini and early Apollo programs. He has worked as a computer programmer for Burroughs Corporation (now UNISYS) and Xerox Corporation. Bill lives in Dallas, Texas with his wife Pat and two cats.